Secrets
of the Untold

by
Carly Robbins

DORRANCE
PUBLISHING CO
EST. 1920
PITTSBURGH, PENNSYLVANIA 15222

The contents of this work, including, but not limited to, the accuracy of events, people, and places depicted; opinions expressed; permission to use previously published materials included; and any advice given or actions advocated are solely the responsibility of the author, who assumes all liability for said work and indemnifies the publisher against any claims stemming from publication of the work.

All Rights Reserved
Copyright © 2015 by Carly Robbins

No part of this book may be reproduced or transmitted, downloaded, distributed, reverse engineered, or stored in or introduced into any information storage and retrieval system, in any form or by any means, including photocopying and recording, whether electronic or mechanical, now known or hereinafter invented without permission in writing from the publisher.

Dorrance Publishing Co
701 Smithfield Street
Pittsburgh, PA 15222
Visit our website at *www.dorrancebookstore.com*

ISBN: 978-1-4809-1909-9
eISBN: 978-1-4809-1886-3

Prologue

As I look out over the rolling hills of my beloved Scotland, I'm taken aback by all that I have been part of or witness to. From the time I took my first breath, brought to life by the will of a powerful wizard, it was a gift, an odd gift, but it was all he had to give. From that time forward I have taken quite seriously all that have been placed in my charge to care for and protect. Why it was in these very halls where I witnessed our Lord Navar, Zoul, and their closest comrades as they struggled with the brutality of what a vampire must do. Vampire or no, Lord Navar always knew that humanity was meant for more. More is what demanded from the men that were to be his knights. There was one, evil to his very being, who would not live by the code of Lord Navar's knights; this dark one was banished. The evil one did not go quietly; he left with a threat, one he would keep.

I was saddened on the day that our Lord Navar had to walk away from us. As he had come to the end of his time here, when he could no longer blend in, he had no other choice but to leave. I almost could not conceal my joy when he had regained his humanity, for it was all he ever wanted. Then I was plunged into the depths of despair as he newly found humanity led him to discover what it would mean to be mortal, as they lay him to rest just over there in the cemetery. The life-size bronze statue may bear his likeness but nothing could capture his spirit.

Now they have brought Lord Navar's love, Lera McConall, home to rest at his side. I am consumed with grief as I am reminded once more of all that we have lost. Through all the sadness, a ray of joy, for the one to whom Lera chose to entrust all her secrets, the one who is to now be our new Lord, and the one who brought Lera home, goes by the name of Katelynn Anthony. She is strong, wise, and beautiful. She comes from a faraway land, and she will be our mortal guardian although she is not quite all mortal.

I feel Katelynn's pain as she stands at the grave of Lera with her love, Corbin, one of Lords Navar's trusted comrades, by her side. There are secrets for her to learn. Secrets such as a grand wizard in her bloodline. His name was Kayland. She holds a bit of his power still. He is her namesake. She will befriend a fairy, a beautiful fairy; this fragile fairy will be her rescuer. Katelynn will come to know many while she is here. Some will be more important to her than other but all will be loved.

There is one thing I fear above all else; it is the dark, evil one. He will come for her; he will have all of Lera's secrets whatever the cost. Oh, sweet Katelynn, my child, my new Lord, if arms I had I would comfort you in your grief. As for now my sadness is made sadder for you cannot hear me, not yet. Soon you will hear me and understand my soft warning. Soon you will know things that are neither probable nor possible—are. Until then, please be careful the evil one is here, please be careful....

The castle sighed as her unheard words fell upon unhearing ears.

Chapter One

It had started to rain. Corbin took me by the arm.

"Come on, Katelynn; you're going to get soaked. There's nothing more we can do here."

The rose I held in my hand slipped from my fingers, landing on the top of Ms. Lera's grave with a soft bounce and causing one of the petals to break off, mirroring my broken heart.

We reached the entrance to Castle Go-Brath. Standing there in the entrance hall, I looked up at Corbin. He took the cuff of his shirt and wiped the mix of rain and tears from my face.

"As sad as I am to lose her, I'm glad that she has made it home to Navar," I said, smiling as I walked into Corbin's open arms.

"Navar and Lera, together now and for all eternity; Theirs is one of the great love stories, each willing to give their life for the other," Corbin whispered.

I looked back at their graves.

"I'm so glad we could bring her here. It's just as it should be," I said.

Corbin tilted my face up to meet his gaze.

"You know, she loved you as though you were her own child, the one that she and Navar might have had. Did you know she was the one who recommended you for the job at Silver Cove? She carried a lot of power. She had watched you for years," Corbin said as he brushed a stray hair from my face. "I have truly fallen in love with you, my beautiful, dark-haired mortal. I don't know what has captivated me more: your shiny black hair, those amazing crystal-cut blue eyes, or that smile that could melt the polar ice caps." He pulled me in closer. "I know that you're tall and lean and every man's dream; even if you don't see it, the rest of the world does. However, it takes more than just a great pair of legs to impress a vampire, although they certainly don't hurt. It's here," he placed his hand over my heart. "This is where you touch me in my heart."

I lay my face against his chest.

"I love you, too, my handsome, strong, vam-Spiderman." I heard his soft chuckle.

"You do have an issue with that word," he said, his voice edged with sadness. He placed his finger under my chin, gently raising my face to meet his gaze. "It is what I am," Corbin said, and a sad smile touched his lips.

"I prefer to think of you as an ordinary man trapped in an extraordinary life, wielding your powers for good; but if we can resurrect Ms. Lera's cure, we might be able to change that." I gave him a sweet kiss. "May I ask how you know that Ms. Lera had been looking for and watching over me? I thought you had lost touch with her," I said.

"I did; Tanarr, however, did not. He kept me informed," Corbin said.

"Ah," I said.

Note to self, I thought, *ask Tanarr about all this later.* For now, I was happy to be in the safety and comfort of Corbin's arms. I turned to look at the breathtaking castle that stood before us. *I can't believe she left all this to me.* The pain of all I had lost came flooding back. I began to weep, not cry but weep—that sadness that only comes from that heartbreaking loss of a loved one.

"Corbin, what will I do without her?" I sobbed.

"We will do as we promised; we will continue with her work," he said as he gently stroked my back, trying to comfort me.

"I know I told her we would," I shook my head. "But I'm not smart enough or strong enough or anything enough. I can't do this!"

Corbin held me at arm's length.

"Yes, you are. You can do anything that you believe you can," he said with a warm smile that said, "I believe in you."

"But how?" I asked.

"You have all of Lera's research papers and a good portion of her courage. That's quite all you may need." Corbin said

"That's not all I need," I said, never taking my eyes off his.

"What else could you possibly need?" He paused to think "Oh, yeah, a lab. We'll build that," he said.

"That's still not it," I said, still not looking away.

"What, then?" he asked, throwing his hands in the air in frustration.

I leaned over and whispered in his ear.

"You," I said, kissing him on the cheek. "Without you I wouldn't have the heart or the courage to go on."

He didn't say a word as he scooped me up in his arms. His reply was a soft kiss that crumpled my recants and built up my courage. That kiss held as much power and magic as the place in which we stood.

I was so lost in the moment that I didn't hear the soft footsteps of Calldoon. I had no idea he was there until he cleared his throat. I jumped and turned a childish shade of red. Calldoon didn't notice because of the dim lighting, or maybe he was just being nice. I thought it was the latter of the two, for that's the way he seemed: a true gentleman from the old world and the old ways trapped in an existence not of his making. He, too, was one of them: a vampire and a good man. With his platinum blond hair, square chin and shoulders, he carried himself well when he so chose. His white-blond hair color allowed him to appear older or younger, whichever he needed to be, as he recreated himself to maintain his position here at the castle. He wore green contacts to cloak his amber eyes; he was very handsome in a quiet kind of way. I hoped that we would be friends, for although he was a quiet gentleman of the old world, I did not want to get on his bad side.

"M'lady, pardon, but the kitchen staff would be needin' to know what time ye would be liking yer evening meal."

I stopped to think.

"You know, I'm not very hungry. It's all been too much today. If it's okay with everyone, I'll just have a bowl of soup and half of a sandwich. I think I would like to have my supper in the library by the fireplace, if that's all right," I said, looking from Calldoon to Corbin.

They gave each other a knowing nod. It was one of understanding, for they knew all that was in and around this mystical place, and they knew things that I could only imagine.

"Yes, M'lady, as you wish." Calldoon said with a bow.

"Thank you," I said as he left the room. "Do you think he doesn't like me?" I asked Corbin as the door closed behind Calldoon.

"Nah, he's just sizing you up. He doesn't know if he quite trusts you yet," Corbin said. Then, with a mischievous twinkle in his eye, he turned slowly, looking out from under his eyelashes.

"Or maybe he's trying to decide if you would be as tasty as you look; after all, he is one of us," Corbin said.

"Yeah, right," I said, giving him a thump on the chest. "You are kidding me, right?" He didn't reply. I swallowed hard and turned a little pale. "You *are* kidding, right?" I asked.

He laughed as he put his arms around my shoulders.

"Come here, my sweet, tasty morsel!" He kissed my ear.

"Stop that! You're creeping me out!" I said, giving him a jab to the ribs.

He laughed again.

"You know I'm just messing with you," he said. "I would never let anyone harm you. I love you," he whispered into my hair.

We walked hand-in-hand into the library, where Corbin built a roaring fire, just for my pleasure.

"How's that?" he asked, dusting off his hands and sliding into his chair.

"That's nice," I said as I snuggled back into my chair. We had had the two big leather wingbacks that had been in Ms. Lera's room flown over so we could sit in them by the fireplace. We thought it fitting for Lera and Navar's chairs to be here together in the castle. I lovingly stroked the arm of the chair I was occupying.

As hard as I tried, I could not prevent the small tear from escaping the realm of my lashes. That little tear held a mix of sadness and joy: sadness for the loss of my precious friend and joy for having known her. She had given me a small glimmer into her life with Navar. Oh, how I would have loved to have known that gallant, gentle man who was for most of his life a vampire! What a couple they must have made, an amazing mix of old world power and knowledge: dark hair, amber eyes, tall and handsome, with a good and kind heart. That would have been Navar. Short, sweet, crazy curly red hair, and sparkly green eyes: she had cared deeply for all but loved only one. She possessed more knowledge than most people of her age, and that would have been Lera.

I truly wished I could have seen the two of them together; everyone said they were the perfect fit. She had given me a lot, including this grand old castle and a whole lot more. The greatest gifts were her friendship, her love, and her hope.

"I'll always think of her when I sit here," I said with a smile.

"She would like that," Corbin said, propping his feet up in front of the fire.

"You're getting better at that," I said with a wink.

"Better at what?" he asked.

"Putting your feet up. Do you remember when you tried to kick off your shoes and put your feet up at my apartment? My candy dish never quite recovered," I laughed.

"It did take me a while to conquer the skill of relaxing," he said, leaning his head back and closing his eyes.

We sat in silence while the fire crackled and popped, enjoying just being with each other. Sometimes words get in the way of our time with the ones we love.

Deireadh brought the food in. She placed the tray on the table, making no eye contact and speaking no words.

"Thank you," I said. She only nodded and bowed. As soon as the tray was out of her hands, she left.

"Now, that's one odd chick," I said, taking my bowl of soup and sandwich that were all on the same big plate.

Just as I was preparing to snuggle back in my chair, I stopped. I looked at my food, then at the chair, then back down to the floor.

"I think I'm going to do this picnic style," I said, giving the floor a nod. "You know how much I love a picnic!" I made my way to the floor, which was covered with a rich, thick rug. Fat pillows were scattered around and about the fireplace, inviting one to snuggle down.

"That I do," Corbin said, slipping out of his chair to join me on the pillows.

The soup was tasty; it warmed my stomach. The fire was toasty, and it warmed my feet. None of these were as satisfying as this man, who warmed my heart. I finished my soup, watching as the firelight played off his chiseled profile. I took a deep breath and slowly exhaled. I knew in my heart that our love story would play out to be quite an adventure, filled with all kinds of new people, places, and hopefully at least one big cure for the man I loved.

I just knew that if it could cure Navar of the vampire virus, it would work for Corbin. Maybe, just maybe, we would find that this orchid held many more secrets than even Ms. Lera could have dreamed. We might quite possibly impact the whole world *if* we could get that blasted thing to work. Wow! What a difference we could make.

I set my bowl down and scooted over, giving him a loving kiss on the lips, sweet and slow.

"What was that for?" he asked.

"That was for all you do, all you give. You didn't have to come with me. You didn't have to help, but you did." I looked deep into his beautiful amber eyes. "I believe we can make a big difference in the world." I took a deep breath. "I know that I've made a big deal about you being cured." I paused and looked down at our hands that were linked together and lying on top of our knees, which were barely touching. "It has occurred to me that you haven't been as talkative about this as I have. I need you to know that—" I stopped again, looking back into his eyes. "You don't have to take the cure. You don't need to change for me. I love you regardless; I've never met anyone like you, my Spiderman."

He didn't say a word: just smiled. He placed one hand on the side of my face. The other he wrapped around my waist, pulling us closer together for a breathtaking, earth-shattering kiss. When at last the kiss ended, my heart was pounding so hard I could barely breathe. He pulled back, looked at me, and smiled. With his hand resting on my face, he stroked the corner of my mouth with the edge of his thumb.

"I know I haven't said a lot about my being cured. That's because I wasn't sure it was what I wanted," he said.

I looked away.

"Oh. I'm sorry. I wouldn't pressure you into anything. You know that, don't you?" I said.

"Yes, I do know that, and I thank you," he said, turning my face to meet his. "I have come to some conclusions on my own. First, I love you more." He paused. "I can't even think of anything that comes close to you. After talking to Zoul, seeing his pain at losing his beloved wife, Kasandra: she was the reason for his existence. I can't imagine having to stand by and watch as time consumed the one you loved. I know that I never want to be on this planet one second of one day without you, ever. So please know that I so want that cure. I myself have outlived many people that I cared for, but this love that we share is so much more. You are my breath, my life. First, there are some things I have to see to. At the top of that list is Blake," Corbin said.

I shivered at the thought of him.

"Do you have to?" I asked.

"Yes, I do," he said as he put his finger over my lips. "But not tonight. However, he is at the top. He'll not be dogging us for the rest of our days. After that, I only have a few other little things to take care of, then I'm all yours."

"Hmmm, that sounds nice," I said as we snuggled together in front of the fire. We stayed there for a good long time until at last the fire was beginning to fade.

I yawned.

"Oh, goodness, my eyes are getting heavy," I said.

Corbin scooped me up. "Let me see you to your room."

"Hey!" I started to kick. "Put me down! I can walk. I'm not that tired."

"I know. I just like carrying you," he said.

"No, no, no! What will the castle people say?" I asked.

"Woo hoo! What a lucky man! That's what they would say," Corbin replied with a big smile.

"I don't think so. Now put me down!" I said.

As he put me down, I gave him a good back handed whack to the chest, all in good fun.

"Ha! They might be saying woo hoo! What a lucky woman!" I said. He popped me on the butt and smiled.

"Either way, I win," he said with a wink.

"Ah, you," I said as I spun him around and linked my arm through his.

"Let's call it a night, and you, my Spidey, may walk me to my room," I said, leaning my head on his shoulder.

"I still don't get how you can deal with a spider bite better than a vampire bite." He leaned in and whispered in my ear. "You do know that a bite is a bite, and I am what I am: a vampire." He gave me a kiss on the cheek. "But if it makes you happy to call me Spiderman, call me Spiderman. What is it that they say? A rose by any other name?"

"Yeah, but some roses have bigger thorns than others. So for now, I'm going to call my rose Spiderman. I know I'm only tricking myself, but I'm good with that," I said with a smile and an eye flutter.

We stepped out of the library and into the hall.

"Man, castles are cold!" I said, pulling in close to Corbin, which was no help at all. He was as cold as the night air. That always shocked me; I knew he was a vampire, and I knew they were cold. I guessed that was because this man that I held by the arm warmed my heart more than any one or thing that I had ever known. I shivered.

"You're colder than I am. I'm sorry," he said as he started to pull away.

"Oh no," I said, pulling him back. "You're not that cold, and besides, it might be fun to try to warm you up."

We both laughed. As he tightened his hold on me, he leaned over and kissed the top of my head.

"I've heard that friction is a good way to get some heat going on," he said, rubbing his hands and jiggling his eyebrows. "You know friction?"

I leaned my head over on his shoulder as we walked.

"Oh, you," I laughed. He knew how I felt about that kind of thing.

My quiet laughter bounced around the vacant stone hall. Everyone else in the castle had long since retired for the evening. The halls were dimly lit by electric lights that were on timed dimmer switches. The ornate wall lighting had long ago replaced the torch sconces. Detailed, handwoven rugs draped the walls. They had been placed there hundreds of years ago, not only to add a splash of color to the gray stone; they also proved to be a small barrier against the cold nights. They were so intricately designed; in today's market, they would be priceless, for no one did work like that anymore.

We moved on down the hall toward the marble staircase. For the first time, I took a good look at it. As we headed up the stairs, I ran my hand over the railing.

"Wow! This is beautiful!" I said, not bothering to hide the awe in my voice.

The stair treads were a soft, tan marble. The railings were a hand-carved wood. I was not really sure what kind of wood it was, but it matched the marble perfectly. The beginning of the railing was a bold curve giving the feeling that the entire rail emanated from that spot.

We were at the second floor; one more flight and we would be to the Lord of the castle's floor. That was where I was expected to stay. I had had a big "girly bed" and some other things moved in, but I also asked them to leave the three pieces of Navar's furnishings. They consisted of his armoire, chair, and table. These pieces would forever stay where they were, if for no other reason than respect for a man I never knew but had grown to love. His sword was prominently displayed over the fireplace; that, too, would never be removed. I loved seeing it there. It made me feel safe. In some strange way, it felt like he was protecting me, like the sword itself had power.

As for Corbin, my strong man with sandy brown hair that framed a chiseled face, he could have been a sculpture come to life. His very presence made you aware of him. He was tall and muscular, designed for the chase, built for the kill but still so gentle that he could hold a woman in his arms and make her feel safe and cared for.

I didn't know where he went at night. He hadn't said, and I never asked. I knew that he was close. I asked him to take the room closest to mine, which was a floor down. I didn't think that he stayed there, but that was okay. He is where he needs to be when he is needed. That's what matters. I gave him a little squeeze and a smile, and he smiled back.

We got to my room.

"Here we are, safe and sound," he opened the door for me and gave me a kiss. "I'll see you in the morning," he said, giving the end of my nose a flick. "Remember, if you need me, I can be here in a heartbeat." He put his hands at my waist and pulled me in close, putting his forehead to mine, "unless you would feel safer with Spiderman beside you."

"I do thank you for that offer, but you know this old-fashioned daughter of the South will have to pass on that for now. Besides, Momma would cut a switch for both of us if she got wind of anything like that," I said with grin.

"Yeah, but you can't blame a Spiderman for trying," Corbin said.

"Yeah, well, I guess the only spiders I'll be seeing tonight will have eight legs." I started to go into my room then stopped short. "Uh, you don't think there are any *real* spiders in there, do you?" I asked, looking at with him with my best puppy dog face.

He rolled his eyes.

"Do you want me to check?"

I nodded. He went to check all the corners.

I turned to yell into the room, "Don't forget under the bed!" just as he appeared at the door.

"Oh, I'm sorry! I didn't mean to yell in your face!" I sheepishly said.

"I can't believe the girl that faced down and even threatened a vampire is afraid of teeny little spiders," he said.

"Yeah, but technically I threatened the vampire with you. The teeny little spiders don't seem to be as afraid of you as he is," I said with a flutter of my eyelashes.

He smiled and brushed the side of my face with the edge of his fingers.

"Okay, you win; I now leave you to your peaceful, spider-free slumber. I love you," he said as he closed the door. Behind him I caught the door before it closed all the way.

"Were there any spiders?" I sheepishly asked.

"Only one, and he's dead now," he replied.

"Thank you, and I love you, too," I whispered.

I heard him chuckling as the door closed.

Chapter Two

I made sure the door was locked.

"Well," I said out loud. "Now what? No TV, no radio. I have my iPod, but I'm not in the mood for that."

I rifled through my suitcase. I knew I had brought some books. I dug all the way to the bottom of my case. *Katelynn*, I thought, *you are going to have to upgrade to one of those computerized, handheld reader things.*

I picked up one of the books that was hiding at the bottom. *Nah, I like the feel of a book in my hand, and there's no possibility that I might sit on it and break it.*

"Now, let me see, what I have found," I said, flipping open the book as I made my way to my chair or, shall I say, Navar's chair. It was not just a four-legs, two-arms kind of chair. His chair had two large paws carved out of dark wood for the front legs. The back legs looked like they had detailed vines winding into the fabric carved from the same wood. The fabric itself was a strong weave. It appeared to be hard and scratchy, but it wasn't. On the contrary, it was soft and comfy in shades of brown and tan with threads of royal blue and gold that ran through it.

The arms rolled to the side, inviting one to sit, to rest, even to take a nap in its protective care. There in the center of the back, neatly created in rich detail, was Navar's crest. The needlework had that amazing medieval detail that you just didn't see anymore. Each stitch was done by hand with love and care. I ran my fingers over the beautiful handiwork. The shield that was at the heart of the crest was colored in shades of black and deep red-amber, much like the eye color of a vampire after a successful hunt.

The bird that flew in the center of the shield was not like a real bird. Instead, it resembled a mythical creature: wings open, talons extended, prepared for the kill. The bird itself was stitched in gold threads, all but its eye. The eye was sewn in the same red-amber that was in the shield. It made me wonder if whoever stitched his shield might have known what he was. If they did, I'm sure they keep it to themselves, for this man carried as much power as a king. It must have been hard for him to walk away from all of this, as they all must do as time catches up with them.

I decided that I would leave the chair in front of the fireplace, just as he had left it. Corbin had started a fire for me earlier that had almost gone out by now. It was the first fire to be kindled there. With a little TLC, it sprang back to life. The light of the fire glinted off Navar's sword. I reached up to touch it. "You must have been some kind of a person to still command such respect. I wish I had known you," I said, giving the sword a gentle pat. I took my seat in front of the fire and opened my book.

I was going along pretty good, hanging on every word, until the murderer reared his evil head. I snapped the book closed. "Oh no! Not tonight! I have had quite enough bad guys to last me for a while." I picked up another book. Ah, yes, a love story. *Okay, this could work.* I read until I started to get sleepy.

I folded the corner of my page so I wouldn't lose my place then placed it on the table by the chair. As the book hit the table, I remembered that I needed to brush my teeth. I ran my tongue over my teeth. *Yuck! Aw man, I have to go all the way downstairs just to brush my teeth or anything else I might need to do in the bathroom.* One of the next things I was going to ask about was having an en-suite bathroom put in. For now, I was happy to have some lamps hooked up. I knew that it had taken some doing: some really long extension cords and a lot of thank you's. I really would have hated to have to stay in here in the total dark. In my little apartment back in New York, I always had a light on. I didn't like the dark.

I put my toothbrush, my toothpaste, and my favorite shower items in my overnight bag. I headed out the door and down the stairs in search of the closest bathroom. I ran smack-dab into Calldoon, who always said very little to me; mostly he talked to Corbin or Tanarr.

"Pardon me, m'lady," he said as we collided.

"Oh, no, it was my fault; I wasn't looking where I was going. I'm so sorry," I said.

He nodded in acknowledgement as we moved on in different directions.

"Calldoon," I said quickly before he got completely out of sight. He stopped and slowly turned back to me.

"Yes, m'lady?" he said in a very professional tone. I walked to meet him where he had stopped on the stairs.

"May I ask you something?" I asked.

"Yes, m'lady," he said with a nod.

"Well, it's really two questions," I said with a smile. "Will you show me the nearest bathroom?" I held up my overnight bag, "but first I need to know… " I paused for a breath to choose my words. "Does it bother you that there is a woman occupying the Lord's chamber, or is it that there is a human there?" I asked in a matter-of-fact way.

He gazed at my face like he was trying to read my thoughts then quickly looked at the floor before he spoke.

"No, m'lady, 'tis meself that would be wondering if ye be displeased with the likes of me being in charge of yer holdings," he said, never meeting my eyes.

I thought for a moment.

"What do you mean, 'the likes of you,'" I said with a puzzled look and tone to match. "What's wrong with you?"

He finally looked back up at my face.

"Ye know, with me being what I am and all," he said.

It still didn't sink in. I stood there not saying a word until he turned his pleading amber eyes on me. He had removed his contacts for the night. They were still a little burgundy/amber after a recent successful hunt.

"Oh! You mean that thing about you being a vam—" I stopped and lowered my voice. "You mean the vampire thing?"

He raised his head, his eyes darting about to see if anyone who was out and about might have heard.

"Oh, m'lady, please do not say such out loud within the walls of the castle. There are too many ears around that do not know." He gently waved his hand. "Too many hearts that would not understand."

I stepped closer and put my hand on his shoulder.

"Rest assured, if that's all it is. I trust you like I do Tanarr and Zoul, and let's not forget Corbin; you have been the guardian of this grand place for," I paused, "I don't know how long. You have proven to everyone who lives here that you are a good man. Trust me; you're good with me," I said with a wink.

"Thank ye, m'lady. I will honor ye as I have Lord Navar," he said with his hand going over his heart. "I must know," he stopped.

"Go on," I said.

He looked back at the floor then up to me.

"With ye knowing what ye know, do ye not fear me?" he asked.

"Well, no, not with all I've learned about you," *and not with Corbin at my side*, I thought, "and how you've honored your pact with Navar. When I think of the time and care you have put into the upkeep of such a large castle and surrounding estate," I made a motion with my hands displaying the castle, "not even counting all the people that you have looked after, how could I have anything less than the highest of respect for you, not fear?"

A broad smile came across his face. "Thank you, m'lady, I'll not be lettin' ye down. My alliance will forever be with ye."

"No one could ask for more," I said, tucking my arm through the crook of his arm. "Now, with that out of the way, will you please show me the way to the bathroom?" I said with a big smile.

"Yes, m'lady, this way," Calldoon said, returning my smile with one of his own.

As we walked down the dimly lit hall arm in arm, I thought about how I would be the envy of many a woman with such a handsome man on my arm.

"Do you think we can have a bathroom put in my room?" I asked, looking up at him sideways. "Do you think that's a doable thing?"

He stopped and looked down at me with an odd look on his face.

"Ye do not get it, do ye?" he said.

"Get what?" I asked.

"Ye may do whatever ye please; she is all yers," he said.

"You know," I said with a shake of my head. "I really don't get it. I probably will always ask you."

He shook his head and chuckled as we continued on down the hall.

In a short time we came to a halt in front of a very large, arched door. It was much newer than the rest of the structure, even though the craftsman had taken great pains to make it look as old as the rest of the castle. As I looked at the door before me, I thought, *Good job*. I would have had a hard time picking it out from the other doors.

"Here ye go, m'lady," Calldoon said with a bow.

"Thank you," I said, looking up at him. I gave him a wink. "I think you and I are going to be great friends."

"I hope so, m'lady," he said.

"Hey, what happened to Katelynn?" I said, thumping myself on the chest.

"I'm sorry," he said, "but for now ye are the new Lord of the castle. I canna call ye by yer Christian name. It would not be proper."

"Ah, come on now!" I gave him a pouty face. "You're making me feel like an old lady!"

He bowed his head.

"'Tis not my intention; 'tis only respect."

"All right, for now, but I'm going to keep working on you," I said with a wink and a finger wag.

I timidly opened the bathroom door and flicked on the light. Calldoon stopped and turned back.

"Would ye like me to check for spiders?" he asked.

I looked at him, put my hands on my hips, rolled my eyes, and let out a huff. "No, I can do this."

About that time I saw something scurry across the floor. I squealed and jumped back into the hall, grabbing Calldoon by the arm. I almost threw him into the bathroom.

"Okay, if you insist, and only if it makes you feel better!"

He gave me a polite smile and went into the bathroom to see if he could find anything. He hadn't been in there but a moment when I heard a stomp. I swallowed hard. I heard Calldoon's footsteps coming back out of the bathroom.

"All offending parties have been eradicated," he said.

"Was it very big?" I asked.

He adjusted his sweater.

"Well, it was no small one; by me measuring, it was the biggest spider I've ever acquainted," he said.

"Oh, my!" I said.

"It is all clear now," he said with an assuring nod and smile.

"Thank you," I said.

"Tomorrow we will see about having a full bath installed in the master chamber," Calldoon said.

"Thank you, again," I said.

He gave me a polite bow as he took his leave. I took care of business as quickly as possible. I knew it would be a long walk back to my room. I had thought that I would be scared to be all by myself in these long, old, dimly lit halls. To my surprise, I felt safe and cared for here in this unfamiliar land, surrounded by the unknown, and even worse, knowing the unknown or the unbelievable. For now, Zoul and Tanarr had both decided to stay for a while. I would think that having four vampires as constant company, I would feel at least a little uneasy. What was I thinking? Just saying "vampire" should have made me uneasy, but it did not. I felt so very safe, I thought with a shake of my head. Who would have thought? I was so lost in my own little world that I almost didn't see the woman, girl, lady…I wasn't sure of her age, but I was sure that it was the same woman who had brought my supper last night. I couldn't tell what was up with her. I couldn't tell if she were mad at the world, sad, shy, or maybe her elevator just didn't go to the top floor; perhaps something tragic had happened in her life. One day I hoped I would get to talk to her. I pondered all this as I made my way up the last flight of stairs.

Now with my teeth brushed and having had a good, hot shower, I slid between clean, fresh-smelling sheets. I could have sworn that they must have been washed in lavender and sunshine. I was asleep before my head hit the pillow.

Chapter Three

The next morning I awoke to sunlight streaming through my bedroom window. My room was so high up that it hadn't made any sense to wrestle those heavy drapes closed. With a stretch and a yawn, I came slowly but fully awake. After all the rain of yesterday, the sun was a nice reprieve. Looking out the window, over the rolling hills framed by a perfect sunrise, I could see that the sky was streaked red, pink, orange, and grey. *Wow! This was a visual holiday: amazing!*

In the courtyard below, something caught my eye. Who was that? I squinted my eyes, trying to focus. It looked like Tanarr; it looked like he was talking to Navar and Lera's graves. Her statue had just been place there beside Navar's, as it should be. *What on earth was he doing?* I couldn't take my eyes away, and that was not just because this man was easy on the eyes. His strawberry blond hair sparkled in the morning sun. Even from this distance, I could see the detail on his perfectly tanned face. I knew it was only a spray tan. Corbin had told me that one day, but it worked for him. That face commanded your attention.

I didn't know if he was wearing his green contacts or not. His straight nose, not too big, not too small, gave him an air of importance, but the high cheekbone and that small cleft in his chin toned down some of his formal look to give him a smoking, sexy profile. He was wearing a crisp, white shirt and well-worn jeans. I didn't even have to see his shoes to know that they were expensive; he always wore expensive shoes. *Whoa there, girl!* I gave myself a good mental shake. I already had my very own very handsome, very sweet vam… Spiderman. I didn't even like to think that word. So I would keep a friendly distance from Tanarr, but I still wondered what he was saying.

"My old, trusted friend, I've missed you." Tanarr looked up at the bronze face of Navar. "I tried my best to look out for her," he smiled, chuckled, and shook his head. "You know how headstrong Lera always was. She never let me know where she was most of the time. Being what she was, I couldn't feel where she was." His smile faded. "I loved her; you know that. I'm not sorry; you know that too. I would have taken her from you if I could have." He shook his head. "She never even gave me a second look."

He bent down, sitting back on his heels. He reached down and broke off a blade of grass. As he rolled the blade of grass between his thumb and forefinger, he looked back up at the bronze face, lit by the morning sunlight, and continued his conversation with his long-gone friend. "Do you know where I found Lera, after your services, when everyone thought that she had disappeared?" He tossed the blade of grass to the ground. "In the Amazon! Yeah, you heard me, the Amazon. I think her mother was right to call her a little Irish spitfire."

He took a deep breath. "I found her there in the shadow of that blasted orchid, caring for the people of the Kee-Ka-Na tribe. I tried to get her to leave with me, but she wouldn't. So for a short time I stayed with her there. I borrowed your life for a short season, although not completely, as she never loved me, not like she loved you." He said it so sadly that he could feel his heart break all over again. He slowly turned to Lera's bronze figure. He placed his hand lovingly on the cold bronze face, colder now than his own hand. He shook his head. "I wanted you so badly my bones ached. If only I could have made you love me. I would have given all I possessed to have had just a small portion of what you gave to Navar." As his hand slid from the bronze face, his head bowed. Tanaar's shoulders slumped, and he walked away.

I watched the whole scene unfold from my lofty perch. There was no way that I could tell what he was saying, but I still felt like I had witnessed something profoundly personal. I felt as if I were intruding. With the look on his face and his body language, I could almost feel his pain. I knew he and Navar had been good friends. Perhaps he was saddened to lose his last link to his old friend. There was so much in this magical place that I didn't understand.

There was a soft knock at my door.

"Who is it?" I asked.

"Meself, 'tis only," came a soft voice.

I opened the door to the odd lady who has been assigned to care for my needs.

"Hi!" I paused; her name had left me. "I'm sorry. What is your name again? I know Calldoon told me, but for the life of me, I can't remember."

Never raising her head, she gave a little bob for a curtsey. "Deireadh, 'tis the name given," she replied softly.

"Now, that's quite a mouthful. I don't believe I've heard it before; whatever does it mean? I know most names have a meaning. I don't think mine does. I was named after some great-great-great-grandmother. There is a Katelynn that pops up now and then along the way in our family. I guess it was time for it to turn up again." I was rambling to fill in the awkward silence. When I finally took a breath, she quickly spoke up.

"The last one," she whispered. "Me name: that would be the meaning of me name."

"Girl, one of these days you and I have got to sit down and talk, but for now, what's on your mind?" I asked.

"Would like to be knowin', the kitchen would, if ye be takin yer mornin' meal here, or would ye be comin' to the dining hall?" she asked, still never looking me in the eyes.

"I don't know. I had not thought much about it," I said.

Deireadh sheepishly cleared her throat.

"'Tis none of me concern, it is. However, sittin' at the table, Sir Corbin would be," she said.

"Oh, really? In that case, I'm eating in the dining hall." I held my hand up to stop her. "Wait one second. I'll walk down with you," I said.

"But, but, m'lady," she stuttered, "ye can no be goin' to the dining hall in ye nightdress."

I looked down at what I had on. I was still wearing the big over-sized football jersey that I had slept in. I had stolen it (well, not really stolen, more like in the borrowed-but-never-planned-to-return-it kind of way) from Moose. Back home, Moose was the biggest football player on our high school team. He had let me borrow his gold and blue jersey. I proudly wore it during homecoming week and kind of never gave it back. (Sorry, Moose.) Here I stood in this football jersey, which came all the way to my knees, in my bare feet and with my hair uncombed. I looked down at what I had on.

"Okay, make that two seconds!" I said.

"No, m'lady!" she protested.

"Really, I'm pretty fast at changing; it won't take long!" I said as I dashed behind a vanity screen.

"No, m'lady, 'tis not fittin'. I be but yer maid," she said as I jumped into my jeans. I stepped out from behind the screen wearing jeans, a sweatshirt, and sneaks. I pulled my hair back in a ponytail.

"Now, listen here, sweetie; if I'm the Lord of all of this," I said with a chuckle, "I still find that hard to believe! Then I get to say who I can walk to breakfast with, all right?"

"Right," she said back with a smile in her voice.

She and I were about the same height, so it was easy for me to slip my arm through the crook of her arm.

"Now that we have that straight, let's you and me head down to breakfast," I said with a smile and a nod. For the first time since having met her, she raised her face to meet mine.

"As ye wish, m'lady," she replied with a broad smile of her own. She looked down at her hands.

"No one has ever asked me to walk anywhere with them; honor ye forever I will!" her eyes fluttered open wide. My breath caught in my chest.

"You are cute as a button, and your eyes are, are—" I couldn't even think of a good word to describe them. "They're purple! Not blue, but purple!"

Her eyes dropped to the floor.

"Strange, odd, bewitched, weird, freakish. Be that it would, some of the words ye be looking for. Go ahead, heard them I have." I could feel the pain of each one as they sliced through her heart. I stopped before we went any further.

"No, the words are more like breathtaking, beautiful, lovely, amazing, and words like envious, because that's what I am." I tilted her chin up. "Any man would be proud to have you on his arm. Any woman would be green with envy to see you there!" She smiled back at me.

"Thank ye. I've never been told that I be pretty," she said.

I gave her a good finger wag.

"Not pretty," I said.

Her beautiful, happy face fell. Sadness returned, and her eyes dropped to the floor. I took the tip end of my index finger, placed it under her chin, and tilted her face up so we were eye to eye.

"But—" I said, with a big emphasis on that word, "you are drop-dead gorgeous!" I said with a smile.

The light came back to her eyes, and the smile returned to her lips.

"You got that, girl?" I added. She nodded; I spun her around and linked arms with her. "Now that we have that out of the way, I have a sexy guy waiting for me at the table, so let's go! However, tomorrow or the next day we are going to have lunch. You know, while the guys are doing guy stuff, we will have some chick time."

"Chick time?" Deireadh said with a puzzled look. "Going to the chicken coop are we?"

"No, no, no, we are going to eat chocolate, drink coffee, and giggle. You know, gal time: just the two of us." I said.

"Oh," she said, opening her eyes wide and giving a little giggle, and we were off.

We were about to step into the dining hall. As soon as Deireadh caught sight of Corbin, she immediately released my arm and hurried off. Corbin looked up.

"Who were you talking to?" he asked as he got up to pull my chair out for me.

"Deireadh," I said, looking down the hall after her.

"Who?" he asked again.

"You know, the girl that brought my soup last night?" I said.

"Oh, really? I've never heard her speak. I don't even know what she looks like. She's a little bit like a mouse: always hiding behind things then scurrying away before she's seen," Corbin said as he took his chair. "Wait, is this the same crazy old woman who cares for the rose garden, the one the castle is supposed to talk to?"

"One and the same, but I don't know how old she is. She doesn't look that old, and I don't know if she's crazy. I like her," I said.

Corbin moved the paper he had been reading to reveal one very large, very steamy cup of coffee.

"Your food is on the way. I knew you couldn't make it much longer without this," he said, pushing the mug under my nose. I wrapped both my hands around it, lifted it up, inhaled slowly, and took a big gulp

"Ah, now, that's perfect!" I said.

About the time my food came, we heard Tanarr and Calldoon return from a night of hunting. Tanarr came into the dining hall.

"Katelynn, could we meet this morning to start getting all the paperwork in order?" he asked.

"Sure, where?" I asked with a perfectly browned scone on its way to my mouth.

"Calldoon said we could use his office," Tanarr said.

"Okay, what time?" I asked

Tamarr glanced at his watch.

"Let me see; I need a shower." He held out the corner of his shirt. "I hate the stench that hunting leaves on me. How about ten thirty? We'll get some of it done. Then we'll do the rest later," he said.

"Sounds great; I'll see you at ten thirty in Calldoon's office," I said.

Corbin shook his head.

"Lawyers! They never stop," he said with a chuckle.

With my breakfast finished, all the dishes cleared, and my coffee refilled, Corbin and I just enjoyed being in the dining hall with all its splendor. The grand fireplace took up the whole end of the room; it was so big that you could stand up in it. Large wooden beams supported the high ceiling. Hanging from the center beam was a huge, ornate, wrought-iron chandelier. It had long since been converted to gas lights. They flickered like candles, but there was no mess. The dining table was thick, strong wood, so dark it must have been walnut or mahogany. The grain of the wood stood out from years of use. The top of the table rested atop six hand-carved legs. The base of each leg looked like a bear's paw, or perhaps a lion's paw. Either way, it was meant to be as strong as the men that had once dined here.

At the other end of the hall, above the large, arched opening, Navar's coat of arms was proudly displayed. So much detail had been put into it. The shield was black and then trimmed in burgundy. In the center of the shield was a bird, wings outstretched and claws ready for the kill. The bird was raised and etched in gold, or maybe it was solid gold; I couldn't tell from where I was seated. Just below the shield was a pair of swords crossed in unity and protection.

I thought of Ms. Lera's description of the only man she ever loved. Navar: black hair, English profile, strong and handsome and very much in love with a human woman, willing to do whatever it took to be human again; human so he could be with his love, Lera; human, to have a normal life with all its bumps and bruises, laughter, and love.

After this invincible vampire was cured by the nectar from the same orchid that could kill him, the cure that Lera had discovered, he once more became susceptible to everything. The price for his love of life and Lera was the end of his life. All these thoughts ran through my mind as I sat in this magnificent old world, filled with all of Navar's treasures that he had had to leave behind. I smiled up at Corbin as I dragged my thoughts back to the present.

We had been talking for a while when Corbin moved the conversation to Deireadh.

"Did you and your maid have a good morning?" he asked

"Her name is Deireadh; did you know that her name means, "the last one?" I asked.

"Well, yes, I did. I am well versed in Gaelic," Corbin said.

"Isn't that an odd name for a young woman? And speaking of odd, she has the most amazing eyes; they're purple." Corbin's eyebrows went up. "And her hair is red blond and gold. It sparkles like it has glitter in it," I said.

Corbin leaned in.

"Did you say her eyes are purple?" he asked.

"Yeah, purple." I placed my coffee cup down on the table. "Why?" I asked.

"No reason. I just haven't seen purple eyes in a long time," he said.

"Really? I don't think I've ever seen purple eyes before. Are they common here?" I asked.

"No. I wouldn't say common, but I have seen them. Hey, what time are you going to meet Tanarr?" Corbin asked.

I could tell he was trying to discreetly change the subject for some reason. "We said ten thirty, I think." I said. I looked down at what I was wearing. "Do I need to change?" I asked.

He reached over and brushed the side of my face with the back of his hand, capturing a stray strand of hair and tucking it behind my ear.

"Not one hair," he said with a smile that melted my heart.

"Are you sure?" I asked.

"I'm sure," he winked. "You're perfect. Besides, it's just Tanarr, and you're just signing some papers."

Tanarr fit well in his role as a lawyer. He was Ms. Lera's lawyer, and no mortal would have guessed that some of his nights were spent draining animals of their blood in lieu of humans, to fill his hunger and sustain his life. Thankfully for us all, he was one of the good guys, I thought.

"Good point," I said with one last gulp of coffee. I glanced at my watch. "Oh, my! I didn't realize it was so late. If I run, I can make it to Calldoon's office on time." I leaned over and gave Corbin a quick peck on the lips. "I got to run!"

"I think I'm going to see if I can find Calldoon and see how he is doing. See if I can do anything to help," he said.

"Okay." I said as I headed off for my meeting with Tanarr.

Chapter Four

Corbin found Calldoon in the courtyard. "Calldoon, a word, please," Corbin said.

"Yes, Sir Corbin," Calldoon replied.

When he got close enough so others could not hear, he began his inquiry.

"I have one question," Corbin said.

"Yes, Sir?" Calldoon nodded.

"Is there a fairy living here in Castle Go-Brath?" Corbin asked frankly.

Calldoon's mouth almost fell open.

"A what, Sir??" Calldoon asked as shock spread over his face.

"You heard me: a fairy!" Corbin said.

"No, Sir. I would never allow a fairy to stay within the walls of the castle. Ye know how dangerous they can be for us." He stopped and looked out over the rolling hills, then back to Corbin. "Why did ye think that there would be such a being here, anyway?" Calldoon asked.

"Katelynn told me that her maid has purple eyes." Corbin now had Calldoon's full attention.

"Purple eyes, ye say?" Calldoon said.

"Yes, and we both know that only fairies have purple eyes," Corbin said.

"That be true; it must surely have been a trick of the light," Calldoon said.

"She also said that her hair looked like she had glitter in it," Corbin said.

"That does sound like a fairy." Calldoon paused for a moment. "No, it could not be. I would know if Deireadh was a fairy."

"But what if, as her name implies, she is the last one?" The concern was building in Corbin's voice.

"Do not fret yerself. I'll be seein' about this at once," Calldoon said as he started to leave.

"Calldoon," Corbin called after him. "Be careful; you know what they're capable of."

"That I do, Sir, that I do," Calldoon said.

Chapter Five

I knocked softly at Calldoon's office door. I had started to walk straight in but changed my mind, as that seemed a little disrespectful. After all, I didn't want Tanarr to think I had no raising. About that time, the door opened. My breath caught; *wow, this man was hot!!* He had showered, donned a crisp, white shirt and designer jeans that fit well, very well! His hair was a bit tousled, and he had put his green contacts back in place. I was so at ease that I almost forgot what he was. *Mental shake! One vampire at a time, please*! I was quite happy with the one that I had.

"Katelynn, please come in." His voice was like a purr as he led me to my seat. He walked around Calldoon's heavy oak desk and took a seat in the high-back leather chair. His well-made leather briefcase sat open on the desk.

"Shall we get started?" he said.

I perched myself on the edge of my chair so I could watch everything he was doing. The first thing he withdrew was the deed to the castle.

"I thought perhaps you might want to start with Go-Brath herself?" He put his pen down and looked around the room. "I know she doesn't mean much to you now, but those of us who have been with her from the beginning would very much like to see her cared for." He leaned in close, his green eyes looking so intense that I felt as though he could see right into my soul. "We all hope you will grow to love her as we do. I know you didn't know Navar. He was kind, strong, gracious, and a good man. He loved this place more than anything in the world." Sadness washed over his face, "save one thing alone he loved more," he stopped.

"What was that?" I asked, not waiting for him to finish. He ran his hand across his forehead.

"Lera," was all he said. Her name hung in the air as if her very presence was there in the room with us. Neither of us said a word for a while. Call it respect; call it fear. I didn't know what to say. His reaction was so strong, and I just waited for him to pull himself together.

"Are you okay?" I asked after a while.

"Yes, I'm fine. She has always had this effect on me. You would think after all this time it wouldn't matter; it wouldn't hurt." I didn't know if he was talking to me or to himself. My curiosity got the best of me.

"Tanarr, is there something you would like to talk about?" I asked.

He lowered his eyes.

"What is it about you? I've already said things to you that I have never even said out loud before. I can see how Lera would trust you," he said.

I reached out and touched his hand. It always surprised me at how cold their hands were.

"If she can trust me, so can you. Whatever you say, I promise it will go no further," I said with a smile.

He put his hand on top of mine.

"Thank you; it would be nice to talk to someone. I've never had that privilege," he said with a soft smile

A chill ran up my spine. What had I done? I hoped I had not opened that proverbial Pandora's Box.

He ran his hand over the deed, which was now yellowed with age.

"Navar was my best and oldest friend; there was nothing I would not do for him. That went both ways with almost everything. When we were here, we—the three of us—were kings. I know that Navar held the title, but the three of us took care of everything together. He taught us how to be noble: how to walk with our heads held high. He taught us that even though we were vampires, we were still among the human race. We still mattered. To return evil for evil is unacceptable and no way to live one's life. Navar taught us to always choose the truth over a lie. Chose to do right over wrong, and always choose love over hate. The stronger you are, the larger your responsibility. Care for the ones that cannot care for themselves." Tanarr took a beep breath and smiled a little crooked smile at me.

Oh my, this man is...wow! I thought. If I had been standing, my knees would have buckled. I had to remind myself that he was talking and I was supposed to be listening—no, I needed to be listening. He went back to his memories. "We all, even the human knights, lived by that same code. If you could not, then you had to leave."

"Did anyone ever have to leave?" I asked.

"Only once," he said.

"Really?" I said, moving to the edge of my seat and waiting for him to answer. He didn't say anything. "Well, aren't you going to tell me who?" I said.

He looked at me out from under thick eyelashes.

"Blake," he said as he went back to the task at hand without missing a beat.

I sucked in my breath so fast and hard that I choked myself.

"What? Are you serious? Not the same Blake that killed Ms. Lera, and the same Blake that was driving the truck that killed Navar?"

Tanarr was completely silent. Then, so softly that I could barely hear him, he growled through clinched teeth.

"What did you say?!"

This time he scared me: the look on his face, the tone of his voice, and the fact that every muscle in his body had come to full attention and was ready to pounce. This reaction made me flinch and slide back in my chair.

"I—I—I'm sorry. I thought you knew," I began to stutter. He stood and walked over to the far end of the room. I could tell he was trying to regain his composure. When he turned back to face me, I could see that he had pulled himself back together. He calmly walked back around the desk to take his seat across from me once more. He leaned across the papers that lay on the desk before him.

"Would you please tell me what you're talking about?" Tanarr asked.

I swallowed hard, took a deep breath, and began.

"One night when Blake was trying to intimidate Ms. Lera's work out of me, he confessed that he had been the one that was driving the truck that killed Navar."

I could see the pain flash across his face. He closed his eyes and turned his face away.

"Does Corbin know this?" he asked.

"Yes, he does. I told him just after it happened," I said.

He turned back to face me.

"And he did nothing?" he asked slowly.

"He said he wanted to take care of Ms. Lera's arrangements first. Then he said he would deal with Blake," I said.

Tanarr wrote something down on a pad and slipped it into his briefcase. "Corbin and I will talk later," he said just barely under his breath. It made me think that he was not talking to me. I opted to keep my mouth shut and wait for the first chance to change the subject.

Straightway he went back to the task at hand. He turned the deed around for me to sign, making the castle one hundred percent mine.

"Tanarr, may I ask you something?" I asked, looking up at him as I finished signing the deed.

He nodded as he checked to make sure everything was in order.

"Calldoon told me that there was a person who chose to remain anonymous that kept the castle funded all these years. Do you know who that was?" I asked.

"Lera," he said in a matter-of-fact way.

"Did she ever come here?" I asked.

"No, she never set one foot on the property. She couldn't; her heart was too broken. She did, however, want to make sure it was restored and maintained in the style that would make Navar proud. She did fly over it from time to time, just to see how it was going." Tanarr said.

"Ah, that's so cool. Did she hire a helicopter or something?" I asked, looking up from the freshly completed deed. He was smiling, almost laughing in fact.

"What?" he chuckled. "Lera never hired anyone. She flew herself."

"She had her pilot's license?" I said with a squeak in my voice.

He tilted his face up, closed his eyes, and smiled.

"I can still see her standing there in those ridiculously baggie pants, cinched in tightly with a thick belt. A long-sleeve man's shirt tucked in, all the same shade of tan, and one of those—" he paused. "Oh, what do you call it? It's one of those tight-fitting caps with the bug-eyed goggles strapped across the top of it. Whatever it's called, it took my breath. She was a vision standing there all fluttering in the wind. One rebel strand of curly red hair had escaped out from under her cap. That little red curl danced around the edge of her sparkly green eyes. Oh, how I loved to see that sparkle in her eyes. It always made my hands sweat, and that's a hard thing to do to a vampire," he said with a smile of remembrance. "She was standing beside her very own plane, jumping up and down waving her brand-new license. A bigger smile I had never seen. I walked over and gave her a big hug. While I had her in my arms, I couldn't resist giving her a kiss."

"A kiss?" I said, interrupting him.

"Yes, a kiss. It didn't mean much to her, but to me, it sent my world out of control. I remember for one brief moment, her melting into my arms." He closed his eyes. "She relaxed and was enjoying herself; she was enjoying us. She had forgotten who I was; I knew she was thinking of Navar. I didn't care. I felt her stiffen, and she pushed away from me. 'Tanarr,' she said as her eyes fluttered open. 'I'm so sorry.' She stepped back looking embarrassed, awkward, and shy. She turned her back to me. 'It's okay,' I said as I slipped my arms around her waist, pulling her back against my chest. 'No, it's not okay. If I had only left things alone, Navar would still be with us.'"

"Lera didn't often cry. For the first time since the funeral, she started to cry. 'Lera, it wasn't your fault.' I said as I put my chin on top of her head. 'You know he wanted his life back, as much as you wanted him to have it back. You know I loved him like a brother. But he is gone, and it's not your fault. I know you loved him. Don't spend the rest of your life mourning him. He wouldn't want that for you.' She relaxed back against my chest. I slowly turned her in my arms, took my finger and lifted her face to meet my eyes."

"'He's gone, Lera,' I said, smiling down at her. 'But I'm here, and I love you.' I lowered my head to kiss her. She closed her eyes. I was so close I could feel her warm breath and smell the blood coursing through her heart. 'No, Tanarr, I can't. It wouldn't be fair to you. You deserve more than this,' she said without opening her eyes. One single tear remained on her eyelash. It broke my heart."

"Instead of a kiss, I scooped her up and held her tight in my arms. 'Lera, please let me love you. I've loved you so long that I can't remember when I first fell for you,' I said into her ear. 'No, please. I don't need someone to love me now. Right now I need a friend,' she whispered."

"I stood there cradling her like a small child. 'I'll always be your friend: your friend that will always be hoping for more.' I said with my head against hers. 'Maybe later: maybe someday I'll love again, but not now. Now I feel too much pain, too much responsibility. There's no room for love,' she said. I gave her a soft kiss on the cheek. 'Someday,' I said. 'I'll wait if it takes forever. I love you enough for the both of us, so I can wait.'"

There was a knock at the door. I was so caught up in what Tanarr was telling me that I jumped at the sound. Tanarr got up and went to the door. I was still so lost in his world that I didn't hear what was being said at the door. As soon as Tanarr finished his conversation, he came back to where I sat and placed his hand on my shoulder. I jumped again. Tanarr chuckled.

"I'm sorry, but I said your name twice, and you didn't respond," he said.

"I'm sorry!" I said, looking up into his handsome face. "You were in love with her all along, weren't you?" I asked.

His smile faded.

"Yes, I loved her so much. I would have done anything for her, taken her anywhere, given her anything she wanted." He shook his head. "But she wanted the only thing I couldn't give her." He went silent.

"What was that?" I couldn't help but ask.

Tanarr raised his head toward the portrait of Navar hanging prominently on the office wall.

"Him." I could hear the pain in his voice.

"Oh, Navar," I whispered.

"Yes," he said so softly that I could barely hear him. "He was all she ever wanted."

Tanarr walked around the desk and took his seat. It creaked in protest as he settled back in. He quickly changed the subject with a shuffle of the papers that were spread about the desk.

"The young man that was at the door said that Calldoon has requested that you meet him in the library."

As I got up from my chair, I looked back at Tanarr. He seemed a little sadder now than when we had begun.

"Are we through here?" I asked.

"No, we have more to do, but we can take care of it later," he said, stacking papers into his briefcase. I had my hand on the door handle but stopped and looked over my shoulder.

"Can we talk later?" I asked.

"Sure; we have a lot more paperwork to do," he said.

"I don't mean talk about all this," I said, motioning to the papers we had been going through. "I mean about Lera." I paused. "It's just that you seem to know more about her than anyone else."

"Sure. How about tonight over coffee, in the library? I've heard you have quite a taste for the stuff." He got a little twinkle back in his eye and then shook his head. "I don't get it: a hot black liquid in a hard stone mug." He made a distasteful face. "I prefer a warm red drink in a soft, shapely container; ahh!"

"Hey, quit that!" I said with my best stern face.

"I'm just messing with you," he said with a chuckle, "but just so we're straight, I do not abide by the hunter's code. I like people to feel safe around me. Edge fear is not my thing," he said.

"Good; as long as we're clear on that, I'll see you tonight in front of the fireplace." I gave him a playful finger wag. "Coffee only, deal?"

"Deal!" he replied with that crooked smile.

Chapter Six

I found Calldoon at the table in the library.

"Hi! I got word that you wanted to see me," I said.

"Yes, m'lady," he said, looking up from the table.

"Hey!" I said, holding up my hands. "What did I say about that m'lady thing?"

"I know," he said with a sheepish grin. "Katelynn is hard for meself to be sayin': too many years of training."

"We'll go slowly; I'll try not to feel like I need to be in a long dress and a pointy hat if you'll try to call me Katelynn." I said, stepping to his side of the table. "What do we have here?" The papers spread before me appeared to be blueprints.

"I have been thinking about ye having to come all the way down the stairs for yer evening grooming. As we agreed last night, ye have need of a well-lit ladies' room in yer suite," Calldoon said.

"Oh, wow! This looks great! Who did the drawing, and how did you get him to get it done so fast?" I said, running my hand over the freshly drawn blueprint.

"I did this," Calldoon said with pride.

"You're very good. Did you go to school for this?" I asked, still not taking my eyes off the paper.

"Living as long as we do, one tends to pick up a thing or two," he said with a touch of sadness in his voice.

"Well, I think you have this down pat," I said.

"May I show ye what I have in mind?" He straightened out the blueprints and used the flat end of the pencil as a pointer. "The room will be placed in this corner of yer suite. It will be set up as two rooms in one, with the first room a dressing room. One wall will be mirrored. This side will be for yer hanging clothing; here, shoes, and all these drawers will be prepared to receive all your jewels."

"Jewels!" I laughed. "Don't waste your time; all I have, I wear," I said, wiggling my fingers that showed off Lera's ring that was to be her wedding ring. Around my neck was a thick silver chain that held Navar's ring: bold, ornate, and the key to his castle. "I do have some costume things, but don't you think this would be overkill? It's just junk."

Calldoon looked up from his blueprints. He tilted his face to the side and gave me a smile.

"When we be done here, I'll be showin' ye the basement."

I swallowed hard.

"Do you mean the dungeon?"

He chuckled.

"I guess so, but we've had no need for a dungeon in a long, long time. Now 'tis used for storage only," he said.

"Ah, okay. As long as no one is planning a hostile takeover, it's all good," I said, trying to sound funny and not scared.

He grinned.

"No hostile takeover, just stuff," he said, going back to the blueprints. Using the flat end of his pencil, he pointed out the entry to what he called the bathing room. "Here we will be puttin' a large, marble counter top with a sink in the center. What color would ye be likin' it to be?" he asked, looking up from his work.

"Hmm... how about white? No, no, no; black with small, white lines in it. I think it will match the strength of the castle," I said.

Calldoon nodded his approval.

"Very good. I think that would be perfect," he said with a smile. "Here we will put the toilet; this long space will be for a multi-headed shower that will be glass enclosed. Then here under a large skylight, there will be a hand-carved black marble tub, big enough for two, if ye be so inclined," he said with a sheepish grin.

"Hmm...," was all I said to that. "This looks perfect; thank you so much!"

"You're welcome," Calldoon said as he rolled up the blueprint. "Now to the dungeon with us!" he said with a nod.

"Great, to the dungeon." I said. *Great*, I thought, *I hope I'm not in over my head.*

Chapter Seven

In New York, Blake Klavell climbed on board a jumbo jet. As he made his way to the first-class section, he turned the head of every woman, even the nun, fresh off her mission trip.

Tall, lean, unbelievably good-looking, and well cared for—from his handmade Italian shoes, made from the most exotic of skins, all the way up to his striking, navy blue contacts and perfectly trimmed jet black hair—Blake always made an impression. As he glided down the aisle, lipsticks were dropped, magazines were fumbled, and every female's mouth went dry. Each woman slowly inhaled as he passed by. The lady behind him closed her eyes and breathed in slowly. She leaned over to her friend.

"Oh my, he smells...," she paused to search for the right word, "delicious. That's it; he smells delicious. I wonder if he would tell me who makes his cologne. I would love to get some for my husband."

Blake gracefully rose to his feet, stepped back to stand by her seat, and knelt down so they would be eye to eye.

"Thank you," he whispered in her ear, "but it's been formulated just for me. It's so very kind of you to notice."

He took the woman's hand and kissed the edge of her knuckles. He could smell the blood that rushed through her veins.

"Mmm...you smell pretty tasty yourself." Blake's silky voice played with the woman's heart. She blushed and giggled. It had been a long time since she had done either. Blake winked at her and returned to his seat.

With a low rumble of laughter, he shook his head in disgust. *Yuck! Old woman: now there's a taste that was hard to get out of your mouth.* He thought it quite a shame that he hadn't met her years earlier. She would have been an easy snack. *But now*, he thought, *I never want that taste in my mouth again.*

Tiffany was a young flight attendant with sparkly brown eyes that had gold flecks dancing about in the brown. Her bouncy blond hair tumbled down her back, and she had a body that would no doubt have been perfect for *Playboy*.

Dramatically, she leaned over to expose her ample cleavage. The woman behind Blake rolled her eyes in disgust. Blake, however, had to restrain to keep from licking his lips. *Now this is more like it*, he thought. Tiffany put on her sexiest voice (Blake always did that to a woman).

"May I get you anything?" she giggled. "You know, coffee, tea, or me?"

Blake winked at her.

"I'll have a glass of wine, red, at room temperature for now; the last part we'll see about later," Blake said with a sadistic smile. As she walked away, she ran her fingers across his chest and over his shoulder.

"You promise?" she whined.

Blake caught her hand, turned it over, and nipped the center.

"Oh, yeah, I promise," he almost purred when he spoke.

Anyone who cared to could see the excitement on Tiffany's face. This gave Blake a great deal of pleasure; he loved to play with pretty young things.

As soon as Tiffany got back to the attendant's station, the spell was broken. She shook her head.

"Are you okay?" April asked.

"I think so," she said, rubbing her hand over her face. "Have you seen the guy in first class?"

"Oh, yeah! Everyone on the plane is talking about him," April said, leaning back against the counter.

"Whoa," Tiffany said as she poured the red wine. "He can get under your skin." She cleared her throat and squared her shoulders. "Just my luck, he's in my section." She gave her friend a nervous smile and headed back to first class, wine in hand.

"Here you go, Mr. Klavell," Tiffany said, handing the glass of wine to Blake.

"Call me Blake; all my friends do," he said, taking the glass from her hand. As he did so, he wrapped his hand around hers so she couldn't let go of the glass. Blake looked deep into her eyes, so intently that she could not even blink. His silky voice caressed her ears. "I do hope we will be friends." His presence had stolen her voice; she could only nod.

"Tiffany!" April called from the entrance of first class.

Tiffany snapped back to reality with a jump.

"Yes, yes, April. I'm coming," Tiffany said, still never taking her eyes off Blake. "Excuse me, sir, I need to get back to work," she said as she slipped her hand from between the glass and Blake's hand.

"Of course. I didn't mean to monopolize your time. Perhaps when we land in Paris, we can catch a bite together," Blake said with a smile.

"Sure, maybe; we'll see," she stuttered.

"Tiffany!" April impatiently called her name again.

"Coming!" She nodded goodbye to Blake.

He chuckled to himself. "Now that was fun, but not as fun as it will be." He lifted the glass, took a sniff, snarled his nose, and immediately set it aside. "I don't see the appeal," he thought.

The flight continued on uneventfully. They touched down in Paris on time. As each person slowly filed off, Blake purposely held back so he would be the last one off the plane. He waited to make his exit. Just at the right moment he stood, almost pinning Tiffany to the seat across from his.

"I'm so sorry," he whispered, stepping closer instead of backing up.

"No, no, it's my fault," she nervously stammered.

He took his finger and lifted her chin.

"No, it's my pleasure," he said, moving in even closer. Tiffany tried to step back, but she had nowhere to go.

"How about dinner, tonight at my hotel?" he asked.

Tiffany knew in the back of her mind that this was not a good idea. Try as she may, she could not say no to this handsome man who held some kind of power over her, or was it just lust?

"I'm staying at the St. Marritze, and I'm all alone," he added.

She blinked a couple times; everyone knew that that was the most expensive place in the world. Money, looks, and sex appeal to spare made the whole evening that more alluring. *There is no way I'm going to miss this*, she thought. Tiffany paused for a moment to make it look like she wasn't easy.

"Sure, what time?" She knew there would be a lot of people there; she could see no harm. Besides that, she had always wanted to see that place.

"How about eight? I prefer to feed, I mean, *eat*, late," Blake said, almost misspeaking. She didn't even catch the glitch; she was looking forward to the evening too much.

"Eight sounds great to me. It will give me time to get cleaned up," she said.

He leaned down and ran his nose around the side of her neck, inhaling as he went.

"Mmm…you smell delicious." He couldn't resist licking the artery that throbbed just below the skin. "And you taste even better." He chuckled, then under his breath he said, "I'm sure."

Tiffany shivered. She placed her hand in the center of his chest, pushing him back so she could pass.

"Until tonight," she said.

As Blake watched her walk away, he slowly licked his lips.

"You won't be walking away tonight," he whispered.

Gail caught Tiffany by the arm.

"What are you doing?" Gail asked, the concern rising in her voice.

Tiffany jerked loose. "I'm having dinner at the St. Marritze tonight," she said.

"You be careful," Gail warned. "He looks like a big old bag of heartache."

"I will. There is something about him; I couldn't say no, and besides, we'll be in that grand dining room with all those people. What could possibly go wrong? I'll be fine; you worry too much," Tiffany said with a big smile.

Later that night, Blake was standing in front of the lounge. Between his thumb and forefinger he held one long-stemmed rose. Each woman that passed by him secretly wished it was for her.

Tiffany arrived at 8:00 P.M. on the dot. Not sure how to dress, she had chosen a shell pink, strappy evening dress. Thin and clingy, it showed her perfect curves flawlessly.

Blake spotted her across the room.

Hmm…I do like my dinner to arrive on time and hot, and she is both, he thought.

He locked eyes with her then made his way straight to where she stood.

"Good evening, my dear. You look ravishing," he said, leaning in to give her a light kiss on the cheek. Then he presented her with the rose.

"Thank you," she said as she accepted the flower.

"I thought we would have dinner in my suite, if you don't mind?" Blake asked.

"But I thought we were eating in the dining room," Tiffany said with a touch of disappointment in her voice.

"Well," he said pulling her in close, "when one has such a tasty morsel, one does not see the need to share said morsel. Besides, we have a fresh, crisp salad, lobster with melted butter, asparagus with a lemon sauce, and a warm crème brulee just waiting for us to pierce the crust, followed by an old black-and-white movie," he said.

"Well…what's the name of the movie?" she asked in a feeble attempt to seem unconcerned and uninterested. She knew she could not say no to this man.

"*Casablanca*; we'll sit on the couch, watch the movie, and talk," he said, giving her a little fake pouty face. "If you say no, we'll eat down here, in the crowd, where we can't talk."

Tiffany was twisting the rose between her fingers. She knew she should say no, but she was going to say yes anyway.

"I don't think—ouch!" she yelped.

"What's wrong?" Blake asked.

She held up her finger.

"The rose got me," she said with a whine.

The bright red blood oozed down the side of her finger.

"Now, that just won't do; let me kiss it and make it better," he said, raising the injured finger to his lips. He gave it a gentle kiss. Her eyes fluttered closed, trying to act shy. In that flutter of her eye, he completely consumed the trickle of blood that had run down her finger. Like sampling a fine wine, he couldn't wait to drain the bottle. "All right, now it's your call. If you say no, I'll abide by that. It will break my heart," he said, clutching at his chest. "I'll call the kitchen and have someone take all the tasty food away. Then I'll watch *Casablanca* all by myself later." He let out a long sigh. "So, what do you say?"

"Okay, dinner and a movie, and that's all," she said with fake resistance. He nodded. "As you wish, so it shall be," he said with a smile. Blake offered her his arm.

"Shall we?" he asked.

"We shall," she replied.

Chapter Eight

Blake took out his gold-plated key. He slid it in, and the door came open to the penthouse suite. Tiffany's mouth gaped. She was almost overwhelmed by the splendor that besieged her.

"This is the most amazing place I have ever seen, and exactly what I expected!" she said as the aroma of the perfectly prepared food swirled around her head. "Wow! Dinner smells great!"

Blake stepped close behind her, slid his arms around her waist, and nuzzled the back of her ear.

"Yes, it does; come on in and eat, while it's hot. Then we'll settle down and enjoy the movie," Blake said with a smile as he pulled out her chair. He then slowly walked around the small table, enjoying the view. He took his seat across from her.

The meal was spent in pleasant conversation. He intently watched as she enjoyed her meal, and yes, she did know which fork to use. Handling herself in social settings was not new to her. Tiffany had been well schooled, not only in the world of books but also in the social world. She was accustomed to being wined and dined by well-heeled men of all nationalities. Her job and her looks had opened a lot of doors for her. She knew what she wanted, and she knew how to get it. *This guy is different*, she thought. *He knows how to get what he wants, too. I'll have to keep my guard up.*

Tiffany looked over at Blake's plate.

"You're not eating," she said.

"I have eaten some; I'm not terribly hungry." A wicked little smile crept across his face. "Not for lobster, anyway."

She looked up from her food and gave him a sexy little smile accompanied by a suggestive eye flutter, which invoked a rich rumble of laughter form Blake.

When they were ready for dessert, the crème brulee with its sugar crust browned to perfection sat in the center of the small table.

"What a perfect ending to a perfect meal!" Tiffany said, picking up her spoon and preparing to break through the crust. Just before the spoon touched the crisp sugar shell, Blake stopped her.

"Wait, please; let me," he said.

She stopped; he took his spoon, tapped it gently then broke through the crust. He took a small bite and offered it to her.

"I like to be the first one to break the crust; it's my favorite part of the meal. There is something about hearing that crack as the crust gives in, knowing what lies below. Ah…," he said as she took the bite offered her.

"That's very good," she said. He started to feed her another bite. She held up her hand in protest.

"No, thank you, I'm full. If I eat any more, I'll sleep right through the movie; it was a long flight," she said.

He put the spoon back down on the plate with the bite still intact.

"Well, now, we don't want that to happen. I like my dinner fully awake," Blake said.

"What?" Tiffany asked.

"What, what?" Blake replied, trying to act like he had said nothing strange, but he knew exactly what he was talking about. He laughed. "I like my dinner guest awake and able to carry on a coherent conversation, don't you?" He let out a huff and rolled his eyes. "What did you think I was talking about? Did you think I meant that you were dinner?" he said with laughter edging each word. Unbeknownst to her, his statement was dripping with sarcasm.

"Well, no," she said, feeling a little uncomfortable. "I guess I just misunderstood you."

He reached over the small table and cupped her face in his cold hand. She repressed a shiver, not willing to risk offending him further.

"No harm, no folly," he said. His hand slid to her chin, giving it a little shake much like teasing a small child. He laughed. "You thought you were the meal." He slowly stood, offering her his hand. "Come, let's move to the sofa. We'll pop the move in and get comfortable for a delightfully tasty, stress-free evening."

"Okay…," she said, accepting the hand he offered her. The whole time Tiffany was thinking *he has the most unusual way of saying things. I don't know what he wants. That's just fine; he'll get no more than I'm willing to give him!* Little did she know that he would take what he wanted. That was the way he rolled, and no human could stop him.

They were almost to the sofa, Tiffany stopped.

"If you don't mind, I'm going to freshen up first."

"Sure; the bathroom is just through the bedroom," he said.

"Thanks. I'll be right back," she said as she made her exit.

"I'll get the movie ready," Blake said, picking up the DVD box. By the time she got back, the lights were dimmed and the movie was playing. When

Tiffany stepped through the doors, she started to protest the degree of darkness. Before she had the chance to do so, Blake scooped her up into his arms; the music from *Casablanca* was playing in the background.

"Dance with me," he whispered in her ear.

He smelled so good; the soft light and the sound of the familiar soulful song all overpowered her. She didn't say a word as her body fell in step with his.

His linen shirt and her thin dress were all that separated them. Tiffany laid her head against Blake's cold chest.

"This is nice," she said as they swayed to the music.

"Yes, it is," he whispered, lowering his head to kiss the artery just below her ear, his favored spot. She giggled.

"Ooo…that tickles!" she said.

"Mmm…," was his only reply as his fangs pierced the throbbing artery just beneath the soft skin. Tiffany was so caught up in the dance of the evening that she didn't notice until it was too late.

"I feel, I feel," were her last words before the ashen face of death overtook her as Blake claimed another victim. She collapsed white and lifeless in his arms. He still would not release her until there was not one drop of blood left in her perfect body.

Blake raised his head. With a twinkle in his eye, he grinned.

"Now, that was a perfect meal delivered in a perfect package, although next time I would prefer less garlic." He chuckled, lowering her to the sofa. He then made his way to the bathroom to clean up. He wanted no evidence of the evening left on him.

With his teeth brushed, his face washed, and a quick check in the mirror, he exited the bathroom. In the sitting room, Tiffany's cold, stiff body lay on the sofa where he had placed her. He knelt beside her; he closed her eyes for the last time with his fingers. He removed the long-stemmed rose from the bud vase in the center of the table at the side of the sofa and kissed its fragrant head, for it had been the one to introduce him to his first taste of her.

"You called this one right," he said, placing the flower in her cold hands. He ran his knuckles across the white cheeks. "Thanks, baby, you were—" he ran his tongue across his teeth, "a delicious ending to a perfect evening!" He threw his head back and let out a deep, roaring kind of crazy laugh: the kind that made the hair stand up on the back of a person's neck. He patted her folded hands. "That's enough fun for tonight; I have an appointment in Scotland to keep." With his hand on the door handle, he looked back over his shoulder. "Someday I'm going to have to select myself a mate. Nah…," he said with a shrug of his shoulders. "Who am I kidding? This is way too much fun. Next time, I'll take my time. It'll be even more fun." He chuckled, "for me, at least. For now, there is one pretty Katelynn needing my attention. I will know all her secrets." He nodded as he closed the door on another life.

Chapter Nine

Standing at the door that led to the castle dungeon/basement, I couldn't help but feel a little nervous.

"Now, let me get this straight," I said, trying to keep the crack of nerves out of my voice. "Do we need torches or lanterns?" I asked Calldoon. He crooked his head to the side and scrunched up his eyebrows.

"Duh—Katelynn!" I said, hitting my forehead with the palm of my hand. "We do live in the twenty first century! We'll use flashlights, right?"

"Nah, Ms. Katelynn," he said with a glint of amusement in his eye. As he opened the door, he slid his hand up the wall, hitting the light switch. "We have electric lights. Ye do know that, don't ye?"

Feeling more than a little embarrassed, I rolled my eyes. "I know that," I said as the bright light flooded the stairwell.

Descending the stairs into the bowels of the castle, I had to admit that I was a little anxious. The spiral stone steps were worn from the millions of feet that had treaded them over the centuries. Who knew for what reasons? I did know that my crazy imagination was cooking up some pretty bad things. The lower we went, the cooler the temperature got, but not my nerves. To break the awkward silence between myself and this man, this stranger, this vampire, I decided it was time to get to know him better.

"Calldoon, may I ask you something?" I asked.

"Sure," he replied.

I ran my hand over the expertly carved ancient stones to steady my steps as well as my nerves.

"Have you always been a guardian?" I asked. The question caught him off guard; he stopped so quickly that I almost plowed right into his back. I grabbed at the wall to balance myself and kept on babbling away. "I mean, I think you must be a guardian to be here at Navar's castle. I mean, I'm not afraid of you. I think I'm under Corbin's protection; you do know that?" I said, looking at him to get his reaction. He didn't say a word; he just stood there. "Okay…I'm out of here!" I said as I turned to make my exit. After all, I didn't know this guy at all. This was probably not my best move, coming down here, just me and this vampire dude, not smart!

I had taken only one step back up the steps when I felt his cold hand on my arm. I stopped; I knew I was at his mercy at this point.

"Sorry, m'lady; I did not mean to frighten ye. It's just that I've not thought of that period in me being for a long time," he said softly.

"If it's too personal, you don't have to tell me about it." I could see the pain in his eyes.

"No, m'lady. Ye need to know; ye need to trust me," he said.

"I do trust you," I said.

He just looked at me.

"Okay, I will try to trust you," I said.

"Let me tell ye but a part of me story for now," Calldoon said as we began our journey down the stairs once more. "Shortly after I arrived here with Lord Navar, I was befriended by Sir Blake. One evening he came to me. 'Hey, boy,' he said. 'How would you like to have some fun tonight?' Being so new, I was very surprised that a knight would speak to me, much less ask me to do something with him and not for him. 'Yes, Sir,' I said, starry eyed. 'Meet me in the courtyard at midnight,' Blake told me as he cuffed me on the back of the head. 'I'll be there,' I told him."

"I met him there under the cover of darkness. I looked around. 'Where are the horses?' I asked him. 'Horses, horses!' he laughed. 'We don't need horses.' He put his hand on me shoulder and looked me in the eye. 'Why, you don't even know what we are or what we are capable of, do you, boy?' I shook me head; I really had no knowledge of what he was talking about. 'Follow me, boy.' He began running so fast that me mouth gaped. To me surprise, I caught up with him and keep up with him easily."

Calldoon smiled at the memory. "It was exhilarating: such freedom. I soon began to follow his lead. It was not long before we came upon two men hunting. Sir Blake jumped on the first man before he even knew we were there. I took down the second one. When we were through feeding on them, I was filled with a mix of remorse and excitement. I had never tasted human blood before."

He bowed his head. "I must admit it was good; it was very good. On the other hand, I knew it was wrong to take a human life. I also knew that Lord Navar would be very cross with us. With that in mind, I decided to tell Lord Navar what we had done. Lord Navar was more disappointed than mad and that hurt meself the most. In his kind way, he sat me down and explained the choice he had made to be a guardian and only drink animal blood, never human. He told me that I must choose my path. If I chose the path of a guardian, I could be stayin', but if I'd be takin' the path of the hunter for me-self, I must leave; it must be me own choice."

Calldoon turned to see what my reaction was to what he had just told me.

I tried to show no emotion, even though the thought of this big boy en-joying the taste of human blood made my insides shake just a little bit, not to mention the fact that I was alone with him. *Get a grip, Katelynn! You're safe! I think*...I tried to get the image out of my mind while Calldoon continued with his story.

"I was all but sure that Lord Navar would be having nothing more to do with me after I told him. Late one evening, Sir Blake found me alone in the stables. It had been almost two weeks since last I had fed. He stopped at the door of the stable, where I was caring for the Lord's horse; the grand animal had thrown a shoe and was in need of assistance. 'Boy,' he said, causing me to jump. 'Meet me here at midnight. If you enjoyed the other night, you are really going to like this.' I didn't even look up from my task. 'I don't know, Sir. I be thinking that Lord Navar would be nailing our hides to yonder wall, if he caught wind of this.' Blake then stepped in where I was working. He bent down so close to me back that I could feel his breath on me neck. He took hold of me hair and pulled me head back. 'Boy,' he said. 'Meet me here, or I'll have a talk with Navar.' " Calldoon stopped and took a deep breath.

"Did you meet him?" I asked.

"Yes, I was afraid not to. I did not know what he would tell Lord Navar. So midnight found me waiting in the stable. As soon as he arrived, we took off. I followed him to a remote village. It was really too small to be called a village; it was but three or four houses grouped together for protection, which did not work. As soon as we arrived at the village, the horror began." Calldoon closed his eyes and shook his head.

"Are you okay?" I asked.

"Sometimes the memories are so strong, they still haunt me: what I saw." he closed his eyes again and rubbed his hand over his face. "It was the most unbelievable thing I had ever witnessed. I did not participate, nor did I stay. I left well before his carnage ended. This time I went straight to Lord Navar. I found him sitting in the library. I ran in and fell at his feet, trembling like a leaf in a storm. He spoke to me in his kind, soft voice."

"He said, 'Boy, what has you in such a state?' I could not stop trembling; such a bloodcurdling sight I had never seen before. When me words began, they all tumbled out at once. With me tellin' done, I could see the anger rising in Lord Navar's face. He stood and walked over to the fireplace. With his back to me and his hands clasped behind him, his head bowed."

"At last he spoke. 'I hope you have learned something from all of this.' I could once again hear the disappointment in his voice. 'Yes, my Lord. I never want to see anything like that again. I'm so very sorry I have disappointed you again, after all you have done for meself.' Lord Navar turned and slowly walked over to me. He placed his hand on me shoulder. 'Rise, boy. You knew no better; go now and understand why I chose the path of the guardian. I choose to protect and care for those who are weaker, unlike Blake. He has chosen the path of the hunter; he cares for no one but himself.' He looked me in the eye. 'Choose your path well.'

"'Yes, my Lord,' I said as I rose to take me leave. He stopped me before I got to the door. 'Boy, stay out of Blake's way. I promise that by the next full moon, you will not have to worry about him anymore.'"

By the time Calldoon had gotten to this point of his story, we had reached the door to the dungeon. With his hand on the door handle, he stopped and looked over his shoulder.

"Are ye ready for this, m'lady?" he asked. I couldn't tell if it was humor or fear in his voice. Whichever one it was, it made me nervous. I blinked a couple times, swallowed hard, and nodded.

Slowly he turned the handle and pushed hard against the heavy wooden door. It came open with a slow creak: that same sound that the door makes in horror movies just before the creepy guy pounces on you. The little hairs on my arm were beginning to prickle. As the door came open I smelled the cool, stale basement air. I was so close to Calldoon that you couldn't have gotten an envelope between us. I had my eyes closed and would have buried my face in his shirt if I had known him better. Calldoon extended his left arm and flipped on the lights. Stepping to the side. I opened my eyes slowly, not knowing what I would see.

"Well, um…it's just furniture!" I said with a sigh of relief.

"Yes, m'lady; what were ye expecting?" he said, and this time I could see the humor dancing in his eyes.

I started to give him a good finger wag; instead, I decided to play along.

"Oh…I don't know," I said, running my fingers over one of the tables. "Maybe a skeleton or two chained to the wall, or an old man huddling in the corner begging for a crust of bread." I raised my finger to inspect it for dust. "Hey! There's no dust on this!" I looked around. "Or on anything else, for that matter!"

"That's correct; housekeeping cleans down here at least once a month," Calldoon said.

"Wow!" I said, still looking at my finger.

Calldoon shook his head.

"No, m'lady; save the wows for the next room."

"Okay, but why?" I asked.

"Ye'll see; come this way," he said.

We walked past more old furniture, trunks, racks of vintage wine, lamps, and all kinds of stuff. The next door we came to had a series of elaborate locks.

It required two keys to unlock it. Calldoon gave me one of the keys, and he kept the other. As he handed me the key, he explained how the lock worked.

"I'll put me key in the upper left hand lock; ye insert yer key in the lower right hand lock," he said.

"Well, now, this is quite a set up. My uncle Thad would have loved to have this on his basement door. It would have kept the Donavain brothers out of his secret stash," I said with a chuckle.

Calldoon looked at me and grinned.

"Secret stash?"

"Yeah…it's what we called his white lightning." Calldoon gave me an odd look. "You know, homemade liquor." I laughed. "Uncle Thad thought Aunt Dot didn't know about it, but she did. If he had this kind of lock, they would never have gotten in." I tilted my head to the side. "Sheesh…this seems like a lot of work for a basement door."

"Ye won't think so when ye see what's on the other side. When I say now, we must turn our keys at the same time or it will not open," he said.

"Really, at the same time?" I asked.

"Yes, at the same time. It's a safety feature; this way, no one person can open the door," he said.

"What ya got in there, the crown jewels?" I said, trying my best to be light-hearted. For the life me, I couldn't figure out what was so important as to require all this.

"Ye'll see; now, on three we'll turn our keys. I will say one, two, three, then we will turn our keys," he said.

"What happens if I turn on four and you turn on three?" I asked.

"Absolutely nothing, and we won't be able to try again for twenty-four hours," he replied.

"All righty then, let's do this right the first time," I said getting my key ready to go on cue.

He began the countdown.

"One-two-three, now."

We both turned our keys at the same time. I heard the locks disengage. Calldoon turned the handles first to the right then to the left, gave it a pull, and the door came open with ease. He hit the light switch; lights came on all over the place. My chin hit my chest as I gasped in shock at what lay before me.

"WOW!" I turned around and around. "Wow-wow!"

"I told ye," he said.

I simply could not believe what I was seeing. There twinkling before me were some of the most splendid pieces of jewelry I had ever seen. Diamonds, emeralds, rubies, and pearls set in gold and silver. Some pieces were under spotlights, making them dance as we moved around. I looked up at Calldoon.

"May I touch them?" I asked.

He smiled and shook his head.

"Ye still do not get it; they're yers. Ye may do with them as ye please."

I closed my mouth and blinked a few times. Then I started to laugh.

"Yeah, right; that's a good one! Now, who do they really belong to?" I said.

"Ye," he said.

"That's not possible," I said in total disbelief.

"But it is; this all belonged to Lord Navar. Now, as is the castle, this is yers," he said with a bow.

"That's not fair; it should be yours. You are the one who has cared for this for all these years," I said in protest.

"No, m'lady, for what would such as I have need of this?" he said with a smile.

I picked up one of the large pieces and ran my thumb over the large ruby that was imbedded in the gold pendant.

"May I ask you something?" I said, looking up at him.

"Sure," he said with a nod.

"Why did you stay all these years?" I asked.

He smiled.

"It all goes back to that gruesome night with Blake and Lord Navar's kind reaction to me misplaced trust. He never made me feel at fault," he said.

My curiosity got the best of me.

"What did he do with Blake?" I asked.

"Lord Navar brought him before his most trusted of trusted, that bein' Sir Tanarr and Sir Corbin. I was there only as Lord Navar's armor bearer. I remember Blake standing there in front of them, boldly defiant and daring them to challenge him. There was no challenge but a statement instead. Lord Navar rose from his chair. 'Sir Blake, it has come to my attention that you have chosen to no longer live by our code of conduct.' Blake glared at me."

Calldoon grimaced. "I can still feel his eyes boring holes through meself with pure hate. 'What say you?' Lord Navar asked. 'What is this ye speak of?' Blake said, his eyes moving from me to Lord Navar. 'It has come to my attention that you not only have found pleasure in the blood of humans but you take enjoyment in their pain and terror. This will not be tolerated in my home. My knights will honor their pledge to protect those who cannot protect themselves, or they will leave. As for you, Sir Blake, just as the rest of us in this room, the power you possess is great; therefore, the responsibility is greater. Can you not live by your pledge any longer?' Navar asked, never taking his eyes off Blake's eyes."

Calldoon continued. "Blake threw his head back and laughed out loud. With an evil twinkle in his eyes, he walked around the room. As he did so he looked each man in the eye.

'Do you honestly think that we have any responsibility to these fragile beings? We could be gods among them!' Blake yelled. He walked in front of Sir Corbin then turned to Sir Tanarr. 'Come with me! Join me! We will rule!' He waited for an answer that did not come. 'Cowards!' Blake hissed as he slammed his fist onto the table."

"Sir Corbin spoke. 'No, we are not cowards, nor would we be gods. We would be devils instead. Soon, they would seek to destroy us, and just how long do you think it would be before a hero would rise up among them, one that would discover the orchid and its power therein?' It was Sir Tanarr's turn to speak. 'If I must choose between love and respect or hate and fear, I choose love.'"

"Blake was so mad he could no longer speak. 'So you have made your choice,' Lord Navar said with deep regret. Blake raised his chin, his eyes darkened with anger and defiance. 'I will be a god; you will see!' he hissed. 'Not in my home,' Lord Navar answered. 'I will give you but one choice; you may take your leave now and never return. For on the day that you do, I will see you sealed up in the dungeon. When I say sealed up, that is to say, bricked and mortared into a room never to see daylight again. Do I make myself clear?' 'Crystal,' Blake said. 'I will be gone within the hour.' He turned on his heel. As he passed me, he hissed, 'Watch your back, boy!' Navar had caught a little of what he had said to me. He put his strong hand on me shoulder. 'Let not your fear overtake you, for that one is little more than a coward. The would-be god could only be one if he had someone of strength to back him.'"

"Navar then turned to the men who stood behind him. I could hear the pride and gratitude in his voice. 'Thank you for your choice; you took a stand for the right. I knew I could trust and believe in you,' he paused, 'and I was right. Thank you, my friends; thank you.'"

"Blake left, and our lives went back to normal," Calldoon laughed. "Or as normal as a vampire can be until that mournful day, the day Lord Navar chose to walk away, that plunged us all into darkness, but we survived." Calldoon took a deep breath. "Now with all that said, I hope ye understand that I stayed because I chose to be a guardian: a guardian of this place and all who dwell therein. The kind heart of one noble vampire taught us that we can be more than what we are left with; this man made a difference in us all. I chose to honor that and all that it stands for. He was a good man."

I looked at this strong man, who now looked a little older from the wear of telling his tale. I touched his cold arm.

"I do understand; like Navar, I think you made a good decision. I thank you," I reached up and kissed him on the cheek. He looked surprised, and I think I even saw a little blush. "I also thank you for sharing your story with me. It helps me to understand one more piece of this huge puzzle. That's why Blake was so proud to tell me he had killed Navar," I said.

This information hit Calldoon like a ton of bricks. He took a step back in shock and pain. "You didn't know Blake was driving the truck that ran Navar off the road?" I said.

Calldoon closed his eyes and shook his head. "The three of us should have seen this coming; we should have had his back."

I couldn't stand to see him in so much uncomforted pain. I put my arms around him and gave him a big momma hug.

"It's okay; no one could have known what lengths Blake would go to for revenge," I said as I patted his back. "It's okay."

I took a deep breath, dried my eyes, and was determined to lighten the mood.

"How about you give me a tour of this sparkly box that you say is all mine," I said, rubbing my hands together. We spent a goodly amount of time looking at each piece. Some were Calldoon's favorites, usually because of a memory they invoked. Then there were the ones that caught my eye: an odd design or an unusual cut of the stone. I picked up one of the large pieces, turned it over in my hand.

"To be perfectly honest, I don't think I will ever feel like all this could ever be mine," I said.

Calldoon just smiled.

"Ah, but it is," he said.

Chapter Ten

That evening we were all together for dinner. I knew the men wouldn't eat, and I didn't care. I was going to eat my dinner and enjoy it. I was also very glad to have them all present. As I sat there sipping my sweet iced tea and waiting for my evening meal, I thought to myself, *Boy, I didn't see this coming. Here I sit in my very own castle, in the company of four amazing men, wise, strong, caring men who just happen to be vampires. Wow!*

To my left sat Zoul, roughly handsome with tousled, thick, gold hair, a thick mustache, a square chin and, of course, those amazing amber eyes. He had that outdoor look going on: a hero who could take care of business. Zoul was the oldest of all the vampires, the one from where I thought the whole virus began. *I've got to talk to him before I leave the castle, if I can.*

Tanarr sat by Zoul. Ah, Tanarr, a gorgeous man. He had red hair that he kept manicured at one of the most expensive salons. His amber eyes were hooded in green; he had never mentioned it, but I believed that he wore green contacts because Lera had green eyes. The sparkle in his eyes matched the spark in his voice, and that little cleft in his chin, oooh! You couldn't help but love and trust this man, but it was that sparkle in his eyes that let you know that there was a touch of the rogue in this one, so guard your heart.

Next was Calldoon, the constant caretaker of this grand old castle. He had done a great job with her. He also had done a great job at blending. Until he wanted me to know, I had no idea what he was. His platinum blond hair allowed him to take on the persona of a very old or very young person. He had learned to embrace the use of contacts to disguise his eye color.

There sitting to my right, laughing and smiling with his friends, was Corbin. My heart almost skipped a beat. I did love this man: my friend, my love, my guardian, and the best-looking man at the table. His brown hair was cut perfectly: not too long, not too short, with the gold highlights sparkling in the dim light. His chiseled face always made my mouth go dry. And when you added in the perfectly formed lips and rich baritone voice: wow! He chose not to cover his amber eyes, and it worked for him. I couldn't even get started on the rest of him. *Okay, Katelynn, you need to reign those thoughts in.* Mental ice water: yep, that's what I needed.

These men I would trust with my life. What was it that Ms. Lera used to say? Ah, yes: "These are good men." These men all chose to do the right thing, to take the path of the guardians. They did this for the love of humanity, for the love of themselves, and the love of their best friend, Lord Navar Hamlet.

My food arrived amidst the chatter of friends and heartfelt laughter. This time, my food was delivered by a boy, not the shy Deireadh. As he set my food in front of me, out of the corner of my eye I caught movement at the doorway.

"Excuse me, guys; I'll be right back," I said.

Corbin looked at my steaming plate.

"But your food just got here," he said.

"I know. I'll be right back," I said.

They each stood as I got up from my seat.

"Thanks, guys. Y'all know you don't have to do that for me. I'm coming right back," I said over my shoulder. They each nodded.

Out in the hall I saw the edge of Deireadh's skirt rounding the corner.

"Deireadh," I softly called her name. We met halfway; she did her little bob of a curtsey.

"Yes, m'lady, something for ye?" she asked.

"No, no," I said with a wave. "However, I would like for you to come have dinner with us. I have four very handsome men: a captive audience," I said, wiggling my eyebrows up and down. I didn't wait for her to answer. I grabbed her by the wrist and started to take off, but I pulled up short.

"Come on; the food is getting cold," I said, turning to look at her. She had turned a little pale, and she was shaking her head.

"No, m'lady, I canna'," she said.

"It's just the guys, and I'll be with you," I said.

"No, m'lady," she said one last time as she broke free and bolted from the room. I gave my head a shake; *Ah…she is so pretty to be so shy*, I thought.

As I entered the dining hall, the guys all stood, again. I rolled my eyes and clapped my hands.

"Now stop that!" I said, taking my seat.

Corbin leaned over.

"Is everything okay?" he asked.

"Yeah. I saw Deireadh in the hall. I went to see if she would have dinner with us," I said.

"Is she? I would really like to meet this purple-eyed girl," Corbin said.

At the mention of purple eyes, everyone went silent.

Zoul was the first to speak.

"Did you say purple eyes?" he asked me, but he was looking at Corbin.

"Yeah, I did. They're beautiful; I've never seen anything like them!" I said.

"And does she have sparkly hair?" Tanarr asked.

"Yes, she does," I answered.

The men all exchanged some kind of knowing look.

"Okay, what's going on?" I asked, giving them my best motherly look.

"Nothing," Tanarr said with a twinkle in his eye. "She sounds like a dream; I'd like to meet this vision."

All four men laughed, but it was not the same happy laughter that they had shared before. This time it was more a laughter of nerves. I had opened my mouth to question them about what was going on, but I was interrupted before I could begin.

"How's your food?" Corbin asked.

I had almost forgotten how hungry I was.

"Oh, I don't know" I said, taking a good sniff. "It smells great." I took a big forkful of something green with some meat. "Mmm…what is this?"

Corbin looked at my plate.

"If memory serves me right, it looks like turnip greens and venison," he said.

"Well, whatever it is, it's delicious!" I declared.

The men went back to their conversation while I cleaned my plate. The boy came back to clear the dishes.

"Pardon, but would ye be carin' for any dessert this evenin'?" the boy asked.

"Oh, no! I'm stuffed," I replied.

He picked up my dishes and started to leave.

"Hold on. If I could have dessert, what would that be?" I asked with a sheepish grin, "I do love dessert."

The boy stopped and squinted one eye; he bit the corner of his lip.

"Let me think; there is a berry cobbler, some kind of cream pie, and the most beautiful seven-layer chocolate cake ever did I see!" the boy said with longing in his eyes: you know, that look that a boy gets when chocolate cake is involved.

"You know, I think I might have a very small slice of that chocolate cake with a large cup of coffee." I leaned over, motioning him to come closer. "And while they're cutting a small slice for me, have them cut a large slice for you."

The boy's eyes lit up.

"Oh, thank ye, m'lady, I will!" he said as he hurried off.

I looked up. All four men had stopped their conversation to listen to my chat with the boy, and they were all smiling.

"What? I mean really, have you ever seen a boy who didn't like chocolate cake?"

"Well done, missy," Zoul said.

"Great call, Katelynn. He won't ever forget you," Tanarr said with his crooked smile and a wink.

"Aye, m'lady, 'twas a grand and kind touch," Calldoon nodded.

Corbin just smiled and squeezed my hand. "Love you," he whispered in my hair.

"Come on, guys; it's just cake!" I said.

"Nay, m'lady, here you are queen. The queen does not often speak to children in the house, much less offer them cake," Calldoon said with a smile of approval.

"Oh, but you see, castle or no castle," I patted my chest over my heart, "here in my heart, where it counts the most, I am now and will always be a Southern girl. If I'm having cake and there is a child or an adult in the same room, it's just plain old good manners to offer them cake."

"It may be good manners in the South, but here it is a grand gesture," Calldoon said. They were all smiling at me.

"Ah, come on, guys! It's only cake. Quit it!" I said with a shake of my head. I leaned over toward Calldoon. "So, do we employ children here in the castle? I mean, really! That boy can't be more than seven or eight, maybe nine. I don't like the thought of a small child having to do hard work. That sweet little boy should be out chasing frogs, not working in the kitchen."

A big smile came across Calldoon's face.

"No, Katelynn, ye'll be thinkin' about this all wrong. The child is the young son of the stable master. They came here when the child was just born. As he grew, we each and every one fell in love with the freckled-faced little boy. He loves to help about the castle, and I'd be thinkin' that you'd be likin' to acquaint the child. His name is Charles; he has meself wrapped around his wee finger. I see that he gets some spending money each week, and set up a trust fund for him I have. When he turns twenty-one, he will have enough money to go on to school or start his own business with a goodly portion left over. Fret not, Katelynn. He does very little work; most of the time he is but playin' about the grounds. His biggest job is to make the lot of us smile, and that he does very well," Calldoon smiled with pride as he finished his explanation.

"I'm sorry. I should have known that you would not let a little boy to do hard work, and you're right. He is absolutely adorable. I can see how everyone could fall in love with him. If there is anything I can do to help, just let me know, okay? Now that that is settled," I turned my attention on Tanarr. "Tanarr, if you don't mind," I paused for a sip of coffee and to wonder if I were about to overstep my bounds, but I decided to ask anyway. "May I ask, where did Lera go after Navar's death?"

He looked up without saying a word. Although I felt a little uneasy, I kept talking.

"Well, I thought you might know, since you knew about the airplane thing."

The others were looking a little lost.

"Tanarr was telling me about Lera getting her pilot license," I explained.

Corbin smiled.

"I could see that; she loved adventure," he said.

"That she did," Tanarr chimed in.

I looked at him with pleading eyes.

"Do you know where she went?" I asked.

"I do; she contacted me shortly after his death. She wanted to know if she could borrow a little of Navar's money. She wanted to finish something she was working on," Tanarr said.

"Borrow?" I said with surprise.

He looked over at me.

"She had no idea that as soon as Navar could, after he got home from the compound, knowing his newfound humanity came with a price, he called me and had a will prepared so that everything went to Lera in the event that something happened to him. He wanted to make sure she would want for nothing."

"Oh...," I said with a nod. "What did you tell her?"

"It was late one afternoon when a messenger arrived with a brief note. At this point I had no idea anything had happened. The note only ask to borrow a small amount of money and listed where to send it." He paused. "Let me think." He looked down at his hands, talking as much to himself as to us. "It had been a day or two. I believe the note said:

> *Dear, Tanarr...stop...may I borrow $100.00...stop...if yes... stop...Send to the fishing village of Bockson on the Amazon...stop...Thank you, Lera . . ."*

"What did you do?" I asked.

"I didn't send the money," he said with a shake of his head.

"What?!" we all said at the same time.

"But it was her money! What if she was hurt or in trouble or something worse?" I said.

We all started to question him at the same time. Tanarr put his hands up both in defense and to stop our verbal assault.

"Whoa!" he said. "I didn't *send* her the money; I took it to her. I had to see for myself that she was safe."

"I arrived at the dock of Bockson late at night; the fog hung like a mix of old cotton candy and thick spider webs: sticking to everything, obscuring the world around me, and giving what faint specks of light that were in the small huts an eerie, lonesome feeling. The air was heavy with the smell of dead fish and unsanitary living conditions. I couldn't think of one reason for her to be there. I went straight to the address she had given me, hoping she wouldn't be there," he said, shaking his head.

"It was a small grass-topped hut; no door, just a ragged curtain. I knocked at the edge of the door opening. 'Come in,' I heard her lovely voice waft through the curtain. I pulled the curtain to the side and stepped through the opening. 'Lera, what are you doing here?' I asked her. The next thing I knew she was in my arms, and I wasn't complaining. I loved the feeling of her arms around my neck."

"She started to cry. 'Tanarr, of all the people in the world I expected to see!' then she stepped back. 'What are you doing here?' Lera asked. I put my hand to the side of her face. 'I believe I asked that question first,' I said. She turned away from me.

'I've come to put an end to the two things that killed Navar,' she said. 'What are you talking about? Who killed Navar?' I asked her.

'Me.' she said in a matter-of-fact way. 'Me and that blasted orchid!' I grabbed her by the shoulders. 'What are you talking about? Sit down, and tell me what's going on!'

We sat there in her dingy one-room hut while she unfurled her story. It was well into dawn by the time she was finished. I took her by the hand.

'If I got this whole story straight, it wasn't you who killed him but his love for that motorcycle of his and the truck that was on the wrong side of the road.'

'No, if I had stayed out of his life and never introduced him to that blasted cure from that stupid flower, he'd still be here!' she raved.

'That might be true, but do you remember how he hated what he was, what it took to maintain that way of life?'

'Yes,' she said, looking out the window. I placed my finger to the side of her face. As gently as I could, I turned her face to meet my gaze.

'Do you remember the pure joy he got from being human again?' She said nothing. I pulled her into my arms and just held her. 'I do,' I said. 'He loved it and you.' With my chin on the top of her head, I told her, 'he knew that he wanted to grow old with you, and he knew what the risks were. He didn't care; he only wanted you.' I gave her a soft hug because I knew how he felt. 'What did you have in mind?'

She shrugged her shoulders. 'I don't know. I was going to sneak into that village and see what happened,' she said with a sniff. I had to laugh. 'Now, there's a plan,' I said. 'Okay, so I don't have a plan. I'm mad. I'm mad at myself. I'm mad at that blasted flower, and I'm mad at Navar for leaving me. I begged him not to get on that ridiculous motorcycle, but would he listen to me? NO!' she said.

The more we talked, the more her emotions got the best of her. 'It's all right. We'll be fine,' I whispered over her head. 'What do you mean, we'll be fine?' she asked, trying to push back. 'We: you and I. You don't think I'm leaving you here, do you?' I said. 'Well, yes! Why would you leave your law practice and stay here, in this disgusting jungle, with me? I know how you detest dirt and filth!' she said, blinking up at me.

'Because I love you,' I said. 'No, Tanarr, you can't love me; no one should love me,' Lera said. 'But I do,' I told her. She pushed back from me and shook her head. 'But I can't love you back: not now, and maybe never,' she said softly. 'We'll see. I can wait. For now, let me be with you and keep you safe.'"

Tanarr looked down at his hands folded on the table. I could tell that he was trying to hide the feelings he still had for a love he could only borrow but never have, not truly have. He took a deep breath and went on.

"'She didn't say yes; however...,'" he put a great deal of emphasis on that word, "she didn't say no, either. I took it as a foot in the door.'"

His story and our thoughts were interrupted by someone at the door.

"Excuse me, Master Calldoon," one of the stable hands said. Calldoon looked around at us.

"Pardon me," he said as he got up to see what the young man wanted. He soon returned to the table. "I'm sorry; it seems that one of the horses has acquired a nasty gash on its leg, and the stable master would like a word with me. If you please, I will take me leave."

We all nodded our recognition of his explanation. After Calldoon had left the room, I looked back to Tanarr.

"Would you please go on?" I asked.

Tanarr looked at his watch.

"It's getting late, and I have dominated the conversation long enough for tonight," he said.

"No, just a little longer, please?" I asked.

"Later," he said with a nod.

"Tomorrow, maybe?" I asked hopefully, although with a look at my watch I knew he was right. "How on earth did it get so late? Y'all may not need sleep, but I do. I think I'm headed to the barn," I said with a yawn.

Zoul and Tanarr both at the same time gave me a confused look.

"Why would you go to the stable at this late hour?" Tanarr asked with his brows drawn together.

Corbin leaned in.

"She isn't going to the stable; she is going to her room," he said.

"Really?" Tanarr asked.

"Yeah," Corbin said with a chuckle.

I said my good nights as I got up, and so did Corbin.

"I'll walk you to your room," he said.

"That would be nice, Spidey," I said with a wink.

Zoul leaned toward Tanarr.

"Did she just call him Spidey?" he asked.

"Yes, I believe she did," Tanarr replied with a chuckle. "That I've got to find out about," he said from behind the back of his hand.

"Good night, boys," I said, slipping my hand through the crook of Corbin's arm. I looked back over my shoulder at Zoul and Tanarr. "Someday I'll tell you all about the Spidey thing," I said from behind my hand, giving them a wink. Both men laughed.

"This will be the last night in my room before they start renovations." I took a deep breath and smiled "Ah…a bathroom, in my room, sweet! No more hiking all the way across this place just to take a shower," I smiled.

Halfway to my room, I leaned my head over on Corbin's shoulder.

"He really loved her, didn't he?" I said.

"Yes, he did. He was in and out of her life the entire time she was with Navar," Corbin said.

"Really? She never mentioned him except to say he was the lawyer I was to contact if I needed anything at any time because he knew it all," I said.

"That's because she only had eyes for Navar. She never looked at another man," Corbin said.

"Was Tanarr ever in love with anyone else?" I asked.

"He flirted around with a lot of other women, and I do mean a lot, but love, no. He only ever loved Lera," Corbin said.

"That's sad, in a sweet sort of way," I said, giving a very unladylike yawn. Corbin kissed the top of my head.

"You're tired," he said.

"More than I thought," I replied with a little nod. "It's been a long day."

We stopped at my door. He took my hand, kissed the top edge of my knuckles, then turned my hand over and placed a soft kiss in the center of my palm. He looked up at me and smiled.

"That was a nice move with little Charles and the cake," he said.

"It was just a piece of cake: no big deal!" I said with a wave of my hand.

"It was a big deal here in this place. To that little boy, you are his hero," he said, looking into my eyes and smiling.

"Yeah, right!" I said as I gave him a peck on the check. "Well, this hero is tired and going to bed."

Corbin stepped closer, giving me a slow kiss on the lips. "I'll see you to-morrow. I love you," he said with his lips still just barely touching mine.

He turned and disappeared down the steps. I slid into my room; no sooner had the door closed than I realized what I had forgotten.

"Dang it!" I said with a stomp of my foot. "I'm going to have to go all the way back down all those steps just to shower and brush my teeth. Dang it, dang it, dang it!!" I gathered up all my stuff with a huff and a grumble. Down two flights of stairs and all the way to the far end of the castle I went.

I took care of business as quickly as possible, grumbling the whole time.

"I can't wait till I have my own bathroom!" As soon as the words were out of my mouth, I looked at myself in the mirror. With toothpaste all around my mouth, I asked myself: "Katelynn, just how long do you plan on staying here? Have you forgotten that you have a life and a job and a home back in New York?" I took a mouthful of water, swished it about in my mouth, and spit into the sink. "I think I'm going to pull a Scarlett and think about this tomorrow; besides, I still want that bathroom."

Chapter Eleven

Back in my room, the once sleepy head was now fully awake. I tried to go to sleep anyway, to no avail. I flipped and flopped, pulled the covers off and back on again, plumped up my pillow then punched it down. Fully and completely frustrated, I kicked the covers off and took a stroll over to the window.

Standing there looking out over the countryside, I saw that it was a beautiful night. There wasn't a cloud in the sky. The stars were twinkling like diamonds. The moon was full; it lit up the fields so clearly that I could see all the way to the edge of the woods. There, just inside the tree line, I saw something. "What is that? Is it something glowing or just a reflection?" Squinting my eyes, I still couldn't tell. My curiosity got the best of me once more. I jumped into my jeans, a good, thick sweatshirt, and slid on my sneaks. "I'll be back before anyone knows I'm gone. It's probably only a piece of broken glass or tin can lid that has caught the moonlight. Yeah, that's it."

I took one more look out the window before taking off. It was still there, still glowing. I didn't know what it was, but I was going to find out. I felt a bit like I was sneaking out of my mom's house to go to a party. *Katelynn, snap out of it! Not only are you not sneaking out, but this is your house, and you're a big girl. If you want to go, go!* I told myself as I went out of the castle and over the arched bridge.

At the edge of the woods I ducked behind a bush. It was definitely not a broken bottle or a tin can. It was a GIRL! Or, at least, I thought it was, and she was glowing, shimmering; I wasn't sure what to call it. Not only was she the most devastatingly beautiful thing I had ever seen, but she had wings! Big, beautiful, gossamer, shimmering wings. They were almost clear except for an iridescent shimmer of purple. *Okay, Katelynn, you must be asleep. This is some kind of freaky weird dream brought on by too much coffee.* But no, according to the bush that was sticking in my side, this was no dream.

Slowly she turned so I could see her face. Oh my goodness! I had to clamp my hand over my mouth; this beautiful creature was Deireadh. Her hair was sparkling, and her wings were shimmering. Her dress looked to be very old: a medieval style that laced up the front. The sleeves were fitted to her elbow, and then they belled out to a point and draped to just below her hand. The dress was a soft, light purple that was trimmed in dark purple. She looked like she should have been on the cover of a fairy tale book.

I was so lost in what was going on in front of me that I didn't hear the footsteps behind me. Then all of a sudden I felt a man's heavy hand come down hard on my shoulder. I jumped and spun around to come face to face with none other than Blake Klavell!

His eyes glared at me as he hissed. "I think we have some unfinished business to attend to!"

I was so caught off guard that it took me a while to find my voice.

"I don't think so, now unhand me!" I said with more strength than I felt. I started to punch him with my fist but he caught it in midflight and began to squeeze.

"Stop it! You're hurting me!" I said.

"Good," he said with a smirk.

"I'll scream!" I said.

"Go ahead; they're all on the other side of the village hunting. They'll never hear you, not in time, anyway. However, I will give you some choices. You can give me that cure, I can make you my mate, or I can make you a snack," Blake said, toying with a lock of my hair. "Hmm…I'd be happy with any of the above."

"You know what? None of that works for me, so I think I'll just be going back to the castle," I said as I started to walk away. He grabbed my arm and spun me around.

"I don't think so," he said, pulling me against his chest and almost knocking the breath out of me.

A sparkle at his right shoulder caught my eye. Long, slender, feminine fingers slowly, one at a time, curled over his shoulder. *What on earth?* I thought. I saw this look come over Blake's face. It was almost like some of his power left him.

It was Deireadh; she turned him to face her with little effort. He was completely powerless, his mission forgotten. I watched the whole drama unfold before my eyes as she worked this—this magic of sorts.

"Ye, sir, will bother not this lady; turn ye will, and take yer leave ye shall." She clapped her hands. "Shoo, shoo! Say not a word; leave us." She waved her hands like she was waving away a fly. Blake turned and left without saying a word.

"How did you do that? Where are you from? How did you know he was here?" I stammered.

She grabbed my arm.

"Question me not now, m'lady," she said as she all but dragged me toward the castle.

"But why? You can handle anything! You're amazing!" I said as I stared at her, halfway afraid she would just disappear.

"There be things afoot that I can do nothing about," she said with a little panic in her voice.

"Yeah, right! Did you see how you handled Blake, and he's a vampire! You did know that he is a vampire, didn't you?" I whispered the last part.

"Yes, m'lady, know that I do," she said with a nod.

I stopped still in my tracks, causing Deireadh to come to jerking halt.

"How did you know that?" I asked, squinting one eye as I spoke.

"M'lady, please, come! Talk later we shall." This time I could hear fear in her voice.

"What are you so afraid of? You can obviously handle yourself just fine," I said.

She grabbed my arm once more; she was talking as we were walking, almost running, toward the castle.

"M'lady, vampires handle I can; 'Tis part of me gift," she said.

"Gift?" I said, completely confused.

"Yes, me gift; work it does not on snakes, wolves, and bears. If any of them find us, eat you they will, for see me they canna'," she said.

"Girl, what are you talking about?" I asked.

"Please, m'lady, please!" she said.

"Okay, fine. As my Grandma would say, you can lead a horse to water, but you can't make it drink," I said with a huff.

Deireadh looked at me sideways.

"I know it doesn't exactly apply, but it comes close," I said.

By now we were back on the arched bridge leading into the castle. I could feel some of the tension leaving Deireadh's body.

"Better now?" I asked.

"Almost," she said as we hurried over the bridge. We didn't talk as we went through the courtyard, into the castle, and up the stairs. She never left my side, for she was making sure that I got to my room safely.

I had my hand on the door handle, ready to go in.

"What have you been doing?"

I jumped, spun on my heels, and grabbed my chest.

"Jeez Louise! Corbin, you scared the living daylights out of me!" I said.

Corbin tried to suppress a chuckle.

"I do know you are about the jumpiest little thing I have ever met," he said, reaching out to flick the end of my nose. "It's just one more thing I love about you; however, it is late. Is everything all right?"

"I think so. Deireadh and I were…," my words faded as I looked around to see that Deireadh was no longer anywhere to be found.

"You and who?" Corbin asked.

"Deireadh. Deireadh, you know, my lady's maid. She was with me," I said looking around.

"Really?" Corbin said with a touch of humor in his voice.

"Yes, really; she was with me," I said in my defense.

"Are you sure that it wasn't fatigue that was with you?" he asked.

"I'm sure, or at least I think I'm sure," I said, blinking a few times and trying to clear my thoughts.

Corbin turned me toward my door and popped me on my butt.

"I think you are in serious need of sleep," he said as he guided me through the door. "Love you."

"Okay...," I said, slowly walking into my room. I closed the door and leaned back against it, giving myself a good mental shake.

"All right, now, Katelynn. Maybe you are asleep; that would explain a lot. Just roll over, give your pillow a big hug, and tell it you're sorry for beating it up. Tighten the covers up around your ears, and you will be awake in a little while. A yummy breakfast and a steamy cup of coffee will be waiting for you." I had to be asleep. Girls didn't glow, they didn't have wings, and they surely couldn't make vampires do whatever they said.

I pushed away from the door and began to laugh. "Girls with wings, vampires! I'm asleep, and all this is a dream. Except...," I grabbed my side and pulled up my sweatshirt to reveal a cut where the branch from that bush had stabbed me when Blake scared me. I opened and closed my fist. Yep, it hurt, too, where Blake had almost crushed it in his anger. "Okay, so it wasn't a dream, so what was it? That I don't know, but tomorrow I'm going to find out. For now, sleep! I need sleep!"

Chapter Twelve

"Ah, man, what day is it" I said, trying my best to clear the fog that was my sleepy brain. I lay still, trying to think. I finally kicked the covers off. "Christie is going to kill me if I'm late to work." The instant my feet hit the cold stone floor, I came fully awake. I was not going to be late for work. Then I realized I wasn't even at home in my little apartment.

Everything slowly started to come into focus. I opened my eyes. "Yep, I'm still in Scotland: still in the castle, my castle."

As the rest of my brain fog cleared, all the events of the previous night came back with crystal clarity. I went to my door and stuck my head out. I saw one of the housemaids.

"Excuse me," I said, trying to get her attention. I had no idea what her name was.

"Excuse me, sweetie?" I said again, and this time the young woman turned to see what I wanted.

"Sorry, m'lady, ye be talking to me?" the young woman said.

"Yes, yes. Could you come here for just a jiff?" I asked.

"A jiff?" she looked confused. "What is a jiff?" she asked.

"It means a minute or for just a little while," I said, motioning her to come closer. "Just come here, please."

She came over and stopped in front of me.

"Yes, m'lady," she said with a curtsey.

"First, what is your name?" I asked.

"Rosey, m'lady," she said.

"Hi, Rosey. I'm Katelynn," I said.

"Oh, yes, I know! Ye be all the little Charles is talking about. He thinks ye be the best thing since sliced bread. We all be thinking that he just might be right," she said with a smile.

"Ah, that's sweet, but what I really need, if you can, is I need for you to find my lady's maid, Deireadh," I said.

"Yes, m'lady; she be in the kitchen preparing yer breakfast tray. She said she would be a'bringing it up to ye. She said ye had a late night, that ye would more than likely be taking yer breakfast in yer room," Rosey said.

"Thank you, Rosey, and she is right. If you would, please tell her I'm awake. Thank you," I said.

In no time at all I heard a tap at my door.

"Come in, Deireadh," I said as I continued to make up my bed, putting each pillow where I wanted it to be.

"You know that Deireadh will do that for you, right?" the person at the door said. It was not Deireadh; I knew that soft, baritone voice.

"Well, good morning, Sir Corbin! How's Spidey doing this morning?" I asked.

"Spidey is doing fine," he said as he wrapped his arms around me. "No matter what's going on in my life, when you're in my arms, it's all good."

"Now that's just what a girl wants to hear first thing in the morning," I said with an eye flutter.

Corbin kissed my forehead.

"Seriously, you do know that you don't have to clean your room?" Corbin said.

"Yeah, I know. But I like doing things for myself. It's the way I was raised. Momma's motto is 'if you mess it up, you clean it up.' Besides that, I'm the only one who knows how I want those pillows to look."

Corbin looked from me to the pillows.

"They look perfect, along with the rest of the room. Poor Deireadh! She won't have anything to do today," he said.

"She'll live, and I won't get used to a lifestyle that I won't have when I get back home," I said.

Corbin gave me a little hug.

"This can be your home; you don't have to go back," he said.

"I know, but I want to see Christie; best friends are hard to come by. And I want to see Momma and Daddy," I said.

He smiled at me.

"You can go anywhere you want. You're not a prisoner here; you own it all," he said.

I gave him a little sideways look.

"You know, I still can't wrap my head around that. I still feel like that small-town nurse who can't afford to buy a used car. This rich thing—" I trailed off.

"Very rich," Corbin added.

"Okay, very rich: whatever. It's having a hard time sinking in," I said with a head shake.

"Give it time; it will," Corbin said. "Speaking of time, I have lost track of it. Calldoon is waiting for me downstairs. We'll be out all day; we're checking on the north borders today. Zoul and Tanarr will both be here if you need them."

"Thank you, but I'm sure I'll be fine. I'm going to have breakfast with Deireadh. I want to talk to her," I said.

Corbin looked a little confused.

"Why?" he said.

"Last night, hello!" I answered.

He still had a blank look.

"What about last night?" he asked.

"I saw her in the woods," I said.

"You were in the woods last night?!" Panic began to rise in his voice. "Do not go out in the woods at night by yourself! Too much could happen!"

"You're telling me, 'cause you're not going to believe who else was in the woods," I said.

"Who?" Corbin asked.

"Blake," I said. The muscle in his jaw began to twitch.

"Did he touch you?" he asked through clenched teeth.

"Well, yeah, he snuck up on me. I thought it was the end. Then, and you're not going to believe this, Deireadh stopped him," I said.

"She did? How?" Corbin asked.

"It was the coolest thing. She just told him to go away, and he did," I said with a shrug.

"Really…he just left?" Corbin said with an arched eyebrow.

"Yeah, he just left," I said.

"Hmm . . .I think you were having a bad dream," he said, walking toward the door.

I picked up a pillow and threw it; the pillow caught him in the back of the head.

"Hey!" he said, throwing it back at me.

"Two things," I said, catching the pillow. "One: you know I'm always straight with you, and two: we never leave each other without a kiss goodbye!"

"I know. I wasn't leaving; I was thinking." He walked back and gave me a long, slow kiss. "Now I'm leaving. I'll see you tonight; love you."

"Love you, too," I said as he went through the door.

Not long after Corbin left there was another tap at my door. This time I was going to know who was out there before I asked them in.

"Who's there?" I yelled through the door.

"Deireadh, it be."

I ran to the door, opening it quickly.

"Come in, come in," I said, taking the tray from her hands. "I hope you brought two of these."

"Pardon?" she said with a blink.

"We are so eating breakfast together!" I said.

"Proper, that would not be," she protested.

"Yeah, sure it is! Here, have a seat. I'll have another tray sent up." I stuck my head out the door. Rosey was still cleaning the stairs. "Rosey?" I called.

"Yes, m'lady?" she answered.

"Will you have another breakfast tray sent up?" I asked.

"Right away," she said with a bob.

Rosey returned quickly with the other tray. I put the second on the table beside the one that Deireadh had just brought; they both had the exact same things on them. I pulled the chair out for her to have a seat.

"You sit here. I'll sit there," I said, and we took our places. As we ate, she slowly became more comfortable with me. We talked and munched on crusty bread, fruit, and cheeses and sipped out of two very large mugs of coffee.

I took a big gulp of my coffee and leaned in close.

"Now, just between you, me, and the fencepost," I said.

Deireadh's eyebrows went up.

"Pardon?" she said.

"Oh… that only means that no one else needs to know," I said with a wave.

"Ah…," she said with an uneasy smile.

"Anyway…how did you make Blake leave us last night? I mean, he turned and left just like you told him to. How did you do that?" I asked.

She didn't say a word; she only played with her food, not meeting my eyes. I waited, but she still didn't say anything.

"Come on, you have to fill me in on how that works!" I took another sip of my coffee, and she still said nothing. "How did you know that he was a vampire, and why didn't that freak you out? When my friend Christie found out about vampires, she completely freaked." Deireadh still said nothing. "Please, tell me! I won't tell anyone if you tell me not to. I won't!"

She looked at me shyly.

"Nice it would be, to tell someone. Long it has been since I had anyone to talk to," she said.

"You can trust me, Deireadh. I would never betray your confidence," I said.

"I knew what he was and how to make him do my will because of what I am," she began.

"Go on," I encouraged her.

She took a deep breath and looked at me with her purple eyes twinkling.

"I be a fairy," she said in a very matter-of-fact way. Neither of us said a word for a while. Then I slapped my leg, threw my head back, and laughed out loud.

"Yeah, right, that's a good one!" When I stopped laughing and took a good look at her face, the look of sadness and disappointment almost broke my heart. "Oh my, you're serious!" I blinked a couple of times. "I am *so* sorry! Let's do this one more time. I mean, if there can be vampires, why can't there be fairies? I'm sorry; please, forgive me?" She smiled at me. "Can we start over again?" I asked. She nodded.

"Okay, Deireadh, fairy…," She nodded with half a smile. "So how did you make him leave?" I asked.

She squared her shoulders and folded her hands in her lap.

"All fairies have powers. Each fairy's power be as different as she. Some fairies put that unexpected smile on yer face, they do. Others help with art or music. Then there was one who would trip people just for the giggle of it. Do ye understand the power of a power?" she asked.

"I think I got it. They're kind of like the daughters of Zeus, the muses in Greek mythology," I said.

"Yes. One thing be not the same," she said.

"What's that?" I asked.

"Real we be, or were," she said.

"What do you mean, 'were' real?" I asked.

"Remember, I told ye, I did; me name means the last one," she said.

"Yeah, but I thought that it was just a fluke: you know, a cool name with an odd meaning," I said.

"No; me name was given to me by me father because the time of fairies had come to an end. He knew the last one I would be," she said.

"Was your father a fairy?" I asked.

"No, for a fairy be the child of a wizard and a mortal. Me father, a powerful wizard he was: the very wizard who gave the castle her name. Me mother was a beautiful kitchen maid. Worked she did, here at the castle. They fell in love." She threw her hands up in the air, "and voila! Here be me," she smiled.

"Wow! How long have you been a fairy?" I asked in complete wonder.

"All me life," she said with a giggle.

"And that has been how long?" I asked.

"Let me think." She thought for a while, rolling her purple eyes from one side to the other. "This I do not know: hundreds of years," she said with a shrug. "I never keep up. Matter it does not, for I be the last one. I live the lost years."

I looked at her with unanswered question in my eyes, and she continued.

"Lost I have been; the years have rolled over me unnoticed. It mattered not, for I will be till I be no longer," she said.

"How have you survived so long on your own?" I asked.

"I have borrowed seasons, lived in lost years. No one knows what I am, for to look at me they choose not. As needful as the breeze, see they canna'. There be it anyway. They pay me no mind and canna' see me, for they do not look. So I matter not to the mortal heart. Fine it be, for hurt me, no. For one of the only things that can kill a fairy is herself," she said.

"Okay, okay," I said, holding up my hands. "Now I'm really confused."

"It be like this," she folded her hands on the table. "Me power be like sand in an hourglass; when the last grain of sand drops, the time for it is done. The same is with me power; when me power is gone, so am I," she said with a shrug.

"So when your power is used up, you die?" I asked.

She nodded.

"May I ask what your power is?"

"A will bender I be; works on most it does," she said.

"A bender?" I questioned because I had no earthly idea what she was talking about.

She thought for a breath before she spoke. As she thought, she scrunched up her face.

"Bender…have me an odd power, but to bend ye own power to do me will. 'Tis but an odd power, think ye so?" she said with a giggle.

"When you do something like make Blake go away, do you lose some of your power?" I asked.

"Yes," she replied.

"How much more do you have left, power that is?" I knew it was none of my business, but now I was concerned about her.

"Know this, I do not, for I have not used it in a long time," she said.

"Can you do something to regain some of the power?" I asked.

"This I do not know, for by the time I was of age, none there were left. What I know, I learned on me own." She shook her head. "That be not much." She looked at me with pleading eyes. "This that I have told ye, ye must never tell anyone. No one can know." It was as if it had just sunk in that she had told all her secrets, and now she was scared.

"You say that your power works on almost everyone, right? So just use it on me so I don't remember. I don't mind. Then you will feel better in knowing that I won't accidentally tell someone," I said.

She placed her hand on the side of my face and shook her head.

"Work it will not. The best I can figure is ye have wizard blood in ye somewhere," she said.

"Wizard, now that really is a good one!" I said with a little nervous laugh.

"No way! I can't even make my car start most of the time, much less do some kind of a spell," I said, whirling my hands around my head. "What makes you say something like that, anyway?"

"Because the only person I canna' affect is a wizard," she leaned in close. "Ye, m'lady, have wizard blood in ye, somewhere. It's in there. That would be why Ms. Lera trusted ye, she did; feel it she could. Did ye not tell me that yer name is an old family name that comes up to be used every so often? I'll bet me wings that ye name goes back to wizard time, and his name would be something like Keeland or Carland. I'll bet me wings."

"Speaking of wings, you do have wings, right?" I inquired.

"Ah, that I do," she said with a hint of pride in her voice. "Love me wings, this is true. The only time I get to see them is in the light of the full moon. That's what I be doin' last night," she smiled. "I be enjoying me pride."

"I must say, they are the most magnificent things I have ever seen," I said in complete agreement. "I couldn't take my eyes off them. That's how Blake could sneak up on me." I stood up and walked over to the window. I looked out at nothing in particular, trying to gather my thoughts. I turned and went back to where Deireadh sat. "Why didn't Blake know that you were there? He didn't pay any attention to you at all, and that's not like him. He likes pretty girls, a lot."

She giggled.

"That's why vampires be afraid of fairies, see our true nature they canna'. Look for us they do not, for the power of a fairy they canna' feel. Play with them as we please," she giggled. "Stand at his side, even that he could not tell that fairies we be," she looked down at her hands. "Or I should say, me. From the stories I used to hear, fairies once wreaked havoc on the lot of them. Turned their world upside down, they did. I make them a little nervous," she giggled again. "If a fairy they could see me as," she smiled. "Meself, a great deal of fun have me had at their expense."

"Wow! That's why Corbin didn't notice you last night," I said.

She only nodded; I sat back down beside her.

"May I tell Corbin?" I asked with a plea.

"Waste not yer time, for I canna' allow him to remember and run the risk of being banished from me home: the only home ever I know. That I will not do," she said in a matter-of-fact way.

"Banish? No, he won't do that. I won't let him; after all, I do own this place, so I get to make the rules," I said.

She lowered her head.

"You ask too much of him. His fear will be too strong," she whispered.

I shook my head.

"I can't believe that Corbin, who is afraid of nothing that I know of, could possibly be afraid of someone as delicate and as pretty as you," I said with a huff.

She looked out from under her eyelashes.

"Delicate and pretty," she fluttered her lashes. "These are the words I have heard used to describe the vampire orchid; it is the only other thing they fear."

My mouth gaped. I was speechless. I got up and walked to the window and back. Actually, it was more like pacing. I came back and kneeled in front of her.

"What did you say?" I whispered.

She blinked a few times.

"I thought you knew about the flower; wrong was I?" she asked.

"No, I mean yes. No, you weren't wrong, and yes, I do know about the orchid. How did you know about it?" I asked.

She giggled and shrugged her shoulders.

"All fairies know about the vampire flower."

"Do you know where the orchid grows?" I asked slowly.

"Sure. Me father took me to see it when I was but a child. A warning he gave me, for this be the one thing that can kill all creatures of great power, from vampires to fairies. He wanted me to know what it looked like, for with knowledge comes power. Told me he did that there would be no more after me. All he could tell me, he would," she said.

"What happened to your father?" I asked.

"He went the way of all wizards; his time was over, so he was no more," she said.

"What?" I asked.

"Sorry be, there is no more I know. He went away one day, and saw him no more, I did," she said

"I'm sorry. You must miss him," I said.

"That I do. I miss them all," she whispered. "When I was but a child, there were still quite a few fairies left. Play about we would, with the moonlight playing off our wings." She closed her eyes and smiled at the memories. "A grand time it was to be a fairy, but as with all things, be they good or bad, they have a time to be and a time to be no more." She dropped her head in a sadness that no one could miss. I put my hand on top of hers, trying to share her pain.

"Is there anything I can do to help?" I asked.

As quickly as the sadness has descended upon her, the twinkle came back to her eyes and a smile back to her lips.

"Ah, but help me ye have, to share all that I am, glorious it be," she giggled. "Hope I do, friends we will be forever, or at least as long as I am." She took a nibble of her cheese and a bite of grape. "Grapes and cheese be me favorite," she said.

"What?" I said. What she had just shared had nothing to do with what we were talking about. Her mind had hopped from one thing to the other without much warning.

She held up the half-eaten grape.

"Grapes, love them I do: small, sweet. They come in bunches; ye can make wine of them or make a whole meal of them. See? Love them, I do," she said.

I had to smile as she inspected her half-eaten grape.

"Sure, everyone should love grapes," I agreed.

Chapter Thrirteen

There was a knock at the door. *Oh shoot! I forgot they were supposed to start on my new bathroom today*, I thought.

"Who is it?" I yelled through the door.

"Chuck Roberts, contractor," came a very husky voice.

"I knew it!" I said, turning to Deireadh. "They're here to start on the bathroom. Can we talk later?"

"Sure. I would like that very much, m'lady," she said with a nod.

I gave her a little finger wag.

"It's Katelynn, okay?" I said.

"O—kay," she said with a smile and a giggle.

"Just give us a minute, please!" I yelled though the door.

I started to pick up the trays.

"I will get it, m'la—Katelynn," Deireadh corrected herself.

"Are you sure? I can help," I said.

"Sure," she said.

"Thank you," I said as I began helping her put everything back on the tray. I pulled open the door; there, filling the entire entrance of the door, was Mr. Roberts. This big, burly, barrel-chested man sported a well-worn cap with a fishing design on it. At one time there had been some writing around the fish that had long since worn off, and his dark brown hair just barely peeked out around the edges. His face was covered with a thick but well-trimmed beard. His clean tan shirt was rolled up to the elbow and tucked in, showing a well-stocked tool belt. His jeans were clean, but I could tell that these were his work jeans. His outfit was finished off with good heavy work boots; this man was here to get his job done.

The contractor passed Deireadh as she was leaving. When the big, burly contractor caught sight of her, he dropped his toolbox and tripped over the rug as he plowed right into the table. I heard Deireadh giggle as she left the room without even looking back. After the contractor regained his composure (almost), he turned all the way around, hitting the edge of a very expensive vase with the back of his hand. I made a dive for and caught the vase before it hit the floor. I stood there cradling the vase; the contractor rocked back on his heels, paying little attention to me or the very expensive vase that I was still holding.

"Who was that?" he asked.

I do believe that man was drooling. I looked at him and rolled my eyes.

"Good grief, man! Put your eyeballs back in your head and roll that tongue back up before you step on it. We can't afford for you to crash into anything else."

"Oh…pardon me, miss, but that's just about the prettiest dang thing I ever did see. Why, she is prettier than the sunset from the top of Newfound Gap or the frost frozen in the trees atop Water Rock Knob. Dang!" he said with a shake of his head.

"Well, now, you're not from around these parts," I said with a big grin.

"No, miss, I'm not. I reckon you ain't, either," he said with a nod.

"What makes you think that?" I asked, setting the vase back in its place.

"I hear people all over this castle talking about the new Lord. They're saying how she talks funny, gives cake to little boys, and has breakfast with her maid." He looked up from spreading his blueprints out on the table. "And, again, I got to say, that girl is fine."

I put my hand on his shoulder and shook my head.

"Let it go man, let it go."

He gave me a sideways glance.

"I'm not her type," he said.

"That's an understatement!" I said with a huff.

"What?" he asked.

"Never mind," I said. "But hey, where are you from?" I asked as I retrieved my sneaker from under the edge of the bed.

"I was raised in the Great Smoky Mountains," he said with pride.

"Really? What part of the Smokies?" I asked.

"Let's just say in the Smokies," Chuck said with a chuckle.

"Wow! That must have been fun! I heard stories about and I saw some pictures of the mountains. I think it was my great-great grandpa that worked on the road that went over the park. He built tunnels, or something like that," I said with a shrug. "If you don't mind, I'd love to hear about them. Do those mountains really touch the sky?"

Chuck opened his thermos and poured himself a cup.

"Would you care for a cup?" he asked, holding up the thermos.

"I'd love some," I said, holding up my empty cup that I had kept from breakfast.

"Well," he said as he placed his cup on the edge of the blueprint to hold it in place, "I'll tell you about where I grew up if you will tell me about your home place, 'cause I know this ain't it."

I put my hands on my hips.

"Just what makes you say that?" I said.

"Well, now, let's take a little test. If I were to say 'how's your brother's younguns', what would you say?" he asked.

"I'd say my nieces are fine," I answered.

"Then if I were to ask, 'how do you like your tea,' what would you say?"

"That's a no brainer: on ice and sweet, of course, with a sprig of mint if you have it," I said with a smile and an eye flutter.

Chuck threw his head back, and a deep, rich laughter came rolling out of his chest.

"Girl, if you ain't from south of the Mason-Dixon line, then the sun don't set in the west," he said.

"Guilty as charged. I grew up in a small town in south Alabama. Small town, big family: everyone knew us," I said with a smile that let him know just how proud I was of it.

"How the dickens did you come into all of this?" he said with a wave of his hind.

I took a big gulp of my coffee. "That's a long story, but the bottom line is, I inherited it," I said.

"Nice," he said with a nod.

"Now it's your turn," I said.

"Like I said, I grew up in the heart of the Great Smoky Mountains. We zigzagged between the North Carolina side and the Tennessee side most of my life. Them mountains are truly God's country. I love 'em. The peaks hold up the very heavens. In the spring, the flowers bloom. In summer, the bugs sing. For fall, the leaves turn, and in winter, the snow flies. Elk, bear, and mountain lion roam free. Fish are jumpin' onto the banks just a beggin' to be rolled in corn meal and fried. Sometimes Dad didn't have work, so we were happy that the fish were glad to be rolled in corn meal and fried." Chuck picked up his cup and took a gulp.

"One summer, on one of our trips back over the mountains, we went through the Cherokee Reservation. We stopped to have a picnic. There we met an old Cherokee man. His name was Running Wolf. We became quick friends. Each time we came over the mountains we would stop and visit. One summer, when I was about thirteen, he asked if I would like to stay the summer with him. After much beggin' and a wagon load of promises, Dad let me stay for the summer."

"The whole summer?" I asked.

"Yeah, the whole summer. I learned how to trap and hunt. We never wasted a thing. If we took a deer, we used it all, from the tip of the antler all the way to the white tip on the end of the tail. I learned how to dig ramps; that's a wild onion. It's pretty darn good fried with potatoes. He also taught me all about the different wild greens and mushrooms. We gathered yellow root, ginseng, and lamb's tongue for medicinal use. Everything we did was an adventure; let's just say I had the summer of my life," Chuck smiled.

"That makes my summers swinging on the front porch seem kind of lame. You have to tell me how a mountain man like you made his way here," I said with a shake of my head.

"It was that summer with Running Wolf that made me realize that I wanted to see as much and do as much as I could. I studied hard in school, got myself a scholarship to one of the top colleges in the south: U.N.C. Chapel Hill, of course. There I got a master's degree in engineering. I came here to build bridges; I do this kind of work just for fun. This way, I get to meet some of the local folks. So, missy, now that you know my history, how about hooking me up with that pretty maid of yours?" he said with a jiggle of his eyebrows.

"Again, I say, she is not your type. I'll ask anyway, but don't hold your breath," I said with a shake of my head.

"Thanks," he said with a wink. "Now, I had better get to work before Mr. Calldoon gets back and nothing has been done. I don't think I want to have to explain that," he said, half muttering the last part.

"I'll get out of your way," I said as I extended my hand for a parting handshake. "Chuck, it's a pleasure to meet another Southerner."

"The pleasure is all mine," he said with a nod.

I headed out the door, and Chuck started on my bathroom.

Chapter Fourteen

Down the stairs, I turned the corner and ran right into Tanarr. It was like hitting a brick wall: a very handsome, green-eyed, delicious-smelling brick wall.

"Oh my gosh, I'm so sorry, Tanarr!" I said.

It didn't even faze him. He flashed me one of his infamous crooked smiles, and I could see a twinkle of amusement in his eye.

"If not for Corbin, I might say it was truly all my pleasure," he said.

I didn't say a word; I crossed my arms over my chest and tried to give him my best stern look, even though I was having some very pleasant brick wall thoughts.

"Come on, Katelynn; I'm only kidding. You're Corbin's; I know that. I still have an alliance to this place and all who dwell therein." He turned serious. "Now, that includes you. I know the time of knights has passed, or at least, the way we were is no more. Today it's but a title. However, if you would have me, I will still be a knight of Go-Brath." He raised my hand to meet his lips. "That is, if you will still have the lot of us."

"Really?" I squeaked.

"Really," he smiled. "We promised Navar that as long as we were here, we would care for all that he loved. Now that I find myself back here, I feel my oath still intact, as is the castle herself. I am yours to command," he said as he went down on one knee and his fist went over his heart. He bowed his head.

I almost jumped back.

"What are you doing?" I said with a little panic in my voice as I reached down and took him by the arm. "Get up!"

"I pledge myself, my sword, and my honor to you," he said.

"That's all fine and dandy, but I have no idea how I should react to this. So let's just say we did, you did, and it's all good," I stammered as my face turned a little red.

Tanarr chuckled as he came to his feet.

"You are the most delightful creature I have ever met. I most certainly can see what Corbin loves about you. What I am saying is I will never harm you, nor will I allow anyone or anything to bring harm to you: not within the walls of this castle. I will serve and protect you," Tanarr said.

"Pfffft!" I said with a wave of my hand. "You can't do that. You're a big city lawyer; you don't have time for that."

"While I am here, I am a knight of Go-Brath: your knight," he said.

"Well, Sir Knight, my very first command is…is…um…nope. I got nothing. See ya!" I said with a grin.

"How about," he said, running his arm through the crook of mine, "if I might be so bold, how about we go finish signing all the papers to make all this and more yours?"

"Okay, but can we do this after lunch? I'm on my way to the library. I'd like to give my friend Christie a call. If I call her now, she'll be home." I stopped, squinted my eyes, and started to count on my fingers. "If we are five or six hours ahead of them, it should be somewhere between 5:30 and 6:00; she will be home and not in the bed yet. So, if it's not a problem, I would love to work on the papers later, okay?" I said with my hands folded under my chin. "Please, Sir, your knightship?" *Eye flutter, eye flutter*, I thought.

"How could anyone say no to that?" he said with his crooked smile that I bet had melted many a maiden's heart. "You go on, call your friend; the papers can wait. I'm sure you have a lot to catch up on."

"More than she is going to believe," I said with a roll of my eyes. I smiled up at him. "Thank you for understanding." I reached up and gave him a peck on the cheek. "I would use my cell phone, but it's dead, and I can't find my charger." I turned to leave. "I'll see you after lunch. Bye, now." I took off for the library as quick as a wink.

It's nice to know that I have a guardian protector even when my Spidey is away, I thought as I made my way down the hall. I was really starting to love this place with its mix of very old and very new: from the kitchen with its centuries-old, open-hearth cooking spit to the new-fangled microwave (as Doulsie would call it) that sat on the foot-thick, well-worn butcher block that was as old as the castle herself.

I opened the door that led into the library; the smell of old books mingled with leather and wood smoke from the fireplace. Even in here, there were books hundreds of years old, as well as new releases sharing the same shelf. Then there were paintings by the old masters hanging on the wall behind a state-of-the-art computer setup. It sat on a very old, hand-carved oak desk. To the left of the computer on the same desk was a phone that would do everything short of talking for you, and it might even have been able to do that.

I pulled out the desk chair and got as comfortable as possible; this might take a while. I hadn't talked to Christie in what seemed like forever, and I couldn't wait to hear her voice. We were used to talking every day.

I could hear her phone ringing. "Hello?" the moment I heard Christie's voice I could picture her sitting there in her kitchen in New York, her blue eyes sparkling as she and her husband, Hank, talked over the day's events. She would have her thick blond hair pulled back in a ponytail, with her feet in those big fuzzy slippers, coffee in hand. Both kids would be playing around them, asking all kinds of questions, like where do rainbows come from and why can't the dog talk? *Man, I love that place!*

"Hey, Christie, it's me. How are you doing?" I said.

"I'm fine, girl. How on earth is everything on the other side of the planet?" she said, adding a fake British accent.

"Things are, um, how are they? You won't believe how they are," I said.

"What does that mean?" Christie chuckled.

"It means I so wish you were here," I replied with a sigh.

"I do, too; I miss my Southern sassy gal pal and her amazing Spiderman. No one else calls me Wonder Woman." Christie paused. "I do miss that," she said.

"I think that Corbin came up with a great superhero name for you. You are pretty much a wonder woman the way you handle the kids, work, and home; you rock!" I had to say that to the one person I wanted to be more like. We both laughed.

"Tell me how it is over there, Miss Lord of the Castle," Christie laughed.

I put my feet up on the desk and leaned back. My feet flew up in the air as the chair went back farther than I meant for it to, and I almost lost my balance.

"Wowooo!" I squeaked.

"What was that?" Christie almost yelled.

"Nothing, except that the Lord of the Castle almost dumped herself in the floor. Isn't it nice to know some things never change?" I said, and we both laughed some more.

"Oh, where to start? It's amazing over here: the crisp air, rolling hills, and this castle. Oh, Christie, you have to see this. It's beautiful. It's big and old, new and exciting. Art of all kinds hang on the walls. There are tall ceilings, tapestries that line the halls, and huge fireplaces. In the dungeon—"

Christie interrupted me. "Dungeon?" she squeaked.

"Okay, it's no longer used as a dungeon; it's just storage now, but hold onto your hat. Just guess what is stored down there." Before she could answer, I blurted it out. "Jewels! Lots and lots of jewels: diamonds, rubies, emeralds, and pearls set in gold and silver, but mostly gold," I said. I wouldn't have told just anybody about all this, but with Christie I could and did tell her everything. *Shoot, I trust this girl with my life; she's the best!*

"Wow, you're kidding me!" Christie said.

"Nope," I said.

"Who do they belong to?" she asked.

"Calldoon, he's the caretaker. Well, he said it's all mine!" I said with a squeal. Christie squealed with me.

"Jump back; you are kidding me!" she gasped.

"All I know is what he said, and that is what he said." I let out another squeal. "But seriously, Christie, I don't know exactly how much Ms. Lera has left me, but I do know it's a lot." I took a deep breath. "Now, don't say anything, and just let me talk, okay?" I asked with a small plea in my voice.

"Okay...," Christie replied with a little suspicion.

"I know you're not going to want me to, but just like you have always had my back, now I have got yours. I had Tanarr set up trust funds for both of the kids." She started to protest. "Now, Christie, please let me do this. I love those two. As for you and Hank, there are plane tickets, room reservations, and money for you to go anywhere in the world you want to go. All you have to do is call Tanarr or me, 'cause I love you two, too. If this were all reversed, you would do the same. So give me this, please...."

"Thank you, Katelynn, but you don't have to do all that," she said softly.

"I know, but I really want to," I said.

"Well, thank you, and I will let you know about that trip; it sounds like fun!" she laughed. "Wow, girl, this is too much!" Christie took a deep breath, and I could hear her tone change. "I'm so glad things are going well, but I must admit that I have been worried about you. Speaking about things that worry me, have you seen or heard from tall, gorgeous, and scary since you have been over there?" she asked.

"Do you mean Blake?" I asked. I slung my feet back to the floor, leaned over the phone and lowered my voice so no one else would hear. "Oh, yes I have; he caught me off guard in the woods last night." I heard the sharp intake of Christie's breath on the other end of the phone.

"Katelynn, what did you do? Are you all right? He didn't hurt you, did he?" she asked.

"I'm fine, but you're never going to believe who came to my rescue," I said.

"Who?" Christie asked.

"My lady's maid," I said.

"Your what?" she asked.

"I know that sounds completely ridiculous, but I have one, and she is the one who rescued me," I said.

"And how on earth did she do that?" Christie asked.

"I can't tell you yet; I have to talk to her first. She is kind of shy about things. She doesn't like people to know much about her; she's funny like that," I said.

"Okay, let me get this straight. You have a lady's maid who can stop vampires?" Christie said with doubt edging her voice.

"Something like that," I said.

There was a knock at the door.

"Christie, hold on; there is someone at the door," I said,

"Hey, Rosey, what's up?" I said, holding the phone against my shoulder.

"M'lady," she said with a little bob. "Mr. Roberts the carpenter wishes to see you upstairs, at your convenience, of course."

"Tell him I'll be right there," I said.

"Yes, m'lady," Rosey said with another bob as she left the room.

"Christie, hey," I could hear her laughing on the other end.

"Sorry! I've never heard you called 'm'lady' before." She stopped laughing. "Come to think of it, I've never heard anyone called that before. I thought that was a storybook line," she said.

"Storybook? That does fit; this place comes as close to a storybook as it gets. I do wish you could see it," I said.

"Someday, I hope," Christie said with a sigh. "I might just use my plane tickets to come there," she laughed.

"Christie, I'll have to call you back later. I need to see how my new bathroom is coming. I have to take a serious hike just to take my shower and brush my teeth. So let me see what is going on; I'll call you back as soon as I can," I said.

"Hey, you be careful over there with Blake running around," I could hear the worry in her voice.

"I'll be fine; remember, I have my Spidey with me," I said with a little laugh.

"Be sure to tell Spidey I said hi," she said.

"I will. Love ya! Talk to you later, bye," I said.

"Bye, love ya!" she said.

As I put the phone back in place, I had to smile. I did miss my best friend. A shiver ran up my spine. Now that she had brought that Blake thing up, I wondered where he was and what he was up to. It had been my experience that evil does not give up this easily. But first things first, I had to get up to my room and see what was going on there.

Chapter Fifteen

Softly I tapped at the door to my suite. There was no answer. I went in talking so I wouldn't startle Chuck.

"Rosey said you wanted to see me," my words fell away. "Chuck?" I called out. "Chuck, where are you?" About that time I heard the sound of a hammer making contact with a nail, followed by his voice.

"I'll be darn; that makes no sense whatsoever, hmm...."

My room was shaped a little strangely; you entered into a lovely sitting room with a large double fireplace. On the other side of the fireplace was where the bedroom was and where my new bathroom would be. This is where I found Chuck.

"Here you are; what can I do for you?" I inquired.

He held up his hand to stop me. He set another nail to the wall, drew back with the hammer, and hit the nail on the head. It bent in half. He gave me an odd look.

"Do you see that pile of nails?" he pointed to a bucket on the floor that was half full; sure enough, they were all bent.

"Yeah...?" I said.

"Watch this." He took another nail, set it, and with just a few hard strikes of his hammer the nail went straight in. "Hmm...well, I'll be," he said.

I stood there with my hands on my hips.

"Okay, that was fascinating, but I have seen a hammer at work before," I said sarcastically. "I've even been known to set a few nails myself."

"Here, you try," he said, handing me the hammer. "That is the first nail I've got to go in without bending. That's why I had the girl go get you. I didn't think we were going to be able to build anything in here."

I took the hammer he held out to me. I chose my nail and picked out my spot.

"I wouldn't try there if I were you; I've bent at least ten nails there," Chuck said.

"But it looks like there should be a nail there," I said, giving the 2x4 a good look over. "I us to help my grandpa build dog houses, chicken coops, and repair the barn. I really do know what I'm doing."

"All righty, go for it," Chuck said as he took a step back.

I set my nail, drew back, and gave my best swing. The hammer made contact with the nail head, driving it straight in all the way. Chuck's chin almost hit his chest.

"How did you do that? I've been trying all morning to get just one nail to go in that spot," he said.

I blew on my fingernails and buffed them on my shirt, giving my hair a little flip.

"I'm just good; I told you, this is not the first nail I have ever set." I reached out and rubbed the head of the sunken nail. "My grandpa would be proud."

"Never did I ever see anyone sink a nail with just one hit: impressive," he said.

I put the hammer down on his toolbox and dusted off my hands.

"Anything else I can do for you?" I said.

"No, I guess you broke the hammer-nail spell," he said jokingly with a shake. "Or maybe you have the touch, 'cause that was the first nail that's gone in right all day. Now I hope I can get to work," he said.

"If my work here is done, I think I'm going to grab myself a bite of lunch. After that, I have a meeting with a lawyer" I said as I headed out of the room.

"Good luck with that," Chuck said as he loaded his teeth with a few nails.

I stopped and turned back.

"Just out of curiosity, why aren't you using a nail gun? And why don't you have a crew working with you?" I asked.

He took the nails out of his mouth.

"First, I don't use a nail gun because I like to have more control when I'm working on old wood like this. I think you need to use the old ways; if for no other reason, I do it out of respect. I also want it to look as old as the work around it. You just can't get that look using new-fangled tools. The other, I work best by myself; I don't want to have to be going back fixing what someone else has messed up. I know how I want it to look; I'm kind of picky," he said.

"Ah, that would be why Calldoon chose you; he likes picky," I said with a wink.

"I'll try my best not to let him down. We'll do this till it's the way you want it," he said.

"Thanks, Chuck. I got to run, or I'm not getting my lunch," I said as I left the room.

"Bye, miss," Chuck said in a muffled tone as he placed each nail back between his teeth, one at a time like still cigarettes dangling, ready to be put to work.

Chapter Sixteen

I ran down the stairs and straight to the kitchen.

"Good day, Ms. Doulsie," I said with as much respect as I could. Doulsie was the head cook and the one that everyone in this house came to for answers. She looked to be about seventy years old and short and round with a little chubby red face. Her Scottish accent was so thick that I had to listen really closely to understand her.

I fell in love with her the very first time we met. She felt like family from the start. Instead of a formal curtsey like the rest of the staff, when I was introduced to Doulsie, she had given me a soft but firm bear hug.

"Ah, what a sweet child. If I don't be liking ye from the start, ye have a kind heart. I'll just be knowing that ye'll be good for this old place. We welcome ye home, child," she had said in her thick Scottish accent. She released me from her hug and took both of my hands in hers. "Welcome!" she had said with a wink and a smile. "We've been a waitin' for ye!"

Who couldn't love her? I thought, although I had heard whispers about her hurling a meat cleaver across the kitchen when two kitchen girls were not taking their task seriously enough. She ran a tight ship.

"Yes, Ms. Katelynn, what can I be doin' fer ye today?" Doulsie looked at me over the top of her little glasses that were perched on the end of her nose. "I'd be thinking that ye might be in need of a bite of lunch," she said.

"Oh, you read me like a book, Ms. Doulsie. If I could, please, I would love to have a half of a turkey sandwich on your world-famous sourdough bread," I said.

"Only a half! Child, all ye had for breakfast was fruit and cheese!" she said.

"I know. I don't eat much, but it's all I can hold," I said.

She waved her wooden spoon at me.

"Ye'll blow away if ye don't put some meat on them bones," she gave me a wink. "If ye want to be catchin' and keepin' a man, ye got to give him a little something to hang onto," she said, giving her ample hips a little shimmy as she tapped them with her wooden spoon. "That be how I kept my mister for all these many years."

"Now, now, Ms. Doulsie, I think there is a little bit more to it than that. I can tell by that twinkle in your eyes," I said

She turned a little red and gave her spoon a wave in the air like the magic wand of a fairy godmother.

"Ah, there is some more to it than that," she winked. "Someday, you'll know," she giggled.

I perched on the stool at her side as she began to assemble my half sandwich. With my coffee in hand, I watched as she worked her magic. By the time she had finished, it was all I could do to pick it up.

"Wow! Ms. Doulsie, now this is a sandwich," I patted the stool beside me. "Sit, please. Have a cup of coffee and sandwich with me," I asked.

"Nay, I be done with me eatin' a long time ago," she said.

"At least sit. Have a cup of coffee with me and keep me company," I said.

She walked over to the refrigerator and poured herself a big glass of buttermilk.

"If it be all right with ye, I'll be havin' buttermilk; don't care much for coffee or tea. Buttermilk—" she said, raising her glass, "makes yer hair shiny." She cut herself a thick slice of sourdough bread and took the stool across the counter from me.

I took a big bite of my sandwich.

"This is the best thing," I paused. "It may be the best thing I have ever had," I said, filling my mouth again.

"Thank ye," Doulsie said with a nod.

"Someday you will have to show me how to make this bread." I took another bite. "I think I just might be in love."

She waved her little pudgy hand.

"My, how ye do go on. I'll be making bread tomorrow, if you'd like to stop by the kitchen," she said.

"I'd love to," I said, excitement gleaming in my voice and eyes. Not only did I want to learn how to make this wonderful bread, but I couldn't wait to spend some time with Doulsie. I looked at her across the counter and smiled. I could tell that there were some stories just waiting to bubble to the top.

I finished the last bite of my sandwich and licked my fingers.

"Now, that was a meal fit for a king," I said, dusting the crumbs off my lap. "Thank you, Ms. Doulsie, for keeping me company. I know you have a very busy day. You didn't have to stop and waste time on me," I said.

"Nay, Ms. Katelynn, ye did not have to be spending ye time here in the kitchen with the likes of me. In all me days, I never saw not one of the high ups come here to visit with the likes of me, much less ask me to eat with 'em."

She paused and tilted her head to the side. "Come to think of it, we've had no Lord for a long time. They all be thinking that we be nothing more than orphans. Some thought that we would be doomed to be that way forever."

She leaned in and gave me a wink. "Ah, but I knew that ye'd be a coming, and I be thankful that I lived to see ye. We've a kindred spirit. I knew it from the first time I laid me eyes on ye. I knew. Then, after ye made our very own Charles so happy to be having a slice of yer cake," she wagged her little pudgy finger in the air, "then they all knew, for we all be lovin' that child as our own."

"Ms. Doulsie, it was only a slice of cake," I said playing with a crumb at the edge of the table.

"Nay, 'twas much more. It showed a kindness that few have: an understanding of the little ones. Then ye have breakfast with yer maid and lunch with plain old me. You've made us all fall in love with ye, ye have," Doulsie said.

"That's what my Momma called following the golden rule; do unto others as you would have them do unto you." I gave her a wink and a nod. "I call it the Southern way, 'cause that's how we were raised back home."

She patted my hand.

"And a fine way it was, my child," she nodded. "For now, if I don't be getting back to me chores, they'll be no supper for ye tonight," she said.

I took my dishes to the sink. Before I left the kitchen, I stopped on impulse and gave her a kiss on the cheek.

"Thanks, Ms. Doulsie. I'll see you later," I said.

I glanced back as I was leaving the kitchen. Doulsie was rubbing her little face where I had kissed her. *She does so melt my heart, but still, I wouldn't want to cross her.*

When I stepped out into the hall, I glanced at my watch. It was time to meet with Tanarr, but before that, I thought I would grab another cup of coffee to take with me. *Man, I miss that coffee shop back in New York*, I thought. By now Doulsie was back at work.

"Excuse me, Mss Doulsie? Could I bother you for another cup of coffee to take with me to my meeting?" I asked.

"Sure, but ye know that buttermilk will make yer hair shine?" she said, offering the thick white stuff in place of my dark, rich coffee.

"That's all good and dandy, and I do like shiny hair. Nevertheless, I need my coffee more. I have a strong dislike of meetings and paperwork. Next stop: Tanarr and a very large stack of papers," I said with a sigh.

Doulsie chuckled.

"Would be a terrible task to be a sitting across the table from the face of an angel, and I'd be thinking, under all them fancy coverings of his, there would be quite a treat," she chuckled again. "Poor, poor child; I'll be thinking about ye."

"Ms. Doulsie!" I said with a shocked tone.

She handed me my coffee.

"I be old, not dead, and me eyes are very good with me glasses on," she sighed. "That lad is easy to gaze on, with them sparkly green eyes and his chest as broad as a bear."

I leaned in.

"You do know that he wears contacts to give those sparkly eyes their green?" I said.

"I though as much; I do not care as long as ye don't go tellin' me that glorious chest is not real," she said with a wink.

I took my coffee cup from her and gave her a good finger wag.

"I'm going to have to keep an eye on you, missy," I teased.

"Hmm…don't be wasting yer eye on the likes of me, with the likes of himself sitting across from ye," she said under her breath.

"Ms. Doulsie, I heard that. You do know that I have a fellow already?" I said.

She pointed to my left hand with her spoon.

"I don't be seeing a ring on that finger, so look, child, look," she winked. "Touch if ye can, till ye be getting' a ring, that is."

"Ms. Doulsie!" was all I said as I giggled my way out of the kitchen.

Chapter Seventeen

With coffee in hand, I made my way to my meeting with Tanarr, Ms. Doulsie's secret crush. I had to suppress a giggle. I smiled into my coffee cup. *What a lady!* I thought.

The door was ajar. I tapped softly.

"Hello, may I come in?" I asked.

"Yes, please come on in," came Tanarr's masculine voice from the other side of the door. I walked over to his desk. "Have a seat; I think I have everything in order."

I took my seat and set my coffee cup down on the desk. It made a much bigger thud than I had intended.

"Oh, I'm sorry! I didn't mean to make that much noise." I looked up at him from under my eyelashes. "Do you mind that I brought my coffee with me?"

"No, not at all; make yourself comfortable. We may be here for a while," he said, straightening the stack of papers. "By the way, how was your phone call to your friend? Did it go through with no problems?"

"It was great," I smiled. "It was so nice to talk to her. Christie is my best friend. She is going to let us do the trust fund, and she said she would take the trip sometime. Isn't that great?" I said.

He picked up a pen and handed it to me.

"Yes, it is. It's good to have friends one can count on. She should come visit," he said.

"That's what I told her. She said she might use the plane tickets to come here." I leaned in. "Did you know that she knows about Corbin and Blake?"

He looked up from his paperwork and squinted his eyes.

"She knows all?"

"Yeah, all; she knows that they're, you know?" I said, trying to avoid the V-word.

He didn't say anything, only shook his head.

"Tanarr…you know…vampire," I whispered behind my hand.

"Oh, that? You do know that the word itself won't harm you?" he said with amusement tugging at the corner of his mouth.

"I know, but I still can't believe I've found myself in the middle of all this," I said, propping my elbows on the desk.

He leaned in.

"You do know that I also am one?" he whispered.

"Yes, I do. I think I'm going to call you…," I put my finger to the side of my mouth. "I don't know yet; I'll have to think on it."

"Call me? You call me Tanarr or Tad," he said with some confusion.

"No, not your name: instead of calling you a vam…I call you something like Green Hornet or the Hulk. That's why I call Corbin Spiderman," I said.

"Oh! We were all wondering why you called him that." Tanarr said.

"Yeah, he thought it was weird at first, but I can deal with a superhero much easier than I can," I paused. "You know."

"Vampire?" he said.

"Yeah, that," I said with a big gulp of coffee.

Tanarr had a twinkle of humor in his eye.

"Do I get to choose my superhero name?" he asked.

"No, you do not; I told you I would have to think on it for a spell to see what works for you. I am leaning toward something green," I said.

"Oh, really?" he said.

"It's all about those green contacts. I think Ms. Doulsie has a crush on you and your twinkly green eyes," I said, looking at him over the rim of my coffee cup.

"Do you mean Doulsie, the little round cook?" he said.

"I do indeed. Let me see. What was it she said; you were easy to gaze on with your sparkly green eyes," I said.

He chuckled and rolled his eyes.

"Just my luck. Do you think that anyone a little younger and perhaps just a little, well, littler, has shown any interest in me?" he said with a shake of his head.

"Now that you mention it, have you seen my maid? She is so sweet," I said with a smile.

He rolled his eyes.

"Sweet? We all know what that means."

I gave him a frown.

"No, we don't; just because one is nice does not mean she can't be beautiful," I said with a flutter of my eyes.

He lifted his hands in defense.

"You are absolutely correct; the evidence sits before me," he said.

"Ooh, good answer, Clark," I said.

"Who?" he asked.

"Clark, you know, Clark Kent, the alter ego of Superman. You slip on your designer glasses and go among the world unnoticed. When you take off those glasses, you can save the world," I said.

He took off his glasses and put the end of the earpiece in the edge of his mouth.

"Clark Kent/Superman. Hmm…I like that," he said.

"Yeah, me too," I said as I drained the last of my coffee. "Now, Clark, let's get on with this business."

"Let's see," he said laying the glasses aside; they really were only a prop. "You have already signed the deed, making the castle and all that lies within and all her lands yours." He patted the time-yellowed document that lay on the desk at his left hand. He reached for the top document on the stack to his right. "Next, let's take care of the banking," he said.

"How much are we talking about?" I asked.

"A lot," Tanarr said, studying the paper in his hand.

"How did Ms. Lera amass such wealth?" I asked as I inspected the bank records.

"A lot came from Navar; he had done quite well over the centuries. He could blend with the best of us. Then, with some advice from me, Lera made some very wise investments," he said.

I propped my elbows on the edge of the desk.

"Last night, you said that she had planned to do away with the two things responsible for Navar's death. Do you think she meant to destroy the orchid and herself?" I asked.

"Yes, I think that was her plan," he said.

"Wow. How on earth did you ever stop her?" I asked.

"I didn't. I went with her instead," he said.

"What! Why didn't you stop her?" I said.

"If you had known her then, you would understand. She was the most beautiful, headstrong little piece of dynamite I ever had the privilege to meet. I couldn't stop myself from falling in love with her. If I had said, 'No, you can't do that,' she would have been even more determined. Instead, I went with her to keep her safe from others and herself. Just as I knew it would, as her pain and anger cooled her passion, and her compassion returned," he said, sliding the bank documents in front of me; he placed the tip of his pen on a blank line. "Sign here, please."

I didn't even look at what I was signing. I barely glanced at the line I scribbled my name on. I so wanted to know more about this sweet lady who had brought so much to me in so many ways.

"Tell me, please, what happened? Where did you go?" I asked, placing the pen back on the desk.

He picked up the papers and inspected them, tapping the bottom edge on the desktop. Then he placed them in the stack with the deed to the castle. As he started his story again, I could almost see the mist of the past as it began to overtake the present.

"Early the next morning, while the fog was still clinging to the world like old spider webs, we climbed into a small one-cabin boat, if you could call that a boat. It was more like three walls and a bad roof on a raft. With what little gear we had, we climbed on board, and up the Amazon we went. Luckily, the elderly man who piloted our boat spoke English, broken though it was. We still could communicate with each other. He also spoke the language of the river. All up and down the banks there were so many things we dealt with, from the water itself to the people that dwelled along the water's edge. Even though the languages were almost the same, the dialects were distinctly different."

"By the time the sun was rising, we were well on our way. Even though the day had just begun, the air was thick with humidity and bugs. By the time the sun was high in the sky, the humidity was clinging to our skin, and the air felt like thick soup."

I interrupted him.

"Sorry, but I remember Ms. Lera telling me about how painful the sun was to her, that brief time she was…was…you know," I said.

"Vampire?" Tanarr whispered.

"Yeah, that. Does it affect you the same way?" I asked.

"Certainly. It's the same way for all of us. We have to learn to deal with it. I always try to mentally go somewhere else. On that trip up the Amazon, I spent my time and energy trying to talk to Lera. She was so lost in her grief that conversation was not high on her list of things to do. I finally gave up and found myself a spot to sit and observe. The river was wide and flat, and the only ripple on the water was the one made by our boat. Crocodiles lined the banks on each side," he chuckled. "Them bad boys even made the lot of us seem tame. Flocks of white birds flew overhead. That truly was a different world."

"Having given up on any hope of conversation with Lera, I decided to see if I could engage our captain. 'Hey…ah…Captain…sir, by the way, what is your name?' I asked.

'Tom. Everyone calls me Tom,' he said.

'Okay, Tom, do you know where we're going?' I asked.

His only reply was a nod.

'How long before we get there?' I asked with my hand hooding my eyes.

'Long time, short time; we be there when we get there,' Tom replied, never taking his eyes off the horizon.

'What?' I turned my gaze on him. 'Do you really know where we're going?' I asked.

He nodded again.

'I not take you all the way to the village. I no go past the big pink fish,' Tom said.

'What?' I asked.

'He means the pink dolphins. There is only one place on the planet where the pink freshwater dolphin exist,' Lera said in a flat, monotone voice. She sounded like she was in a trance. There was no emotion in her voice or face. 'The pink dolphins are the first sign that we are going in the right direction.'

'What does he mean, he won't take us all the way?' I asked.

'They think it a curse to cross the pink fish; to do so would mean certain death, they think. Tom will not cross them; he'll leave us on the banks.' Lera said.

'Are you kidding me? Don't tell me we are going to have to walk the rest of the way, 'cause I don't have my hiking boots on.' I stuck my foot up, exposing my very expensive shoe. 'These babies are crocodile, and I don't want a relative making friends with them, as said relative could turn on us,' I said.

Lera smiled and even gave a little laugh.

'You can't tell me you're afraid of a little bite,' she nodded toward one fat croc. 'He's the one that should be nervous.'

I rolled my eyes.

'No, I'm not the least bit worried about him, but these,' I pointed at my shoes, 'these are new and very expensive,' I told her. What I was really worried about was her.

'Relax, city boy. Tom is leaving the boat with us. He has someone coming to pick him up,' she said as she stood there with her back leaning against the side of the boat.

'That's good,' I grumbled. 'How long before we get there?'

She shielded her eyes against the sun and looked from one side to the other. 'My best guess is that it will be three or four days before we get to where the pink dolphins are. After that, I don't know.'

I squinted my eyes at her.

'Are you sure?' I said with a roll of my eyes.

'Quite,' she said, pushing away from the boat. 'You don't have to go on with me. I can and will continue by myself. You can go back with Tom.'

'Forget that. I'm not going to leave you out here by yourself to become some creature's next meal,' I all but shouted.

'Oh, really?' she said, leaning back against the boat with her eyes closed and her hat pulled down. 'Oh, wait,' she said, pushing her hat back. 'I don't tempt you at all, do I?' She tilted her head to the side."

Tanarr smiled as he paused in the middle of his story, staring off at nothing in particular. Then, in a very soft voice, he said, "Ah, if she had only known just how temping she was to me, but not in the way she was implying." He looked back at the desk, tapping the end of his pen on the stack of papers. "She was on a completely different level; she was more temping than anything I had ever encountered. She was my world, a world in which I was not permitted to live."

He continued with his story: "Lera gave me a little smile. 'Matter of fact, I probably repulse you. I know that one of the side effects of the cure is that I am completely immune to anything to do with…' She giggled, raising her eyebrows in lieu of saying the word 'vampire'; she knew that would unsettle Tom. After all, he was very fluent in English; he might choose to jump off the boat right into the river, feeling safer with the crocs than a vampire. As it was, he probably thought our verbal exchange was nothing more than odd flirting. I moved closer to Lera; we were shoulder-to-shoulder and hip-to-hip with our backs against the railing. I slid my arm across the rail and around her waist. Tom looked at me and gave me a wink. I had to suppress a laugh," Tanarr said with a nod.

"Smooth move; I'm sure Lera knew what you were up to," I said.

"Oh, yeah, smooth," he said with a big smile. "I'm not so sure she thought so."

"Tanarr, that sounds like a move my boyfriend in high school tried on me at the drive-in," I said.

"Well, now, Katelynn, did it get him very far?" Tanarr asked.

"Did you ever hear about the boy I shot in my car?" I asked.

Tanarr was so caught by that statement that he almost choked.

"You shot some boy for trying to put his arm around you?" he said.

I wrinkled my nose.

"I did shoot him, but not that time." I looked at him from under my lashes. "I didn't kill him; I only nicked him. He learned not to push me. I don't push easy."

"I will remember that piece of information," Tanarr said as he picked up another set of papers.

"Now, what are these papers for?" I asked.

"The first set of papers you signed were to transfer all American funds into your name. This next set will make the Swiss accounts all yours," he said.

I watched as he flipped through all the papers, marking each place I was to sign. After he looked over the last page, he slid them over to me. I picked up the pen and took a deep breath.

"Wow! This accounts for a lot of Swiss!" I said.

He smiled.

"Lera was a lot of things, from explorer to homemaker, research scientist, and even a chief medicine man. She started out with very little and ended up one of the richest women in the world." Tanarr said with a smile and a touch of pride.

"Hold it; did you say medicine man?" I asked.

"I did," he nodded.

"Medicine man? Ms. Lera?" I squeaked.

"Yes, that's in all reality what saved her life," he said.

"Are you sure?" I asked.

"Very!" he replied.

I had started to open my mouth to say more when there was a soft tap at the door. I got up from my seat to see who was there. With one hand on the door handle, I turned back to Tanarr.

"Hold that thought; I have got to hear the rest of this," I said as I opened the door.

Standing on the other side was Rosey.

"What can I do for you, Rosey?" I asked.

She did her little bob curtsey thing.

"So sorry to be bothering ye, 'tis Mr. Roberts. He be asking to see ye again," Rosey said with a huff. She rolled her eyes toward the stairs.

"Okay," I said, trying to suppress the laughter that threatened to spill over. Patient, quiet, polite little Rosey was obviously not impressed with the needy carpenter. "Tell him I'll be up in just a little while; there is one more thing I need to see to."

"Yes, m'lady, as ye wish," Rosey said with a bob. As she was walking away, I could hear her mumbling. "Blasted man, canna' hit a nail without assistance. If I'd be doing me own work so poorly, ha! I'd be banished to the hog pens to care for the swine. They would not be caring if I slopped them just right or not!"

I gave my head a shake, closed the door, and returned to my seat across from Tanarr.

"Now, you have to tell me about that medicine man thing," I said, sliding back in my chair, crossing my legs, and getting comfortable.

Tanarr leaned back in the leather chair. It creaked a little in protest. As he, too, got a little more comfortable, he cleared his throat and continued on with what he was telling.

"After Tom left us, we continued on upstream. The large pink dolphin played alongside of our boat. I asked Lera if she wanted me to drive.

'Hmm…If you call it driving, then you don't know what you're doing. I got it.' she said with a roll of her eyes. 'At the next village we will either have to trade this for a smaller boat or walk: your choice,' she grinned. 'You're the one with the fancy shoes.'

I looked at my shoes, then back to her.

'Boat,' I said.

'I know that money is not a problem, so the shoes aren't it. And you don't get tired, so having a ride is not it. So what is the real deal? Why are you here?' Lera asked, never taking her eyes off the horizon."

"I walked up behind her. I wanted so badly to wrap my arms around her, to protect her, to love her." Tanarr looked up at me and gave his head a sideways nod. "But she would have taken my head off, no doubt about it. I could tell by her body language that she was in no mood to be touched, not by me or anyone. She could barely stand for her own skin to touch her." He took a deep breath and exhaled slowly. "I refrained from telling her the truth."

I leaned forward in my chair, placed my forearm on the desk, and gave Tanarr a good old-fashioned Southern eye flutter.

"And the truth was?" I asked, fluttering my eyes.

He smiled his crooked smile, which by the way I'm sure had gotten him almost anything he ever wanted, almost.

"I wanted to grab Lera and run, to comfort her, to protect her, and to get her out of that mosquito-infested, croc-laden death trap that she had chosen for herself. Instead of the truth, I choose the comic route. I flicked the rim of her hat.

"'Let's see; I think I've come too far to get back on my own.' I threw my hands up in the air. 'Just picture this: a directionally challenged vampire, who by the way can find all the best places in New York, LA, and Paris with no problem, gets lost in this huge swamp, crosses paths with a she-croc, who falls madly in love with my insanely expensive crocodile shoes, all while trying not to get speared by one of those blasted poison arrows.' At the end of my speech I gave her my best little boy pouty face. 'You don't want me to be the laughingstock of the vampire community, now do you?'

'No...,' she replied.

'I know that you would be just as happy for me to leave as to stay, but please let me stay?' I pleaded.

She said nothing.

'Come on; I'll behave. I promise,' I said.

'Okay, you can stay, but do not get in my way!' she demanded.

'What do you mean, get in your way?' I said.

She just looked at me.

'Is this getting in your way?' I asked, popping right in front of her. 'Or is this what you call getting in your way?' I grabbed the captain's wheel and gave it a jerk; the boat veered to the left. I turned from the captain's wheel and ran my knuckles along her jawline. 'Or is this in your way?'

She rolled her eyes.

'No. All this is only getting on my last nerve, so stop it!' she said.

I cleared my throat.

'All right,' I said.

'Trust me,' she said, taking the wheel back. 'You'll know when you're getting in my way. Everyone will know when you're in my way.'

'Deal. I'll stay out of your way, and you won't make me walk home,' I said as I extended my hand. 'Let's shake on it.'"

"We pulled over at the next little village to trade boats. The young boy who helped us dock our boat was happy to see new faces and as equally excited to know where we were going and why. When we told him we were going to Kee-Ka-Na, he turned a little pale. At that point, he no longer cared about the new people. The once-friendly boy had nothing more to say; he just took off. We finished docking our boat and continued in our search to find someone to trade with."

"As we walked through the village, we did not see one single person. We could see where they had been, but there were no people around."

I straightened in my chair, cleared my throat, and interrupted him. My curiosity got the best of me.

"What do you mean, you couldn't find anyone? Where did they go?" I asked.

Tanarr leaned in close and lowered his voice.

"They were hiding," he said.

"Hiding from what? Surely not you and Lera?" I asked.

"Yes," he said.

"Why?" I slapped my hand over my mouth. "Oh! Was it because they knew that you were a vam—" I stopped.

"—pire," Tanarr finished my word with that crooked smile. "Katelynn, my friend, you have a problem with that word, don't you?"

"I do, Clark." I said putting a little extra emphasis on the new name I had given him.

A flash of confusion crossed his face, and then he laughed.

"You are a funny little human," he said, picking up his glasses that lay to the side of the stack of documents. He looked at the designer frames then back at me. "I am beginning to see what Corbin sees in you." He shook his head. "Why is it that all my friends found the one thing that slips through my fingers?"

He was so distant. I could feel his pain.

"I don't know. I guess us human women are like parking places at the mall on a busy day," I said, trying to lighten the mood.

Tanarr looked at me over the top of his fake glasses with his brows scrunched together. "What?"

"You know, all the good ones are taken. All the rest are either door bangers or not worth the walk," I said with a big, goofy grin.

He gave it a little thought then threw his head back and laughed so hard and loud that I thought the books would come off the wall. The sparkle that had left his green eyes from the remembering of his tale came springing back. My little joke had worked just as I had hoped.

"You are a true diamond; are you sure that you are one-hundred-percent happy with that boring old Corbin?" he said with a wink.

I knew that he was kidding, as he and Corbin were way too good of friends to let me come between them. I could also tell that there was only room for Lera in his heart; he still loved her. I waved my hand.

"Yeah, yeah, yeah. I know; I'm the best thing since sliced bread. And yes, I am completely happy with my Spiderman. Now, with that out of the way, can we get back to the story, please? I have a 'needful' carpenter, as Rosey

90 • Carly Robbins

would say, waiting for me so he can finish my new bathroom. I would like to hear where the people all were."

"Ah, yes, the village people," Tanarr said.

"Yeah. If they weren't hiding because they knew what you were, then why?" I asked, sitting on the side of my chair.

"Well," he said rubbing his chin with the back of his hand, "It was definitely not on my account. The Chief finally came out of his hut. Timidly he approached us."

"'Why you go to Kee-Ka-Na?' the Chief asked.

I looked at Lera, waiting for her to reply.

She shrugged her shoulders.

'Just never been there," she said.

'No good, no good. You no go there,' the Chief said.

'Why?' I asked.

'Bad spirit walks in them, makes them bark like wild dog. It try to get out of them,' he waved his hands. 'You no go there. They must drive out the evil spirit; it kills their little ones and the old ones alike. It tries to take the rest. Kill it they must, as they did the winged creature of long ago,' the Chief said.

'What do you mean, bad spirit?' Lera asked.

'Bad spirit, bad spirit: you no go there,' the Chief said as he started to walk away.

'But wait, what has happened to the people?' Lera asked.

The chief slowly turned.

'Bad spirit kill them,' the Chief replied.

'Yes, I got that,' Lera said a little more passionately than she might have meant it to sound. She took a deep breath and tried to calm herself. 'But how?' she asked.

'It go in,' the Chief shook his head. 'It trapped.' The Chief hit his chest with his fist. 'Inside, bad spirit trapped, make bad sound when try to get out.' "

'What kind of sound?' Lera asked.

'Much loud, much loud,' the Chief said.

Lera squinted her eyes and stepped closer to the Chief.

'Can you show me? Can you make the sound?' she asked.

The Chief shook his head.

'No can make sound: much bad, much bad,' he said.

'Could you try for me, please?' Lera pleaded.

'I try for you,' the Chief said with a nod. He placed his hands on his throat and made this horrible choking, strangling, coughing sound.

'Whooping cough!' she said instantly, with fear in her eyes and concern in her voice. 'We've got to get there now!'

'You no go there,' the Chief kept repeating.

'We have to go! I think I can help!' Lera said.

The chief stepped in front of her.

'You no go. You only a woman,' he said.

She looked at me with pleading eyes.

'Help me! Help me explain!' she whispered.

I got between Lera and the chief, looked back over my shoulder, and whispered out of the corner of my mouth, 'Is this getting in your way?'

Tanarr laughed at the memory. He smiled and winked.

My reward for that wise crack was a good, hard pinch.

'Hey, I like that. Do it again,' I said, trying not to grin in the Chief's face.

'Rrrr…would you please?' she said, pushing me forward.

'Okay, okay; I can handle this,' I said with my hand behind my back. I waved her back, and then I made an elaborate bow.

'Oh, great Chief, forgive me for not making her presence known.' Next, I bowed to Lera, stepping to the side to allow the Chief to gaze at all five feet of her, while I made up an explanation.

"There she stood in her perfectly fitted shorts, rolled pretty high, hiking boots with socks peeking out of the top of them that framed her legs. Short though they were, no legs were ever more perfect. She had a man's white shirt tucked into those short shorts. Her curly red hair was stuffed into a big hat with only a strand or two that had freed themselves and hung along the sides of her face.

'This is the great medicine man, come from far, far away to protect the people of Kee-Ka-Na. There is no one like her in the whole jungle; at last, she has come. You must grant us safe passage, or the Kee-Ka-Na's deaths will be on you all,' I said.

"The Chief squinted his eyes and looked her up and down. At this point I was pretty sure he wasn't buying our act. Lera had a flashlight in her back pocket; I remembered seeing it there as she walked in front of me. I reached my hand behind her like I was going to present her to the Chief. When she felt my hand at her backside, the look that flashed across her face…,' Tanarr smiled and shook his head. 'I could see her coiling to strike and strike hard. I was close enough to whisper in her ear, 'Work with me! Please, just work with me!' She relaxed, and I hit the on button on the flashlight in her pocket. The light beam came on, streaming up her back and causing a halo to appear at just the right time. The Chief drew his breath in sharply out of fear and awe. He then took a step back and fell to his knees in front of her.

'Oh, great medicine man, how we help?' the Chief said.

"Lera nodded and instructed me to help the Chief to his feet. She had played the part to the tee. The flashlight had achieved what I had hoped it would. The Chief thought Lera to be a god: a great white medicine man. From that point on, anything she wanted, she got; the Chief saw to that."

'All we require is a small boat,' she said.

The Chief lead us to the edge of the water.

'You choose; take what you want,' he said.

'Thank you,' Lera said as she walked along the water's edge, looking at each boat. 'This one will do nicely. We will leave ours in exchange, if that's okay?' she asked.

The Chief nodded his approval. We loaded our meager supplies into the small boat and shoved off. Slowly we made our way upstream toward the village. The jungle took on a strange silence as we got closer. No wildlife moved about, not on the banks or in the water. It was as if the Amazon herself were warning us to stay away.

'Lera, if this is whooping cough, won't you be in danger?' I asked.

She shook her head.

'No. Do you remember my telling you about the side effects of the antidote made from the orchid? It not only cured me from the vampire virus, but it also gave me an amazing immunity to almost everything,' she said.

'Do you think it is whooping cough?' I asked as our boat slid through the water.

'I don't know; we'll see,' she said.

Chapter Eighteen

"Tanarr, wait, stop! Don't tell me any more. I really want to hear what you and Lera found when you got to the village. However, to quote Rosey, I have a needful carpenter waiting for me in my suite," I said.

I started to stand; Tanarr shuffled the stack of papers in front of him.

"That will be fine, but you know we still have more things to take care of," he said.

"Is it something that will keep?" I asked as I made my way to the door.

"Yes, for now; it's the rest of the land deeds," he said.

With my hand on the door handle, I looked back over my shoulder.

"Will tomorrow be okay?" I asked.

"Yes, we can do that," he replied.

"You just tell me the time, and I'll be here," I said with a nod.

He took off his glasses and put them to the side.

"How about in the morning after breakfast?" he said with a crooked smile.

"So you'll be at breakfast?" I asked.

He nodded.

"Great, it's a date. I'll see you in the morning," I said as I left the room.

I almost sprinted from the office to my room. I knew I had kept Mr. Roberts waiting longer than I meant to. Gently I slid the door to my room open.

"Hello?" No response. "Hello? Chuck, where are you?" My voice bounced around the apparently empty room. I walked around the fireplace to where my new bathroom would be, and there was still no Chuck. There on the table, by the blueprints, was a note.

Dear Katelynn,

I'll be back in the morning: bad nails. All but two of them bent. I'm taking them back to the hardware store.

With the note still in hand, I walked over to the two-by-four with the two nails firmly imbedded. One was the one that I heard Chuck hit when I first came into the room. The other was the one I had sunk, with one swing, I might add. I rubbed the heads of the nails.

"Hmm…that's odd. How could all but two of the nails be bad?" Still pondering that thought, I moved over to the window. The view took my breath away every time. The evening was well spent, and the shadows were getting long. The day was cooling off, preparing for the coming of the night. The hills took on a dark shade of blue green. There, where the meadow met the forest, lay a dark ring of deep shadows. In that ring, my curiosity and imagination collided. Their collision either got me in trouble or scared the ever-loving daylights out of me. Either way, I wasn't going there. Back home, this would have been the time of the evening when I would be heading to the old porch swing, sweet tea in hand. With the bugs singing, I would await the coming sunset while dreaming about my knight in shining armor. Who would have ever guessed I would find one: a real one! It was more like he had found me. Then, to top it all off, here we were in a castle, *my* castle. I let out a sigh as I let my mind wander. *Yipes! Stay away from that dark ring, and keep close to the porch swing….*

Chapter Nineteen

I hurried down to breakfast only to discover that Corbin and Calldoon had not yet returned from checking on the borders. Tanarr had some kind of international banking thing going on, and Zoul, who knew where he was? I decided to have my light breakfast of fruit and toast in my room. With my steaming cup of coffee in my hand, I strolled over to the window. From this lofty height, I could see Deireadh in the rose garden talking to the roses, or maybe it was the castle. Whichever did not matter; I only hoped she would talk to me. I thought I would try to spend some time with her today, if she would let me.

I made as much noise as I could as I went into the garden. I banged the gate. I shuffled my feet on the path, and I even hummed. I didn't want to startle her.

"Hear ye, there I do," Deireadh said, not even looking up from her task.

"Oh, good. I didn't want to startle you."

"That ye canna' do; lets me know who is about, she does," Deireadh said.

"She who?" I asked, looking around. "There's no one here but you."

She nodded toward the exterior wall of the castle that stood tall and proud, protecting all that dwelled within.

"She knows all," Deireadh said.

"Are you talking about the castle?" I asked with a little hesitation.

"Aye," she said with a nod.

"The castle told you?" I said with a huff.

She looked up from her work, her purple eyes sparkling.

"Aye," she said with a giggle. "She does. Many are the things she tells meself. There be someone about yer room, this she tells me today, it be." She gave her head a little shake. "Give her permission to let him be there, ye must, to let him do anything; she won't if ye do not," Deireadh said.

I fluttered my eyes and shook my head. I truly had no idea what on earth she was talking about.

"Okay, Deireadh, tell me one more time, 'cause I didn't get any of that."

She giggled and took a seat on the stone bench that sat at the edge of the rose garden; she patted the bench beside her.

"Come sit with me, m'lady," she said   .

"Arr! Please call me Katelynn," I asked her.

"As ye wish, Katelynn," she said, giving the bench another pat.

I heard the unmistakable sound of the soft tinkle of gold against stone. I took the seat offered me at her side. I lifted her delicate hand to inspect the source of the soft sound. There on her middle finger was this ring, this amazing ring. There was no single word to describe it. It almost looked like a daisy that had been gently wrapped around her finger, and the stone that was at the very heart of the ring, oh my! That stone! The more I looked at it, the more it drew me in.

It was a clear stone, I think. In the midst of all that clear smokiness, I could see shoots of every color under the rainbow; each facet held a different color. Around the edges of this large stone was an inscription: *That which is true may only be true to whom it appears*. She removed her hand from mine. Lovingly, she rocked the ring back and forth on her finger, making the stone explode in a whirl of color.

"Queen of the fairies, she was," Deireadh whispered.

"Excuse me?" I questioned.

"She be from where such came," she said, still rocking the ring.

I said nothing, only waited for her to tell me what she wanted me to know. I had learned this strategy from Ms. Lera; don't rush the tale or the teller. Wait for it, and it will unfold as it needs to, as it's meant to be.

She took a deep breath, exhaled slowly, and began.

"When she slid it on me finger, I did not want it, so unworthy I be," she shrugged her shoulders. "I be but a mind bender."

"But Deireadh, that's a lot. I most certainly don't know anyone else who can do that," I said with a squeak. "Even back home in Alabama, Dory, who claimed to have all kinds of power, couldn't do that. Hmm…," I said, looking off to the side. "Come to think of it, I never saw her do anything." I turned back to Deireadh. "You do know your power saved my life the other night?" I said.

She shook her head.

"Ye do not be understanding; some there were whose powers were more than most could believe."

"Really?" I said.

"Really. There were those, there were, who could change the weather. Some the waters they could command. There be one, I knew, who change the very dimensions of time itself she could." She shook her head. "Ah, but she did not last, for her power was too strong. Consumed her it did; she was no more. Every glimmer of her left."

"Wow!" I said in a whisper of awe. "How did you wind up with the ring?" I asked.

She sighed and looked up at the sky.

"I being the last, there was none left to care for it. So Queen Ceela, with sadness of the knowledge, passed her on to meself. As she did so, told me she did, 'Wear it; wear it well. Be proud. Protect that which ye are, for there shall be no more after ye. For this I am so very sorry, for it has been a grand time to be.' " Deireadh looked down at her ring. She ran her finger across the stone. "She is but a fairy stone."

She had said it so quietly that I could barely hear her.

"A fairy stone?" I repeated. "Where does a fairy stone come from?"

"It came from the heart of the oldest fairy circle, which lay deep in the dark forest. In the very center of the dark forest clearing, beautiful and bright, the sun came streaming through. It be in that very fairy circle, there be the birthplace of the fairy stone. She holds all that we are." She looked at me from under her lashes. With a sad smile tugging at the corners of her mouth, she ran her thumb over the stone. "Like meself, she is the last of her kind."

"May I ask about the words around the stone?" I timidly asked.

She repeated the inscription.

"That which is true, may only be true to whom it appears." She paused and smiled. "It matters not what be the truth, if the truth won't show herself to ye."

I didn't say a word, only looked at her with that blank stare that said, "I have no earthly idea what you are talking about." She took my hand in hers.

"If we do not want them to know of us, they won't. It is that simple," she said. Releasing my hand, she prepared to leave.

"But wait! You said 'they' could not see you?" I said.

She nodded.

"See us, speak wrong I may, see us they may, know us," she giggled. "See our wings that be, they will not till it be their will. As for ye 'they,' among them ye are not counted, almost one of us ye be. Hide from you, never could I, for it is in that wee touch of wizard that sees all it does. If the truth bein', and she does not care fer ye to see her, ye will not do, for the truth takes on a truth of her own," she said with a smile.

I decided to let that wizard thing go. There were some things I just didn't want to know about yet.

We had been talking for a while. It was getting close to dinnertime, and I still wanted to know about those wings of hers. I gave her a sideways look and decided to just jump in and ask.

"May I ask you one more thing before it gets too late and we get interrupted by Rosey coming to get us for dinner?" I asked.

"Aye," she said with a nod.

"It's about your wings," I said.

She looked at me and smiled; she said nothing, just smiled. I plowed ahead with my question.

"Where are those glorious, lavender, sparkly, gossamer wings? I know I saw them. Do you have the power to just pop them in and out at will?" I asked.

She covered her mouth as a little giggle escaped.

"Silly that would be; just because ye canna' see them does not mean they be not there. Their truth simply does not want to be seen," she said, rubbing the stone in her ring "'Tis what the ring is, after all."

"Are you saying that if I really want to, I can see them? If I'm looking for them, I can?" I asked.

"Maybe, if they want to be seen," Deireadh said.

"Let me put it this way; if I wanted to see them right now, could I?" I asked.

Her head shot up, and her eyes were darting around.

"No, my Katelynn," she shook her head. "No, for there are too many folks about." She got so upset that her words got even more jumbled. "Too many eyes there be. Me heart will not allow. Ears hear what we do not want: pain. No, m'lady. Do not ask…."

I put my arm around her shoulders to comfort her. In doing so, I do believe that I saw a sparkle in the air about her shoulders and back, but Deireadh was so upset, so discombobulated that I didn't have time to think about that sparkle.

"Shh…shh…it's okay. They will be our secret; no one needs to know," I cooed.

She quickly calmed herself.

"Thank ye, for they can never know. It be on that day I will be gone. They would have no understanding; meself would be consumed," she said with a little panic still in her voice.

I sat there silently, letting her speak her concerns. All the while my brain was spinning like a top out of control. I was having a hard time wrapping my little mind around all she had said. I decided that I would write all this down as soon as I got back to my room to see if that would help sort it all out.

When she had completely calmed down, I thought that it would be a good idea to change the subject to get it off that wing thing.

I took a deep breath and exhaled slowly, swinging my feet above the ground like a bored child waiting for her turn on the merry-go-round.

"Well, I have nothing to do; it's too early for dinner, and I can't work on the bathroom. Speaking of my bathroom," I said, happy to be onto another subject.

"Aye, ye new bathroom," she repeated.

I gave her a sideways look.

"Is there something about that room that I need to know? Earlier you said something about the castle knowing? " I asked.

She giggled.

"Ye do not know?" she said.

"Know what?" I asked.

"Ye must give her permission, or she will not allow anyone to do anything in yer space," she said.

I ran my hand down my face.

"Give her permission, for real? Permission? And just how do I do that?" I asked.

She gave her head a little shake.

"All ye do is go into yer chamber and tell her," she said.

I gave her a sideways look.

"How do you know this?" I asked.

"It is part of the gift me father gave Lord Navar. She be a bit alive," Deireadh said.

"The castle, *this* castle, is alive? Are you messing with me?" I asked with a squeak.

She giggled.

"Messing…that be a silly word, thinks me do what this messing with means, I assure you, I do. I not be messing with ye, and that it be true. Ye must talk to her. Ye do know that her name, Go-Brath, means forever? Me father's gift was that she would forever be. If ye do her harm, a curse will be on ye, but if ye restore her, blessed ye shall be." She gave my shoulder a nudge with her own. "The latter of the two be ye; she knows that she now belongs to ye. So she will allow whatever ye ask." All of a sudden she got very quiet. "Shh!"

"What is it?" I asked.

"Shh…someone comes," she said. "Ah, 'tis only Rosey."

At that moment I heard the crunch of Rosey's feet on the path. I got up to meet her and see what she wanted.

"Good evening, Rosey, what's up?" I said.

She curtsied.

"Good eve, m'lady. Ms. Doulsie has sent me to fetch ye, for yer dinner is a waitin'," Rosey said.

"Oh yeah, I'm starving! Deireadh, come on, and din—" My words fell on empty space. "Arrr…I hate it when she does that!"

"Who does what, m'lady?" Rosey asked, innocently blinking up at me.

"Nothing," I said as we started back to the dining hall.

Chapter Twenty

I was not looking forward to eating all by myself in that big old dining hall. Corbin and Calldoon were still not back from their border patrol. I decided I might as well get on with it; I trudged on into the dining hall. To my surprise, there set Tanarr.

"What are you doing here?" I ask with a sharp intake of breath and a big smile. I walked over to my seat. Tanarr instantly stood, pulling out my chair for me.

"Your chair, m'lady," he said with a bow.

"Oh, thank you, my kind knight, sir, dude," I said with a lavish curtsy. "I really didn't expect to see you here tonight. I thought that all that big banking stuff would still have you all tied up."

"The bank issue is all well at hand, and even if it were not, I couldn't let you have dinner all by yourself, now could I? If I did, Corbin would not be very happy with me," he said.

"Do you know when they will be back?" I asked.

"It won't be too long, I'm sure," he said as he took his seat.

Charles came in with my food on a tray.

"Thank you," I said as the young boy with the big eyes and an even bigger smile set my food on the table in front of me. "Please tell Ms. Doulsie that this looks great."

He gave me his best grown-up bow.

"Yes, m'lady," he said.

I had to smile. I could see how everyone, including me, had fallen in love with this sparkly eyed little young man.

Before he left the room, I motioned for him to come closer. I put my arm around his waist and pulled him close, like I had done with my little brother when I was in high school.

"Hey, how was your cake?" I asked.

His eyes lit up.

"It was wonderful, m'lady," he said.

"Ooh, so was mine. You know what? We just might need another slice tonight," I said, giving him a wink.

He gave me a smile.

"If ye really think so," he said with a big smile.

"I do," I replied as I ruffled his hair.

He left the room so fast that I could tell it was all he could do not to run, although walking that fast could have been called running. Tanarr looked at me and smiled that crooked smile that he was infamous for.

"You know that kid loves you," he said.

"That kind of goes both ways," I said, looking down at my plate of steaming food. I inhaled deeply. "Oh, wow! This smells great. Oh! Sorry!" I said, glancing up at Tanarr.

"Don't be," he said with a wave of his hand. "I lost my fascination with that stuff long ago. I'm just here to talk and watch."

"Are you here to watch" I said, pointing at myself, "or are you here to watch," this time I pointed at my food as I prepared to shovel a loaded forkful in my mouth.

"Well, yes and yes," he said.

"So you've heard about my encounter with Blake?" I asked.

He nodded.

"Corbin has filled me in. I can assure you that coward won't bother you on my watch. I have less tolerance for that piece of slime than Corbin. Corbin has always had more patience than I; he tries to find some good in everyone." He gave his head a shake. "Some just have no good in them; don't waste your time with them."

I took a large mouthful of mashed potatoes that were covered in pot roast gravy, or as my Grandpa would call it, pot liquor. Whatever it may have been called, it was delicious. I chased it with a big gulp of tea.

"Oh, really?" I said. It was an observation more than a question.

"Really," he said in a matter-of-fact kind of way. "I have only one request."

"That would be?" I paused before loading my fork again.

"Stay within the walls of the castle," he said.

"That's no problem," I said, paying more attention to my potatoes than to our conversation. He reached over and touched my arm.

"Katelynn, pay attention; do not leave the castle grounds. Not till the others get back anyway, okay?" he said.

"Okay, I won't, but I have a request of my own," I said.

"That would be?" he said, repeating what I had said earlier.

"Tell me some more about Lera. Pleeeeeeease?" I asked.

The usually sparkly eyed Tanarr took a serious turn as he settled back in his chair. He was stone-faced and so quiet for so long that I thought he had decided not to say any more.

With his head bowed and his eyes focused on his folded hands, he began.

"Our canoe slid onto the bank. The only sound that could be heard was the crunch the nose of the boat made as it ran aground. No sooner had our feet made shorefall than we heard this…this," he paused and raised his head, looking off into the distant past. I could only assume that he was remembering what they had encountered.

"The sound, it still haunts me. It wasn't human, or at least it didn't sound human. It was a barking, strangling sound: a cough that wouldn't allow whoever or whatever to catch their breath, and it was close. We both stopped dead still in our tracks, listing to see if we could determine where the sound was coming from. The coughing stopped, and we looked around. Then it began again. It didn't take long to find the source. There, crumpled behind a thicket of brush, was a dirty child gasping for breath between fits of coughing. Lera pushed back the bushes."

'Tanarr, oh, my, it's a child!' She knelt and took the small child's face in her hands. She looked up at me. 'Oh, Tanarr, oh no!'

'What is it?' I asked as I tried to break the shrubs away without harming the child.

'It's much worse than we had thought,' she said.

I stopped in midmotion; she looked a little pale and very scared.

'This child not only has whooping cough; she also has the measles,' Lera said."

Tanarr took a deep breath; his brow had furrowed from the memory of the worry.

"I shook my head and shrugged my shoulders. 'But Lera, kids get the measles all the time!' I told her. I just didn't see why she should be so concerned; it was just measles with a cough.

'That's true; in the States it is no big deal when you have doctors, medicine, clean water, and sanitary conditions. There was a time in America when the measles completely wiped out whole Indian tribes.' The whooping cough, along with the measles, not only could but was killing the whole village of Kee-Ka-Na.

Lera had started to pick up the small girl. I touched her arm to stop her.

'Please, let me,' I said.

She moved back. I stepped in and knelt, scooping up the child." Tanarr closed his eyes and shook his head. "The little girl was light as a feather; I could feel each of her ribs. Her face was gaunt and pale with red splotches. I looked over at Lera.

'Now what do we do?' I asked.

She took charge from that point on.

'Let's head up to the village. If we're lucky, there will only be a few cases,' she said as we followed a narrow path that lead through the jungle.

"It quickly became apparent that this village was in trouble and under siege; this child was not the only one infected. The closer we got, the louder we could hear the classic whooping cough along with the moans of the sick and dying.

"As we stepped into the clearing of the village, this eerie, creepy feeling climbed up my spine. There were no fires burning and no people moving about."

'Hello, hello? Is there anyone here?' Lera began to yell.

"A young woman stepped out from one of the huts. Pale and exhausted, she stumbled toward us only to collapse at our feet. Lera fell on her knees at the woman's side, gathering her up in her arms. I looked down at the two women. With the child still in my arms, I didn't know what to do.

'Lera, is she all right?' I asked.

'I think so. I think she is just tired,' Lera brushed the hair out of her face. 'Hey, lady. Hey.'

"The woman's eyes fluttered open. In broken English, she began to try to communicate.

'Tank you, tank you. Need, need,' she motioned toward the other huts. 'We need,' she said again. She was trying to tell us that they were in need of help. Lera helped her to her feet.

"One by one, we went into every hut. The stench was horrible; there were unwashed, fevered bodies everywhere. To the best we could tell, this one exhausted woman was the only one left to care for all the sick. Some had expired, and she left them where they died. She had no other choice. I was completely overwhelmed. With the child still in my arms, I looked at Lera, trying to keep the panic out of my voice.

'Now what!?' I asked.

'First,' she said, taking the small child out of my arms, 'let's put her down here.' She lay the girl on a vacant cot. 'Next, I need you to go as quickly as we know you are capable of going. Bring back these medications.' She pulled a pen and a small notepad out of her backpack. Quickly she wrote down a list of things she needed and handed me the list.

'Do you have any money?' she asked. Before I could reply, she reached into her pocket and pulled out what little money she had. 'Here, take this. I know it's not much, but add it to whatever you have. I know you will do your best.'"

Tanarr looked up at me, breaking the spell of his tale.

"To this day, I carry a substantial amount of cash on me all the time. It was such a frightening thing to think that just because I had not brought enough cash, I might not be able to help these people," he said.

"Did you have money on you?" I asked. I was so caught up in his story that I wanted to know everything.

"I did, but not a lot. I had brought Lera's hundred. I had some on me, and between what she had and what I brought, we barely had enough for what she needed."

"It only took me one day to get back to civilization, and I don't mean that wretched fishing village I found Lera in; I mean civilization. There was a good-sized city downstream. I don't know what the name was. It didn't matter; it was irrelevant to my mission. I went to the closest medical center. Luckily the doctor on staff had heard about what was happening to the people of the village."

At this point I interrupted him.

"But Tanarr, if they knew what was going on, why on earth didn't they do something to help?" I asked. With my food cold and forgotten, I pushed my plate aside. "Were they just hoping that everyone would just stay away and it wouldn't spread?"

"I seriously don't know what they were thinking; I only knew they were more than willing to supply me with whatever I needed. However, no one was willing to go back with me. I don't know if they were afraid of the people or the disease. We loaded a small boat, and I left by myself," Tanarr said.

I leaned in close.

"As I recall, Ms. Lera told me that the people of Kee-Ka-Na were notorious for killing trespassers first and asking questions never," I said.

"Yes, and I do believe that is exactly what Navar and Zoul told me also."

Tanarr leaned back in his chair, making himself more comfortable as he prepared to unfold more of his memories.

"With my boat loaded, I began the trip back. I pushed as hard as I could, and it still took me four full days, pushing as hard as the boat would allow. This time I paid no attention to my surroundings. I didn't care at all what was around me; all I could think of was Lera and the horror I had left her in.

"The boat had barely touched land before I was out and making sure it was tied to the shore, and then I took off to find Lera. I found her there just as I had left her, caring for the village people. She didn't see me until I spoke.

'Lera,' I softly said her name. She turned. Blinking back tears, she fell around my neck.

'Oh, Tanarr. I'm so glad you're back. I've been so scared.' Immediately she took a step back. With a deep, trembling breath, she squared her shoulders and took control of her emotions. 'Did you get all the things I needed?' she asked as if she had not just been melted around my neck.

'Yes,' I said with a nod, all the while hating her strength that wouldn't let me hold her longer.

'Well, then, let's get started,' she said.

We headed back to the boat to get the supplies.

'How's the little girl doing?' I asked."

'She's holding her own, but her cough seems to be getting worse, and her fever has been steadily climbing,' she said.

'Do you think she'll make it?' I asked.

'I don't know. I hope so. Now that we have medical supplies and clean water, I think they all will have a good chance,' she said with a smile.

When she opened the supplies on the boat, tears welled up in her eyes. She looked up with an angelic face of hope.

'You got food! I didn't have food on the list, but you got food!' she said, cradling the can of chicken broth.

"At that moment, the weight of all that was happening around her hit full impact. She crumpled on the crate of chicken broth and began to sob. She held the can up to me.

'How did you know to get broth?' she said between sobs as one fat tear slid down her cheek and landed on the lid with a splat.

I knelt in front of her and gathered her in my arms.

'It's all right; let it all out. You've been through a lot these past five days,' I told her.

'I can't!' she said as she melted onto my shoulder. 'I have too much to do!' she sobbed. 'They need us!'

'I know,' I said, rubbing her hair and loving every second of being there for her, being the one she turned to, even if it was only for that moment. It was worth my very being to be there for her," he said as his fist slammed into the table, making me jump and all the dishes rattle.

"Why wouldn't she let me love her?" he said, his voice dripping with pain.

I didn't know whether to stay quiet and let him talk or to try to comfort him by saying something that might only make it worse. He looked at me, and to my sadness, that sparkle that was usually in his eyes was gone, replaced with pain of the memory of lost love, lost years. He slowly stood.

"I'm sorry. I need to go and be alone. We'll talk later," he said as he started to leave.

"But wait! What can I do to help?" I said, reaching for his hand.

He put his finger on my lips.

"Shh...I'll be fine. I've learned how to deal with this. I just need to be alone," he said.

"Are you sure?" I asked.

He only nodded as he left the room.

As the sound of his footsteps disappeared down the hall, I suddenly felt more alone than I ever had. Tanarr's sadness hung in the air like the stench of love denied, and my heart broke for him.

At the complete opposite end of the emotional spectrum, the adorable Charles entered the room. He came over to where I sat and took one look at my half-eaten meal. His face drooped.

"Was yer meal not to yer liking?" he asked.

I was still a little lost in Tanarr's world and not quite sure what the boy was talking about.

"I'm sorry, what?" I said with a shake and a flutter of my eyes.

"Yer meal," he said, motioning to my plate. "Was it no good?"

"Oh, no! I was talking. I lost track of time, and my food got cold," I said, wrinkling my nose.

"Yuck! I do not like cold food, either," he said, giving his nose a wrinkle, too. "But do ye know what is very good cold?" he said with a smile and a twinkle in his eye.

"Let me guess," I squinted one eye and bit my lip. "Chocolate cake!" I said.

"Yes!" he said, coming up on his toes and raising both his hands. You would have thought I had just scored the winning touchdown at the homecoming football game. I flicked the end of his nose.

"How about you have someone bring me a large mug of coffee to the library, then have Ms. Doulsie cut a large slice of that cake and have yourself a big old glass of cold milk to go with it, okay?" I said. The boy smiled even wider, nodded, and left the room. He stopped at the doorjamb and popped his angelic face back around the corner.

"Oh, thank ye, m'lady. Ye be the best ever!"

Chapter Twenty-One

I was still smiling as I settled into Navar's big wingback. Someone on the house staff had started a nice fire burning in the large fireplace. *I do love this library*, I thought. Charles had decided that he was big enough to bring my coffee himself; Doulsie had only filled the cup half full so it would not splash on him.

"Thank you, sir," I said as I took the cup from the tray. He smiled and turned and hurried off to his cake. *It just doesn't get better than this*, I thought. *Well, if Corbin were here, it would be better, but I can make do for now.*

I stared into the fire with my coffee perched under my nose because after all, the smell was as much a part of the flavor as the taste. My mind began to wander over the events of the day. Tanarr going up the Amazon with Lera; I really couldn't wait to hear the rest of that story. And how about Mr. Roberts with all those defective nails that Deireadh says aren't defective at all but that it's the castle herself that won't allow the nails to be driven in? Now, I just didn't know if I believed that the castle had a life of her own or not. I just didn't see how that could be. I took in a deep breath and exhaled it with a huff. *Probably the same way there could be vampires, fairies, and wizards*, I thought. Maybe there were things just under the vision of mortals' eyes, things we wouldn't or couldn't understand. *Why have I been selected to witness them?* I didn't know the answer to that question, either. Then something came to mind, something that Deireadh had said; I had wizard blood running in my veins. Hmm…wizard blood? I shook my head. I didn't know about that, either, but when I got back home, Momma and I were going to get down the family albums and see what we could find out.

I looked around the library and wondered if there were any books that could give me any insight on the folklore of the castle. I set my mug down to take a cruise through the books that lined the walls.

The shelves were filled with first edition classics. It was fascinating exploring some of the time-aged leather-bound books. Some of them were signed by the author, personalized for Navar. They always included a thank you for some brave act of kindness. I couldn't resist reading some of the personalized notes.

There was one in particular that wasn't from an author but a king. The book had been part of a thank you gift to Navar for rescuing the king's child from kidnappers.

Lord Navar,

I call you Lord out of respect for your title. I do hope I may be permitted to call you Navar out of friendship. I would truly be honored to do so. To you, dear friend, along with the stable of thoroughbreds, a trunk filled with the finest of silks, a strong box of gold, and this book of sonnets, I have also taken the liberty and have commissioned the most skilled of silversmiths to design the greatest suit of armor ever. Still all this pales in comparison to your bravery. Thank you for returning to me the life of my beloved child. We are forever grateful.

Forever in your debt,
Your friend
King Darr

I ran my fingers over the yellowed page.

"So that's where that magnificent suit of armor came from!" I whispered just under my breath. I gently slid the book back in to its slot. While reading the spines of the various books, some were impressive, others unknown, at least to me. I ran right past one book that at first glance one might have mistaken for a fairy tale book, but something drew me back to it. It was almost calling my name. I took a step back and read the spine out loud.

"*Truths of Those That Be*," I whispered. "Hmm…" I read it one more time. "*Truths of Those That Be*." I gave my shoulders a shrug. *That sounds like something Deireadh would say*, I thought as I started to move on to the next book. Then I stopped.

"That-sounds-like-something-Deireadh-would-say." I said each word slowly and out loud as I turned back to the book one more time. I reached for and slowly pulled the ancient, wooden-bound book from its perch. Carefully I placed it on the table and nervously I took the wooden cover in hand. I took a deep breath and braced myself for whatever I was about to see. Slowly I pulled back the cover and nothing…nada…nothing…not a word; the pages were blank.

"Okay, now; that was not what I was expecting," I said out loud as my shoulders deflated and my imagination bar went flat. Grumbling to myself, I put the book back in its space. *Well, that was a big old sack of disappointment*, I thought. It was almost like expecting peach cobbler and getting brussels sprouts instead. Just before pushing the book all the way back, I saw something. The light had reflected off something on the back of the shelf. I drug a chair over, climbed up in it, and stuck my hand all the way to the backside. I could feel something metallic.

"What is that?" I said as I jumped back down. I ran over to the desk and rummaged around in the drawers.

"Aha!" I found a small flashlight in the bottom drawer. Back up on the chair I went with flashlight in hand, there it was. Oh, my! It was a crest, just like the one that was on Navar's door, the crest that was the key to owning the whole castle.

"What are you doing all the way back there?" I said, tracing the crest with the tip of my finger. "That's odd; it even feels the same." Then the realization that this must unlock something sunk in, and I reeled back so fast that I almost fell off the chair. I made a mad grab for the bookshelf, bringing my backward motion to a halt and causing Navar's heavy ring (that I wore on a chain around my neck) to hit my chest with a thud. I took hold of the chain and withdrew the ring from my blouse.

"Let's just see what, if anything, happens if I do this," I said as I took the ring off the chain. Carefully I put the ring on my middle finger and lined up the crest in the ring with the crest in the back of the bookcase, just as I had done when I unlocked Navar's room for the first time. I gave the ring a gentle push and a turn and heard the soft click as the lock disengaged. The bookcase next to me didn't slide to the side or spin around; instead, it simply lurched forward ever so slightly.

I jumped down off the chair. My imagination and curiosity that had previously been flatlined now were jumping off the chart. Stepping closer, I could tell that there were slots on the side designed for fingers to fit into. With my heart racing, I slid my fingers into the slots. Ever so slowly I gave the case a pull; with very little effort, it glided forward, allowing a soft wisp of cool air to escape. The air smelled of dirt, basements, and unearthed secrets; chill bumps immediately broke out all over me.

"Oh, my goodness! What have I found?" I said.

With my flashlight in hand and my courage not quite at hand, I went no farther than the mouth of what appeared to be a very long, very dark hallway.

"I swear, this place has more secrets than, than, I don't know, anyplace with this much going on!" I said as I timidly looked around. I still was not brave enough to go all the way in. I swallowed hard. "I'll bet there are spiders in there big enough to carry someone off, and I want to make sure that someone isn't me." I shined the light on every corner.

"No webs! Man, it's like this place cleans itself" I said. I shined the light from the ceiling to the floor and the light flicked on something in the floor. On closer inspection, I could tell it was another crest.

"This must be an exit lock, Okay, that's it for me. I can just see it now. The bookshelf closes, the battery in my flashlight goes dead, and so do I. *Oh no! Call me chicken, but I have no intention of becoming a permanent part of this castle.* Between my dislike of pitch-dark places and my unnatural fear of spiders, this adventure would have to wait until my superhero got back; *as soon as my Spidey gets here, we'll see where this hall goes! I'm definitely not going down that hall by myself!*

As easily as the bookcase opened, it slid back into place. I took a breath and leaned back against the shelf. What on earth was down there? It could be more treasure, or maybe it connected to the outside like an escape tunnel; it could even be a root cellar for turnips and potatoes. I pushed myself off the shelf and gave my shoulders a shrug. Or maybe it was just a hall with nothing at the end. Either way, I wasn't going to find out tonight.

I walked over to the table where my coffee mug sat and took a big gulp. Yuck! It was cold. *I'll just bet that there is some hot coffee in the kitchen.* I thought it would be a much safer adventure to seek out hot coffee then what was at the end of that hall.

After I get some hot coffee, I'm going to find a TV and catch up on some world events. Okay, what I really want to catch up on is some of my favorite sitcoms.

Chapter Twenty-Two

Cup in hand, I rounded the corner out of the library and plowed right into Tanarr. The cold coffee sloshed all over the front of his very expensive, very white shirt. I was so mortified that all I could do was stand there gaping at the dark, black, cold coffee running down his chest.

"Whoa, there! Where are you going in such a hurry?" he said with a twinkle of humor in his eye as he wiped at the cold liquid that was seeping into that beautiful shirt.

"Oh, oh, I'm so sorry!" I stammered. "I'll run to the kitchen and get a towel. You stay put; I'll be right back!" I said as I started to take off.

"No, no, it's all right. It's just coffee on a shirt. I think I'll survive; I have been through much worse battles," he gave me wink.

My shoulders sank.

"I truly am sorry," I said.

"Don't give it a second thought; I have a closet full of white shirts. I was coming to see if you would like some company. Were you turning in for the night?" he asked.

"No," I said with a shake of my head, lifting my now empty cup. "I was going after a refill."

"Why don't you go find your coffee, and I'll go get out of your coffee. Then let's meet back in the library, and we'll keep each other company for a while. After all, the evening is still young," he said.

I tilted my head to the side.

"Will you tell me some more about what happened while you were in the Amazon with Ms. Lera?" I asked with a flutter of my eyes.

Tanarr took a deep breath.

"If you would like," he said.

"Oh, I would like; I would like that a lot. I'll meet you back at the library, toot sweet!" I said with a nod.

Tanarr gave me a blank look.

"You'll do what?" he asked.

"I'll be back toot sweet, you know: fast, waste no time. My Grandma used to say that all the time. I don't know exactly what it means, but I think that's what it means. In any event, I'll hurry!" I said as I took off.

By the time I got back to the library with my hot coffee, Tanarr was already there, sitting in one of the wingbacks and looking drop-dead gorgeous in what else but another white shirt.

He looked at me and gave the collar a tug.

"See? I told you I have a closet full of these."

I smiled back at him.

"You are so kind," I said, tucking my legs under me as I got comfortable in the other wingback. With an elbow on each arm of the chair and my coffee perched under my nose, we sat in silence and stared into the fire. I was trying to decide whether to start the conversation or to allow Tanarr to take the lead. He propped his heels on the edge of the hearth and leaned his head back.

"You want to know what happened to the people of Kee-Ka-Na?" Tanarr said, breaking the silence.

I lowered my cup, balancing it on the thick leather chair arm.

"I would love to hear more, if you wouldn't mind sharing it with me," I said.

He rolled his head to the side so he could see my face.

"Sorry I took off so fast at dinner. Sometimes the fact that I can no longer see her or talk to her gets the best of me. I know she will always be the love of my heart." He looked back into the fire, his voice taking on a sudden dark tone. "Someday, I will make Blake pay for that."

"Hold on," I said, setting my cup to the side and leaning forward in my chair. "When was the last time you saw her?" I asked.

He turned back to face me.

"In her room, at Silver Cove, the day before she died," he answered in a matter-of-fact kind of way.

"What!" I said.

"Oh, yes. I saw her at least every other day," he said.

"No way! Why did I not know about you or see you coming or going?" I said.

He leaned forward in his chair and held up two fingers.

"Two reasons: One, I went in the morning before you came in. I knew she was telling you her story," he shrugged his shoulders. "I didn't see the need to interfere."

I interrupted him.

"But she never once said that anyone else had ever been to see her," I said.

"I'm not surprised that she never said anything about me, and that brings me to the second reason," he said with sadness in his voice.

"What would that be?" I asked.

"I never meant as much to her as she did to me," he said.

"What are you talking about?" I asked. I had to ask; I had to try to understand.

He leaned forward over his knees, staring into the fire again.

"It wasn't her fault. She couldn't help it any more than I could help loving her, but she loved Navar only. Both of us were trapped in worlds that we had no control over: worlds that we loved and hated at the same time, and worlds that we couldn't change, wouldn't change, even if we could." He looked down at his feet and swallowed hard. His voice cracked when he spoke again.

"I remember that last morning; she must have felt something was about to happen. You know, she had that power: almost a vampire but without the horrific things and not quite as strong. I was sitting on the edge of her bed, and we had been talking about you." He looked up at me and smiled. "We had been talking about you and how she had been right; you were the one. How happy she was to have you with her at last!"

"Before I left her for the night, she gathered both my hands in her frail little ones; she looked me in the eye."

'Dear Tanarr, you have been the best friend I have ever known. I am truly sorry I could not love you, not in that way. You deserved so much more.' I started to say something, but she stopped me, placing her small finger over my lips. 'Shh…don't say anything; let me finish. I know as well as I know my next breath that I don't have much time left. You must promise me that you will not mourn for me. We did what we could. You will need to move on. Find someone to love you the way you deserve to be: the way I could not. Do this for me,' she cupped my face in her hands. 'In some way, I have loved you. I could surely not have survived without you, but now go on; find your love,' Lera whispered.

This time I gathered her up in my arms and kissed the top of her head.

'I have found my love, the love of my life, and I plan to hold onto you for as long as I can. I would gladly borrow from all my tomorrows for just one more hour with you today,' I whispered into her hair.

'No, my sweet, sparkly eyed Tanarr, for I have no more tomorrows left. But you do; make the best of them,' she pushed back from me. 'I would ask one thing.'

'Anything; it's yours,' I said.

'Look out for Katelynn; she will need guidance,' she said.

'That I will do,' I said as I stood to leave, 'and I will see you tomorrow. As for now, I must go; I have court in about two hours.' I gave her a kiss on the cheek and left her smiling. That was the last time I saw her alive," he said with a shake of his head.

"I'm so very sorry; she was truly an amazing woman," I said with a smile.

"That she was," he looked at me and smiled back. "You know she loved you like a daughter, right?"

"I loved her right back." I shook my head. "I can't believe that she asked you to look out for me."

"She knew you would have a lot of questions that only I could answer. I was the one she came to first. She knew that Navar had trusted me with all his legal work. Then she learned she, too, could trust me: not only with her legal work but with everything: even her heart."

I took a big gulp of coffee.

"I'll bet I know where she learned to trust you," I said.

"Really? And where would that be?" he asked.

I looked at him sideways.

"The Amazon: nothing builds trust like someone leaving everything, going halfway around the world to help you do whatever you needed help with even when you didn't know you needed that help," I said with a salute of my coffee cup.

He took a deep breath.

"One thing is for sure, she didn't know just how much help she would need. I will never forget seeing her so completely exhausted, working day and night trying to save the people of Kee-Ka-Na," he said.

He folded his hands, sinking back in his chair as he sank back into his memories. He was remembering those lost years when he was the only one who knew where Lera was, the only one she could turn to or trust.

"We dragged all the supplies up to the village. I told her I could get it all by myself, but she would not hear of it. She loaded herself down to the point where she could barely walk. I remember telling her, 'Lera, please. I really don't need help.' As she loaded her arms, she didn't even look up.

'I know that, but I need to help, and this is something I know I can complete. When we get back to the village, I can only hope that I can do something, that all this is not too late,' she said as she finished loading her arms.

"The closer we got to the village, the more we could hear the moans and groans of the sick and dying." Tanarr shook his head like he was trying to block out the memory of the sounds. "Then there was that soul-rattling sound brought on by the whooping cough."

He closed his eyes. "Once you hear that sound, you don't ever forget it."

"The moment we arrived at the village, Lera squared her shoulders and cleared her throat and her mind. She went from a broken, scared little girl to a strong, self-confident medical person, taking charge and giving instructions. She only had one village woman and me to help her, but she knew what had to be done.

"The three of us went from hut to hut. Lera made a quick assessment of each situation. She then moved the less sick out and into one section of the village. The ones that were very sick were taken to the council hut; she thought that it would be much easier to care for them all in one place. The dead," he let out a huff. "That was my job; I took care of that quickly. I took the bodies deep into the jungle to burn; it was the best way to make sure that all contaminants were destroyed."

"We opened the case of chicken broth. I had to show Maleeka how to use a can opener. It was the old crank style type, and it only took her a few cans to master opening them. She got the broth ready; we started to feed those that were able to take nourishment. Lera began to dispense the medications. When a person vacated their cot either by death or by being moved to the recovery section of the village, I quickly sanitized the cot and got it ready for the next victim. The ones that had survived and were showing no more symptoms were allowed to go back to their newly cleaned huts. Maleeka brought hot broth and clean water to each recovering person. The chief or the king, whichever you wanted to call him, was treated no differently; there was no time for pomp and circumstance; this was life and death.

"One night, everyone was settled down, and even Maleeka had gone to bed. She had been on call all day, keeping up with us and doing whatever was asked of her," Tanarr shook his head. "As I recall, she was quite a trooper. Lera and I were sitting by the fire. I reached over and took her hand.

'Why don't you turn in? I'll keep an eye on everyone,' I told her.

'Nah, I'm okay. Someone might need me,' she said.

'They will be fine, and you need the rest,' I said.

'No, really, I'm okay,' she said with a yawn.

I kissed the top of her head.

'How much longer do you think this siege will last?' I asked.

'I don't know,' she said with a drowsy tone. 'If everyone keeps on the way they're going and no one takes a turn for the worse, we might just have this thing on the run.'

I poked the fire with a stick I had been using to play in the dirt.

'I must admit, this has been one of the hardest things I have ever been part of. And you: you have been amazing: taking charge and doing what no one else could have done, working till you drop to help these people who, if they were well, would have killed you the instant they caught sight of you. You knew all this, and it didn't matter. You saw a need, jumped in, and worked as hard as you could, using all of your skills and knowledge. What makes you like that?' I asked.

'Like what?' she said, snuggling up close and finding a comfy spot on my shoulder with her head.

'What makes you work so hard for a people that would kill you? Where does that kind of caring and kindness come from?' I took a deep breath. I knew that I should let it go at that. I knew that I was pushing her, but I couldn't stop; she had to know how I felt. 'It's that side of you that I fell in love with. I know that you still love Navar. But he's gone, Lera. I'm here. Let go of the past; grab onto the present, and we can start anew. You and I can have it all; I will love you like no one else ever will. We will go and do whatever you say, just let go and love me. I'm all yours; I always will be.'

I looked down at her curly red hair all tumbled and back in a make-shift ponytail. One stray curl lay lazily over one eye. It was at that moment I realized that my lady love was sound asleep. I bent my head down so I could look at her face. I gave my shoulder a little jiggle.

'Lera. Lera,' I whispered, but there was no response."

Tanarr smiled and closed his eyes in sweet memory. He opened his eyes, looked over at me, and gave me a wink.

"Yep, she was asleep, so asleep that a small trickle of drool was running down my white shirt; it left a spot there." He gave me a smile followed by a sad little chuckle. "You know, I still have that shirt. I never washed it; that was one of my best nights ever: the night air, the songs of the jungle, her sweet curly head on my shoulder, and the simple fact that she felt safe enough to relax and to fall asleep on my shoulder," he exhaled slowly. "That was the best. I know that she didn't hear a word that I said, and that was okay; the universe heard it. I know that she knew; that's all that mattered.

I scooped her up in my arms and carried her to a freshly cleaned cot. Ever so gently, I placed her there. I stayed there all night by her side; not even a mosquito landed on her. I loved her so much that even if she couldn't love me then, I had high hopes that I would win her over. I reached down, gently cupping her face in my hands. In her sleep, she curled around my arm.

'Thank you,' she whispered.

I had to smile; I was winning her over.

'I love you,' she sighed.

My heart melted.

'Good night, Navar,' she said as sleep completely overtook her.

Then it broke."

"Oh, Tanarr!" was all I could say as I clutched at my heart and slid back in my chair.

He nodded his head.

"Yeah, that was a kick in the gut, but you know what, Katelynn?" he said, squinting his eyes. "It only made me more determined. I wanted to hear her say that to me and know it to be me. I would not give up." He looked away. "I never got to hear that. Oh, she said 'I love you' from time to time, but not like that; it was more like a best-friend kind of love or a brother-sister kind of love: not that earth-shaking, rock-your-world kind of love. She only ever had that type of love for Navar and only Navar."

Tanarr unfolded his hands and shrugged his shoulders. "I still never gave up. I loved her too much, and I always will."

He took a deep cleansing breath, swallowed his emotions, and then continued on with his telling.

"It still took another four weeks before everyone was back up and able to get about. For the first time in a long time, we were able to relax.

"One evening the king sent word for Maleeka, Lera, and myself to meet him in the counsel house. When we arrived, there stood Maleeka waiting at the entrance, not daring to go in by herself; she looked at us with a little fear showing in her face."

'What he want? We do good, yes?' Maleeka asked with a little tremble in her voice.

'Yes, Maleeka, we did very well,' Lera said, putting her hand on Maleeka's shoulder. 'It will be fine; you'll see.'

"As we stepped through the entrance and looked around, it was easy to see that everyone who had survived and was able was there. As soon as someone noticed that we had arrived, a hush came over the room. An unnerving silence spread like the sickness that had almost consumed their village.

"At the very front of the room sat the King. By his side stood his woman, and sitting at his feet was their child, a daughter. It was the same child I had carried on the first day we were there. She gave me a little sweet smile. I had made it a point to check on her several times a day. I had been the one to feed broth to her and to make sure she had plenty of clean water. It made my heart soar to see her sitting with both her parents.

There were now a lot of children without parents and a lot of parents without children, so it was good to see one family left intact.

"The King motioned for us to step forward. When we stood before him, Maleeka fell to her knees, never looking him in the eye. Lera and I both gave low, sweeping bows. The King stood in his full regalia, his long robe made of exotic feathers and leopard skin. A leopard's head appeared at his right shoulder. The eyes were two large diamonds, and his crown was made of hand-hammered gold. It was not very elaborate; there were no jewels, just a thick band of this exquisite pure gold.

"The King stepped down from his throne and knelt, gathering Maleeka in his arms. His beautiful robe engulfed her. He helped her to stand and tilted her face up to meet his grateful eyes. When he spoke, his voice was deep and rich. In the silent room it resounded like thunder in a quiet valley. He spoke with as much eloquence and authority as the educated man that he was."

I interrupted Tanarr.

"Educated?" I said with a shake of my head.

"Yes. One day while caring for him and his family, he had told me of some missionaries that had been allowed to spend time in the village. Among the missionaries were two professors. They had taught him a lot in the time they were permitted to stay. His father died, leaving him a crown to wear and a village to care for."

"What happened to the missionaries?" I asked.

"I don't know; the King didn't say," Tanarr gave his shoulders a shrug. "Anyway, back to our story, or shall I say, our history."

"'Maleeka,' the King said, turning her to face the people. 'From this day on, your name shall mean "great one," "hero," "caregiver." We shall build a great home. As your husband is listed among the lost, you may choose a new one from our strongest and bravest young men.' He turned her to face the group of males, who were all standing tall and proud. 'They are all that is left of us. They are yours to choose from, if you like. Know this; you will never want for anything.'

Next, he turned to Lera and me. Gathering our hands in his, he looked from her face to mine.

'You two: what can I say? Without you, we would surely have perished. You came in where no one else would and did what none other was able. You cared for a people that you should have feared; if things had been different, they would have killed you. You knew this, yet you came anyway. We thank you; anything you would like, it's yours.' He waited for one of us to answer him. 'Please, anything: just name it, and it's yours.'

Lera timidly began.

'You have already given me all I needed,' she said.

The King looked puzzled.

'But we've given you nothing!' the King answered.

'Oh, but you have; you gave me back my life,' she said.

"The King looked even more puzzled, but he remained silent, letting her continue. She looked up at me and gave me a sad little smile, then looked back at our hands all joined together. 'I had come here to kill myself.' She gave a little chuckle and a nervous smile. 'Or I guess I had hoped that you would kill me and save me the effort, but first I had intended to destroy an innocent, valuable orchid.' She wouldn't look at any of us as she unfolded her story. My heart was breaking for her; all I could do was stand there and listen to her.

She took a deep, shaking breath.

'You see, I felt responsible for the death of the man I loved.'

The King, who had been intently listening, now spoke.

'You? You could never hurt anyone. You care too much for humanity. If you care this much for a people that you didn't know, I can't imagine the depth you would go to for the man you love.' He nodded toward me. 'Is this not the man you love? You two worked so well together that I assumed he was your man,' the King said.

Lera looked at me with apology in her sad eyes. I gave her an understanding nod.

'I do love this man,' she began, 'but not that way.'

I could tell by her eyes and her body language that she was trying to explain things without hurting me or giving away what I was. She was trying her best to protect me. For that I loved her even more, if that were possible.

'You see, sir, I am a research scientist. My love, Navar, was very sick and had been for a very long time.'

'Was he near death, as we were?' the King asked.

'You might say so,' Lera replied, picking her words carefully. 'I wanted so badly to help him, so I did a lot of research on his condition.' She stopped and looked up at the king, who still had our hands firmly locked together in his. 'Do you know about the orchid that grows here in your village?' she asked.

'Yes, if the flower you speak of is the white orchid; we call her the kee-nan-twa,' the king said.

Lera scrunched up her face.

'The kee...what?' she asked.

The king looked at her with a smile then pronounced the name of the flower very slowly. 'Kee-nan-twa: it means twin protectors, those that protect us from the fanged ones,' he said.

I looked over at Lera and gave her a smile. Now, you see, I was pretty sure I knew who he was talking about when he said 'fanged ones,' but I still wanted to hear his take on the story, so I asked him.

'What kind of fanged things are you talking about?'

He released our hands.

'These are the fables that have been told around our fires forever, and if they are true, I never want to live in a world without the kee-nan-twa.' He stopped and held up his hand. 'I will tell you this, but be prepared not to believe what you are about to hear.' He motioned for us to take a seat on the floor around the throne. With us seated, he then took his place and began his tale.

'Many, many rainy seasons ago, the young prince, fair of face and strong in body, the would-be King of Kee-Ka-Na, was attacked by the last of the winged demons. He should have died. Instead, he could never die; so possessed was he that he began to feed off the blood of his own people, like the winged dark one had once done. Much to the King's heartbreak, he knew that his only son must die to save the village. Try as they may, they could not kill him or the ones that came from his bite: the ones that survived the prince's attacks. Nothing worked: not poison, not spears, not fire. In his despair, the King prayed to the Great One. He asked for help, for on their own, the village soon would be consumed.'

"The King stopped and lifted his face toward the sky. A smile touched his lips. 'His prayers were answered. The Great One sent the King a gift; he sent him the kee-nan-twa, but only two, a sister pair. There are never more than two at a time. The nectar, the very blood of the kee-nan-twa, is the only thing that could kill the fanged creatures that were created by the prince.'

Lera reached over and took my hand; I don't know if it was out of fear for herself or me. You know what? I didn't care. I loved that she wanted to touch me, so I told myself that she did it because she cared for me. I encouraged the King to go on with his story, and with my next question, she moved even closer.

'Did it work? Did it kill the fanged ones?' I asked.

I could feel Lera shiver as she moved as close as she could get to me.

'It did work; most were killed, and some escaped into the jungle,' the King said.

'Did they kill the prince?' I asked.

'No, they did not kill the prince. The King could not bring himself to let that happen; his love for his sun was too deep,' the King said.

'What happened to the ones who escaped?' I asked.

'At night they would come out, seeking the blood of the village people. They would attack, leaving bodies lying where they fell. The King ordered that each hut have a pot of nectar and spears at all times,' the King said.

'What happened to the prince?' I asked.

'Legend has it that his father told him to leave: to take what was his and never return. For on the day that he returned, the king himself would strike the fatal blow. With that decree, he was banished. As long as we have the sister kee-nan-twa, we the people of Kee-Ka-Na are forever safe,' the King said with a nod.

'Have there always been two orchids?' I asked.

'Yes,' the King said, then paused. 'There was a time about a year and half ago. Someone in the village came to me. They had noticed that something was wrong in the high place of the kee-nan-twa; one of them was missing,' the King said.

'Missing? What do you mean, missing?' Lera asked.

The King turned to Lera. In his most regal tone, he replied, 'Missing, as in no longer present, gone,' he said.

'What happened to it?' Lera said as she pushed a stray curl behind her ear.

The King straightened his shoulders.

'I went straight to the High Priest,' he said.

Lera squinted her eyes.

'High Priest?' she said.

'Yes, the High Priest; he not only cares for our spirits, but he is also the village doctor.'

Lera interrupted. 'But wait, if he is the doctor, why was he not helping with the sick?' she asked.

People brought their sick to him, but he had never seen such. He was in counsel with the kee-nan-twa when you arrived,' he said.

Lera looked at me. 'Counsel with a flower?' she whispered.

'He is also the only one who cares for the kee-nan-twa; he cannot leave the protection of the temple. I can tell you no more; the telling is his alone,' the King said. 'I knew if anyone would know what had happened, it would be him, so I went to the temple in search of the High Priest,' the King said as he motioned toward a structure that had been built around a large tree in the center of the village.

We both turned toward the structure.

'I asked him if he knew what had happened to the kee-nan-twa.'

'"A friend was in need," was all he would say.'

'"But the village needs the sisters to keep her safe; we need both of them!" I protested,' the King said.

'"The two have been restored. We were not without protection," the High Priest said.'

Lera shook her head.

'What did he mean by that?' she asked.

The King looked back at the temple.

'I truly do not know; that is all he would say,' the King said."

Tanarr was now slouched over his lap with his hands dangling between his knees. He just sat there, not saying a word. I couldn't tell if he was getting comfortable or struggling with his memories. He took a deep breath and cleared his throat.

"You know, I had seen and walked past that place, I don't even know how many times. I had no idea that was it. I had thought that there would be this ominous cloud of fear that would surround that thing, or at the very least I would feel something when I was around it," Tanarr said.

"You mean like kryptonite?" I could not resist, especially since I had decided to call him Superman/Clark Kent.

He looked over at me with his crooked smile and chuckled.

"Yeah, like kryptonite," he said as he flipped open his hands to emphasize his next statement. "But there was nothing: no overwhelming feeling of dread, no loss of power, nothing but a flower in the top of a very tall tree." He shook his head and let out a long breath before he started on his story again.

"Lera turned to the King.

'May I talk to the High Priest?' she asked.

The King nodded.

'I will ask if he will speak with you.'

'Thank you,' she replied with a smile.

The King took Lera by the hand.

'For now, let me get back to why I have requested your presence.' He paused and looked around at the people, then back to Lera. 'In order to thank you properly, we, the people of Kee-Ka-Na, have come up with this.' He motioned for one of the villagers to step forward. In his hand was a tray, and on the tray lay a scroll. The King reached for the scroll, unfurled it, and began to read. 'We the people of Kee-Ka-Na, with full knowledge that we would not be here were it not for your skill and kindness, we ask you to be one of us, to take control of all that we have. With that, we freely give to you our lands.'

Her jaw dropped.

'What? No, you don't mean it?' she stuttered.

'Yes, we do. You are the one who saved us all; you were the only one who knew what to do.' Lera started to protest, and the King held up his hand to stop her. 'You were the only ones who were willing to risk themselves to help such a people as we,' the King said.

She looked up at me with big, round, surprised, scared eyes, and then she shook her head.

'I can't; it's too much. A simple thank you will do,' she said with a sad tear tugging at the corner of her eye.

The King looked down at her, his dark eyes getting even darker.

'You would insult us thus? This honor has never been bestowed on any other person ever; this kind of trust has never been given. It is a great gift,' the King said.

'I would never do that. I only meant that it is too much. I don't deserve all this. Like I told you, you saved me,' she said.

'But none of us would be here if not for you,' he paused. 'Will you take us?'

Lera looked up at me and mouthed the words, 'What should I do?'

I nodded my approval. She looked back up at the King and nodded her acceptance. A roar of approval rose from the crowd of village people that had gathered in the council house.

'Now, we feast,' the King said, lifting his scepter.

"The rest of the night was spent in celebration, and that's how Lera wound up owning the land where the orchid grows," Tanarr said with a wink and a nod.

"Did Ms. Lera ever get to talk to the High Priest?" I asked.

"Oh, yes," Tanarr said with an arch of his eyebrows. "Now, that was an interesting encounter; one that caught us both a little by surprise." He glanced at his Rolex. "Good grief! It's much later than I thought; you must be tired."

"No, no, I'm fine. Please go on," I said with a yawn.

"I don't think so. I can tell you're worn out," he said. "We can talk later."

"Please!" I said with my best puppy-dog face.

Chapter Twenty-Three

I stretched and yawned. Tanarr gave me one of those I-told-you-so looks.

"No, really; I'm not sleepy. Please, just tell me what happened with the High Priest?" I pleaded.

"But Katelynn, it really is getting late," he said.

"I don't care! Tomorrow the guys will be back. Things will get busy, and the next thing you know, we won't have time. Please, just a little while longer! I really do want to hear it all at the same time so I don't forget anything," I said.

He raised his hands in surrender.

"If you insist. I can go on all night; I don't need sleep," he said with a grin.

"I do insist," I said as I snuggled back in my chair.

Tanarr took a deep breath and continued.

"As I said, the encounter with the High Priest was quite a surprise. The High Priest had not been in the counsel house with the rest of the villagers. He never leaves the temple," Tanarr said.

"Never?" I said with a squeak.

"Never. His food, water, and everything he needs is brought to him. His main job is to care for the kee-nan-twa. If someone needed his special talents, they came to him. He is not physically attached to the kee-nan-twa, but he is part of the flower in every other way. He must stay within the midst of their power or risk all; that's the best way I can explain it."

"The King entered the temple first. It was apparent even from the outside that this was much more than a little grass hut built around a very large tree. And when I say a very large tree," he stood up and stretched out his arms as far as he could, "just imagine a tree so large that 20 people couldn't reach around it. It was so tall that seeing the top of it was not possible from the ground. Its bark was almost like skin: thick, weather-worn, time-aged skin with vines wrapped around one side of it, giving it a feeling of being more than just a tree. It had a power, a silent strength, but it was still a tree." He gave his shoulders a shrug. "I guess that's why I didn't see it as a tree. You know, it was that classic can't-see-the-tree-for-the-forest thing. Its canopy was so broad it shadowed the whole village. I realized there was no jungle towering above the huts; it was only a single tree. The darn thing was that massive!"

"Anyway, when the King came back out of the temple, he motioned us forward.

'The High Priest will grant you audience,' the King said.

Lera looked up at the King.

'Thank you,' she said with her sweet little smile.

"We entered the temple not knowing what to expect. Would he be tall or short, old, mean, kind, ugly, fair of face, elusive, or friendly?

"It was surprisingly light inside, unlike the other dark little huts in the village we had grown accustomed to. The air smelled fresh and clean, and the sunlight streamed in all around the top of the temple. There in the center of it all stood that huge tree that shot up through the very middle."

I interrupted him.

"What were you expecting?" I asked.

Tanarr looked over at me with that crooked smile.

"I honestly don't know: dark, smoky, the shrunken heads of vampires that dared to enter," he said.

I looked over at him and bit my lip, trying to hold back the giggle that was doing its best to escape.

"Shrunken heads? Really?" I asked as that giggle came rolling on out.

He laughed with me.

"Okay, maybe not shrunken heads, but I definitely was not expecting what we found."

"What about the High Priest? Was he as much a surprise as the temple?" I asked.

"Even more," Tanarr said with a shake of his head. "From around the corner there appeared this tall, slim man who was what most women would call handsome, or at least that's what Lera called him." He closed his eyes and put his hand to his forehead.

"Let's see, what was it Lera said under her breath? She thought I didn't hear her. Oh, yeah," he said with a nod. "I believe it was, 'Oh, my, what a hunk!' She almost swooned. His straight black hair came to just past his shoulders. His eyes were so dark that they were almost black; you could all but see your reflection in them. He had a bronzed skin tone with a sharp face but still an air of royalty. He wore a band of silver around his head that crossed his forehead, holding his thick hair in place. He also had a thick band of silver around the top of one of his arms, and I must admit that they were impressive arms. His appearance fascinated me; he didn't look like the rest of the tribe. He looked as if he, himself, were out of place and time. Lera extended her hand to him.

'Sir, it is very nice to meet you. What may I call you?' she asked.

Before he answered her, his attention was directed fully on me.

'You are one of them?' he asked as he took my hand for a firm handshake. I froze. I was pretty sure he wasn't asking if I were one of the local guys."

"Oh, no, Tanarr! What did you do?" I asked as my hand went to my mouth.

"Well, I looked him in the eye and tried my best to bluff my way out. I tried to act like I had no idea what he was talking about. As I tried to escape his handshake, I innocently asked, 'One of what?'

He held firm to my hand and leaned in.

'One of the fanged ones likened unto Prince Zoul and Lord Navar, for your hands are as cold as theirs were. Your eyes, even though you have disguised them with some kind of covering are as amber as theirs, and I feel the hunger that runs in your veins,' he whispered.

"I blinked a few times and swallowed hard. I knew that he had me, and there was nothing I could do." Tanarr stood and walked over to the fireplace. He ran his fingers through his thick red hair. "I was completely at his mercy; he had this…this power over me. The minute he took my hand, all my power left me. My speed and strength were all gone," he said.

"What? How could that be? What happened?" I asked as I sat straight up in my chair.

Tanarr turned to face me.

"It was the most," he paused, grappling for words. "It was the most…it's so hard to explain. I wasn't the least bit scared. There was a calm feeling that came over me. My power was gone, and I was fine with it. Later Lera explained to me that he had absorbed some of the power of the orchid as he worked with and cared for them over the years," Tanarr said.

"But wait, how did he know Zoul, and why did he call him a prince? How about Navar? He called him Lord," I said.

"Correct. That caught our attention, too, but I'll get to that in a little while. When I realized he had me, all I could do was come clean with the hope that he would take mercy on me. He knew I had cared for all the villagers, and I hoped he would take that into consideration. However, if it were time for me to leave this world, so be it. I would do so with courage; Lera would be proud to say that she had known me and loved me.

I squared my shoulders and raised my chin. With a clear, strong voice I answered him. 'Yes, I am. I was very honored to have known both men. I don't know Zoul as well as I did Lord Navar. Navar was a good man, both while he was a vampire and when he was human.'

The High Priest interrupted me.

'You said "was." Are you telling me that Lord Navar is dead?' he asked.

'Yes, he is,' I answered with pain in my voice: the same pain I felt in my heart.

The High Priest shook his head.

'But they said the kee-nan-twa would cure him!'

'It was not the kee-nan-twa that took his life; it was that stupid motorcycle,' Lera answered as a tear slid down her cheek.

All I could do was put my arm around her and try to comfort her.

'I know not what a "stupid motorcycle" is. But I must know; did the kee-nan-twa work? Was the sacrifice worth it?' he said.

Lera looked up at him from under her tear-soaked lashes.

'Yes, it worked just as we had hoped it would. He simply forgot that he was no longer immortal,' she said with regret in her voice.

The High Priest took Lera by the hand and led us both into the most beautiful garden. It was a space between the body of the tree and the temple. There he offered us a seat at a table that was laden with fresh fruit, clean water, and some kind of bread.

'First, we eat. Then you can tell me more,' he said.

"We both took the seats he offered, and the Priest sat down right across from us. My guess is that he was ensuring we would both be included in the conversation, or he could have wanted to keep an eye on us both from that vantage point.

The High Priest pulled in close to the table. He leaned in to give me a closer inspection. He didn't say a word; he just looked me up and down. Then he turned to Lera.

'If it works as well as you say,' he nodded in my direction, 'why have you not made him whole?'

Lera lowered her head.

'It was our plan to offer the cure to anyone who was in need and wanted it.' She shook her head. 'After Navar's death, I just no longer cared. I didn't want to live, much less worry about whether anyone else did. I came here to die. I was hoping the flower and I would die together,' she said.

"I could see the shock on the Priest's face, and so could Lera. She threw up her hands. 'But since coming here, I've seen all the sickness that the people went through, all the hardship, the hard work, the pain and death. And I know that it all could have been avoided with just a little work with the kee-nan-twa,' Lera said.

The Priest's face went from shocked to puzzled.

'How?' he asked.

'With a little work, I think the nectar of the flower not only can cure the vampire virus but much more. I think the bounds of its power may be limitless. It could quite possibly keep this village safe from all sickness,' Lera said.

The High Priest took her hand and looked her in the eye.

'Then it is you; you are the one!' he said.

I could hear the wonder in his voice and see the respect mirrored in his eyes.

Lera looked at me then back at the Priest.

'What are you talking about?' she asked.

"He folded his hands on the table and straightened his back. Closing his eyes, he took a deep breath. As he exhaled, his eyes came open; his focus was solely on Lera.

'When the Great One asked me to care for the kee-nan-twa, he said that one day, one would come who would know all about the kee-nan-twa; this one would know all that she was capable of. This one would come from far away; he would rescue the people and would also be accompanied by a fanged one. I could never have believed that the "he" could be a she!' he said.

Lera looked him in the eye; one stray red curl hung over her eye.

'I'm not really sure who or what you're talking about,' she said.

'I am talking about you. I have been waiting for you for a long time,' he said.

'Me?' Lera said with a squeak.

'Yes, you. You will know what to do with the orchid; she will trust you,' he said.

Lera stood. With one hand on her hip and the other on her forehead, she began to pace. 'Wait! Wait just one minute. I have so many questions swirling around in my head that I don't know where to start,' she said.

The Priest also stood and began to pace with her. The two of them were making me a little dizzy.

'Start at the beginning; it is the only place to start,' he said.

'Start at the beginning?' she repeated.

'Yes, at the beginning,' he answered.

'Okay, then; let's start at your beginning,' Lera said.

The priest nodded his approval.

'But first, let's sit back down,' he said, pulling out the chair for her.

She did as he asked. When they were both seated, Lera offered up her first question.

'How long have you been waiting for the one to come?' she asked.

'From the beginning,' he replied.

'From the beginning of what?' she said with a shake of her head. 'Would that be the beginning of your ministry?'

'Something like that,' he said.

'When did your work here begin?' she asked.

He looked up at the canopy of the giant tree.

'It began when the Great One gifted us with the kee-nan-twa.'

'Do you mean that your ancestors were here at the beginning?' Lera asked.

'No, I mean I was there,' he said.

'But wait, that's not possible! You would be thousands of years old!' she said.

At that, he only smiled.

'You were here at the beginning of the beginning?' she asked, her voice a mix of puzzlement and fascination.

The Priest nodded as he began to speak.

'Yes, I was here in the beginning; I was here when the dark winged creature preyed on our people. I was here as we battled it and slowly we won.' He paused and looked from Lera to me and then back to Lera. When his eyes had fallen on Lera, he spoke again, this time in a soft whisper. 'I was also there when the last of the winged creatures struck its final blow. I was the one who carried the young prince back to his father. Then, by their sides, I awaited his death.' He bowed his head. 'We all knew the horror that would be in his death, for we had seen these attacks many times before.'

He shook his head and raised his chin so he could look us in the eye. 'Extreme pain, vomiting, dehydration, and finally, thankfully, death. We knew that all the winged creatures were now gone, but they had taken their toll. This was their last victory and the loss of our most prized possession as we awaited the death of our prince.' He paused. 'For without a king, we could not go on.'

'We waited for death. The pain came, the sweats, convulsions, and everything just as we had expected, but still no death. Then one night as we slept, he disappeared. I found him the next day huddled in the back of one of the huts, racked in pain, his face dripping with blood. I ran to him and took him by the shoulders, trying to get him to look at me. Giving his shoulders a little shake, I called his name. Zoul!' The Priest could not even look at me, he was in so much pain.

"I could see the shock on Lera's face; it was the same shock that was mirrored in my own. Lera held up her hand to interrupt him.

'Did you say, Zoul?' Her question hung thick in the air.

'Yes, Zoul,' he said, looking off into the distance. 'I thought you knew him. He is the one that brought your Lord Navar here at great risk to himself. For he was all but sure he would be killed; this promise had come from his father.'

Lera tapped her fingernails on the table as she thought.

'Oh, yes, I know Zoul. Navar had told me that Zoul was the oldest of vampires. I just had no idea he was the first vampire,' she said.

The Priest nodded.

'Yes, he was the first; it took some time before we knew what he was. By the time we had knowledge of what he was capable of, it was too late. Many of our villagers and those in the nearby village had been killed. Some had been changed into the same kind of creature as he. With the help of the kee-nan-twa, we killed most of them. Some escaped into the jungle. Prince Zoul was allowed to leave if he promised never to return. When he came to me late that night two years ago, I knew he was in need of help. He told me of your plan to create this cure with the help of the kee-nan-twa. My hopes were high that you could do this thing you call a cure, that maybe, just maybe, our Prince would be restored to us. My hopes were so high that I allowed him to take one of the sister orchids.'

Lera adjusted her position in her chair.

'The King said that without the power of the twin sisters, your village would not be safe,' she turned and looked at me, squinting one eye as she thought. 'Wait, wait! What was it that he said? I believe that he said that you said the village was not left without protection.'

The High Priest nodded.

'What did he mean?' Lera asked.

The Priest took a deep breath.

'When Prince Zoul made his request, I knew the risk, and so did he. We knew that he would be risking his very being; the village would be left without enough protection, but the Prince had a plan,' the High Priest said.

'A plan?' both Lera and I said at the same time.

'Yes, a plan,' he said with a nod.

'Prince Zoul and Lord Navar were standing shoulder to shoulder. The moon was full, allowing for a well-lit night. We were just over there in a small clearing. This was the one and only time I ever left the temple. That small journey cost me about 10 of your years, for when I am away for any amount of time, the years catch up with me quickly. The Great One granted me time so I could care for the sisters. Still, I wanted…I *needed* to hear their plan regardless of the cost to me. There he unfolded his plan that would allow him to borrow one of the sisters. For this sacrifice, he would provide us with a guardian. With their plan unfurled, each man stepped to the side to reveal the most beautiful creature I had ever seen.'

"This time it was I who chimed in," Tanarr said.

'What kind of creature?' I asked.

'A woman,' he said with wonder in his voice. 'She was tall and willowy but with a perfect shape. Her long black hair glistened in the moonlight. She had high cheekbones that gave her face a most perfect heart shape. When she spoke,' he closed his eyes and smiled at the memory, 'it was like the whisper of a butterfly's wing or soft rain on parched earth. I could tell even in this light that she was one of them. It was in her eyes; that color was unmistakable even in the filtered light.' He nodded toward me, 'like yours; even with that green film, I can see that they are amber in color. This you cannot hide, not from me.'

I gave him a slight nod to let him know that I understood that he knew what I was and that he was okay with it, at least for now.

'What was his plan?' Lera asked.

'Her: she was a strong one and well-schooled in how to protect "the weak ones," as they called the mere humans. She was to take the place of the sister until she could be restored, and so she did."'

Tanarr stopped his story. He gave me a sideways look.

"You know, I saw something in that man's eyes; it was the same thing I saw in Navar's eyes: that spark."

"A spark?" I repeated.

"Yes, Katelynn; it's the same spark I now see in Corbin's eyes. It's that spark of love. Once it's there, it never goes away. I saw it in the Priest's eyes that night as he told us this story. I wondered if he would tell us what was in his heart, so I waited."

"Did he?" I asked.

"He did, but only briefly. The Priest cleared his throat and looked away."

"'I fell so deeply in love with her that when her time was up, I begged her to take me with her. Whatever was required, I would do it. I would become whatever I needed to just to be with her. Alas, we both knew that for me to leave would mean certain death for me. I could never be one like her, for the power of the kee-nan-twa would not allow it. And if I were to just leave, time would soon consume me. I would have gladly given the rest of my time just to have one year with her.'"

"'She would not allow this. She said the kee-nan-twa would not survive without me, and the world would not survive without the kee-nan-twa. I knew that she was right. She also told me that she could not bear it if she were the cause of my end. I knew that I must stay.' The Priest closed his eyes and raised his chin. We could see the pain of the memories. 'So she left. I stayed, and here I will be until I am no more. I will never forget that beautiful creature; as long as time shall spin, she shall be in my heart. We had but a borrowed season, and until now, our secret was untold.'

'What was her name?' Lera whispered.

'Grace,' he said with a smile. 'From my understanding of your language, she was the very embodiment of grace. With every word she spoke and every movement she made, she was grace.'

For a while we all sat in silence. Lera finally broke the spell.

'May I see the kee-nan-twa?' she asked.

The Priest looked at Lera.

'You may go.' He nodded at me. 'He cannot.'

I started to protest, but he stopped me.

'It would kill you to be that close; you will stay here,' the Priest said in a very matter-of-fact way.

"I stood as they ascended into the canopy of the forest by the way of this ladder on the trunk of the tree itself. The ladder was made of a vine that was growing on the side of the tree. By the looks of it, it was used often; the edges were quite worn. As they vanished into the canopy, I began to walk around the garden, not daring to touch anything." He shrugged his shoulders.

"I didn't know if the plants that were around the base of the tree were part of the lethal orchid that grew at the top or not." He gave his hands a shake. "I was taking no chance. Then it occurred to me that I was not a very good guardian. I had allowed Lera, my charge, to go somewhere I could not; I had no way to control what was going on around her. I had let her go with a man that could do with her as he pleased; she was at his mercy.

Tanarr stopped his story and began to laugh. He ran his hand over his face. I couldn't tell if it was out of frustration or the fog of the memory. Either way, his laughter faded. When he spoke again, it was a whisper. "As if I could have kept her from doing anything she decided she wanted to do. It would have been like trying to keep the sun from rising."

"Tanarr," I said, "just one more question, then I'll let you go for tonight."

"Okay, but tomorrow we'll finish the paperwork that will turn the estate over to you, deal?" he asked.

"Deal!" I replied with a nod.

"What's your question?" he asked, leaning back in his chair.

"What was at the top of that tree?" I asked.

With each elbow propped on the arms of the chair and his chin resting on his fist, he began once more.

"It seemed like forever before I caught sight of them coming back out of the canopy. When they finally made their way to the ground, Lera thanked the Priest for letting her see the sister, and we left the temple. It was almost dark by then. I took her by the hand.

'Lera, walk with me, please,' I asked.

When we had gotten out of earshot, I stopped her.

'You've got to tell me what's up there,' I said, looking up into the trees.

We had stopped in a small clearing. In the time that it had taken us to get there, Lera was about to burst. She simply couldn't wait any longer to tell me what she had seen.

'You're just not going to believe what's up there!' she said, almost bubbling.

Tanarr took a deep breath and smiled.

"When she looked up at me with those green eyes sparkling, it was a sparkle I had not seen there in a long time. You know, those green eyes always took my breath away; they are why I chose green contacts for my eye color, her green eyes." His smile lent a touch of sadness to his handsome face: a sadness that broke my heart for a love that could not be.

Tanarr took a deep breath before going back to his memories.

"I did it to honor her."

I put my hand over my heart and said nothing; I only nodded because in my heart I had known that was why he had chosen that color for himself. I sat there in silence as he went back to his story…their story.

"As we stood there in that clearing, she took both of my hands in hers, and my spirits soared. She was talking, but my ears had disengaged and my heart had taken complete control. All I wanted to do was grab her and run,

run as far and as fast as I could with her and never let her go. All I wanted was to love and protect her. Instead, I stood there trying to listen, all the while drowning in those glorious green eyes.

She gave my hands a little shake as she emphasized a part of what she was telling me; that little shake jerked me back to what she was saying. I gave myself a good mental shake. I knew I needed to calm down and pay attention. She only wanted to tell me what she had seen and why she was so excited. I had to tell myself that she wasn't excited about me, and it was important for me to understand what she was talking about. I tried to hear each word as she spoke.

'Oh, Tanarr! I wish you could have been with me. It was amazing. First, the climb to the top of that tree was worth being here. It was like being at the top of the world. I could see all the way to the end of the earth. I mean, I could actually see the curve of the earth!' She clenched her fists and almost squealed as she bounced up and down on her toes. 'The sun, the air, the treetops! It was breathtaking!' Her voice got very low. 'There, at the very top of the tree, in what was almost like a nest, was the kee-nan-twa, the sisters. It was beautiful! It was amazing, and it was surreal. Their faces are huge; they're the size of a dish tub.' She hooped her arms by touching the tips of her fingers to further emphasize the size of the flower. 'They look just like the orchid that Navar and Zoul had retrieved for my work, but much larger.'

'That was only two years ago; how could they grow that fast?' I asked.

Lera looked up and me. She was so pleased with herself.

'I asked him the same question. He told me that they were only that large when they were in the top of the tree. As soon as you began to descend with one of the sisters, they would start to shrink in size until by the time you reached the ground, they were of normal size,' she said, looking up at the canopy.

'Now, just how does that work?' I inquired as my curiosity began to climb.

'I don't know, but there are a lot of things here that I don't understand,' she replied, looking around at the forest that seemed to swallow everything past the edge of the village.

'Amazing . . .' was all I could say to her.

'Yes, amazing. The Priest also said I could go on with our work as long as I did it here. The kee-nan-twa will never be apart again. The Priest said that after the first sister was removed, the sister that remained began to wither until a bud appeared. It grew as the vampire guardian, Grace, kept watch over them. When it opened, it revealed a beautiful, strong sister. Then the other was restored to the same. It seems that the one cannot be on its own. There are only ever two, but there must also always be two. I will not risk the sisters again; it would not be worth the price of losing what the Great One has gifted us with and their protection.'

I raised my hand to cup the side of Lera's face.

'Now what?' I asked. All the while I was hoping that I could whisk her away to someplace like Paris or the Caribbean: anywhere except here.

'I'm going to stay here and work with the orchid to see what it will yield,' she said with a nod. I dropped my hands, and my shoulders sank.

"'I knew you were going to say that. I'll send my office a message that I'll be delayed.'

Lera looked up at me with those big, beautiful green eyes.

'You don't have to do that. I'll be fine. You can go back to work. I know how busy you are. After all, I think you have wasted enough time on me.'

I put my finger over her lips.

'First, you will never be a waste of my time; nothing will ever come before you. My business can go on whether I'm there or not; that's what associates are for. As for the part about your being fine, there is no question about that; you are fine in every way possible.'

For that I got an eye roll and a head shake. Before she had the chance to start with me, I held up my hand to stop her.

'But, shall we say, it will make me feel much better to know that my lady love is—' She started to protest, and I stopped her once more. 'Let me finish before you say anything, please.'

She said nothing, just stared at me."

Tanarr shook his head.

"I know I went too far with that lady love bit." He gave me a little nod. "I couldn't help myself. Anyway, she let me go on. I tried to dig myself out."

"'What would my friend and Lord say if I left you here by yourself to fall prey to whoever or whatever? I made a promise that I plan to keep: a promise to protect all that belonged to our Lord. After all, I am and will always be a knight of Go-Brath.'

That statement caught her off guard because she knew I was talking about Navar.

'Okay, you win; you can stay,' she said, looking down at her hands. 'I'm sorry,' she whispered.

I took my finger and gently raised her chin.

'Sorry for what?'

'I'm sorry that Navar died. I'm sorry that you had to come looking for me. I'm sorry for all the people we couldn't save,' she said as tears threatened to spill over her lashes. 'I'm sorry you lost your best friend. I'm sorry I'm keeping you from your work, but I'm not sorry we're here. We made differences here; we did a good thing.'

I grabbed her in a crushing hug. It was a brother's hug or a father's hug, not a lover's hug.

'Yes, we did a good thing,' I whispered over her head. 'See how much you have to offer? How much you still have left? All the things you have to do? And I'll be here for you to help in any way I can.'

I held her at arm's length and cupped her face in my hands. I brushed away a stray tear that had escaped and started down her face with my thumb.

'From what I understand, we have a lot of work ahead of us, so I recommend we get started,' I spun her around and gave her cute little backside a good pop. 'Now march, young lady!'"

Tanarr closed his eyes and smiled. It was like he could still see her.

"Man, I loved to see her walk in front of me. Aw…"

With that I reached over from my chair and gave him a good backhanded whack on the shoulder.

"Tanarr! Shame on you!" I said in a teasing tone.

"Oh, sorry, Katelynn, but she did have a fine backside. I always loved walking behind her." He rubbed his hands together. "AND…that's how Lera wound up with the land where the kee-nan-twa grows. It's also how the Kee-Ka-Na people became the healthiest people in the world." He paused. "I think that *National Geographic* did a story on them; I'll have to look that up for you."

"All of her work paid off?" I asked.

"It did for the people of Kee-Ka-Na; they took the vaccination Lera made from the orchid. They never got any of the sicknesses that most would have, so they lived longer, too."

"Wow!" I said.

"Yes, wow. And that's all for now. You need your sleep, and I need to go in search of nourishment."

"Just one more thing?" I asked with a plea.

"Katelynn…It's getting late," Tanarr said with a shake of his head.

"Please?" I said with a flutter of my eyes.

"Okay, what?" he said with a roll of his eyes and a soft chuckle.

"What did you do about…you know…feeding? You all had so much to do. You don't have to tell me if you don't want to; I'll understand. I was just curious."

He stopped and took a deep breath.

"At dawn, while everyone except for Lera was still asleep, I would go hunt. If anyone ever knew what I was doing or what I was, they never said. There was too much need for anyone to think about what I was doing at night as long as I kept helping Lera."

"Oh…," was all I said.

With that he stood and gave the top of my head a soft kiss. "Now good night, m'lady." He turned and headed for the door. He stopped with his hand on the door handle and looked back over his shoulder. "Tomorrow we can complete our work," he winked. "Make it all yours, so you can get started on her work once more." With that said, he was gone, leaving me all alone and very, very tired.

I stood and gave a nice, long stretch and a loud yawn. I took a quick look at the clock; it was one o'clock in the morning! The evening had gone so fast. I loved getting glimpses of the young Lera that I never could have known. I walked behind one of the time-worn wingbacks we had been sitting in, the same chairs she and I had spent so much time in as she told me all about her and Navar. They were also the same chairs that she and Navar had kept in front of the fireplace in his West Coast house while they talked about the life they would never get to share. It still surprised me that she never told me about Tanarr and all they had done together and that he had visited her quite often after she came to Silver Cove. She truly was a woman of many facets. My hand lingered there on the back of the chair. I slid my hand along the edges as I passed by. "Good night, Ms. Lera. Good night, Navar. Love ya."

Chapter Twenty-Four

I still had everything on my mind as I followed the path that Tanarr had just taken out the door. Once outside, I looked down the hall toward the bathroom.

"Aww, man! I still have to take my shower." I glanced toward the stairs then back to the bathroom, then from the stairs to the bathroom again. "I could just skip my shower tonight; after all, it is after one. I could just head on up to my room, climb in bed, and go to sleep."

I shook my head. "Yeah, like I could go to sleep without washing off the day. Okay, so here's the new plan. I'll run down to the bathroom, take a quick shower and jump back into my clothes. Then, when I get back to my room, I'll change. That will work, but what about my teeth? I think I saw some toothpaste in one of the drawers. I'll just use my finger for a toothbrush. That could work." I said out loud as I made my way to the bathroom. I hoped that the tube of paste was toothpaste and not something weird like foot cream stuff, or worse, which would be my luck.

In the bathroom, I found everything I needed. The towels were fresh, clean, and hanging on the rack. The shower gel was right where I had left it the night before. And there, in the right-hand drawer, was the tube of paste. *Please let it be for teeth*! I read the label. Blah blah blah, teeth, tartar control. I took off the cap and gave it a little taste. "Ah, minty tasty, yes! It is toothpaste!" It had an odd name, but that was okay; toothpaste was toothpaste.

With minty fresh breath and squeaky clean skin, I looked in the mirror and gave myself a big smile. "Yep, there is more than one way to skin a cat." I scrunched up my face. "That's a gross saying; you just have to wonder who came up with that one and what they were doing." I shivered. "Or maybe not—yuck!"

By the time I got to my room and into my nightshirt (*thanks, Moose*) and slid between the sheets, I was wide awake. *Okay, close your eyes. Breathe. Think pleasant thoughts. Relax*. My eyes popped wide open. *Okay, that didn't work. One more time*. I took a deep breath and repeated the whole thing. Piece by piece, everything that Tanarr had told me about Lera came rushing back into my mind. "Arrrgh!" I wasn't going to lie here fighting with myself and the sheets. I kicked them off and climbed out of bed. I put some big, thick socks on and decided to go prowl through the kitchen.

I didn't even bother with a housecoat; after all, it was after 2:00 A.M. I was pretty sure I wouldn't run into anyone. And if I did, Moose's big old jersey came all the way down to my knees. I did throw my hair back in a ponytail because I couldn't stand having it in my face.

In the kitchen, I began to rummage around in the fridge.

"Let's see...warm milk, yuck! I don't think so," I said with a shiver as I moved on to the cabinets. "Coffee? Yeah, like I need more caffeine." About that time I spotted a canister marked "Chamomile tea."

"Ah, now that sounds kinda castle. I can see a little lady sitting and sipping her chamomile tea, out of a porcelain cup, of course, with her pinky sticking out. Well, let's give her a try." I started to put the teapot on the stove to heat, "Oh, hello, microwave!" We may have been living in a very old castle, but we had access to every modern kitchen gadget under the sun.

With my water now nice and hot, I opened the canister; it was filled with loose tea. I gave it a little sniff. "It doesn't smell like Louisiana tea, but I'll give it a try." I rummaged around in the drawers till I found a little silver tea steeper. I filled it half full with the tea and sunk it into the hot water. I could almost hear the water seep into the tea as it was submerged in the steaming hot water. I gave it a minute or two to steep while I poked around for something to munch on. "Ah-ha!" I spotted the cookie jar. As the lid turned, it made that scraping sound of ceramic on ceramic. Every kid knows and every adult remembers that scrape of anticipation.

The lid came off with a little tug, allowing this heavenly aroma of short-bread cookies to waft out and wrap around my head. My mouth began to water. I placed two cookies on my plate, although I think I could have eaten the whole jarful and maybe even the jar; they smelled so good.

Okay, I started out with three cookies, but I ate one on the way back to where my tea waited for me, and yeah, that cookie was as good as it smelled. I parked myself and my cookies by my cup of tea, leaning over the steaming cup. I gave it a sniff. It smelled a little odd, but sometimes odd could be good. All the folks up north had thought this sassy gal a bit odd, and that was okay. After all, normal wasn't what it was cracked up to be, and ordinary was plain old boring.

With that thought packed under my belt, I gathered up my courage and took a big sip. I was very glad that I was the only one in the kitchen, 'cause no sooner did the tea hit my taste buds than I spit it right back in the cup in a very un-ladylike manner. *Holy! Cow! Ah Yuck! Yuck! Let me say it one more time: Yuck!* I didn't know what a chamomile was, but it must have been one bad mama of a plant. I grabbed the first thing I could find to clean my tongue off, which was a mistake. I didn't know what was on that towel, but it must have been slated for the next wash as it had the distinctive taste of old garlic and way too many hands.

Oh! My! Gosh! Now I was running around the kitchen fanning my tongue, which was hanging out of my mouth. *I think I've killed it! Where are the glasses!* I gave up and went to the sink, where I used my hand for a glass. I took a mouthful of water and swished it around in my mouth before spitting it down the drain and then repeated the whole procedure twice. I wiped my arm across my mouth.

"That's it! I'm done! I'm going to bed!" I muttered. "If I have to whack myself over the head with a frying pan, I am going to sleep."

Back upstairs in my suite, I slid between the sheets. I was much sleepier than I thought. Rolling over, I buried my face in the pillow.

"What is that fragrance? Heather, maybe…," My thoughts began to slur as sleep overtook me.

Chapter Twenty-Five

Morning found me completely exhausted. "Why am I awake?" I muttered through my sleepy fog of exhaustion and irritation. There it was again, the thing that had woken me up: a soft knock followed by the delicate voice of Deireadh.

"Good morning, m'lady."

I could barely hear her through the thick door.

"Morning," I croaked back as I ran my hands over my face, trying to pull myself back into the real world. That thought gave me a mental chuckle. *I'm not sure that this is the real world: castles, books with no words, fairies, vampires, and let's not forget secret passages. Yeah, this is the real world.*

"So sorry I be to be botherin' ye this early in the morning," she paused. "However, Mr. Roberts is here. Ready to start he is, on yer bathroom."

"Ah, shoot!" I had forgotten about that. "Dang it!"

I took a deep breath and exhaled slowly.

"Come on in, Deireadh."

I heard the door open slowly.

"Good morning to ye," she said with that sparkle in her voice that I had come to love.

"How can you be so sparkly so early in the morning?" I said, arching one eyebrow and making a little face at her.

She put her hand over her mouth and let out a little giggle.

"Oh, m'lady, so funny ye be."

I gave her a grumpy look as I flipped back the covers. Sitting there on the edge of my very tall bed with my feet dangling over, I felt much like a small child being dragged out of bed for school, and I was just about as happy. Deireadh looked at me and gave me a little pout.

"Now, now? Be ye not so grumpy, for a perfect day it is," she said, running over to the window. She pulled back the curtains and threw out her arms to greet the day. "See how beautiful it be?"

I looked up at the window and shielded my eyes with my hand.

"Oh, it's just peachy," I said with a fake smile.

"Come, come now," she gave me a big grin. "You can do it, m'lady, know it I do."

"Okay," I said, holding up one finger. "First, my name is Katelynn. If you will call me by my name, I will try my best to happy up and embrace this perfectly beautiful day."

"Do that I can, Katelynn," she said with a wink and a very out-of-character thumbs up. This did, however, make me smile. She clapped her hands together. "See! See, do it ye can, but now get movin' ye must. For keepin' Mr. Roberts from his task we are," Deireadh said with a smile that indicated she had accomplished her mission and she was quite proud of herself.

"All right, all right, I'm moving!" I said with a yawn as my feet met the floor.

"Waitin' for ye I will, yer breakfast will be a waitin', too. Let it not get cold, please," she said with a curtsy as she left the room. "Oh!" she came back in. "Forget not, a happy day will be!" She smiled, gave one more curtsy, and left.

After she had left and the door was closed, I began to get dressed.

"It must be nice to be a fairy and always be happy, sunny, and sparkly." I thought for a second. "Maybe not, 'cause sometimes I don't want to be sparkly. Sometimes I want to be grumpy," I mumbled.

My internal argument continued as I made my way down to breakfast. I rounded the door into the dining hall. There standing at the back of my chair with my coffee in one hand and his elbow casually draped over the back edge of the chair and legs crossed at the ankle was Corbin. He looked just like one of those hot coffee commercials. *Hmm…*I thought. *I'd buy that coffee, oh yeah.*

I didn't say a word. Instead, I sauntered toward him, trying my best to look sexy: unsuccessfully, I might add. The next thing I knew, the toe of my shoe caught on an uneven piece of tile, causing me to lose my footing and balance. I did one of those Three Stooges shuffles/recoveries, coming to a full stop. I threw both my hands in the air.

"Ta da! Just call me grace," I said with a deep and overanimated bow. This extracted a big smile and a rich chuckle from Corbin.

I walked over to where he stood with my coffee in hand.

"That wasn't exactly the response I was going for," I said, taking the steaming cup he offered me. I took a big gulp of the hot coffee then set it down on the table so I could put my hands on each side of his face and look deep into his beautiful eyes.

"Ah, just one smile from you makes my heart melt and my spirit soar," I said as his arms slid around my waist. He pulled me in for a long, slow kiss. We just stood there for a while not caring who came or went.

"Man, I have missed you," he whispered into my ear.

That soft wisp of breath in my ear caused chill bumps to break out all over me.

"Oooh, I missed you, too," I said, moving in as close as I could get. "And I have something to show ya," I said, pulling back just a little. "You know I have to say things when they cross my mind or they may never cross again; that's the way I am. I know it drives everyone crazy...sorry."

He pulled me back

"Well, that's good. I can't wait to see what you have found, and then I have something to tell you."

"What?" I said with my head on his shoulder.

I really didn't care what he said as long as he held me while he said it. He kissed the top of my head then slowly released me and pulled out my chair.

"You can show me later, and I can tell you later, for now you have a hot breakfast to deal with."

"I can live with that," I said almost under my breath. "I am kind of hungry."

No sooner had we settled into our chairs than Charles arrived bearing my piping hot breakfast. Before he took the food off the tray, he set the tray on the floor so he could balance everything. We all chuckled a little and gave him a big smile. Doulsie would have had a fit if she had seen what he was doing. It was just so sweet; who could say anything? I just smiled.

He placed my plate before me; it was laden with two well-prepared eggs, ham, potatoes, and biscuits. One biscuit had slipped off the plate and onto the tray. He picked it up with his fingers. That was okay; I would have eaten it if he had picked it up off the floor. I would never have let him feel anything but proud of what he had done. Butter, jelly, and honey were all spread on the table before me. After he finished placing my plate on the table, I gave him a wink.

"Thank you, Charles," I said. He turned to Corbin. I could see that he was a little embarrassed that he had no food for Corbin.

"Sir Corbin, please forgive. I'd be not knowin' that ye be out here. Ms. Doulsie told me to bring out Lady Katelynn's food. She said nothing about yerself sittin' out here. Will ye be having breakfast with Lady Katelynn?"

Corbin gave the boy a nod and a smile.

"That's all right, son; I've already had my breakfast. I'm only keeping Lady Katelynn company while she enjoys her morning meal."

"Would ye be caring for a cup of coffee, Sir?" Charles asked.

"No thanks; I'm good," Corbin said as he waved Charles to come closer. "But I do thank you for asking." He winked at Charles and handed him twenty pounds sterling.

"Thank you, Sir Corbin. I'll be takin' me leave if there is nothing' more." He gave us both a very grownup bow. Just before he got to the door, he stopped.

"I'll be back in to check on yer coffee, m'lady," he said, and then he was gone.

I buttered my biscuit and set it to the side to let the butter melt. Next I took a big forkful of perfectly prepared eggs followed by a big gulp of steaming coffee.

"Okay, you first or me?" I asked in between bites.

"You first; I do love to hear you talk," he said with a smile. He picked up my napkin and reached over to brush a stray speck of egg off my chin. "Even if you do have egg on your face."

"Oops…I'm sorry. I guess I was a little hungrier than I thought."

"Are you too hungry to talk?"

"Me?" I said with a squeak. "I'm never too anything to talk! Talking is one of the things I do best." I gave him a big smile.

"So," Corbin said, leaning forward over the table and giving me a sideways look. "What do you want to show me?"

I took a big sip of coffee.

"Last night, I was waiting in the library for Tanarr."

Corbin's eyebrows shot up.

"You were?" he said with a hint of jealousy in his voice. I knew that he was messing with me, so I gave him a good eye roll through the steam that was coming off my hot coffee.

"Oh, please! Stop that; you know that Tanarr is telling me about Lera. You also know that he is still very much in love with her. I'm not sure that he will ever get over her." I set my cup down by my plate. "But back to what I found while I was waiting for him. I was looking at some of the books that lined the walls in the library; there are some very interesting books there. I found one book that had a beautiful note to Navar on the inside cover. It was to thank him for saving his child, and it was from a King. Did you know that's where Navar got his armor? It was part of the thank you gift from that same King."

Corbin smiled and looked away.

"No. I didn't. Hmm…that's just like Navar. He would risk all to do the right thing. You'll have to show me that book. I'd like to have it encased and placed with his armor."

"Oh, but that's not all I found!" I said just before I took a big bite of buttered biscuit.

"What else did you find?" he said with smile, like he was watching a child at Christmas.

"As I was reading the spines of each book, I came across this one. Its cover was made of wood, hand-carved wood. I could just tell by the way it looked that it had to be very old. The title is *The Truths of Those That Be*. It caught my full attention. I very gently pulled the book from the shelf and put it on the desk. With much anticipation, I slowly, carefully opened the book." I plopped both my hands down on the table, causing them to make a splat sound. I turned my head, giving Corbin a little odd look with one eye squinted. "Do you know what was in it?" Corbin didn't say a word, only shook his head to indicate that he had no clue. I took a deep breath then exhaled slowly, "NOTHING!"

"Very funny," Corbin said with a smile. "What did it really say?"

"Nothing," I said again with wide eyes. "Absolutely nothing: the pages were blank."

"That's odd," he said with a tilt of his head and his brows scrunched. "Why do you think the book is there if it had no words or at least drawings?"

"I think it's a 'book marker,' no pun intended," I said with a little laugh. "I crack myself up! But seriously, I think it is marking the spot. Just as I started to replace the book where it had been on the shelf, I noticed that on the very back of the shelf was a small crest, just like the one that opens Navar's room. I used his ring like we did when we opened his door. You're not going to believe this, but the shelf beside me came open just a little." I used my fingers to show the space that it had opened. "With a very little tug, it slid all the way open to reveal a secret pathway."

"Did you go in?"

"No way! Not by myself: I am not going to get stuck anywhere in the dark with the possibility of large spiders or even small spiders lurking about!" I smiled, winked, and rubbed my shoulder against his. "That's what my Spider-man is for!"

He rubbed his hands together.

"Sounds like a grand adventure," he wiggled his eyebrows up and down. "You, me, in a dark, tight place." He closed his eyes and smiled. "I can't wait."

"Oh, you!" I said with a shake of my head. I picked up my empty coffee cup. Corbin reached for the warmer pot.

"Here, let me," he said as he refilled my cup.

"Thank you," I took a sip of the hot coffee. "Will you go with me?"

"To the ends of the earth," he said with a smile. "Where are we going?"

I looked at him from under my lashes.

"Wherever that dark hall leads."

"Ah, yes: spiders, long dark hall. Did I say spiders? I will go only if you promise to jump into my arms at the sight of the first spider."

"That's no problem. If I see just one spider, I will be all over you like white on rice."

He looked at me with his steamy amber eyes.

"Oh, how I hope there are spiders!"

"Give me a break! You know there don't have to be any spiders around for me to be in your arms." This time I wiggled my eyebrows.

I took a big sip of coffee.

"You said you had something to tell me."

Corbin folded his hands on the table, bowed his head over them, and took a deep breath. When he lifted his head with those amber eyes sparkling, he had a very somber tone to his voice.

"He's here."

I cocked my head sideways.

"He who?"

"Blake."

The fork that was on its way to my mouth clamored on my plate as it fell from my now shaking hand.

"Did you say Blake?" I shook my head. "No. Where? I thought he would just go away, after, you know, that fairy thing."

"Well, you see," Corbin said with a finger wag, "that's the thing about fairy power. It doesn't last forever. As it fades, you can remember everything right up to the time you encountered the fairy. Blake, being unaware of her presence, thinks that he has just arrived. He will not remember anything about her for now. That's why vampires don't particularly care for the little winged havoc-wreakers. They can make us say things or go places, and we won't know what we have done or why. We have absolutely no control over them. It's maddening."

Panic began to creep into my heart; I put my hand to my forehead.

"How do you know he's here? I mean, I know I told you about seeing him the other night, but when you didn't say any more about it, I assumed he had left."

Corbin leaned back in his chair.

"I was hoping that he had left; however, as you say, evil never gives up that easy. That's why Calldoon and I went out to check on things. I had a bad feeling that I couldn't shake."

"You're sure he's here?"

"Oh, I'm sure."

"Did you see him?" I asked.

"No. I didn't have to," Corbin said, running his hands over his face.

"What do you mean?"

Corbin got up and walked over to the fireplace. He put his forearm against the mantel as he began to speak.

"We came across a small cottage on the northern border of you property." He leaned his head against his arm. "They were all dead."

"But how do you know it was him?"

Corbin came back to my side, knelt at my chair, and took my hand in his.

"I've seen his handiwork; trust me, it was him. We buried the dead and burnt the cottage so there would be no evidence."

I tried to calm myself.

"Do you think he will come after me again?"

"Yes, I do," he shook his head. "I can't believe I'm going to say this." He took a deep breath. "When you can't be with me, stay close to that fairy of yours. She can keep you safe, but tell her to stay away from me, okay?"

"Okay," I said with a nod.

"Between the five of us, you will be safe."

Someone behind me cleared his throat; I jumped and caught my hand on the side of my plate, almost spilling its contents into my lap. Corbin reached over and put his hand over mine.

"It's only Charles."

He pushed back from the table and walked over to where the boy stood. I had scared the child as much as he had scared me. I could not hear what they were saying, nor did I care; all I could think about was Blake. He had always unnerved me, and now that I knew what he was capable of, he just plain old scared me.

Corbin came back to the table.

"The boy said that the carpenter, Mr. Roberts, is here to start on your bathroom: something about nails?"

I waved my hands.

"Oh, that. The nails are fine. Deireadh explained everything to me. I have to give the castle permission for anything to be done on the inside." Corbin gave me a sideways look. "She said it goes back to the spell that the wizard placed on the castle when Navar first built it. Now that I am the Lord of the castle, it will allow nothing to be done without my permission." I arched one eyebrow and shrugged my shoulders. "I don't know; we'll see. I do know that every nail that Mr. Roberts tried to sink bent. When I tried, they went straight in with one hit."

Corbin stood there for a moment. I could see the cogs turning in his head, trying to recall the turn of events.

"I believe she is right; the wizard was caught off guard by the invitation to the ball. He had no gift, so he made this spell his gift. His spell gave the castle life of a kind. No legs or anything like that, but the old gal has a spirit of sorts, as I remember," he turned and gave me an odd look. "How did your fairy know this?"

I had to think fast. I had promised Deireadh that I would not tell anyone who her father was. She had thought that it was enough for them to know what she was. It was more than she could take for them to have that much knowledge of her. She liked to keep her father to herself; she never knew her mother, so her father was special to her. She would allow nothing in that space. It was really kind of sad to be all alone in this world with no one to trust. No matter how much I hated not telling Corbin everything, I would not betray her trust. "Castle talk, I guess. You know what they say."

"No, what do they say?" he asked.

"The maids know everything. If you want to know anything, just ask one," I said.

Corbin laughed.

"You're right on that one."

I felt like a heel not telling him everything, but I couldn't betray Deireadh, as she had no one else. I didn't think that Corbin or any of the others would do anything to her, not after he told me to stay close to her. I thought she just needed to trust someone.

"Katelynn. Katelynn!" I heard Corbin calling my name. I blinked my eyes a couple of times and looked up at him.

"What?" I asked.

"You were staring off into space. Are you okay?"

"Yeah, I'm fine. I was just thinking, but now I'm thinking that if I don't beat Mr. Roberts up to my room and give the old girl permission for the work to be done, he will only be wasting his time and more nails. I'm going to slide around the side and try to beat him to the top. If you see him coming, stall him, please," I said with an eye flutter and a peck on the cheek.

"Sure," Corbin said. "You run on. I'll stall while you talk to the castle."

I crossed my fingers and headed to my room. We were both on our way out when Tanarr arrived.

"Where is everyone going?" he asked.

"I have to give the castle a good talking to while Corbin stalls the carpenter," I said.

"Okay…," Tanarr said.

"I have to catch Mr. Roberts. Would you stay here? I'd like to talk to you about something," I heard Corbin say as I rounded the corner. I could only assume that it was about Blake.

I opened the door to my room and tiptoed in.

"Okay, castle, or lady castle. How about I just call you by your name: Go-Brath. How's that sound to you? Good, I hope. You see, I've never talked to a castle before, so I'm not sure how to address you.

"Go Brath, if you would—I mean, if you don't mind—I would really like to have a new bathroom so I don't have to take a hike every time I need to shower, brush my teeth, or, you know. If you could, please allow Mr. Roberts to do his work," I held up my hand, "I promise he will do a good job. And if he doesn't, Mr. Calldoon will make him redo it or worse. Just trust me; he will do a good job." I stopped and turned around slowly. "Okay, are we good here, I hope?"

I heard a firm knock at my door.

"Who's there?" I called through the door, with my hand on the handle. I was ready to allow entrance. I was almost positive it was Chuck, but I was taking no chances.

"It's just me, Chuck Roberts, the carpenter," he called back.

"Come on in," I said as I pulled the door open.

He walked in with a case of new nails on his shoulder.

"Got some more nails. The store thought it was as odd as I did that every last one of them bent except for the two you sunk. The store manager laid it on the old oak and stone walls; he seemed to think that this new nail that's made of some kind of super steel will work. It makes the claim that it will nail through cement. I can't wait to give them a try," he said as he hoisted the case to the floor. They landed with quite a thud, causing me to jump. "Sorry, miss. Didn't mean to scare ya."

"That's okay. I'm fine; it just startled me. I'm sure that this box will work just fine," I said as I started to leave the room.

"Wait!" he said.

I turned around.

"Did you happen to talk with that pretty little maid of yours? Did she seem to be interested? I mean, would she like to meet me?" he asked.

"I'm sorry. I forgot, but I promise I will ask her today. Don't get your hopes up; I told ya she's a bit different," I said.

Chuck picked up his tool belt and began to fill the front pockets with the new nails.

"Ah, whatever. If it happens, it happens. It ain't no big deal," he said with a shrug as he changed the subject. He rubbed his hands together and fastened his tool belt about his waist.

"Now, back to the business at hand." He walked over and patted the wall. "Now, old girl, we have work at hand if we want to make this little gal happy. I'll do you a good job if ya will let me," he gave a nod to the wall.

Not saying a word, I watched his conversation with the room unfold. He said some words so softly that I couldn't hear what he was saying. When he was done, I couldn't help it; I had to ask.

"What are you doing?" I asked, like I had not been doing the same thing earlier.

"Just askin' for the old gal's permission."

I gave him a blank look.

"I's just thinkin' on my way up those grand old stairs. This place, being of the time she is, she could be under a spell. You know, magic," he said slowly. "The Scots believe that all things have a spirit, and just maybe someone has awakened her spirit. It was too strange how you, the new Lord of the castle, could sink a nail with just one hit, and no matter how hard I tried, every single nail I hit bent." He gave his head a good nod. "It can't hurt to try, now, can it?"

I only nodded as I started to leave, but first I stopped and grabbed the book I had been reading.

"Okay, good luck with all that," I said as I left the room.

Heading down the stairs, I thought to myself, maybe Deireadh did know what she was talking about. We would know by this evening. *We'll see if the castle will let him do any work.*

Back in the dining hall sat Corbin and Tanarr; I had forgotten that Corbin had asked Tanarr to wait there because he had something to talk to him about.

When I stepped into the dining hall, the two of them were sitting there talking in low tones. I walked up, put my book down on the table, and took my seat.

"What's up, guys?"

They both looked at me with a smile, which made me a little more than nervous.

"Okay…again, I say, what's up?"

Tanarr was the first to speak.

"Corbin was just filling me in on what he and Calldoon found on their border patrol."

"Oh, that. Freaky, huh?" I said with a shiver.

"Yes, you might say so. Katelynn, you must listen to me. I know that Corbin has already told you this, and I've already told you this, but I'm going to tell you again. Do not go out on your own alone, please," he said, putting an extra emphasis on each word.

"Oh, don't worry. I have no intention of doing that." I held up my book. "This morning my plan is book, shade, lawn chair, and, hopefully, sleep. Then this evening, you and I will do some more of that paperwork." I paused. "If that's okay with you," I said with an eye flutter.

Tanarr looked over at Corbin.

"How does she do that?"

"Do what?" I said with another eye flutter.

"That. You just flutter those baby blues, and we do whatever you want. And yes, we can meet after your nap," he laughed.

Corbin laughed along with him.

"All I can say is, she is good."

"Boys, boys," I said, this time with an almost cartoon-like eye flutter. "It's not a me thing; it's girl thing. It's something we learn when we're little: really little. It may even be something we're born with. Some of us choose to turn our backs on the power; others run with it." I turned and walked away in sultry old Hollywood style, with my book under my arm. I looked back and blew them both a kiss. I put on my cheap sunglasses and turned around just in time to run smack dab into the door case. I didn't look back, but I heard both men laugh. I flipped my hair and threw up my hand.

"I'm good. I'll be in my lawn chair if anyone needs me."

Chapter Twenty-Six

The morning air felt glorious. The sun had begun to warm the earth. The birds were singing, and the dew had melted away. I looked around the garden in search of the perfect chair. *Ah, yes, a chaise lounge chair, perfect!* I could stretch out and read or sleep with my dark glasses on; who could tell or care? I put my book in the chair and pulled and tugged until I got it dragged into the shade. *Whew! That was not as easy as it looked like it would be*, I thought with a huff.

I plopped down in my chair, which was now in the perfect spot, and opened my book, prepared for a nice, long read. The fragrance of all the beautiful flowers filled the garden. The temperature was perfect; there was a soft breeze flirting with the pages of my book and playing with my hair. I tucked one stray strand back behind my ear as I prepared to get serious.

Two pages in found me sound asleep; in my dream state, I continued the storyline. I had just gotten to where the two young lovers were about to meet. Even before his horse had stopped, he had jumped to the ground and was running into the arms of his love. He had been away on a cattle drive, and she had kept the home fires burning. Softly, sweetly, he took her into his arms. Ever so lightly, he ran the back of his hand across her soft face. He could hear her intake of breath as she awaited the kiss that every reader knew was coming.

There was only one problem; the face that got brushed was mine! But that was okay. I could play along. If Corbin wanted to entertain me, I was in. After all, we played this game back home before I knew what was going on, who the players were, and what they were playing for. This time I was aware, and I was going to enjoy playing along. Without opening my eyes, and with my best Scarlett impression, I stepped into my role.

"Oh, Rhett, I've been awaitin' here for you to return! Now, kiss me, you black-hearted scoundrel, so I know it's really you."

Very male lips touched mine. My eyes flew open, for these were definitely not Corbin's lips. I scrambled out of my chair so fast that I almost fell when my foot got caught in the arm of the chair. With the fog of a dream, my sleep was vanquished. As the nap cleared from my eyes, I knew it was time to truly be scared. There stood Blake, and the only thing between us was a chair. I took a shaky breath and decided to stand my ground. Shaky ground it was, but I sunk my heels in. It was fight or flight time, and I just didn't feel like running.

"What are you doing here?" I hissed thorough clenched teeth.

"I do believe I was being invited to kiss you," Blake purred, his piercing dark blue eyes never leaving mine. It felt as if he could see straight through to my soul. This unnerved me completely; he had that effect on most women. I could only assume that they were so dark blue because his contacts were covering the dark amber eyes, made darker from a recent feeding.

He took a step around the chair; I took a step in the other direction.

"Ah…come now, my sweet little Katelynn, or is it Scarlett?" He gave his shoulders a shrug. "Whichever: it makes little matter. A rose by any other name is still a rose, and," he stepped closer, "I think we were about to enjoy a long-awaited kiss." His face turned somber. "I, for one, am going to enjoy it."

I held up my hand to stop him.

"You know that I thought you were Corbin."

He reached out and grabbed my hand; I was shaking like a leaf.

"Oh, look at you, shaking with anticipation for me, I hope," he purred.

My mouth went dry as I watched helplessly; it was like watching it all unfold on the movie screen. I kept waiting for the scary music to start: da, da, da, daaaa.

He slowly turned my hand palm up, never taking his eyes off mine. He brought my hand to his lips and inhaled slowly.

"Ah, yes, that's the fragrance I can't get out of my mind. Even though it was just a small taste, it has lingered with me."

At first I didn't know what he was talking about, and then it all came rushing back: that night on the lanai at the Silver Cove retirement village where Ms. Lera lived. I had gone out to get a book for one of the residents. I was alone. Blake had appeared out of nowhere, and he grabbed my wrist. His ring cut into my skin from the pressure of his grip, and the blood began to ooze out around his ring. He raised my arm and licked the trickle of blood off. If Christie had not come looking for me, I don't know what would have happened. Now here I was again. *Where is my knight in shining armor?* I screamed in my head.

"Don't look so horrified. I'm not here to do you in. I'm not even hungry; I had my fill the other night," he said with a wicked smile. The thought of what Corbin and Calldoon had cleaned up invoked an involuntary shiver from me. "However," he stepped closer and grabbed me by the shoulders, pulling me against his chest. "If you would like to be my queen, just say the word. One small bite…right here…," He ran his fingers down the side of my neck.

Panic began to flood my very being. I made a lurch forward, shoving him as hard as I could. It caught him so off guard that he stumbled backward.

"I see the kitten still has some fight about her."

"I do, and so do my friends!" I had heard them coming.

The residual effect of the fairy power was still with him. He had not even felt Corbin, Tanarr, and Zoul approaching.

"Your friends!" he said in a mocking tone.

"Yes, my friends," I said with my arms crossed. I gave a nod toward the men that were rapidly gaining ground on him.

"How did I let this happen?" he said more to himself than to me. He looked me in the eye. "We aren't through with this!" were his parting words as he took off like a bullet.

Tanarr started to follow him, but Corbin and Zoul stopped him.

"Now is not the time," Zoul said.

"Then when is? You know he was responsible for Navar's death," Tanarr turned his rage on Zoul. "He also killed Lera. If now is not the time, when is? Who else will have to die? We didn't think he would be so brave as to come back to Go-Brath, but he did. What would have happened if we had not been here, and he had gotten to Katelynn? Would it have been time then?" He threw his hands up and stomped the toe of his shoe into the ground in disgust. "We should have destroyed him that day in the counsel room. I knew he would try to get even with Navar," he turned to face us. I could see panic on his face. "Where is Calldoon? He will be next if we're not careful."

Corbin took him by both shoulders.

"Calm yourself, my friend; we won't let that happen. We'll keep an eye on him. For now, he is in the kitchen with Doulsie. She had some questions for him about the 'newfangled' stove, as she called it. We will warn him. I really don't think Blake will try anything with us all here."

"Oh, really?" Tanarr said with his hands on his hips. "Like he didn't try anything with Katelynn?"

"He wasn't trying to do anything. He had ample time to do whatever he wanted," Corbin said, looking at me with an apologetic smile. "He just enjoys terrorizing her."

"Well, I'm going to terrorize him," Tanarr said with more anger than I had ever heard from him.

"It's okay; our time will come," Zoul said.

Corbin dropped his arm around my still-shaking shoulders.

"It's okay; we're here," he said, giving me a little squeeze. I got as close to him as I could get. The four of us walked back to the castle, Corbin and I in the lead flanked by Zoul on one side and Tanarr on the other.

Chapter Twenty-Seven

Out in the garden, tucked into the shade of the old oak tree with his elbow against the now abandoned chair, stood Blake. Katelynn's book lay in the seat, long forgotten. Blake reached down and picked up the book. He rubbed his hand over the cover, then slowly he raised it to inhale her scent that had been absorbed by the pages.

"Katelynn, Katelynn, Katelynn, my pretty little tasty Katelynn. You will give me what I want; you will see. We can do this rough, or you can make it easy; it makes no difference to me. I will, however, need to catch you without your pets." He raised his chin. "That Tanarr has a nasty temper. Zoul, I just don't know about him. His kind of quiet makes me nervous. Sometimes the quiet ones are the most dangerous. What is it they say; still waters run deep? As for Corbin," he shivered. "He's one tough boy. I've dealt with him in the past. He's powerful and quick. I need to watch my back and every other side with him because not only is he powerful, but he's in love," he said, his voice dripping with sarcasm.

"Ha! What a waste of time and energy. Just take what you want and leave them lay," he said with a chuckle of disgust. He took the book that he held in his hand, ripped it in half, and threw it back on the chair. Looking back at the door that they all had disappeared through, he closed his eyes for a second and then slowly opened them.

"I will get you alone; then we'll see. Live or die; it's up to you. If they think that this old castle can protect you, yeah, right! Spell or no spell; what was it that wizard said?" he mocked. "Oh, yeah. He said, 'alive it will be, protect itself alone with all that it loves.' The castle can do little on its own; they can't be at her side at all times. As Navar found out, I'm quite good at being patient. All I have to do is keep an eye on her. They will mess up, and I'll be there like a cat on a mouse. What a game it will be! Slow and painful: just when she thinks she is going to escape, I'll drag her back, kicking and screaming," he rubbed his hands together. "I hope," he said with a wiggle of his eyebrows. "The little air attendant was way too easy; satisfying enough, but I like a little spice in my meal," he said with a nod of his head and a sinister smile.

The wind caught his shiny black hair; he ran his hand through it to put it back in its perfect place. The same breeze that played with his hair flirted with his shirt, which was unbuttoned almost to his waist. He raised his chin and closed his eyes, slowly, methodically dissecting each odor and each fragrance.

"All clear!" he laughed. "They didn't even check to see if I had left or not. Watch your backs, boys! Ask Navar; oh, wait, you can't. Why? Because he's dead, and who killed him? Let me see. I know the answer to that; it was ME!" He threw his head back and laughed. "He thought that the so-called 'cure' had made him invisible to us, that none of us would care, that we would just leave him to his perfect life with his lady love.

"The day I was forced to leave this place, I swore to myself that I would get even. It was all too easy; all I had to do was wait. Then, bonus! I get his lady love, too," he chuckled. "All I needed was patience! I knew that old Mrs. Jenkins would come in handy. I just didn't know how handy, and to think! I was just messing with her granddaughter, scoring brownie points as it were, doing whatever it took to make her feel obligated to me by being nice to granny. Who would have guessed that she would be roomed just down the hall from Navar's lady love, Lera? Sometimes I just get lucky.

"As for the granddaughter, if nothing else, she is good for some late-night entertainment. Pretty, young, and absolutely no scruples. Hmm...she might make a grand match for me," he smiled. "As I recall, she was only being nice to granny while she waited for her to kick off so she could claim her inheritance." Blake gave himself an evil little smile, for he was quite proud of himself. "I really did her a big favor; she will come to me like bees to honey. Did I really just say that? I think I've been dogging that...that Southern thing too long; I need to end this soon." He arched one eyebrow. "And so I shall, and I will enjoy it. All I have to do is wait; keep my eyes open. Then she will be all mine, or maybe I'll keep her and start my very own harem." He paused to think. "I think I like that thought." He laughed much louder than he had intended. Not wanting to get caught on the grounds again, he decided he better go. Before he turned to leave, he said with a nod toward the castle, "I'm here, and you can do nothing!" Then he was gone on the wind.

Chapter Twenty-Eight

Hiding among the roses, as still as a mouse, was Deireadh. She had heard every word, witnessed every threat. With her heart flying like the wings of a hummingbird, she backed up against the wall of the castle. She laid her face gently against the stone wall; in whispered tones so no one could hear her, she spoke.

"All right, be ye. Returned the dark one has, we will need to be keepin' a close watch over our Katelynn. I know that I should not be callin' her by her Christian name, taught I was not to speak so. I be knowin' that she be the Lord of us, and make her happy it does. I like to make her happy, feels like a friend she does. I've not known that feelin' in forever, and that's a long time." She pushed back from the wall, "I've been thinkin' about this; a plan I have. When ye see the dark one about, let me know ye must. Then what? I'll tell ye what. I know, I know, if I do not think that I can handle him, yes; I will be careful. If it will make me weaker, do nothing I will. I will be seekin' the help of, you know," she said behind her hand, not wanting anyone to hear what she was about to say. "Yes, it be Lord Navar's men. They be here and be one more with them. Aye, it is wonderful, I know. Tell me ye did that they be comin'," she walked along, running her hand against the great wall. Going away from the living quarters, she continued her conversation with the castle.

"Just one more thing be, then goin' back to me roses I must." She paused for a moment. "Two things there may be." She held up one finger. "First, Katelynn is more than we thought. Pretty she be, and smart, kind, witty, and oh! So quick on her feet! Not one thing gives her a fright, save spiders alone. This be where the assistance of ye be required. Please take care that not one be in her path, for that I will be thankin' ye." Now she was holding up two fingers. "Last, when ye know the dark one is about, tell me ye must, as quickly as ye can, for that one, up to no good he is. Scare me he does. Out to do our lady Lord harm he is. How do I know this, ye ask? Heard him I did, with me own ears I did. Threaten our lady Lord he did, mockin' ye, my friend. Sayin' things to the tune of how ye could not be stopping him, nothin' ye could do about him. I know," she said, patting the wall. "Show him we will, won't we? See he will." She started to walk away. "Wait, did she speak to ye about her room? Good, good. Did ye go for understanding? Aye, she speaks odd, aye, but I be getting used to her. Enjoy her company I am. Trust her we can. She will just love her new bathroom she will. For helping with everything I thank ye. All may not know what ye can do, ah, but they will."

Deireadh drew in her breath in surprise "Oooo...found it she did? Surprised was she to see no words on the pages there in. Ah, found the lock so neatly hidden. Told ye she be quick of wit, understanding upon how to use the key. Aye, wise beyond wise. This I knew she be. Stop not there, go on. In the pass did she, and find the secret room? I know, I need to get back to me work. Not till ye tell me all that is the rest. As soon as I know that which I do not, back to me roses I go." She sat on her knees facing the wall, waiting to hear the rest of the story. "Waiting I be. No, there be nothing to tell, into the hall she would not go. Told ye I did that she be afraid of spiders. That be a good idea. I do believe I be the first one to ask ye to get the spiders out." Deireadh patted the wall as she sat there. "When ye know anything more quickly ye shall be to let me know." She blew the castle a kiss. "I'll be goin' back to me roses for now."

Chapter Twenty-Nine

We were all gathered in the dining hall after the encounter with Blake. My nerves were completely shot. I began pacing around the room like a caged cat; Corbin fell in step with me.

"Are you all right?" he asked.

"Not really: that guy gets in my head and under my skin. He scares me worse than anything I can think of. Little prickles run up the back of my neck just at the mention of his name," I shivered.

Corbin stepped in front of me and put his hands on my shoulders to stop my pacing. He looked me in the eye.

"Katelynn, stop this. He's gone, and we are not going to let him get to you. Not physically or mentally, so don't you let him in, okay?" He put his hand to the side of my face. The next thing I knew, Tanarr and Zoul were standing on each side of me.

"He's right," Zoul said.

"Absolutely! We've got your back," Tanarr chimed in.

Corbin took both my hands in his and raised them to his lips.

"See? You're safe. We won't let him harm you. He is but one; we are five."

Tanarr looked at him with his crooked smile, with humor dancing in his sparkly green eyes.

"My friend, you've forgotten how to count. There is you, me, Zoul, and Calldoon; that makes four."

Never taking his eyes off mine, Corbin replied.

"Yes, you are right in your counting, but what you're not counting is her fairy."

Both Tanarr and Zoul stopped in their tracks.

"We suspected, but no one ever said for sure," Zoul said.

"Where—I mean, who is she?" Tanarr asked.

Corbin nodded to me.

"That is not mine to say. I do not have the right."

I looked at the three men standing around me, feeling a bit like I was on the witness stand; I took a step back and held up my hands.

"Now, guys, I'm not telling. I promised her. She said you would banish her. I told her I would not allow that to happen. She said I would be asking too much of you and that your fear would be too strong."

"Normally, she would be correct," Tanarr said.

"But these are not normal times, and we need her assistance," Zoul said as he leaned agents the fireplace.

"She can have her way with us, whatever that is." Tanarr paused. "By the way, what is her special talent?"

"She is a mind bender," I said.

Tanarr laughed nervously.

"That's just great, just great: a mind bender…great."

"Yes, it is great," Corbin said as he looked at me, "as long as you make her promise not to apply her skill to any of us four. If she will promise that, she won't break that promise; it is the fairy way, for most, anyway, that is. You may tell her that as long as she will promise, she is welcome among us. We will not harm her, nor will we ask her to leave, ever. She may stay and know that we are friends."

Tanarr stepped between Corbin and myself, speaking in hushed tones. I could barely hear their conversation.

"Corbin, have you lost your mind? If there is a fairy among us, you know what they have done to us. We all know what she is capable of. Are you sure of this?"

"I thought all the fairy were long gone," Zoul said.

Corbin shrugged.

"I did, too; she must be the last one."

No sooner were the words out of Corbin's mouth that Tanarr slowly turned to me.

"Deireadh, Deireadh," he said over and over.

"Yeah, we got it, Tanarr, the last one. We all speak Gaelic," Zoul said, rubbing his chin. "She still makes me nervous."

Tanarr turned all the way around.

"No. Deireadh: isn't that your lady maid's name?"

"So?" I said, trying to act like nothing was up, like he hadn't struck a chord.

He raised an eyebrow.

"Katelynn."

"What?" I said a little louder and with a little more irritation than I meant to show.

"Katelynn, tell us; is Deireadh the fairy? Tell us, please," Tanarr pleaded.

I dropped into the chair.

"No. Yes. Please don't make me break my promise!" I said with a quiver in my voice.

All heads turned toward the soft sound of someone clearing her throat. Deireadh had entered the room. There was complete silence; all anyone could hear was the soft rustle of her skirt as she glided across the room. She stopped between Corbin and me and took both my hands in hers.

"It will all be fine, m'lady. Tell them together we will."

"Tell them what?" the men clattered all at once when they finally found their voices.

I tried to push her behind me. She would have none of that. Instead we stood side by side. Deireadh spoke, addressing Corbin first.

"Yer declaration, heard it I did. Honest and good I believe ye to be. Look up to ye; most do. Do me no harm, this thing I believe ye to mean. I will in return do ye no harm, nor will I seek to entertain meself at yer cost." She turned to the other two men. "The same shall stand to ye both, if ye will honor what say he."

Both men nodded, and Tanarr stepped forward.

"I have not been this close to a fairy…ever." He smiled his crooked smile. "That I can remember, anyway" he said with complete wonder in his voice. He reached up to brush a stray hair from her face, and she flinched.

"I won't harm you. Know this; I do stand with Corbin. I always have, and yes, we will need to stand together to protect Katelynn." He took a deep breath. "May I say, you are the most beautiful thing I have ever seen, a true vision. Were all fairies as magnificently glorious as you?"

Deireadh covered her mouth and her giggle. She fluttered her stunning purple eyes.

"No, Sir Tanarr, for quite plain was I among the fairies, in face and talent."

"Wow!" I heard Tanarr say just under his breath.

"If a man could do so, happy he would be to live among the fairies," she giggled. "If remember he could."

Tanarr took a step back.

"Hey! You promised no fairy business."

She put her hand over her heart.

"That I did, keep it I will. Trust me ye all can."

She looked around the room.

"Where be Master Calldoon?"

Each looked at the other. Zoul turned toward the door.

"I think he's in the stable," Zoul said.

Deireadh stood on her tiptoes, peering out of the room like she could see all the way to the stables. Then she spoke as if she were talking to us, but she clearly was not.

"Yes, yes, there he be, of this ye be sure, I'll be thankin' ye," she said.

"I think so," Zoul said, a little confused by her statement, "and you're welcome."

Deireadh held up her hand to keep us all from saying anything more.

"Shh...I need to hear," she said.

We each looked at one another.

"Corbin, what is she talking about?" I whispered.

He only shrugged his shoulders. Deireadh continued on with her conversation.

"Be ye sure to be keepin' us knowin' if the dark one is about. If close he get to any of the ones we hold dear, let us know ye must, for this we all be thankin' ye." She turned her attention back to us. "Right ye be, for in danger he is not. She has said that he be in the kitchen with Doulsie." She gave Zoul a little finger wag. "In the stable he is not."

"Who is she?" Tanarr asked.

Deireadh held up both her hands. Slowly she turned to display the whole room.

"Herself," she said, "the lady of stone."

We all looked around, still not sure what she was talking about.

"Are you talking about the castle itself?" Tanarr asked.

She nodded.

"Hear her can ye not?"

We all shook our heads; Deireadh stepped in front of me. She took her finger and lifted my chin so we were eye to eye.

"Remember do ye, the very words that are all about me ring."

"I think so." I closed my eyes, trying my best to recall each word that circled the fairy stone. "That which is true, may only be true to whom it may appear." After reciting the verse, I opened my eyes and smiled. "Just because we can't hear her doesn't mean that she isn't talking."

Deireadh smiled back at me

"True words that ye have spoken, m'lady, for talkin' she is. Tell she does all that goes on in and about her gates. Loves all she does, cares more than most for all that she is in charge of."

I could see the light of remembrance come on in Tanarr's face.

"It's the gift from the old wizard," he said.

"Yes, correct that would be. Me father he was. We loved each one the other," Deireadh said, beaming with pride.

Tanarr walked around to face her.

"Did you say your father?"

She nodded her answer.

Tanarr looked deep into her eyes, preparing to ask her about her father. Or at least, I thought he was.

"Wow, you are amazing. It's in those eyes of yours; I think a man could be completely consumed in them."

"Only if I wish it," she replied.

He moved in a little closer.

"I might wish for that wish; it sounds like it could be fun." We could barely hear what he had said. I turned my face to hide my smile. I think he was flirting with her, and that was a good thing.

Corbin put his hand on Tanarr's shoulder, causing him to step back, trying to break the self-imposed spell that Tanarr had fallen into.

"Deireadh, how much does the castle tell you?" Corbin asked.

"Tells me all, she does."

"Let me get this straight. The castle can let you know if Blake comes back around?" Corbin asked.

She nodded.

"Did ye not listen? Ask her meself I did, and thanked her properly I did."

Corbin walked around the room for a moment then came back to Deireadh.

"Precisely how much can you control Blake?" he asked.

She looked down at her hands then back to me; it was almost like she was seeking my permission, or perhaps it was reassurance that she was needed. Either way, I reached out and took her hand.

"He will keep his word," I told her with a loving squeeze on her hand. "It's okay."

She looked back to Corbin.

"A mind bender be I. Not much of a power it is for a fairy, but control him I will. Wear off we all know it so does. Still, it does have its place to do as I please." She smiled a weak little smile. "However, a price there is to pay. Each time I use me power, in that amount weakens me life light it does."

"What do you mean, 'weakens' your life light?" Tanarr asked with his brows drawn in concern.

"It means only that it drains some of me very life powers within," she said with a sad smile.

"Are you telling us that using that kind of power will kill you?" Tanarr asked, taking a step closer to her.

She bowed her head and turned her back on us so that we could barely hear her next words.

"If that kind of power I use, in a good space of time, no longer will I be, for me time here will be all gone."

Tanarr whipped back around to us, his voice strained with concern.

"We can't let that happen!" he said.

"And we won't," Corbin said.

Tanarr walked over to Deireadh and put his hands on her shoulders, gently pulling her back against his chest.

"We won't let anything happen to you, either," he said.

She leaned her head back against his chest, closed her eyes, and smiled.

"So very pleasant it be, for a long time it has been since someone cared for me. Me heart thanks ye. It thanks ye all," she said without opening her eyes.

Corbin propped his hip on the edge of the table. He sat there rubbing his chin and thinking.

"Deireadh, how much can the castle help us? What is she really capable of?" She shook her head.

"Know that I do not. Only she will know," she said, nodding toward me.

This caught me completely off guard. My mouth gaped, and all eyes were now on me.

"Katelynn, what is she talking about?" Corbin inquired.

"I have no earthly idea," I said with a confused shake of my head.

Deireadh turned to me.

"Told me she did, the book ye found."

I blinked a few times.

"What book?"

"The book," she said with a nod. "Remember ye must. *The Truths of Those That Be* the name shall be."

"Oh, that book!" I confessed. By now, everyone was looking at me, waiting to hear what I was going to say. I leaned close to Deireadh and whispered, "But there were no words in it." She only looked at me. "Really, there was nothing in it; it was blank."

"As it should be, for the words are in you," she said.

I gave her one more blank look because I was really confused.

"What?" I said with a shake of my head.

"For know I do that the lock was also found. With the knowledge that ye have, ye used the key; the path was opened to ye."

"Wait, how did you know all of this?" I asked.

"She told me. She always tells me all," Deireadh shook her head. "She told me that enter ye would not."

I started to protest the fact that there may have been spiders in there.

"Hey, wait, she who?" I asked.

"Again must I say, listening were ye not? For the one of whom we speak is herself, Go Brath."

"Go Brath...," we all repeated softly after her.

I turned toward Corbin and made a face then mouthed, "What is she talking about?"

"I think she's talking about that book and that dark hallway you found. You know, the possible spider cave," he whispered with a wiggle of his brows.

I gave him a playful backhand to the stomach as I turned back to Deireadh.

"What am I supposed to do with a book with no words in it and a long, dark, possibly spider-infested hallway? In my defense, a person can't read a book with no words, and I really, really don't like spiders," I said with my hands on my hips.

"You'll not have to be worryin' about the wee little spiders or the big ones, either. A chat I had, about the creatures, with herself I did. Told me she did, no more bothered will ye be." She stopped and looked at each man like she expected them to know what she was about to say. Her purple eyes at last landed on me.

"Ye be the key."

"I know," I said as I pulled Navar's ring out of my blouse where I kept it safely tucked away in my not so ample cleavage. As I retrieved the ring on its gold chain, Corbin leaned close to my ear.

"Lucky ring," he whispered.

I gave him a good Southern eye flutter and mouthed back, only for him to see, "oh, yes it is," then I gave him a wink. "See?" I said so the others could hear. "I keep the key with me at all times."

"No, no, no," Deireadh said with a little frustration in her voice and a shake of her head. "Ye are the key," she said, this time cupping my chin in her hand.

I shook my head.

"I'm sorry, but I don't understand."

She reached for Navar's ring that still was around my neck. She had the ring on the end of her finger, giving it a good once over.

"I've not seen this for a long time." She held the ring up between us. "The key this be to the door; the key to the rest, be you."

"I still don't get it; you must think that I'm dumber than a sack of rocks. I really am trying," I said.

She took me by the hand.

"Come with me ye must; show ye I will." She motioned for Corbin to follow. "Come ye must, for need ye we will."

"Me?" Corbin asked.

"Yes, and all the rest, come ye may. I must remember all, a while it has been since the Room of Truth I have been there; make it work I hope we can."

We all fell in behind her like a carnival caravan. None of us knew where we were going or why.

Chapter Thirty

When the caravan arrived at our destination, we were standing in the center of the library. *I'm still not sure why we are here other than we have followed a fairy who seems to know something that the rest of us do not.*

"Okay, Deireadh, we're all here; now what?" I said. I knew she had something in mind; I just didn't know what.

"Get the book down, now ye must," she said.

"Okay…," I said as I reached for the empty book.

I took the book in both hands, gently placing it on the table. Slowly and with much care, I opened the ancient book to expose the empty pages. Each of the trusted men stepped forward to examine them. Tanarr was the first to speak, looking over Deireadh's shoulders. It seemed that he was taking every opportunity to be close to her. I did hope she kept her word; he'd been hurt enough. With his crooked smile and that twinkle in his eye he said, "Yep, it's blank all right."

"'Tis only for now," Deireadh said.

Tanarr rubbed his hands together.

"Do we get to fill it in? I always fancied myself a writer."

She ran her glittery fingers over the still empty pages. Never taking her eyes off the book, she spoke in almost mystic tones.

"She will fill in herself."

I turned my head to the side and looked up at Corbin from under my lashes.

"Is she serious?" I whispered.

He gave a short chuckle.

"I think she is."

I didn't think she was paying any attention to us, but I was wrong. "That I am. See ye will," she said.

Deireadh turned back to the slot where the book had been resting undisturbed for years.

"Now, m'lady, the time she is here. If so kind ye would be, the unlocking of the passage is at hand. Only ye this can do."

"All right, I can do that," I said, dragging the chair over to the edge of the bookcase. It was the same chair I had used earlier.

"You know, I could have lifted you up there quite easily," Corbin said while he held the back of the chair to keep it from getting away from me.

"I know," I said, reaching up to get the ring in place, "but you know how I like to do things for myself."

"We know!" they all replied in unison. I stopped what I was doing and turned. From my lofty perch, I gave them all a disapproving hmm!

"Thinkin' they are right, I am. To put a pillow on ye bed, this ye not even allowed meself to do." She put her finger to the side of her mouth. "Said ye did, there be no one but yerself to be knowin' the place to be puttin'. Ye like them to be bein' the way ye like them, takin' care of things, self alone ye could do."

"Okay, so maybe some people might call me a little stubborn," I said as I leaned back into the bookcase to complete my task.

"A little stubborn?!" I heard Corbin say.

"Hey! I heard that; I prefer to call it self-reliance," I said as I went on with my work. I heard Deireadh giggle. I didn't say a word, only shook my head. *I know how I am, and so do they; that's okay. It's easier when we all know where we stand, and yeah, I do like to do for myself.* "Someone hand me a flashlight, please; it's in the bottom drawer."

Tanarr reached in the drawer, retrieved the light, and handed it back up to me.

"Do you need anything else?"

"Nah, that's it; it's just a little hard to see how to line everything up without a little light."

I put the light between my teeth so I could steady myself with one hand and manipulate the ring with the other. I felt the ring go into place and gave it a little turn. I heard the lock disengage, followed by the soft whoosh of cool air as the bookcase to the side of Tanarr lurched forward just enough to expose the finger holds in the side of the case. Tanarr jumped.

"What on earth?" he said.

Deireadh stepped forward, tucking her long, sparkly fingers into the finger holds on the side of the case.

"'Tis but the pathway of truth." I could hear the wonder and awe mixed with the love and respect that she felt for this place in her voice, which was both reassuring and disturbing. *What have I gotten myself into? Am I putting too much trust in beings that only a short time ago I would have scoffed at, that I would have thought to be nothing more than Hollywood smoke and mirrors?* Still, here I was, willing to be led by creatures of mythology, fairy tales, or maybe nightmares, depending on your dreams. I had come to trust these people; heck fire, they had saved my hide more times than I could count. I loved them like family. I looked up at Corbin standing beside me. And some of them I loved a little more than family. I couldn't resist giving his hand a little squeeze. He smiled and squeezed my hand back.

Deireadh's soft voice broke the spell.

"See here ye must but put one's finger in the slot. Only a small tug is all that ye needs be." She did as she told us, and the case slide open just as it had for me.

There we all stood looking down this long dark hall. None of us wanted to be the first to step in. Deireadh fearlessly took the lead.

"Meself ye shall follow," she said, leading us into the pitch-black, dark hall. About the time we were all in the hall and it was getting really dark, I snapped my fingers.

"Oh, shoot! Wait, guys; let me go get the flashlight."

"No, for that there will be no need," I heard Deireadh say.

"Oh, yes there is," I said with a little more force than I meant. "There is no way I'm going anywhere this place leads to in the dark without a light, not even with all you guys at my side. That is just not going to happen…," my words fell off at the sight of Deireadh. She had begun to glow, just like she was that night when I first saw her wings in the forest.

"Truly 'tis no need be," she said.

"Well, I can see that," I said. I ran around in front of her and threw my hand up like a crossing guard, causing everyone to come to a screeching halt. "Now, wait just one doggone minute, will this…," I waved my hand up and down the length of her, "this, this fairy glowstick trick mess with your powers? You know, drain your life power?" I gave my eyes a roll. "Or whatever you call it. 'Cause if it will, I'm going after the flashlight. Flashlight batteries can be replaced easy enough, but you, not so easy."

"M'lady, harm me it will not; part of what I be it is. I can glow as it pleases meself," she said.

"Like a dang jar of fireflies, the lot of them were," Zoul said with a smile of memory.

She gave me a nod.

"Thank ye I do for yer carin'."

"I was going for the flashlight if she wasn't," Tanarr said.

"Oh?" Deireadh said with a twinkle in her eyes and a smile tugging at the corners of her perfect lips. "Do ye get a fright from spiders also?"

We all tried to hide the laughter; it started as a big smile that I attempted to conceal behind my hand. Zoul turned his face toward the darkest part of the hall, but I could see his shoulders shaking with suppressed laughter. Corbin, on the other hand, threw his head back and let it roll, a deep, rich laughter that filled the empty corridor, resounding off the walls like thunder.

Poor Tanarr stood there looking at us like he wanted to wring our collective necks.

"What?" he said out of frustration. "You all know I'm not afraid of little spiders! I was only thinking of Deireadh. I didn't want her harmed for our sakes either."

That statement only invoked another bout of laughter. With a huff of defeat, he rolled his eyes at us and gave his head a shake. Deireadh stepped forward and brushed his face with her long sparkly fingers that glowed as richly as the rest of her did.

"Thankin' ye I will that care for me ye do," she said with a flutter of her purple eyes. She leaned in and gave him a light kiss on the cheek.

Tanarr swallowed hard and cleared his throat then slowly took her hand and raised it to his lips. There, just on the edge of her knuckles, he placed a soft kiss.

"You are so very welcome, our beautiful firefly."

Zoul let out a low rumble of a chuckle and gave Tanarr a hard slap on the back.

"Smooth move, boy, smooth, but for now we do have other matters at hand. So if you don't mind, Romeo, can we please get on with this?" Zoul gave a deep bow and motioned for him to proceed. "Please. I, for one, would like to see what is at the end of this hall."

With a flutter of her purple eyes, Deireadh took the lead. She seemed to know what lay ahead, and the fact that she was our light made her a perfect guide.

All the way down the hall my mind kept racing. What would be at the end of this hall? What did she mean when she said that I was the key to the rest, and why did she want Corbin to come? I was so lost in my thoughts that I plowed right into Corbin's back when everyone stopped except for me.

"Whoa, did you see a spider, or am I just getting lucky, 'cause I'm good either way," he whispered over his shoulder. To that I gave his butt a good pinch. "Ooooh! I'm good with that, too!"

"Arrr...stop that!" I whispered. "Why did we stop?"

"I'm not sure; Deireadh stopped, so we did, too," he replied.

Deireadh turned, reached back between the men, and took my hand.

"Up here ye are needed, up here ye are, m'lady. Sir Corbin, yer presence will be needed, among us ye be."

Ever since we started this journey, she had been calling us by our formal titles. At this point I let it go. She must have felt the need to do so, and I wasn't feeling brave enough to challenge her on it.

With one hand on the door handle, she gathered both our hands in the other. She looked at the door before her then back at us.

"Ready be ye, for the knowin' on the other side be."

I looked at Corbin and gave him a wink. I took a deep breath, exhaled slowly, and gave her a nod. She turned the handle and gave it a gentle push. The door opened with ease like it had been waiting for us.

As soon as we entered the small chapel, Deireadh stopped glowing. There was no need, for the room itself seemed to be well lit. The walls were made of beautiful stained glass; peaceful countryside scenes played out on each panel. The tops arched into clear glass, allowing sunlight to spill in. The window seals were mirrored in a mosaic style all around the small room, magnifying the light and giving off as much light as electric lights would have produced. The only thing in the room was a large carved table. The legs of the table looked like lion's legs, with the muscles rippling and claws extended. They were powerful lion's legs. The top of the table had mirrors. I was sure that it had been designed like that to take even more advantage of every last ray of sunlight.

"If ye would be placin' the book here," Deireadh said as she patted the center of the table.

I had been so engrossed in where we were that I had forgotten why we were here and that I even had a book.

"Oh, oh, the book! Okay, the book, I've got it. But I don't understand what good a book with no words in it can be. I don't see how it can help."

"In time, m'lady, shall be revealed, see ye will," she said as we placed the book in the center of the table.

"Okay, now what?" I asked.

Never taking her eyes off the book, she placed Corbin's hand on the lower edge. "Ye here," she said, placing my hand next on the other edge. "If havin' this right I be, me own be havin' me place here," she said, putting her hands on the top edge.

"Welcome back, Sir Corbin, and welcome home, m'lady!"

The collective intake of breath was so sharp that we almost sucked all the air out of the room. I jerked my hand off the book.

"Did you hear that?" I said in wide-eyed panic.

Everyone in the room nodded. Tanarr put his hand to his forehead.

"Or at least I think I did; it was more in my head and not in my ears."

A wide smile spread over Deireadh's face.

"Right ye be, Sir Tanarr, for in ye head it be. Talk to ye she does without speakin'."

"Do you mean that we are getting all this telepathically?" Tanarr asked.

"Yes," she said with a nod. "Remember I do for the first time ever in her time spoke she has to other than the three." She hooked her finger under his chin. "Last time this will not be that hear ye will her sweet sound in yer head: a true gift it be. Special the two of ye are," She turned back to me. "Now, m'lady, open the great book; any question speak ye therein. Find it ye will, only ask." She laid her hand on top of the book and gave it a little pat. "Answer she so will."

I started to do as she had asked, but just before my fingertips touched the book I stopped and held up my hand.

"Hold it. Why do we need the book if the castle can talk to us telepathically? This seems like a waste of time," I said. More than anything else, I was stalling; I wasn't sure that I wanted to know what my part in this play was. If I had a power or a gift, I didn't know if I wanted it. And if I stepped through this door, could I get back? Sometimes I felt like Alice in Wonderland.

Deireadh stopped and squared her shoulders. I could almost see the wheels turning in her head as she tried to give her best argument on why I should do this her way, the castle's way.

"Ever have had a whisper told in yer ear, secret for no other to hear?"

"Sure," I said with a nod.

"Every word, clear to yer understandin' could it be? Know what ye need to have knowledge did ye?" she asked.

"Not always. Sometimes the words are so quiet that you can't hear what they are saying," I answered.

Deireadh gave a nod and a smile.

"Why that be, have the book we do, some things," she waved her hand, "much too important, be they. Every word must be heard by yer eye, then know ye will."

"Okay, I get that. If you see it in print, you are less likely to get it wrong, but why did you need Corbin and me at this point? And why us three?" I asked.

"Open the book," was all she said.

So I did just as she asked. I opened the book.

"Ask," she said with a nod toward the book.

"Okay…why are Corbin and I here with Deireadh?" I issued my question, turned the page. There, where there had been no words, this flowing script appeared in answer:

Katelynn, you ask a good question. The answer, the reason for the three:

The fairy: she brings the spirit of us here.

The vampire: he brings respect of the one that began us all with the building of us.

You: you stand for the wizard, the life to me.

And yes it can only be the three of you for many reasons. The fairy knows all the secrets because of who her father was; she will need to be with us always. She is the spirit: the very spark of life.

The vampire holds the balance of justice, honor, and death, for everything as sure as it begins must end in cold, white death. He loves you and respects the fairy; he is a good man.

Then you, the wizard: you hold life, warm life: breathing, loving life. You love the vampire, the fairy, and all who dwell herein. However one cannot be without the other; the three of you make one.

I looked up and smiled at all of them.

"I have another question for you," I said.

"Go ahead," I heard her say. I smiled and nodded.

"What of our two dear friends who stand here before us?" I turned the page, and there in the same script was my answer.

They are good men with strong hearts; to them I bequeath a special gift. They may speak with me and I with them; we will watch over all who abide. However, they may not seek me within the pages of this book, for it is only for the three.

Suddenly, all heads whipped toward the door, the book long forgotten.

"Are you sure?" Tanarr asked.

"Let's go!" Corbin said as the three men took off.

We had all heard it. The castle had spoken; Calldoon was in trouble.

"Thank ye," Deireadh said softly; she was thanking the castle. I took her by the hand.

"Do you think we will make it in time?"

"Their best they will do," she replied.

Chapter Thirty-One

We followed close behind the men, making our way to the stable as quickly as possible, or at least as fast as a fairy can go while being slowed down by a human. Never once did Deireadh get even one step ahead of me, even though I knew she could easily keep up with the men.

As soon as we entered the stable, we saw the men standing at the far end. We made our way to them quickly. Deireadh went straight to stand with Tanarr, and I by Corbin.

"What happened?" I asked. I could tell by the look on their faces that something was wrong. Intense anger mixed with fear and frustration was spread across each man's face, although the look on Calldoon's face was a little more fear than anything else. I repeated myself, but this time I turned the volume up and softly asked my question.

"What happened? Is everyone all right?" I asked again.

Corbin was the first to speak.

"It was Blake; he was here."

"Blake!" I almost whispered. My Grandma warned us not to speak of evil things, for they could appear. She said never to invoke the presence of evil. That statement got my attention, and I held to it.

"The dark one," Deireadh said in the same tone.

Slowly I turned to each man, looking for answers in their eyes.

"What was he doing here?" I asked, still searching their faces.

"The castle was right; Calldoon was in trouble." Tanarr said as his hand landed firmly on Calldoon's shoulder.

"As for what he was doing here," Calldoon looked from one to the other. When his eyes came to rest on me, he finished his statement. "I think he be here for the both of us."

I swallowed hard and took a step closer to Corbin.

"What makes you say that?" I asked.

Calldoon started to pace. As he paced, he began to tell us what had happened.

"Blake came in, catchin' me off guard, I bein' by meself with no one about save the horses, as it were. He began to circle me. As he did, he said that there be only four people left that he had a score to settle with: two being Sir Corbin and Sir Tanarr for them not joining him. But they did not seem to concern him at this moment, for he said he would have all things in due time. Ah, but you and meself: the two of us he be havin' a true hate for; loathed us, he said. You for rejecting him: he said you'd not be doing that for much longer. And as for that cursed cure ye have inherited, ye could do not one person any good with it when he finished with ye."

I began to tremble as I scrunched up even closer to Corbin; this was a little more than I cared to deal with. *What if he gets to me?*

Calldoon began to slow his pacing until he came to a full stop in front of us. He laid his hand on his chest.

"As for meself, he said I was the very next one on his list: that I was the true reason for his bein' banished. Had I kept my mouth shut or, even better yet, had I joined him, he would have been Lord of herself. This castle would have been his; he would have been a god," Calldoon said as he closed his eyes and shook his head.

I couldn't help but cringe at the thought of the tyrant Blake would have been on humanity with that kind of power.

Calldoon turned his head, looking off at something or possibly nothing while he gathered his thoughts. When he spoke again, his voice was softer than before.

"He said he would make good on his old promise." He closed his eyes at the memory. "That night when he was forced out of the castle, as he passed by meself he told me that he would get me; that I had better watch me back." He took a deep breath. "Tonight he said something about a ring."

At the mention of this ring I saw the expression change on Zoul's face. I'm not sure what that was about, but I was sure that I would try to find out.

Calldoon shook his head.

"The next thing I knew, here ye all stand, and he is gone."

I stepped forward, placing my hand on his arm. I was trying to let him know that we were here for him now and always.

"Are you all right?" I asked.

Calldoon looked down at me with a smile.

"Perhaps a wee bit worse for the wear but unscathed. I thank ye for yer concern." He raised his head and his voice. "And speaking of that, I thank you all for arriving when ye did. I don't know what would have come of me had ye not showed up as ye did. How on earth was it that ye knew I was in need of yer assistance?"

"Well," Zoul said with a slow shrug of his shoulders and a deep chuckle, "Now that's an odd story: one that I'm not sure anyone will believe. I don't know if I believe it!" Calldoon gave him an odd look, tilting his head to the side.

"This was definitely not something we saw coming. We'll fill you in on the way back to the castle," Tanarr said.

Tanarr and Corbin told Calldoon everything we had witnessed, from the book with no words to a fairy that served as flashlight all the way to the heart of a big old castle that talked to us.

I fell in step with Zoul. I slowed my pace and so did he, just as I had hoped. When there was a little distance between us and the others, I couldn't wait any longer.

"Zoul, may I ask you a question?"

"Sure, pretty little lady; anything I can help you with? Fire at will," Zoul said in that easy way of his like an old cowboy just off the round up. He may have been from the Amazon, but he loved the old west and the old west ways. I must admit he wore them well.

"When Calldoon mentioned the ring, I saw something in your face that was not on the others' faces. Am I looking for something that's not there, or do you know something that the rest don't? I know it's none of my business, and you don't have to tell me," I said, giving him a way out if he really didn't want to tell me.

Zoul tilted his chin to the side, looking me in the eye to let me know that he was not holding anything back.

"It may be nothing at all; it's something I remember from ancient times," he said. Zoul stopped, looking off into the distance of time.

"And…?" I said, encouraging him to go on.

"As I recall, there is a ring, forged from the purest of gold at the request of my father, the king. It was made by the hands of the Great One, a gift to the High Priest of the kee-nan-twa. This ring holds the pure nectar, the very life's blood of the orchid; it holds the exact amount to deliver swift death, no escape. My father told me of this ring with his warning that if I were to ever return to the village, he himself would use the ring." Zoul said with a little worry in his face. "I thought it was only a myth: a story made up to keep me away. But maybe it's real after all."

"Do you know who we can talk to about this ring?" I asked.

He ran his hand through his thick gold hair.

"Only one, and I'll have to think on that one for a while."

By now we had all arrived at the castle, and I could tell that he was done talking about this for now.

We gathered in the dining hall. Calldoon turned to Corbin and pointed over his shoulder in the direction of Deireadh. He very softly asked; it was more like a statement.

"I'll be thinkin' that the crazy rose girl is not so crazy after all, if all that ye be tellin' me is true, and this old pile of rocks really does talk."

Corbin smiled and nodded.

"She doesn't like it when you call her that," Corbin stopped. "She… thinks…it's very disrespectful of you to make fun of her in that manner."

"Well, in that case," Calldoon said at the top of his voice. "I be so very sorry, and I'll not be doin' that again."

"Apology accepted," we all said in unison.

Calldoon shook his head and threw his hands up in the air.

"Great, just what I be needin': five of ye talking to the walls!"

About that time my stomach made itself known with a very loud and long growl. It had decided to make me acknowledge its presence and the fact that I had ignored it ever since breakfast. It was now about 6:00 P.M., which meant dinner time according to my stomach.

All eyes turned to me as my stomach let out another loud ode to hunger.

"Did you hear that? I think she has swallowed a lion, and he wants out," Zoul said with humor tugging at the edges of his lips.

"No, no, I think that perhaps our fair lady may be turning into a bear from the inside out," Tanarr said with that crooked smile and a twinkle in his eye. They all laughed.

I looked up to see Ms. Doulsie arriving with a large tray of wonderful smelling hot food in one hand and a large wooden spoon in the other. She wielded that spoon like a knight with a broadsword headed into battle.

"Ms. Doulsie, you never deliver food. I feel quite special tonight. Thank you!" I said with a smile.

She placed the tray in front of me; I inhaled deeply as the aroma whirled around my head, making my mouth water.

"This smells fan-tas-tic," I said, rubbing my hands together.

"Ye be right about me cartin' food about; I've no time to be chasin' the likes of ye about to see that ye be takin' yer nourishment, but," she said, raising her spoon to make her point, "when ye did not show up for yer midday meal, I begun to be gettin' a wee bit worried about ye." She turned and whacked Corbin on the shoulder with her spoon. "Shame on ye for keepin' the child out all day and not lettin' her have even a crust of bread, shame! Do ye not see that the child is starving, hmm!" She turned back to me and patted me on the head. "I'll be headin' back to me kitchen. If ye be needin' any little thing, the boy will be back out to check on ye. Eat all ye want; there be more if ye like," she gave us a nod as she headed back to her kitchen.

Halfway through my meal, with my stomach pacified, the thought occurred to me that Ms. Doulsie was not the least bit surprised that the men were not being served any food, even though they had been out with me all day. Would it not have made sense to have brought everyone food? Isn't that odd? I wondered if she knew what they were or if her concern was only for me? She was a sweet little old lady, but she was also one smart cookie, so this could go either way. One thing was for sure and certain; I would be checking into this; after all, we did have our bread baking date tomorrow. Or had that been today? "Oh, shoot!" I said just under my breath.

"Something wrong?" Corbin asked as he reached for my hand.

"No. Yes. I just remembered something, I think; something I was supposed to do," I said.

"What?" Corbin inquired.

"I think that Ms. Doulsie was going to teach me how to make her wonderful bread today," I said, scrunching up my face.

Deireadh clapped her hands together.

"Oooh, great fun it sounds to be."

"Would you like to join us? I'm sure Ms. Doulsie wouldn't mind, that is, if she doesn't want to wring my neck for not showing up today. I'll find her after dinner and beg her forgiveness, then I'll see if we can both come tomorrow." I said.

"If ye do not be mindin', enjoy I would; great fun it should be," Deireadh said with a smile and a nod.

I took a big scoop of creamy potatoes.

"It's a date, or at least I think it is."

After I had all but licked my plate clean, one of the kitchen staff came in to clear the dishes and brought me my big cup of coffee. Everyone began to calm down and settle in for the evening. The air was filled with pleasant, light-hearted conversation. I sat sipping my coffee, listing to them all discuss the events of the day, but not one person was willing to bring up what had happen in the stable. It seemed that everyone was happy to forget that Blake had sneaked past us all, that he could get that close. Had it not been for the castle's warning, this could have been a much different gathering. For now, it felt so nice to be safe in the presence of all these strong ones, behind this fortress of stone and spirit, for she had truly proved herself to us all, or at least to we five.

Before long the day had begun to catch up with me. I was full, warm, and, unlike the vampires or the fairy, I did need rest. I covered my mouth to suppress a lazy yawn. Tanarr looked up from their conversation.

"It appears that we should be calling it a night; I think our host may need her rest."

I held up my hand.

"Oh, no, please don't leave. You all stay, enjoy each other's company. But I do think I will call it a night. I am kind of tired." Corbin stood as I did.

"May I see you to your room?" he asked like the gentleman that he was. I reached over and gave him a kiss on the cheek.

"Thank you, but I'll be fine. You stay here with your friends. I'm going to pop into the kitchen and see if I can find Doulsie, see if we can do the bread-making thing tomorrow."

"Are you sure? You know I love to walk with you."

"I'm sure," I said giving his hand a squeeze before I turned to say my good-nights to everyone else.

Chapter Thirty-Two

The kitchen, home and hearth: everyone knew that the kitchen was the very heart and soul of any house. When I stepped through the door, the smells whirled around my head and tugged at my heart. A smile spread across my face: a smile brought on by memories of my childhood because the kitchen always reminded me of my grandmother. If I closed my eyes and stood here with all the smells and sounds, I could almost see her puttering around in her kitchen, all five feet of her. She used to be taller, but time had worn on her, and she had begun to shrink. However, this was only in height; she was ten feet tall in spirit.

She was the sweetest little person in the world. She always wore her silver hair up in little braids that crossed over the top of her head. She had these crazy glasses; I think she called them cat-eye frames. They were black with little fake stones in the top corners. She said she loved them; they made her feel so chic. As a kid I thought they just looked a little funny, but that thought I kept to myself. I don't think I ever saw her without an apron on; it was part of who she was. They were always clean and freshly pressed; she must have had a million of them.

There she would be working away in her kitchen, making her famous sticky buns. The smell of cinnamon, butter, and vanilla wrapped itself around me like a warm embrace that said, "Welcome home!" I could still hear her say, "It's all in the vanilla, that's the secret: good vanilla." We would make a big pan full of them, and while they were still piping hot, we would take a basketful over to Pastor John's house.

He had been the pastor of our home church for as long as I could remember. Everyone loved him. He was short and stout with thinning gray hair and a heart as big as the heavens; he always smelled of Old Spice and peppermint. He had a kind word for everyone he met, and everyone he met had a kind word about him.

Grandma and I would pack that backseat with every sticky bun except for two, leaving one for her and one for me. She would set them on a saucer and put that saucer on the back of the stove. After we returned from Pastor John's home, we would take our wonderful sticky buns along with a tall glass of ice-cold milk and go out onto the front steps. There we would sit, enjoying our tasty treat. We shared much more than those sticky buns; we shared secrets, dreams, sometimes fears, and always giggles. The birds would be singing in the trees. The wind would come whispering across the fields and around the corner of the house, playing with the edges of my hair. This was one of my most favorite memories of my sweet Grandma Annie.

A sharp pain of loss hit my heart. I had to fight back tears. I missed my Grandma Annie. She meant the world to me. I stayed with her till the end; for a short time, I became her constant companion and nurse. I loved her so much. It was quite painful to watch her melt away. Still, through that pain came a strength that I didn't know I possessed, and it brought out a love for nursing that I didn't know was there.

When my Grandma Annie passed away, she left what little she had to me with the request that I go back to school to pursue my newfound strength. Who would have guessed that her small gift would have brought me to all this? Without my nursing degree, I could have never gone to New York or been Ms. Lera's nurse. What a gift she had given me! "Thank you, Grandma. I love you," I whispered.

I couldn't say thank you to Grandma without saying thank you to Ms. Lera, my surrogate grandmother. I now knew that she had planned for my coming to her in New York. She knew things about me that I didn't know about myself. I only wished that I had had more time with her. I was also truly grateful for the time we had and for all she did for me and all she left me with. "Thank you, Ms. Lera. I love you."

Ms. Doulsie was quite easy to spot standing there with her back to the world, concentrating on her newest pot of wonderful for the next day and all the while humming an old Scottish pub song. Trying so very hard not to frighten her, I made as much noise as I could. I even called her name twice, but there was still no response. By now I was at her back.

"Ms. Doulsie?" I softly called her name. She jumped and squealed. Her wooden spoon went flying into the air. A long stream of red sauce came off it like the tail of a comet, and the spoon clattered to the floor. Ms. Doulsie spun on me with fire in her eyes. Before she had the chance to say a word, I began to sputter my apology while scrambling for her spoon and trying to grab a dishcloth to mop up the mess left by the crash. I heard her heartfelt laughter just over my head.

"Ah…child, whatcha doin' down there?" she said, reaching down to help me up. "There be people to do such as that." Her eyes had quickly regained their spark of love.

"I'm so sorry! I didn't mean to scare you," I said.

She let out her little laugh that sounded much like a mother hen clucking for her chicks.

"Oh…child, ye did not scare me, ye did but catch me with me guard down." She pulled a small earphone from her ear. The tiny cord ran down into her apron pocket. She reached her pudgy little hand into the pocket and pulled out a pink iPod. She laughed. "'Tis but a wee gift from one of the kitchen girls," she put her hand to her forehead. "How is it she be putting it? Ah, yes! I do believe the child said I rocked, and I needed something to be rockin' with. It truly is a thing of wonder," she said, handing me the small earpiece. I took it and gave it a good once over.

She nodded for me to listen. "Go 'head; you'll not be believin' whatcha can hear in such a small thing." I did as she asked, thinking that there would be some old classic orchestra or even a beloved hymn. To my surprise, there blaring, and I do mean blaring, in the small earpiece was none other than Britney Spears.

"She is right; you do rock, and so does this," I said. With one earpiece in my ear and the other in hers, we both began dancing around the kitchen through the whole song. Ms. Doulsie pulled the earpiece out and held it up.

"This stuff will be me undoin'! Can't help it, for I be lovin' it!" She plopped down on the stool. "See, it was only that I did not see ye comin', and ye gave me quite a start. I'd be thinking that me time was up and the saints had come to collect me for listening to such in me ears!" She threw her head back and laughed. "Quite a relief it be to know it be only yerself, the Lord of our castle. Now, here, child, have a seat right here." She patted the stool at her side. "Ye can sit here whilst ye tell me what has brought ye this way."

I took the seat offered me.

"Ms. Doulsie, I am sorry that I scared you."

"Ye need to be lettin' that go. As the young ones would say, it's all good," she said with a giggle, taking my chin in her chubby hand and giving it a little shake then flicking the end of my nose with her finger. "Ye be so sweet that I could just eat ye right up with a spoon. Why, I can see why yer young man has set his cap for ye!" She walked over, poured a large mug of coffee, and set it on the counter beside me.

I slipped my fingers through the handle and wrapped my hand around it. I raised it to my lips and took a small sip then placed it back on the counter. I was staring down into the wonderful dark liquid wondering how to approach the question that keep tugging at my brain. It was the same question that was playing on the tip of my tongue.

"Penny for yer thoughts?" I heard Ms. Doulsie ask softly.

I looked up into her soft green eyes with her little glasses perched on the end of her nose.

"Ms. Doulsie…may I ask you something?"

"Sure, but first, come with me. I need but a few sprigs of me herbs for the sauce," she said with a nod toward the door as she gathered her basket and snips.

"But it's dark! And besides, couldn't one of the other kitchen staff do that?" I said.

"True, they could, but ye do know we have a sturdy light out back at the garden. Ye know that be the best place to share all our secrets," she said with a wink. I winked back and followed her out the door.

It was getting late, so we knew that our time would be limited. The outside light was pretty bright, but we still couldn't see to pick all the herbs we wanted. We were only able to pick a few of the top leaves that we gently laid in her basket.

After that, Ms. Doulsie set her basket down on the little bench.

"Now, child, what did ye have on yer mind?"

I took a deep breath, not knowing just where to start. There was no place to start like the beginning. *Plain talk is easiest understood*, I thought.

"Well, Ms. Doulsie, I was just wondering why you were not the least bit surprised that the men didn't eat with me?"

She stammered around for a bit, saying things like they never do; I, I, I did not know they be with ye; and besides that, ye be the only one I should be worried about, anyway. They all be big boys; they can care for themselves. Through her whole speech, she never looked me in the eye. I finally stopped her tale by clearing my throat and looking her straight in the eye.

"All right, fine," she said as she took a defiant seat by her herb basket. "Have it yer way. I never was very good at story tellin'. Never needed to be the teller of them till now," she said, patting the bench on the other side of her basket. "Have yerself a seat here; I'll be tellin' ye all ye want to know. For I know none of it will be of any surprise to ye."

"You know all about them, don't you?" I said as I took the seat offered me.

She lifted her chin and closed her eyes.

"If ye be meanin', do I know what they are, that I do." She slowly opened her eyes and turned her face to meet mine. "They be trusted friends, caretakers of all me hold dear. They be guardians of those who be of need, knights of Go-Brath." She leaned in and lowered her voice to a whisper, "and they be vampires, but most of all, they be good men."

I squinted my eyes and lowered my voice to match hers.

"How do you know this?" I asked.

"Well," she said, "meself and master Calldoon go back a far piece of time. I was but a wee lassie when me Da and me Ma come to this grand castle. For it was one summer that the ground would not give up her bounty. We, being with no money and now no food, all showed up here in search of work. Master Calldoon took us all in. Me Da worked in the stables, and Ma worked in the kitchen. The kindness of himself even let little old me work as a kitchen maid even though

I be way too small to do so. As I grew into a young woman, we became close friends. Saved me he did, and on more than one occasion. It was not long before it became evident to me that meself was aging and he was not; still, I kept quiet."

"One day I was out on a walk in the forest when a wild beast sprang from the shadows, attackin' me. Before I knew what was about, the beast had me down, tearing at me flesh. Master Calldoon came out of nowhere; like lightning he was. He killed the beast with little effort. Then he scooped me up like I was a butterfly, carried me all the way back to the castle, and cared for me for days. It was at this time that he told me what he be. Had me cap set for him I did, but at last I knew it could never be."

"We decided to just be friends, and friends we would forever be. After a bit, I found meself a nice mortal man, I did. Still, Master Calldoon looks out for me and all who are here, and I look out for him." She folded her hands in her lap, swinging her little feet back and forth. They looked a good four inches from touching the ground. "As for yer lady's maid," she paused. "She be a fairy," she said in a very matter-of-fact way. "Did ye be knowin' that? Everyone thinks she to be touched in the head, but she is not that. It's just fairies have an odd way about them. Did ye be knowin' this?" she asked.

"Well, yes, I did," I replied.

Ms. Doulsie's mouth gaped, and her eyes got wide.

"How did ye know such?" she asked.

I moved in a little closer, making sure no one could hear us.

"One night when I couldn't sleep, I saw something from my window: something glowing. So I went to check it out, and bless Pete, it was her. While we were out there in the forest, she saved me from a very bad man. Then all the way back to the castle I kept asking her how she did all that. As she hurried me on our way she said she would tell me everything later if I would just go. That very next morning we had our breakfast together. After much pleading and promising, she told me everything." I stopped and looked around. "Does anyone else know about this?"

She shook her head.

"No, m'lady, I think not," she said. "Just you and meself: that be all. I know I have never said a word to anyone save yerself, never would I ever put her in harm's way. For if they knew, their fear would cause them to seek to destroy her. Humans always want to destroy all that they can't control, and she no one or thing could ever control!"

"You're exactly right, Ms. Doulsie; we'll keep this between the two of us. Deal?"

"Deal," Ms. Doulsie replied. We both sealed it with a nod. Linking our fingers together, we smiled at each other: a smile that acknowledged our shared secret. Together we gathered up the basket and the snips, then arm in arm we walked back into the kitchen.

I took the herbs to the sink to be washed.

"Oh, yeah, the main reason I came looking for you tonight was to ask if it would be all right if Deireadh made bread with us?"

"Sure. The three of us will have a grand time," she said with a broad smile.

"And speaking of time, what time do you want us here?" I asked.

Doulsie thought for a moment.

"How about if we start just after yer midday meal?" she asked.

"That sounds great! That way I can work with Tanarr in the morning," I said.

"Ooh, ye be the lucky gal!" she said with a wink and a grin.

"Now, now, Ms. Doulsie: no touchy, only workie. I do have my own man, remember?" I said.

She arched her eyebrows.

"Again, I'll be sayin, there be no ring on that fourth finger." She patted the pocket where her little pink iPod was tucked away. "As Beyonce would say, if you want it, you ought to put a ring on it. That be the next song on me fancy little music box."

"Ms. Doulsie, stop that!" I walked over and gave her a peck on the cheek. "Thank you, sweetie," I whispered.

"For what?" she asked.

"For everything. You're the best!"

Chapter Thirty-Three

Freshly showered, teeth brushed, pajamas donned, and the long hike from the bathroom to my room completed, I tumbled into bed.

"I can't wait till he's done with my bathroom!" I said with a huff as my head crashed onto my pillow. No sooner were those words out of my mouth then I sat straight up in bed.

"My new bathroom, ha ha! I wonder what he got done today." I couldn't stand it any longer; I had to see how much progress had been made.

I kicked off the covers, slid out of bed, and rounded the corner. *Wow! What a difference a day makes! That and a good talking to with the castle herself.*

Each wall was starting to take shape. I could see where the dressing room would be. I ran my hand down the side of the wall; *this must be where the closet will be.* I turned and walked through the archway into the bathroom itself. I walked around the room. I could just see how truly beautiful this was going to look with the gleaming black countertops. The extravagant shower with the water coming out from all different heads would be here, and the deep soaking tub right there. I could see myself sitting there with my head leaned back, bubbles up to my nose. Oh yeah, I couldn't wait. "Thank you. I really did need this," I whispered to the castle. A soft "you're welcome" came wafting through my mind, and I had to smile.

With my curiosity satisfied, I started to make my way back to bed. I saw a note from Mr. Roberts that he had tacked to the edge of one of the finished door casings.

Kate,

I hope you like the work so far. Dangest thing! For whatever reason, every nail I hit went straight in. Can ya beat that? I'll see ya tomorrow.

Chuck Roberts

P.S. I would still like to meet that pretty little maid.

I had to laugh; if he only knew what he was asking. He wouldn't believe it anyway. I could just see it now:

Deireadh, this is Chuck, Chuck Roberts: you know, the builder who's doing my bathroom. Chuck, this is Deireadh, Deireadh…I don't know her last name; she may not even have one. Deireadh is not just a lady's maid; she's a fairy.

Next! Kerrrrsplat, he hits the floor, or he would throw his head back and laugh so hard that it would be almost impossible for him to hit the numbers on his cell phone while he calls the people in the white coats to come haul me away. Either way, I didn't see much good that could come out of this. Still, I was going to have to tell him something.

This new problem was still running through my thoughts as I climbed into bed.

"Ah ha! I know; I'll tell him that I found out she has a love of her own, so I couldn't ask her, sorry. That way he won't be hurt, and I won't be in a straightjacket. I think that she and Tanarr have a little something going on, anyway, so I'm not really telling a story. Yeah, that will work; I think, or I hope."

All snuggled down in my comfy bed one would think that I would have drifted straight off to sleep, but no! Between the excitement of my new bathroom and all I had to do the next day, I could not sleep! I reached over to retrieve my pen and pad that I kept on my nightstand so I could make a list of all I had to do so I wouldn't forget anything.

Morning:
Breakfast
Time with Corbin
Meet with Tanarr

Surely I must be close to having everything signed? But laying all that aside, I couldn't wait to hear more about Ms. Lera. I couldn't imagine doing all that she had done. I shook my head; what a lady! A ping of sadness hit my heart. Tanarr…how sad to have loved her so completely only to never have that love returned. I hoped to see a spark every time he gets close to Deireadh. Could it be? Is it even possible that there could be a love between them? I guess only time would tell. I turned back to my list.

Midday
Lunch

Check on my bathroom
Make bread

That should be fun: Ms. Doulsie, Deireadh, and me! Now there was a mix: the brassy kitchen queen, the sparkly fairy, and the Southern belle. The first lives in the kitchen, the second has never been in the kitchen, and me? I fall somewhere in the middle. *Oh, my! I do hope I haven't bitten off more than I can chew. What am I thinking? I should have choked by now, I'm so far over my head.* This was my last thought as sleep began to overtake me. The pen slipped from my hand, leaving a long wavy line across my paper as dreamland began to consume me.

There in the fog of my dreamland sat a beautiful black tub filled with a fluffy cloud of sourdough bread rising to be baked. Glittery sparkles flashed off fairy wings, and troops of carpenters laughed crazily while men in white coats with butterfly nets chased me into the woods. All of a sudden, Blake's dark face appeared before me. He had been waiting in the shadows to exact his revenge. I could hear his evil laughter in my ears as he took hold of me. I fought as hard as I could; still, he held tight. I was powerless. I couldn't move my legs or my arms. Panic had seized every muscle in my body except for my heart. It was pounding so hard that the sound in my ears was deafening. I heard Blake purr.

"Ah…keep up your fight. The sound of your heart rate rising is making my mouth water. You can take that however you like; I know I will," his sinister laughter filled my head.

My eyes flew open; relief washed over me as I discovered that my sweat-soaked struggle was only with my sheets. Thank goodness there was no tub of bread dough, no white coats with nets, and most of all, no Blake!

I scrambled out of bed and walked around my room, trying to calm myself down.

"Breathe, Katelynn, breathe," I kept chanting to the point that I almost didn't hear the knock at my door. I stopped at the door with my hand on the handle.

"Who is it?" I yelled through the door.

"Just your friendly neighborhood Spiderman," Corbin replied. I jerked the door open so fast that I surprised him. "Is everything all right in there?" he asked.

"Yeah, everything is fine," I said, motioning him in. "Come on in. I just had a bad dream."

"Bad dream? It sounded more like a war in here!" he said. Walking over to the side of my bed, he bent down and picked up a shard of glass.

In my struggle with my bad dream and sheets, I had taken out the glass of water and the lamp that were on my nightstand. He held the piece of glass up.

"Must have been some dream. I think you have cut your foot," he said.

"What?" I said, looking down to see that I was standing in a small amount of blood that had begun to pool. "Oh, no! I'm so sorry!" I said, hopping toward the chair.

"Why are you sorry?" he asked as he scooped me up and headed toward the door. I threw my arms around his neck and began to explain.

"Because…you see, this is blood."

"No!" he said with a fake shocked expression.

I gave him a big whack on the chest.

"Stop that!" I said, not missing a beat with my explanation. "With blood being what it is and you being what you are, I thought it might make you uncomfortable."

He stopped in midstep.

"What did you think I would do? Lick the floor, or your foot, or worse?" I just looked at him and blinked my eyes. He rolled his eyes and let out a huff of disappointment.

"Oh, please! If hundreds of years of being what I am, as you put it, have taught me anything, it has taught me self-control. You are as safe as you could possibly be, unless you happen to get an odd infection from an unattended cut. That's why we are on our way to the kitchen. I know that Doulsie keeps all kinds of stuff in there for cuts and burns; after all, it is a kitchen"

There in the kitchen we found everything we needed: alcohol, bandages, tape; we even found some antibiotic cream. Corbin set me up on the counter and gently began to clean my foot. He found one fragment of glass and removed it.

"That seems to be all," he said.

When he was absolutely sure all the glass was gone, he cleaned the wound with alcohol, applied the antibiotic cream, and wrapped it with tape.

"There, good as new," he said with a smile.

I reached over and took his face in my hands. I gave him a soft kiss.

"Thank you," I said against his lips.

"You're quite welcome," he said as he picked me back up.

"You know, I think I can walk," I said.

"You probably can, but I had rather do it this way," he said as we headed up the stairs. I snuggled up on his shoulder.

"That works for me," I said with a smile. Even though he was cold as ice, I felt warm and cared for.

He carried me upstairs to my room, tucked me into bed, and gave me a goodnight kiss.

"Goodnight, my love," he whispered.

"I love you," I whispered back.

Chapter Thirty-Four

I awoke slowly, trying to shake the morning fog from my brain. With a stretch and a yawn, I finally tumbled out of bed. The instant my feet hit the floor, a tug of tape and a ping of pain brought the full memory back. My list, the glass of water, and the lamp: well, my list was ruined by the glass of water that the lamp knocked over. As for the lamp, it was gone. I had destroyed it while thrashing my arms about in the middle of my nightmare. A shiver ran down my back.

"Eee . . .what a nightmare!" I said with a cringe. "Now I guess I need to clean up my mess." To my surprise, there was no mess. Had I dreamed it all? With a wiggle of my foot, I saw that my bandage was still there. Ah, that thoughtful Corbin; he must have taken care of it.

Slowly I made my way down the stairs to the dining hall. Standing by my chair was dear sweet Corbin. *Man oh man, he is one fine-looking mister*! I thought. I walked over and gave him a soft kiss on the lips.

"Thank you," I whispered.

"You're welcome," he said with a smile. "I'll gladly get your coffee and pull out your chair any time in exchange for one of those, any time," he said, pulling out my chair.

I took my seat.

"Oh, you silly goose, you know I'm talking about last night," I said.

"How's your foot doing this morning?" he asked.

"Nicely, thanks to you, my superhero Spiderman," I said with an old-fashioned, Southern eye flutter.

He nodded his acceptance of my gratitude.

"It was a pretty good mess. That one shard was really deep." He reached over and clicked me on the chin with his fist. "And you didn't even need a bullet to bite on. What a woman!" We both laughed.

"But really, thank you for cleaning up my lamp mess." I said.

He got a puzzled look on his face. He was about to say something when my breakfast arrived. It was a potato-onion corned beef hash. A heavenly aroma wafted up off the hash, and there was a thick slice of perfectly browned sourdough bread on the side. What a way to start the day!

"This looks de-licious," I said as I took a large forkful of hash.

Corbin smiled and shook his head.

"Girl, you can eat more than any one human I have ever seen."

I gave him a big smile just before another loaded fork went in my mouth. Tanarr stuck his head around the door case.

"Good morning, you two." He started to walk on but stopped, stepped back, and gave the door jamb a loud slap. "Don't forget Calldoon's office after breakfast." He gave us a wink and started to move on before he stopped and stepped back again. "By the way, have you seen that sparkly eyed Deireadh this morning?"

I stopped in mid bite.

"You know, I haven't, and that's odd. She is usually the one that wakes me up in the morning, but that's okay. I'll see her later today; we're making bread together with Ms. Doulsie. If you want me to give her a message for you," this time I gave him a wink. "I will."

"Uh…," he let out a dismissive growl.

"I was just trying to being nice," I said with a giggle.

"After lunch," he said. This time he didn't stop; he headed down the hall toward Calldoon's office. I finished off my hash.

"Don't you think it's unlike Deireadh not to be somewhere about the house in the morning?" I scooted my plate back and moved my coffee forward so I could cradle my warm mug in my hands while I enjoyed every last sip. Corbin rubbed his hand over his chin.

"Come to think of it, I haven't seen her since last night. Speaking of last night, I didn't clean up the lamp mess. It was already taken care of when we got back."

I took a sip of my coffee and smiled.

"It must have been Deireadh; isn't that just like her? I'll be sure to thank her when we do our bread thing, but for now I had better scoot. Tanarr will be waiting."

I gave the door to Calldoon's office a soft knock.

"Enter," came Tanarr's strong voice.

I pushed open the door and put my hand on my hip.

"Why is it that every time I'm at the door, you just yell, 'Enter?'" I said, lowering my voice on the last word to match his tone. "But for everyone else, you get up and open the door to see what you can do to help them?"

He looked up from his paperwork and gave me his infamous crooked smile. He came up out of his chair and gave me a deep bow.

"Forgive me, m'lady. I know not where my mind was. 'Twas an offence worthy of a severe lashing. Shall I commit myself to the dungeon at once?"

I walked over to him; he still had his bow thing going on.

"Stop that!" I said.

"Forgive me, m'lady," he said with his head still down.

I picked up the phone book that was lying on the edge of the desk.

"Forgive this," I said as I knocked him on the back of the head with the phone book.

"Ow!" he yelped as he grabbed his head.

I plopped the phone book back on the desk where I had gotten it.

"Again, I say stop it. I know that didn't hurt you."

He looked up at me and grinned.

"You're right about that, and to answer your question," he motioned for me to take a seat across from him while he eased back into his. "I guess it's because I consider you family; with family, you don't need to be so formal. With family, you can relax, let your guard down. We look out for each other; we love and care for each other. We have each other's backs." He adjusted the papers in front of him, relaxed his shoulders, and smiled. "That's a good feeling, and not one I share with many."

I blinked back tears.

"Thank you," I said with both hands over my heart. "I feel the same way about you guys and this place. You are all family, and this place feels like home. I love it here. I'm sure not looking forward to going back to the States."

He looked at me from behind the stack of papers.

"You don't have to. This is yours; stay."

I propped my face on my hands, took a deep breath, and exhaled slowly.

"That's a lovely thought, but I can't."

"Why not?" he asked.

"Come on, Tanarr! I have family, friends, a job, and an apartment waiting for me back in America."

"Yes, that you do," he said, "and the last two you don't need at all. After all, you have this castle and three other houses, as well as more money than you could spend in ten lifetimes. Go see your family and friends all you want, but come home to here," Tanarr said.

"You know what? I can't think about this right now; let me deal with what's on my plate now, okay? Please?" I asked.

"That sounds like a deal. Let's get on with our work; however, I'm not going to give up on this." He pulled the first sheet off the top of the stack. "We have taken care of the castle and all of her lands, as well as the preserve in the Amazon; we have transferred all bank accounts into your name. That brings us to the house in the Rockies. Well, technically now it's a ski lodge."

"A ski lodge?!" I squeaked.

"Yes. Have you ever heard of the Hamlet Ski Lodge?" he asked.

"Have I! The Travel Channel did a whole series on that place. They said they couldn't cover it all in one show because the place was so sprawling, from its world-class spa to its forty-plus slopes. Oh my gosh, that place has everything! It goes year round: skiing, ice-skating, snowboarding, and snowmobiling in the winter, and horseback riding, fishing, and hiking in the summer. It has five star restaurants! Oh, wow! The accommodations: how was it that the host put it? This place is one of the most magnificent getaways they had ever had the privilege of visiting; it made his job the best job ever. He said that there were small cottages that were so very well decorated that one could get lost for a night or a lifetime. The high-end suites were plush visions for the world's elite to stay and play in. That place is amazing. I always wanted to go there, but I could never afford to go anywhere like that. I couldn't even afford to dream about it."

Tanarr smiled and shook his head.

"Well, now not only can you go there, but it will pay you to do so."

"What? I'm not sure that I'm following you," I said.

"You don't have to follow me or anyone else; just follow yourself because it's yours," he said with a smile.

"Mine?" I said.

"Yes, yours. That was Lera's cabin in the Rockies. Lera and I just tweaked it a little," he said.

"A little? That place is world class!" My heart switched gears. "Did Lera like to ski?" I asked.

Tanarr almost laughed out loud.

"Not at first."

"Then why did she buy a ski lodge?" I asked.

"She didn't; it was Navar's. He did love to ski, and it wasn't a ski lodge then. It was his personal playground. When Lera discovered that, she was determined to learn to love it. It was one more way to keep his memory alive." Tanarr swallowed hard. "And learn to love it she did. She would don that cobalt blue snow suit," he laughed. "I could see her coming from a mile away. She loved it so much that on skis, I could not keep up with her." Tanarr stopped, folded his hands over the deed, and glanced up at Navar's portrait hanging on the wall. Then he turned back to me.

"I asked her one night after we had been skiing till dark." The mist of the years began to cloud his eyes as he went back in time to that ski lodge. He went back to be with her, the one and only person he had ever loved and still loved: the one he could never have. He took a shaky breath. "We were sitting there by the fire," he looked at me and winked. "She loved to sit by that fire, just like you do." He shook his head. "Chicks and fireplaces: I don't get it. Anyway, I handed her a cup of hot tea, earl gray, I believe it was. 'Lera, you're amazing out there,' I said. 'You've gotten so good so fast; how have you mastered it like that?'

"She smiled into the fire. 'I can feel him when I'm out there: the cold wind caressing my face. I can hear his laughter in the trees. If I could stay out on the slopes forever, I would.' She took a sip of her tea and smiled back into the fire. 'I know why he loved it here. It's the solitude; it's just you and the elements when you're flying down the slope. No one else is around, and nothing matters: just you, the snow, and the mountain. There's no vampires, no humans, no blood: just the snow and the mountain.' She took another sip of her tea. She looked so sad. I sat down on the hearth as close to her as I could get. I started to put my arm around her, but she stopped me with one word.

'Don't,' she said, never taking her eyes off the fire.

'Lera, please let me help. Lean on me,' I said, taking her cup from her hand.

'No, Tanarr. Just leave me be for now. Me and the fire will be fine; I'll see you in the morning.'

'But—' I started to protest, but she put up her hand.

'Please, Tanarr. I really will be fine,' she said.

I leaned down to give her a kiss on the cheek, and she ducked her head.

'I'll see you in the morning,' I said as I walked away."

He pushed the deed toward me.

"Sign here," he said, tapping the pen on the line.

"What?" I said with a shake of my head.

"Sign here, and then the ski lodge with all its properties will be all yours," he said.

"But wait! What happened to Lera? Was she okay?" I asked.

"Oh, yes. By the next morning, she was back to herself. We skied, made snowmen, and had a wonderful day." Tanarr paused. "If I'm not mistaken, to this day, before winter is up, they have a snowman contest. It's great fun for everyone. They give out prizes and everything."

"Wait, wait," I said, holding up my hand and closing my eyes. "How did this place go from a skiing cabin in the wildness to a world-class, year-round vacation destination?"

"Quite simple; she and I really made a good team. We saw the potential. What Navar had used for hunting and solitude, she and I, but mostly she, saw the beauty of and knew that others would see it, too. With that in mind, we began to make plans. That place is where she buried herself; she almost gave up on medicine except for the few times she would go back to Kee-Ka-Na."

He ran his hand lovingly over the deed. "Man, she loved that place." He looked up at me. "Did you know that the lodge was where she stayed most of the time?" I shook my head. "She insisted that all the restaurants be the best that they could and that they always have cheesecake and pie: cheesecake for that wonderful meal he had prepared for her at the cabin, and pie because Navar loved pie; it was his favorite. She took great pride in each cabin and every glamorous suite. She chose each piece of rustic furniture and every rug and each towel for the cabins. They were so cozy and welcoming that they worked for everyone, from newlyweds to families."

"She made sure that the large tubs had great bubble baths for the couples and all kinds of board games and cards for the families. The big suites in the lodge were designed to pamper, and I mean extravagantly pamper, from the highest-quality designer sheets all the way to hand-carved Italian tiles on the floors. There is one small cabin that she especially loved," he said, lowering his voice.

"Let me guess; she had it all tricked out. I can just see it now, with all the bells and whistles," I said with a smile.

"On the contrary, it was the most rustic of all, and it was exactly the way Navar had left it. She added only a few personal things. This is where she chose to live; no guest was ever allowed to stay there. In fact, the two large wingback chairs that were in her room in Silver Cove, the same two chairs that are in the library here, were brought from that cabin."

"But I thought they came from the West Coast house. Did she have them moved to the cabin from there?" I asked, trying to keep it all straight. "Is the cabin still there?"

"Yes; it's just the way she left it. She named each cabin, and she called this one Navar's Love. In her will, she asked that you leave it the same for them for their memory," Tanarr said with a sad smile.

"I will," I said, picking up the pen and signing the deed. "So she had a hand in it all?" I asked.

"Yes. She wouldn't have it any other way," he said with a smile "She interviewed each person who worked there, from the head chef to the gardener. She was the one they would answer to. She loved that place; it was her home. It did so well on its own that it would have made her very wealthy. When you add to that all of Navar's wealth, she was more than wealthy."

I handed the pen back to him after signing on the last line.

"Wait…if she was so wealthy, then why didn't I ever see her on one of those lists? You know, like Forbes or People when they do that richest, most-influential people things?" I asked.

He shook his head.

"She was so rich and had so much influence that when she said, 'Don't print my name,' they didn't," he said.

"Really?" I said.

"Really," he replied.

"Why?" I asked.

"Why what?" he asked.

"Why didn't she want people to know?" I asked, giving my eyebrows an arch.

"She said that she preferred to remain anonymous: that people looked at you differently when they knew that you had money. She liked to do things for people without them knowing who was responsible for the kindness. She would pay a medical bill. She would pay for people's kids to go to college or fill pantries that had been empty for too long."

"Each year, on what would have been her anniversary, she would go to a nice restaurant, sometimes alone, sometimes with a group. She would ask whoever was in charge if anyone was having an anniversary. There would always be at least one, usually more. She would pick up their tab and give them a free week at the Hamlet."

"How would she keep all of that quiet?" I asked.

"She always paid in cash, and she always had someone else to give out the gifts so it could never be attached to her," he said.

"Wow!" I said!

"Yes, wow. She was a selfless person who loved to share what she had. Like you, she could never quite get a grip on the depths of her wealth." He shrugged his shoulders. "I guess she never really wanted to for fear it could change her." He ran his fingers over Lera's aged signature and smiled as he looked back through the fog of time. "She was an amazing woman: good to the core, wouldn't harm a fly. She saw the best in everything. She saw potential where most only saw waste, and she saw beauty in things that others found hopelessly despairing. Regardless of whether it was the untouchable side of a raw mountain or a ragtag bunch of vampires, she loved us all. She loved some more that others, but loved us she did." He lay the deed to the side, closed his eyes, and dropped his head. "Man, I miss her."

I reached over and took his hand.

"Me, too," I whispered. "Me, too."

For a little while we sat in silence, each lost in the sweet memories of a person we loved in our own way: memories that were polar opposites. Tanarr's memories were of the love of his life: a young, vibrant, strong-willed, beautiful businesswoman who could move mountains. As for me, I knew a Lera who was much older and wise beyond wise. She took the place of my loving grandmother whom I had lost years before. She touched something inside of me and opened my eyes to things I never dreamed possible. If not for her, I would have none of this; but most of all, I would have never met my Corbin. She passed on so much more than just mere things. She gave me her legacy. I hoped and prayed that I could do right by her memory.

A shuffle of papers brought me back to the task at hand.

"After you sign this, the flat in Paris will be yours, and that leaves only the West Coast house," he said.

"The West Coast house…that's where they were to be married, right?" I asked as he slid the final deed across the desk.

"Yes," he said with a nod. "To my knowledge, her wedding gown still hangs on a hook in her dressing room, just as she left it. I'm not sure; neither she nor I ever returned. When she left that place, she never looked back. She had it locked up. However, the exterior of the house and the grounds have all been well maintained. She didn't want it to be an embarrassment to Navar's memory, but no one has been inside the house since she left. Lots of people ask to buy it, but she would have no part of that. She would not sell it, but she couldn't go back: too much pain."

"Ahhh…," I said, trying my best to fathom the tragedy she had endured.

Tanarr picked up the last deed and handed it to me. I signed the last line and ended it with a dramatic dot. Tanarr's smile was just a little sad.

"Is everything all right?" I couldn't help but ask.

"Sure," he said with a nod. "It just seems that I keep losing her, piece by piece. I'm afraid that one day I'm going to wake up and not be able to remember what color her eyes were or what her laugh sounded like when she was really happy. I never want to forget any of that."

I smiled at him.

"You won't," I said with a tilt of my head. "We will always keep her here." I put my hand over my heart.

"I know," he nodded. "Now, missy, there will be no more talk of sadness. She would not want us to remember her with sadness. She would want us to think of her with laughter."

"And so we shall," I said with a smile.

"Well, young lady," Tanarr said, gathering up all the papers, "this makes you one of, no; this makes you the most wealthy woman in the world."

I sat there for a while posing different scenes in my head. Finally I looked back at Tanarr.

"Nope. I just don't feel any different. I still feel like the girl who can barely pay her bills: the girl who drives an old car that won't start most of the time. That's okay; I kind of like that girl."

Tanarr leaned in smiled that crooked smile. He gave me a wink.

"So do the rest of us."

"Well, if that's all, I'll be heading to the kitchen to make bread with Doulsie and Deireadh," I said with a smile.

He smiled back at me.

"Sounds like fun."

I lowered my head and fluttered my eyes.

"Kind sir, do you have anything you would like me to tell the sparkly Deireadh?"

"What? No. Well, maybe. I don't know," he sputtered.

"What do you mean, you don't know?" I asked.

He looked away as he began to talk.

"I mean that I don't know if I have room for another. Lera has occupied all of what I am for so very long. I don't know if I'm ready to share that space with someone else yet."

"Tanarr," I said, reaching for him. I turned him to face me. "She's gone, and that's a fact. We all loved her, and that's a fact, but she would want more for you. No, she *did* want more for you."

He didn't say a word. I gave his chin a little shake.

"You know that, don't you?" I said. He still said nothing; he only smiled and looked down at the stack of deeds on the desk. Finally he spoke, only to change the subject.

"You better get down to the kitchen. They will have the bread baked and eaten if you hang out here for too long."

With my hand on the door handle, I paused and looked back.

"Are you sure you're going to be all right?" I asked.

"I'm fine," he said, putting everything back in its place in his briefcase.

Chapter Thirty-Five

When I got to the kitchen, Doulsie was standing at the counter, preparing the ingredients needed to start with our bread making. She looked up over the tops of her little glasses.

"Well, saints preserve us! Meself had all but given up on the two of ye." She looked around. "Where be yer maid?"

"Isn't she here?" I asked.

"Nay, I've not seen her. She did not come to fetch yer breakfast this morning, and

I've not seen her about all this day," she said.

I put my hand on top of hers.

"Doulsie, could we put off bread making for a while? I'm really worried about Deireadh," I asked.

"Sure," Doulsie answered.

"Do you know where her room is? You know, where she lives? Where she sleeps? Because I never asked her," I said.

"That I do. It be in the pottin' shed in her beloved rose garden."

I gave her a puzzled look.

"The potting shed?"

She nodded.

"All about this old place thinks it be only for the pots and the shovels, but I know this be where she sleeps. Let's go see if she be there."

Doulsie grabbed my hand, and out the door we went. While tromping across the yard, I kept seeing little shimmery spots on the grass. The closer we got to the potting shed, the more frequent and the larger the spots became. Finally, I stopped Doulsie. I bent down and touched one of the spots, rubbing it between my thumb and forefinger. It was a sticky liquid: a shimmery, sticky liquid.

"What is this?" I asked.

Doulsie looked closely at the shimmery stuff on my fingers. She turned a little pale and clasped her chubby cheeks with both hands.

"Oh, please, Lord! Do not let this be happening again!" No sooner were the words out of her mouth than she spun around and took off running.

"Doulsie, stop! What do you mean, 'not again?'" I yelled while running after her. She didn't answer. I don't think she even heard me. Her focus was full force on that potting shed.

Doulsie burst through the door with me right on her heels. She stopped short with a sharp intake of breath as her hand flew to her mouth. I scrambled to keep from plowing into her back. As soon as I regained my balance, I peered over the top of her head to see what had caused her to come to such an abrupt halt.

"Oh, no, Doulsie!" I said as a crumpled Deireadh came into sight. There she lay so pale that I could almost see right through her. Everything about her was shimmering to the point that I could see the faint outline of her wings; it terrified me to see her like this. We both knelt at her side.

"Doulsie, what can we do? What's wrong with her?"

Deireadh's eyes fluttered open slowly.

"Good day, dear Katelynn, Ms. Doulsie. So sorry I be, missed I did the breadmakin'." She closed her eyes. "So much I did want…being a part of somethin'…Nice, 'twould be." She reached for my hand and didn't quite make it, so I took her soft little hand and just held on.

"Doulsie, what's wrong with her?" I asked, even though I wasn't sure I wanted to know the answer.

Doulsie ran her hand lovingly over her pale face, then she picked up her other hand and turned it palm side up.

"Just as I suspected," she said with a grimace on her face.

"What? What is it?" I asked.

Doulsie looked up at me with sadness in her eyes.

"The poor thing has cut herself' see here in her palm."

"See what?" I asked, searching for something that I was supposed to be seeing. Doulsie ran the tip of her finger along a sparkly ridge in the palm of Deireadh's hand.

"Do ye see this, child? The sparkly liquid and all ye found on the grass is fairy blood," she said.

"But it is clear except for the sparkle," I said.

She nodded.

"That be what makes a fairy sparkle," she said, sitting there holding her hand. "Once, when I was much younger, the dear sweet thing cut her arm, and this same thing happened."

"Will she be all right?" I asked with a mix of fear and sadness in my voice.

I quickly turned toward the sound of footsteps at my back. Corbin and Tanarr were standing there. I turned back to Doulsie.

"What do we do?" I asked, searching for answers in all their faces. I looked back to Deireadh then back to the men. "How did you know we were here?"

"Go-Brath told us," they both said.

"Well, I wish she had told you sooner." I turned back to Deireadh and picked up her hand again. "I hope we aren't too late."

Tanarr knelt and picked her up. I could see the worry in his face. He looked over at Doulsie.

"The castle said you would know what to do; tell us. We can't let her go, not like this."

"Follow me," Doulsie said as she headed out of the potting shed. Tanarr was fast on her heels. I looked up at Corbin with tears threatening to overspill my lashes.

"Do you think she will be all right?" I asked.

"I don't know," he said, reaching for my hand. "She is so pale; it's like she is fading away right before our eyes," he said as we headed out of the potting shed behind Doulsie and Tanarr, who was cradling Deireadh like a small, wounded child.

Doulsie lead us straight to the nearest vacant room. She rolled back the sheets on the bed.

"Here, son, put her here," she said.

Tanarr started to place her on the bed.

"Gently, we were close to being too late," she said.

Tanarr whipped his head toward Doulsie with a frown. He didn't say a word as he slowly placed Deireadh on the bed, like a wounded bird. Ever so carefully, he pulled his arm out from under her. That action extracted a moan of pain; either that, or she wasn't ready for him to leave her. That small sound made everyone in the room turn a worried eye in her direction. Tanarr stepped close to Doulsie.

"Will she survive?" he asked.

"I do not know. The time before, we'd been to her aid much sooner. There be much to worry over, for she has lost a lot of her life juice," she said.

"How did this happen?" I asked.

Doulsie shook her head.

"I do not know. We are just goin' to have to wait for her to tell us." She put her hands on her ample hips. "She knows good and well that she canna' be getting cut. Fairies have a hard time comin' back from a cut." She shook her head and gave a sigh as she looked down at Deireadh. "Most of them could not have survived such." She moved the covers back just enough to find Deireadh's hand. She picked up her hand and carefully turned it over, palm up. Doulsie looked up at me. "Child, go fetch me, me teabox."

"Teabox?" I questioned because frankly, I had no idea what she was talking about.

"Aye, aye!" she said with a wave of her hand. "Me teabox: the one marked chamomile." A flash of the memory of that horrible taste in my mouth made me shiver. With a look of disgust on my face, I repeated her request.

"Did you say chamomile?" I asked.

"Aye, now hurry, child, hurry!" she said.

I ran into the kitchen, remembering exactly where the teabox was. I snatched it up and ran straight back to Doulsie.

I stepped back into the room. They all stood there hovering around Deireadh's bed; each looked so scared and helpless.

"Doulsie, here is the tea," I said, handing her the box.

"Oh, thank ye," she said as she took the box from my hand. Slowly she took the top off the box. "I keep this tucked in the shelf for just such an occasion." She took a pinch of the tea in her fingers and began to pat it into the cut on Deireadh's hand. "Fer ye see, there be more than just tea in this box."

"Really?" I said.

"Oh, aye. Deep in the heart of the dark forest, there is a hidden fairy circle. In the very heart of that circle, there grows the fern of the fairies. That be the only thing in the whole world that can save a fairy." Doulsie kept talking as she was putting the tea on Deireadh's hand. "See here? The little flecks that sparkle? That be the fern. The fern herself sparkles just like the fairies do."

Deireadh's eyes briefly fluttered open and then closed again.

Tanarr bent down and nervously brushed her face with the back of his hand.

"What else can we do?" he asked, his voice so quiet that we could barely hear him.

Doulsie wiped the residue of tea mix along with what little of Deireadh's life juice, as she called it, off her hands and onto her apron.

"No, son, fer now, we wait. If it works, it works. This be all I know to do."

"I'll stay with her," Tanarr insisted.

I put my hand on his shoulder.

"Is it okay if I stay, too?"

"I also will stay," Corbin chimed in.

He looked at us and smiled and nodded.

Doulsie rubbed her hands together.

"I canna be stayin', fer me kitchen be a callin'. If there be a change, someone of ye best be comin' to fetch me."

I gave her a hug.

"We will," I said.

I pulled a chair up to the side of the bed. Corbin stood behind me, while Tanarr paced.

"She will be fine," I said, trying to comfort him. He stopped his pacing, took a deep breath, and exhaled slowly. We all turned our full attention to her as her wings fluttered ever so slightly. They were all but a gossamer wisp, just barely visible.

"She's so pale that I can almost see right through her," Tanarr said, his voice edged with despair. I looked up at him.

"Doulsie said the tea would work."

No one said a word; I looked from one worried man to the other. I stared down at my hands, picking at my thumbnails and trying to hide my own worry, when the teabox caught my eye; I let out a little sigh and shook my head.

"I thought that was really tea."

"What are you talking about?" Corbin asked.

"The teabox," I said, giving my head a nod in the direction of the box. "The teabox…I thought it had teacup tea in it."

"You didn't?" Corbin said with a slight grin on his lips.

"If you mean did I drink a whole cup of the stuff, then you're right, I did not." I held up my hand. "I did, however, have a sip of it."

Both men who had been staring at me now burst out laughing. I crossed my arms over my chest.

"It wasn't that funny," I said with a frown, and they laughed harder. "I'm serious; that stuff was wicked nasty. I spit and spit, then washed out my mouth, then spit some more." They laughed even harder, if that was possible. "Come on, guys; that is really what wore me out. I was just looking for some nice tea to calm me down and help me sleep, and that's what I wound up with." I sat up straight and squared my shoulders. "But they got even worse. The thing with the tea was a couple nights ago. Then last night I crawled into bed, worked on my to-do list 'cause I couldn't sleep and when I finally did go to sleep I had that crazy nightmare, broke my lamp, spilled my water, broke that glass, wrecked my list, and cut my foot." I stuck my foot up in the air to make my point. After returning my injured foot back to the floor, I reached over and patted Corbin on the knee. "Thank you," he stopped laughing long enough to ask a question.

"Thank me for what?"

I fluttered my eyes at him.

"You know, fixing my foot, and cleaning up the mess."

"I did fix your foot, but I'm telling you that I didn't clean up the mess," Corbin said.

"But the glass was all gone when we got back to my room; it was spotless. I had even forgotten that there was a mess to start with," I said, giving him a sideways look. "Then if you didn't clean it up and I didn't clean it up, who did?" At the same time all three of us turned to Deireadh. She was lying there so pale that she was barely a wisp of a shimmer. A tear rolled off her hand and disappeared into the sheet. The tear was mine, for this offence, I knew, belonged to me.

"I'm sorry," I whispered through the tears. "Please forgive me."

Her wings fluttered, and her eyes came open slowly. Tired, drained purple eyes met my tear-filled ones.

"Nay…m'lady. Forgive there is nothing."

"Shhhh," I whispered as I clasped her hand in both of mine. "There will be time to talk later."

Her eyes closed again.

"Maybe that will be, maybe not," Deireadh said as her eyes came open once more. "For that…talk I must…say it…needs to be…there is to be not fault laid at anyone's feet…it is what it is…if me time be past…so be it…for ask me to take care of anything…ye did not." She smiled. "The castle, she had too much on her heart to find me…so blame her not."

She released my hand and reached for Tanarr's. I moved out of the way so he could get closer to her. He took her hand and drew it to his chest. Looking only at Tanarr, Deireadh continued to softly speak. "All did as they could… regret nothing." She closed her eyes and relaxed into her pillow. Tanarr stayed where he was, not moving and barely breathing.

Corbin put his hand on my shoulder. I looked up at him. He motioned his head toward the door then mouthed, "Let's go." I started to protest. Corbin shook his head and mouthed, "Come on." With some hesitation, I left the two of them alone.

In the kitchen I wrapped myself around Corbin, clinging to my rock: the one person I went to, the only one I could always depend on.

"Just think, not so long ago I didn't even know any of this existed. Now I can't imagine life without them. Corbin, do you think she is going to make it?"

He gave me a squeeze and leaned his head against mine.

"I don't know. Right now it doesn't look so good."

I looked back at the door.

"Should I go back in?"

Corbin shook his head.

"No, give them some time. I know what she is, but I see something happening in Tanarr. He's falling for her."

"Do you think it's a fairy thing, or could it be a love thing?" I asked, looking back at the door. He shrugged one shoulder.

"That I don't know, but I do know it's good to see him start to care for someone else. He has loved someone he could not have for so long." Corbin stopped at that; he knew that I knew who he was talking about. He reached for my hand.

"Let's see if we can help Doulsie with anything," he said as we walked back into the kitchen.

"Okay. Hey, I was just thinking; have you seen Calldoon lately?" I asked. Corbin shook his head.

"No, I haven't."

"Do you think he is all right?"

"I am sure he is, or the castle would let us know, like she did with Deireadh," he said.

"Yeah," I said with a huff, "like with Deireadh; it was almost too late," I said, my voice edged with worry.

"He's fine. He's probably out hunting," he said, giving me a nudge as we walked.

"You're probably right. It's just that I haven't seen him for a while, and after this thing with Deireadh, I want to know that everyone is all right," I said.

"Come on. Instead of helping in the kitchen, let's go for a walk and let you clear your head before dinner. Besides, you have scarcely been out of this castle since you've been here. There is a lot to see. You own some of the most beautiful land in Scotland. On second thought, let's go for a ride. You do ride, don't you?" he asked.

"Of course I do; my grandpa owned horses. Okay, so they were work horses, and some of them were mules, but I still rode them," I said.

Corbin laughed.

"Wait till you see the horses in your stables. They are some of the most magnificent steeds in the world," he said.

I rubbed my hands together.

"I can't wait! Lead the way."

When we arrived at the stables, I thought, *Wow*! Corbin had been right; the horses were beautiful and well cared for. I had been to the stables a few days before when Blake had cornered Calldoon there and we had all made a dash to help him at the encouragement of the castle, but I had not taken time to look around. I had had other things on my mind. How I was looking forward to the ride! But something in the back of my mind kept chewing at me.

Chapter Thirty-Six

Just as Corbin had thought, Calldoon was feeding. As he came out of the woods onto the country road that ran along the edge of the forest, he saw someone frantically waving their arms off in the distance. Whoever it was, they were trying their best to get his attention.

Calldoon raised his chin, catching the wind. He could tell from their scent they were human. As he got closer he knew that not only was this one human but female, and a very attractive female at that. She was tall and lean with long legs. Her low-cut jeans fit snugly over her backside, and her blouse was dipped shamelessly low, exposing her ample cleavage. As for her hair, it was bleached blond with the black roots showing just enough to say "This isn't my real color; so what?" It was cut short and choppy, spiking toward her face to frame her sparkling hazel eyes and pouty, full lips.

She was sitting on a stump at the side of the road. As Calldoon got closer, she began to yell.

"Thank goodness! I thought I would never see another human again!" she said.

Calldoon stopped in front of her.

"What are ye doin' out here all by yerself?" he asked.

"I came out for an early morning ride. I love to do that, but then my horse got spooked and took off with me holding on for dear life. He finally threw me. I walked for a while, and then I turned my ankle." She stopped her story to give her injured ankle a rub for effect and to make her sad state a point of sympathy. "So I had to stop…here on this stump." She gave her eyes a flutter. "I'm so glad you came along!" She gave him a little smile. "Do you live around here?"

"I do not; I came only on a walk," Calldoon said.

"Where do you live?" she asked.

"I'm the caretaker for Castle Go-Brath and all her lands. I like to walk them now and again. You are on her lands as we speak." He looked off at the land around them then back to her. "Can you walk?" he asked, offering her his hand.

She tried to stand then grimaced and sat back down as a tear came to her eye.

"No, I don't think I can," she said with a look of pain and a hint of a pout.

Calldoon knelt down to inspect her ankle. As he rubbed the joint, he looked up into her hazel eyes.

"May I enquire of you about your name?" he asked.

"It's Janet, Janet Jenkins," she said with a smile.

"Where might ye be from, Janet, Janet Jenkins?" he asked with a hint of humor in his voice.

"Oh," she said with a giggle and a wave of her hand. "It's just Janet, and I come from the good old U. S. of A."

"What, may I ask, are you doin' all the way over here?" he asked, still holding her ankle.

"Well, you see, my grandmother recently passed away, so my boyfriend thought that it would be good for me to get away. The next thing you know, here we are," she said with a shrug of her shoulders.

"Where be he?" Calldoon asked.

"Oh…he's not exactly what you would call a morning person." She looked at Calldoon, fluttered her eyes, and gave an even bigger pout. "For the record, I'm not having much fun with him."

Calldoon stood and reached down for her hand, feeling a little sorry for this wounded beauty.

"Okay, now up with ye. Let's try to walk once more. This time, lean on me."

Janet stood, stumbled, and landed around Calldoon's neck. She stood there hanging on his neck like a very expensive necklace or perhaps a strangler vine; either way, she was not letting go.

"My, you sure are strong!" she purred in his ear, "and handsome to boot. Of everything that could have found me, I'm very glad it was you!"

Flattery from a beautiful woman is a very strange thing. It had the power to beguile even the normally unmovable and stoic Calldoon.

"Now, that be true; I'm a little stronger than most," he said with a schoolboy's tone in his voice, for he was caught off guard by the words of the beautiful Janet.

"That's a good thing because you may have to carry me," she said with a pout and smoking sultry eyes. "If you don't mind, that is," she almost purred her last words. She reached up and stroked the side of his face, giving him a longing look from under her lashes. "At least till we get to civilization."

"I don't mind," he said, scooping her up in his arms with ease. "I think there be a cottage around the curve."

"Very good," she said as her arm slid around his neck. At the same time she slid the ancient ring on her middle finger around and into position. With her thumb, she moved the crests of the ring to the side, exposing the tiny needle that was dripping with the nectar of the kee-nan-twa, the white orchid of the Amazon: quite lethal to all vampires. She snuggled close to him and caught the very tip of the ring on the back of his collar, releasing a small portion of the nectar. She lay her head on his shoulder and inhaled deeply. "You smell so good! I could just eat you right up!" She raised her head and smiled. "You're so kind; it's a shame that I must do what I have been sent here to do."

Calldoon, who was hanging on her every word, now turned his full attention on her.

"And what have you been sent here to do?" he asked, almost picking fun at her.

"It's a message from an old friend; he said for me to tell you that now you two are even," she said.

He turned his face toward her to inquire further on her comment, but all he managed to get out was "Who—" before she plunged the needle on the head of the ring into his neck. Shock emanated over his face. As pain took control of his being, he dropped the beautiful Janet as gently as this terror that gripped him would allow. As soon as she was out of his arms, he reached for the back of his neck. But before he could discover what was happening, he was well on his way to passing out.

The beautiful Janet stayed with him only long enough to answer his question.

"Blake sends his regards," she laughed and ran into the woods where her small car was hidden. She pulled onto the road and checked her rearview mirror to make sure he still lay dying there in the middle of the road.

"Now," she said out loud to herself, "Blake will have to give me what I want, and what I want is to take my place among the immortals. He will do it this time; he has to." She shifted the small car into fourth gear, heading back to Blake as fast as she could to collect her prize: a single bite, one that held everything she thought she wanted.

Chapter Thirty-Seven

Corbin held the heavy stable door open for me. He tilted his head toward the corral.

"Katelynn, would you pick out a couple of horses for us? I'll check on the saddles. If you have any problems, just ask the stable boys."

"Got it," I said with a double thumbs up as I turned out into the stable yard. When the fresh air hit my face, so did that feeling. There it was, chewing at the pit of my stomach: that something-is-not-right feeling.

I had one of the men help me select two horses: a gentle one for me and a much more spirited one for Corbin. I had both animals by the reigns as I rounded the side of the stable at the same time that Corbin was coming out of the tack room. It hit us both at the same time. We were almost facing each other, and we stopped still in our tracks.

"Calldoon!" we said in unison; the castle had spoken to us.

"But where?" Corbin yelled at the top of his lungs.

"I got it," I said with fear beginning to flood my soul. "I just don't know where that is."

Not only had the castle informed us that Calldoon was in trouble but she had also told us where she thought he was. Since he was outside the castle walls, she could not pinpoint where he was, giving only an overview of where she thought he could be.

We quickly saddled the horses and went in search of Calldoon. We urged our horses to run as fast as they could. We headed out in the direction that he usually went to hunt as well as the way the castle had sent us. For a while I thought we had made the wrong choice; after all, who knew which way he had gone? Even the castle herself couldn't be sure.

Finally, we spotted something off in the distance that was crumpled in the road. We spurred the horses on faster. When we got close, we pulled back hard on the reigns, trying to get the horses to stop. Dirt and small rocks flew up around edges of their hooves; it was the horse version of a screeching halt.

Corbin was off his horse and at Calldoon's side before his horse had completely stopped. I wasn't so agile; I had to wait for my horse to be stationary. It seemed like it took forever. Finally, I made my way to his side. He was just barely alive. I looked up at Corbin.

"What happened to him?" I asked as I cradled Calldoon's head in my lap. His breathing was shallow; he slowly opened his eyes. I motioned to Corbin. "Look! Look at his eyes; they're brown!"

Corbin knelt closer.

"They are?" he said.

Calldoon swallowed hard.

"Her name…Janet," he said as he took another slow breath. "A message… she had from…Blake. 'We're even.' That's what she said: 'we're even.'"

"Shhh…," I whispered. "Don't talk. We'll get you back to the castle, and everything will be fine." I looked up at Corbin. "He looks like he has aged 10 years," I said, brushing the hair off his forehead.

By now both Zoul and Tanarr had arrived. Zoul looked at Corbin and shook his head. Tanarr knelt at my side

"How's Deireadh doing?" I asked, giving him a quick glance to see his reaction.

"She's good," he said with a nod. "I left her in the caring hands of Doulsie."

"That's good," I said, only half listening to what he was saying. Calldoon opened his eyes again but only for a moment. "Did you see that?" I asked the three of them. "Did you see?"

Tanarr nodded.

"Yeah, I did. His eyes, they're brown. I thought he wore green contacts."

"He does except for when he's hunting; then he wears none at all. He says they get in his way," Corbin said.

"Is that his real eye color?" Tanarr asked.

"I don't know," I replied.

Tanarr stood; I could hear the stress and confusion in his voice as he spoke with the others.

"Guys, what's happening here?"

"I don't know," Corbin said as his eyes shifted to Zoul. "Do you have any idea?"

Zoul turned away from Calldoon as he began to speak in his slow, easy way.

"Boys, I'm not sure, but I have my suspicions. I have seen this before; it was the same way with my first mate," Zoul got down at Calldoon's side and put his hand on his forehead. I stood up to give him room to talk with Calldoon. "Son, can you hear me?" he asked.

Calldoon nodded.

"Yes," he said so softly that we could barely hear him.

"What happened? Just take your time; go slow," Zoul said.

Calldoon nodded.

"She was lost…and hurt…when I picked her up…she said she had to do something…didn't want to…something hit me in the back of the neck. She said Blake said we were even."

Zoul gently rolled Calldoon to his side, exposing the back of his neck. We could see an oozing, nasty-looking single hole.

I leaned forward.

"What is that?" I asked as I peered over Zoul's shoulder.

Zoul probed at the edges of the hole. When he did so, Calldoon moaned in pain.

"It is as I had suspected," Zoul said. "He has been injected with the nectar of the kee-nan-twa."

I heard Corbin and Tanarr's sharp intake of breath.

"What does that mean?" I asked.

"It means that we need to get him back to the castle as quickly as possible," Zoul said.

Zoul and Tanarr picked Calldoon up with little effort but with much care. The two of them carried him back to the castle. Corbin and I followed with the horses.

"Corbin, what is going to happen to him? I know that the kee-nan-twa is the orchid that kills—" I paused. Corbin looked over at me then back toward the castle. Without missing a beat, he completed my thought.

"Vampires" he said.

"Yeah, that. So now what? I mean, what is the antidote?" I asked.

"There's not one," he said. "It is the antidote for us. Think back on all that Lera told you. It was sent to destroy us. That's its mission: protection for the world." He let out a sad chuckle. "It was designed to make the world a safer place, free from vampires."

Corbin had ridden a little ahead of me while I let all that he had said soak in. I gave my horse a little nudge to catch up.

"Okay, again I say, now what?" I asked.

"I don't know," Corbin said with a shake of his head. "I have never seen anything like this before."

"What do you mean, 'like this?' " I asked.

"He should have been dead by now; that thing usually works extremely fast," he said.

Back at the castle, they took Calldoon straight to his room. By now the aging process had kicked in; the man that had looked twenty before now appeared to be closer to thirty. We tucked him into bed. I sat on the edge and took his hand in mine. To my surprise, his hand was warm. I looked up at Zoul.

"His hand, it's warm!" Zoul only nodded. I turned my full attention back to Calldoon. "Is there anything I can do for you?" I asked. "Would you like anything?"

He ran the tip of his tongue over his lips.

"Yes…I would very much like a glass of water."

"Sure," I said as I made my way to the door. I put my hand on the handle and then looked over at Corbin. I gave him a nod with a plea to follow me. Out in the hall, I stopped still in my tracks. I took Corbin by the arm.

"Water. He wants water! I have never heard any one of you ask for anything to drink." I began to pace. "What should I do?"

Corbin stopped me with one touch. He had a strength and kindness that came from witnessing all that he had over the years.

"Let's get the water if that is what he wants," he calmly said.

I smiled and gave a nod of my understanding.

"What do you think happened?" I asked on our way to the kitchen.

"I'm not sure, but I will find out. We all know it had something to do with Blake. As soon as Calldoon is stable, that will be a good place to start," he said.

"So you think he will recover, right?" I asked, staring into Corbin's eyes.

He only shook his head as he reached for a glass. I didn't ask any more questions. We walked the rest of the way in silence, each lost in our own tortured thoughts.

With a full glass of water in hand, Corbin stopped me before we entered Calldoon's room.

"I didn't answer your question because I don't know the answer. If we're lucky, Zoul might know something."

I smiled and nodded that I understood his fear and concern, as well as his hope. *We all feel the same way. The unknown does that to you.*

I slowly opened the door, and there stood Zoul and Tanarr. They looked so out of place in the sparsely furnished, drab room. It had always been Calldoon's room; the furnishings were old and the color was ugly, but he had never cared. He didn't come in here often, as he had never had a need for a bed until now.

Corbin took his place by the other two men. They looked every bit as worried as I felt and so very out of character. These three men, the strongest of the strong, forever young immortals, had been brought to their knees by the unknown direction that had been placed at the feet of their friend. The fate of their comrade now hung in the balance.

I sat down on the edge of Calldoon's bed. The instant my weight shifted the covers, his eyes slowly came open.

"Good day, m'lady," he said so very softly.

I smiled and held up the glass of water.

"I have your water. Would like to try some?" I asked.

He nodded. I slid my hand under his shoulders, avoiding the oozing puncture on the back of his neck. I tried my best to assist him to a sitting position so the water would go down the right way. Corbin quickly moved to help me. With our assistance, Calldoon was able to sit up enough to take a sip of water. At first he coughed and seemed to be choking. Panic flashed across my face, but then he looked up at me and smiled.

"Now that be some good water, but now I need rest, if ye would take yer leave," Calldoon said.

I looked up at the men and shook my head.

"No, I think we will stay," I said.

"No," Calldoon said, holding up his hand, "for I only will be sleeping… need sleep," he said as his eyes closed and he turned on his side, exposing the wound on the back of his neck. I couldn't help but cringe at the sight of it.

"Shouldn't we cover that or put some ointment on it?" I asked with a shiver.

"No; it needs to remain open so the air can get to it," Zoul said.

"Does that mean that you think he'll survive?" I asked hopefully.

Zoul shook his head then motioned toward the door.

"Walk with me," he said.

"But what about—?" I inclined my head toward Calldoon.

He dropped his arm around my shoulder.

"The two lads here will take watch over him." Both Corbin and Tanarr nodded.

As we walked down the hall, I looked up at Zoul.

"So what did you not want Calldoon to hear?" I asked.

He smiled down at me.

"I see what Lera saw in you." He flicked the end of my nose.

"That's good," I said. Concern caused me to cut off his compliment; this was not about me.

"Very well," he said with a smile as his voice took on a serious tone. "First, I don't believe he can recover. Time is catching up with him; you can see how much he has aged already. The orchid will take him back to the beginning; that's why his eyes have changed their color." He bowed his head. "All we can do is to keep him comfortable and safe."

"Are you one-hundred-percent sure?" I pleaded.

"Not one hundred percent," he said with a shake of his head. "No one could be one-hundred-percent sure. I just don't think that this will get any better. The only thing that makes me wonder is that he should have already been dead. Every time I have ever seen the kee-nan-twa at work," Zoul took a deep breath and exhaled slowly, "it was fast and violent. For now we will have to wait. For now, we have hope."

Chapter Thirty-Eight

The small car came to a slow, easy stop in the driveway of the spacious country house that Blake had secured for them so they could carry out his plan.

Janet checked her face in the rearview mirror. She wanted to look her best when she told Blake that she had successfully completed her mission. She had done many things for him: some distasteful, some mean, and others pure evil. But this was the first time she had taken a life for him. Oh, sure, she had "set up some meals" for Blake, inviting a dude over for dinner only for him to end up being dinner or having some chick come to do a make-up party complete with snacks, and after giving her spiel, she would be the snack. After Blake was full and satisfied, they would have themselves one more night. Sometimes he liked to play a little rough, and that was okay. Sometimes, she liked it a little rough.

She checked her look. One corner of her lipstick was smudged. She pulled her fireball red lipstick out of her handbag. "I must have brushed it against Calldoon's collar." She laughed under her breath. "What a weak man! All it took was a tight pair of jeans and a few compliments.' She raised her chin. "Hmm, I could do with him as I pleased," she thought as she began to repair her perfect lips. When she was finished, she blotted her lips together.

"I do want my lips to look perfect when I tell Blake how easy it was to fool Calldoon; he was putty in my hands." She winked at herself in the mirror, dug her fingers into her bleached blond hair to give it a good fluffing, and exited the car.

Janet threw her keys on the counter.

"Honey, I'm home!" she yelled then laughed at the innocence of her statement. Standing there at the counter waiting for the reply that didn't come, she finally gave up and went in search of Blake.

She rounded the corner and headed into the great room. She found him there sitting in a large overstuffed chair looking out over the countryside. Janet walked up behind him and ran her fingers through his hair and across his shoulders. She slithered around him like a snake and straddled his lap. She linked her hands behind his neck.

Blake had not moved. His hands were still on the arms of the overstuffed chair. His eyes still stared out the window.

"Well?" he finally said, moving only his eyes to lock a steely stare on Janet's eyes. She snuggled in closer and rubbed her cheek against his.

Just as her perfect lips brushed his ear, she whispered, "piece of cake: devil's food at that."

Blake's eyes sparkled; he curled his fingers around her backside and pulled her closer.

"Good girl," he said as he gave her tight jeans a hard smack.

She pulled her head back only enough to watch his face.

"Now I'll collect my reward," she said, placing her head on his shoulder and exposing her neck to him. Blake lowered his head and began to kiss the throbbing artery located just below the skin.

`"Mmm…," she purred. "That feels good. Do it! Do it now!" she said, gripping the hair at the back of his neck. She prepared herself for the much-anticipated bite and the following transformation.

He laughed and abruptly stood, spilling Janet to the floor. She sprang to her feet.

"Hey! What's this about? You promised!" she yelled as she rubbed her backside where she had bounced hard on the wooden floor.

He came up behind her, wrapped his arms around her waist, and pulled her forcefully against his chest. With the other hand he entwined his fingers in her hair and pulled her head back forcefully to the side. He lowered his lips to hers, grinding a hard, rough kiss on her perfect lips. She jerked her head free of the kiss, but she could not free herself from his grip. He tightened his grip, placing his lips against her ears.

"First, I must know that he is dead," he whispered.

She spun in his arms and put her hands on each side of his face.

"Fine! But you will see. I did it just like you said, and he dropped like a rock." She slid her hands around his neck and returned his rough kiss with one of her own. He threw his head back and laughed.

"Ah, you bad girl! You are one after my own heart. Someday we will be mates in every sense of the word, but for now I need you to be human. The others will never suspect you. Now, tell me everything, and don't leave out one little detail!"

Janet fluttered her long eyelashes.

"Oh, Blake," she said with a pout. "You know I can never stay mad at you." She ran her fingers through his thick black hair. "You also know I would do anything for you." She ran the tip of her tongue over the corner of his mouth.

"I could do a lot with that statement, but for now I will settle for hearing about how you handled the gallant Calldoon," Blake said.

"Phhhh!" she said with a dismissive huff. "That weakling! He was putty in my hands. He didn't even see it coming!" She arched her eyebrows. "Handsome putty, very handsome putty."

Blake pulled her tight against his chest.

"You thought him handsome, did you?"

She reached up and ran her hands through his hair once more. She wound her fingers in the strands then quickly jerked his head back hard. Holding strong to his hair, she looked at him from under hooded eyes.

"I don't like light, soft, handsome men," Janet purred in his ear. She brushed her cheek against his. "I like mine dark, hard, and handsome." They both laughed. "We could talk tomorrow," she whispered against his face. He released her.

"No, we'll talk now," he said.

"Fine!" Janet responded as she flopped down in the overstuffed chair that had been abandoned by Blake.

Chapter Thirty-Nine

My alarm went off early. I had set it to do so because I wanted to check on Deireadh and Calldoon as soon as I had gotten a little rest. When my feet hit the floor, I realized I was still tired, anxious, and now hungry, too. I had been so very worried about my friends and a little tired to boot that I had forgotten to eat supper. Still, as tired as I was, sleep had not come easy. I would have been better off staying up, but Corbin insisted that I needed rest. When I protested that I should go check on Deireadh and I should stay with Calldoon, Corbin had only shaken his head and scooped me up

"Katelynn, you need to rest. Tanarr will stay with Deireadh, and Zoul will be with Calldoon. You won't be able to do anything to help either of them if you are too exhausted to hold your head up." Corbin carried me to my room, tucked me into bed, and gave me a kiss on my forehead. "Now sleep." He turned off the lights as he slipped out the door.

As the door closed, I reached for my cell phone. I set my alarm just in case I did go to sleep. I didn't want to sleep too late; I had people I needed to check on.

The alarm sounded again.

"I'm up! I'm up! I just can't find my dang house slippers!" I yelled at the phone. "Ah ha! There they are." I snatched them out from under the bed, donned my fuzzy housecoat and off I went to see how Deireadh and Calldoon had fared through the night.

Making my way down the stairs, I give my belt a good yank, cinching my housecoat in around me.

"I hope they're both doing well this morning," I said out loud. Rosey, who was busy doing her morning work, stopped and looked up at me.

"Pardon…might ye be in need of somethin'?" she asked.

"No, no, I'm fine. I'm only talking to myself," I said with a wave of my hand.

She gave me a little nervous smile.

I walked on.

"Old habits die hard," I said just under my breath "Arrr…there I go again! I have got to stop talking to myself. I just need to move on quickly; I have places to be and people to see."

I stood in front of the room where Deireadh was. I reached for the door handle and took a deep breath. *She is going to be fine…she is going to be fine*, I kept chanting in my head. Slowly I pushed the door open. To my horror, her bed was empty. I began to tremble as my mind started to race. *What has happened to her? She was getting stronger!*

I ran to her bed, flipped back the covers, and patted down the bed just to make sure she was truly not there. I thought that maybe I could feel what I couldn't see. Was it only the calm before the storm? I whirled around and took off running. I lost one of my slippers in the process, but I didn't care. I needed to find Doulsie or Tanarr; one of them would know what had happened to Deireadh.

I ran from Deireadh's room to the kitchen at a breakneck speed. I slid around the corner and came to an abrupt halt. There, sitting at the kitchen counter, was Doulsie, Tanarr, and yes, Deireadh. There she set, sipping what I could only assume was her special tea: that horrible concoction of chamomile and fairy fern. Relief washed over me like a wave in the ocean from the top of my head all the way down to the bottom of my now cold and unslippered foot. She looked a little pale, but she was smiling, and so was Tanarr. The spark in his eyes was as sparkly as the glitter in Deireadh's hair. Corbin was right; it was good to see this new light in Tanarr. And Doulsie looked like a dear sweet grandmother so happy to see her precious loved one snatched from the cold arms of death.

Doulsie was the first to notice me standing in the doorway.

"Good morning, child!" She patted the stool beside her. "Come have a seat with us; I'll fetch ye a fat mug of coffee," she said with a nod and a smile.

"Thank you," I said, returning her smile with one of my own. I started to take my seat. Deireadh raised her fingers to her mouth to hide a small giggle.

"See I do…this day we may add but one more of the other fairy tales to our strange menagerie, that so dear we hold," Deireadh said.

Doulsie took her seat and handed me the steaming mug of coffee.

"What be that?" she said, settling back onto her perch.

"Well, go like this it does…a vampire have we," she gave Tanarr a nod. "A wonderful fairy godmother: that be ye." She kissed the tip of her finger and placed that kiss on the cheek of a smiling Doulsie. "A fairy be that meself, even if a little broke be me, and as for now we have among us the very likes of one Cinderella," Deireadh gave me a nod.

I looked down at my feet; I had one slipper on and one off. I gave my toes a good wiggle on the slipperless foot. I took the corners of my housecoat and held it up like a grand ball gown. Then I picked up my mug of coffee and lifted it high like I was making a toast and gave a regal bow. We all laughed. I slid onto my stool.

"Where be yer slipper, child?" Doulsie asked with a hint of humor in her voice and a spark of laughter in her eyes.

"In my defense," I said in between large gulps of coffee. "It scared me so badly when I couldn't find Deireadh that all I could think of was finding someone who could tell me what was going on. In doing so, I took off lickety split. I guess I was going faster than my slippers could keep up, and one got left behind. That will teach it not to keep up." I gave my shoulders a shrug. "I hadn't even noticed until now, and you know what?" I gave my bare toe a wiggle. "Now that I think of it, the naked little piggies are getting cold."

Tanarr looked over at me and winked.

"Okay, Cindy. Sit still, and I'll play Prince Charming." He made it almost to the door where he turned and came back to my side of the counter. He leaned in.

"Just don't tell Spiderman," he said with a laugh and took off again.

Tanarr was back with my lost slipper in no time at all. With the slipper in hand, he bowed low and handed me my shoe over his forearm.

"Your slipper, m'lady."

"Thank you, Prince Clark," I said, taking the slipper then playfully whacking him on the shoulder with it. He grabbed his shoulder and gave it a rub.

"That's no way to treat a prince, now is it, Cindy?" he said. We all laughed. I put my shoe back on as we all settled back in place. I took a sip of my coffee and gave Tanarr a smile.

"Thank you for retrieving my slipper. That was very nice, Clark," I said.

"No problem, Cindy," he replied.

"Now, now, guys; we don't want that to stick," I said.

"Oh yeah, we do," Tanarr said with his crooked smile. "You have given almost all of us a nickname; now you have one of your own."

"We'll see," I said.

I set my coffee mug down and turned my attention on Ms. Doulsie.

"I have a question for you," I said.

"Yes, child?" she said with an innocent flutter of her eyes.

"When Deireadh said that we had another to add to us," I paused.

"Yes, child," she said, reaching over to pat my arm. "We all be knowin' that ye not be the real Cinderella." I was so caught up in her twinkling eyes, her sweet, pudgy little face, and that wonderful accent that it took a moment for what she was saying to sink in.

"What? Wait, that's not what I'm talking about!" I said.

"What has vexed ye so?" Doulsie asked as she shifted on her stool.

"What I mean is, you didn't even flinch when Deireadh said we…have… a…vampire." I said the last three words slowly, watching her face to see her reaction.

"What are ye getting' at, child?" Doulsie said with a calmness that comes from knowing what you know.

"What I'm getting at is…how long have you known?" I asked, leaning in toward her. She met me halfway, leaning in so we were face to face.

"Known what?" she asked.

"That Tanarr is a, a—" I was struggling with the word.

"Vampire?" the three of them said in unison.

"Yeah, that," I said, straightening myself on my stool. Tanarr shook his head. Deireadh giggled, and Doulsie just smiled.

"As for Sir Tanarr, I've only just now figured him out. I be thinkin' that your man, Corbin, is one, too," Doulsie said with a smile. I only nodded. "I been knowin' about Master Calldoon for all me life. He came to me rescue from time to time.

Remember me tellin' ye all about himself whilst we was in the garden just last evenin'? All the rest here could or would not notice what I did. I'd be seein' him not gettin' any older. Then he would leave and come back, sayin' that he was someone else, someone like his nephew or grandson. But I always know it be him."

I was sitting there resting my chin on my fist.

"How did you know that?" I asked.

"Wasn't his eyes, no…," she said with a shake of her head. "It was in his heart. A kind heart: a brave heart, a heart of a good man."

"Were you ever afraid of him?" I asked.

Ms. Doulsie smiled.

"I grew up here among fairies, taking walks and hearing stories handed down through generations about the unknown. I've never found meself frightened, for each of us are a bit odd in our own way. As for Master Calldoon, he cares for us all, loves us as if we were his children." She folded her hands on the counter and looked down at them as she patted the top of the counter.

"In a way, I'd be thinkin' we be his children. He looks after us, helps us with all we do, gives of himself, not askin' fer anythin' in return, and stands between us and all harm at the cost of his very own self." She paused and looked up at me with love and admiration in her sparkly eyes, eyes that had seen more than most, that time had now trimmed with deep wrinkles but that still had a beautiful spark of love and laughter.

I was so lost in her sweet face that I almost forgot that she was still talking to me. "That be the actions of a loving father. I be speakin' the truth, am I not?"

I smiled at her as I thought back to my own daddy.

"Yes. Yes, you are," I said.

Doulsie cupped her face with her hands.

"I do not know what will become of us if something is to take the likes of himself from us." I could hear the fear in her voice.

I took Doulsie's hand in mine.

"He is going to be fine; he's one tough old dude. You'll see; we will all see. He is going to be fine," I said, taking a large sip of my coffee. I set the mug back on the table. "We'll see," I whispered. "We'll see."

Zoul stepped into the doorway, and all four of us turned to face the very embodiment of sadness. He was framed on all sides by the thick molding that cased the entrance to the kitchen. My breath caught in my chest, for this was truly a tortured soul. His strong sculpted face looked much older as it bore the pain of watching a friend in tortured agony.

I sprang to my feet, trying to get to him as fast as I could. I just needed to help him somehow. No sooner had I made a move toward him than he held up his hand to stop me. It worked because I stopped.

"Zoul?" I said, watching his face closely. "Is everything okay?"

He shook his head, looking off into a far corner of the kitchen to avoid our stares. When he looked back, the pain was so real and raw. He shook his head once more.

"No, everything is not okay," Zoul said.

By now Tanarr, Deireadh, and Ms. Doulsie stood at my side.

"What has happened?" Tanarr asked.

Zoul shoved his hands into the pockets of his jeans.

"He is getting weaker," he paused and looked down at the floor. "And I don't know what to do."

"What can we do to help ye?" Doulsie said as she straightened her ever-present apron around her ample waist. Zoul took a deep breath.

"I think it is time to say our goodbyes," Zoul said.

"No!" I said with more force than I had the right to.

Zoul closed his eyes then slowly opened them as he turned his full attention on me.

"If we don't do so now, we might miss our opportunity."

"What? No, there has to be something we can do!" I pleaded.

Zoul said nothing, but his sad eyes held my heart. They spoke volumes with their consoling sympathy. He reached for my hands.

"No, dear Katelynn; we have done all that we can do. He has lasted much longer than any other that has been exposed to that blasted flower. Now it is time to say goodbye."

"I'll go find Corbin; he told me that he needs to hunt. Do you know where he goes to do that?" I asked. I had no idea where or how to go about looking for him; I just needed to do something. Zoul nodded.

"We always know," he said with a weak smile as he left the room.

The four of us exchanged looks. No one knew what to say or do; we just stood there. Doulsie cleared her throat and broke the silence. She rubbed her hands down the front of her apron; the action was like a nervous tic for her.

"Well," she said, taking a deep breath. "Best we be getting' on with this." Doulsie made a move toward Calldoon's door. Deireadh reached out and placed her hand on Doulsie's shoulder.

"Wait…please, may I be first goin' in…for ye see…know I do not how much is left of me for this day…hate I would…miss my chance I canna'…for he and I go way back…allow him to remember…this I have not…but remember it all…. This I do."

Doulsie stepped to the side to allow Deireadh to go in to see their friend first. As Deireadh entered Calldoon's room, we heard his weak voice.

"Enter, my beautiful friend, for fairies have no power over me any longer." He waved his finger at her. "You know, I have held a spark longer for you than most have even been." Deireadh smiled and slowly closed the door behind her.

Deireadh had not been in Calldoon's room long before she emerged. She now appeared to be a very sad, very pale, and a somewhat weaker fairy. She was not the same person who had entered only a short time before. Deireadh swayed a bit as she released the door handle. Tanarr was quick to catch her.

"Are you all right?" he asked as he scooped her into his arms. She buried her face in his neck.

"No…not I am," she said with a sniff.

Tanarr looked over at me.

"I'll take her to her room," he said.

"Do you need any help?" I asked, placing my hand on her back and giving her a little back rub. Tanarr kissed the top of her sparkly head.

"Nah, I've got her, if you two will see to Calldoon." He turned and made his way down the hall toward the room that we had claimed for Deireadh.

Doulsie took both of my hands in her own. In a low whisper of a voice, she issued her simple request.

"May I be the next to see the lad?" she asked, releasing my hand as she turned to make her way into her friend's room. I reached for her hand, as it occurred to me that she might not want to go in by herself.

"Do you want me to go in with you?" I asked, holding her little hand in mine. She patted our hands with her other hand.

"No, child. This I'll be doin' by meself; 'tis only fittin', " she said with a sad smile.

"If you're sure," I said.

"I be sure," she said as she turned to enter Calldoon's room.

Doulsie pushed the heavy door open slowly.

I heard Calldoon say, "How fares the queen of the kitchen?" He coughed and took a shallow breath. "And how goes her kingdom?"

Doulsie gave him a deep, rich laugh.

"Aw…my dear son, how fares ye this day?" I heard her say as the door closed tight on her heels.

Standing out in the hall outside of the closed door in the empty space, the cold, silent, stone walls were in good company with the cold sadness in my heart. I had never felt so alone, never. My mind began to wander. What or who could have caught Calldoon so off guard? It couldn't have been Blake; Calldoon would have sensed him and known the danger. He kept mumbling something about a girl; could there have been a girl vamp—? No, he would have seen her, too, and used the same caution. Human? No, there are few humans that know about…them: few that are still alive, anyway, and even fewer that know about the orchid or how to use it.

I had begun to pace the hall with my arms crossed over my chest while the whirl of thoughts in my head was spinning like a top: a top made of disjointed thoughts and worry. I was trying my best to remember everything that Calldoon had said. He had said something about Blake getting even, and a pretty girl with an injured foot; I thought that was what he said. Now I was not so sure anymore; there was so much to think about. The emotions were too raw, and the pain was too deep.

My head was spinning and then my thoughts went still. My breath caught in my chest with the chain of thoughts that began to creep into my mind. If it was this easy for Blake to get to Navar, Lera, and now Calldoon, next could be Tanarr, then…*No! Stop it!* I put my hands over my ears. "No! No! No!" I said out loud, trying to block out the terrifying thoughts that were racing through my mind. "No!"

With my eyes closed tightly, I couldn't see Corbin approaching. I was still whispering my chant when the shock of strong hands gripped my shoulders followed by that reassuring familiar voice.

"Shhh…," He whispered in to my ear at the same time I felt strong arms pulling me close. "It's okay. I'm here. Shhh."

I didn't even have to open my eyes to know that Zoul had found Corbin and then he had found me.

"Oh Corbin, I'm so scared!" I said, and then I buried my face in his chest. He tilted my chin up to meet his smile.

"Why are you scared? Everyone is here inside the walls of the castle; she'll watch over us," he said,

"Yes, while we're all here, but she can't protect us when we go out. You have to go out to feed, and I can't stay here forever, so then what?" I asked, searching his eyes for some kind of hope. Before he had the chance to answer, Calldoon's door opened.

Doulsie stepped out into the hall. One small tear escaped, tracking down her pudgy cheeks. She blinked hard to stave off any other tears and cleared her throat.

"Master Calldoon wishes to speak with ye next, child," she said, reaching out to touch my arm. She gave me a weak smile. "If that be pleasing to ye."

"How is he, Doulsie?" I asked, not knowing if I wanted to hear what she would say. Doulsie said not a word; she only dropped her head and gave it a slow, sad shake. She squeezed my arm and then turned and walked off toward her kitchen.

I looked up at Corbin.

"Would you like me to go with you?" he ask

"No. This seems to be something each of us must do alone." I took a deep breath then put on my brightest smile. I looked back over my shoulder before entering Calldoon's room.

"I love you," I whispered.

Corbin winked and blew me a kiss.

"I'll be here when you come back," he whispered.

Chapter Forty

It was now my turn to say goodbye to our friend. I hadn't known him as long or as well as the rest, but in our short time we had become fast friends. I was really not looking forward to this, but there was no way I would not do this one last thing for my friend. I slowly opened the door and slipped in. He was so still that I thought I might be too late. I took a seat in the chair that had been placed at the side of his bed. He took a deep, raspy breath. His eyes looked puffy as they slowly came open.

"Good day, m'lady," he said with a gravelly voice.

"Hey! What's with this 'm'lady' stuff?" I asked.

His eyes closed as he swallowed hard then smiled.

"Katelynn," he said softly.

"Now that's more like it!" I gave him a wink. "Ms. Doulsie said you would like to talk to me." I reached over and took his warm hand in mine. "What can I do for you, my friend?"

"'Tis good to be counted among yer friends," he said with a smile.

"Well, you know you are and have been ever since you rescued me from that very large spider, remember?"

"Ah, yes, I do," he said as he raised his warm hand to cup my face. "Such a brave young lady to be so frightened by such a small bug." His laughter was silenced by a brief onset of coughing. His lungs must have been beginning to fill with fluid. I fought hard to repress the tears that were trying their hardest to escape. Now was not the time for tears; there would be plenty of time for that later.

I leaned in so we were quite close; this way, neither one of us would need much volume.

"Now, my brave rescuer," I said in a soft voice. "What did you want to talk about?"

He turned his head to the side so he could see me without straining. He swallowed slowly.

"I know that what I am about to request of ye is not proper. If ye think it to be so, ye do not have to grant me this," he said, closing his eyes.

I scrunched my brows together.

"What are you talking about? You have never done or asked or said anything that wasn't proper!"

He held up his hand, and it trembled just a little.

"Wait, Kateylnn. Permit this humble servant to speak his mind."

I took his hand in both of mine and held it to my heart; my only reply was a nod.

"When I be a new being in this existence, I found it sad that when any of them referred to their lives, they never called it living. I did do and witness things." He paused, took a deep breath, and closed his eyes. "Things that still haunt me. Things that are the makings of nightmares. Then, with the help of our beloved Lord Navar, I overcame that horror. I have tried to live with honor in gratitude for that gift." He stopped.

"I know that, Calldoon; we all know that," I said, still clutching his hand. "We all love you and will do anything that is in our power to help you."

A small tear trailed from the corner of his now brown eyes.

"Thank ye, sweet Katelynn, but I fear there is nothing more that ye can do fer me in this life, save one thing." He stopped. I didn't know if he was gathering his courage or his strength, but I said nothing, granting him his time. When he spoke again, his voice cracked, and so did my heart.

"The one thing that I ask is that when I draw me last breath, if ye would please let this old body rest by my Lord Navar and his lady," he looked at me, blinking back tears. "If it would be allowed."

I started to change the subject by saying something silly because I didn't want to face the end of his story: not yet, as I had only just come to know him. But I could see in his sad brown eyes that he needed an answer. I squeezed his hand, kissed the top of it, and swallowed my pain.

"Yes," I said with a smile. "That would be the only place I would have let anyone consider. That is where you would belong." I leaned down and kissed his cheek, "but that's not going to be for a long time from now," I whispered.

He shook his head.

"No, my sweet Katelynn. We both know I'm not long for this world; 'tis fine, though, for I have lived longer than I should have. I've lost more loved ones to the ravages of time than I care to remember. I think it will be a good thing to be leaving this world." He slowly closed his eyes then just as slowly opened them again. He patted my hands that cradled his other hand.

"As fer you, my sweet Katelynn, you need…no, you *must* continue with Ms. Lera's work. 'Tis vital to many; 'tis too late fer meself. There are still others. They need ye." He turned his head to the side to lock eyes with me. "Katelynn, listen to me; heed my warning." I nodded that he had my full attention.

Never taking his eyes from mine, he continued. "Each one of you watch the other. Blake be an evil man; his ways are not to be expected. That's how meself got caught off guard; be ye careful." He put a lot of force on that last word.

By now he was worn out, exhausted, and a little flushed. I thought how sad it was to see that color in his face. He would have loved to have seen it when things were different, but not now, not like this. I leaned in and gave him a kiss on his warm face.

"Calldoon, I'm going to leave for now. You need your rest." As I started to get up, he reached for my hand

"Would you have Zoul, Tanarr, and Corbin come in?" he asked.

I turned to him.

"Wouldn't you like to rest for just a little while before you see anyone else?"

"No, sweet Katelynn. I've no more time left, and soon I'll have all the rest in the world," he said.

I smiled and said nothing. I knew what he meant.

Chapter Forty-One

I stepped outside Calldoon's room, pulling the door closed behind me. I leaned back against the door and closed my eyes. *Bless him*, I thought. *It doesn't matter how long you live; the end is never what you expect.* I took a deep breath and opened my eyes.

"Oh! Hi, guys," I said with a little start, for there, standing in front of me, were Zoul, Tanarr, and Corbin. They had surprised me just a little. I knew that they had not been there when I came out of Calldoon's room, but either way, here they were: three men, each different to the very core but with a tie of brotherhood: a brotherhood of blood.

Zoul, with his easy, slow way reminded me of a ruggedly handsome cowboy with his shaggy golden blond hair: the one who is as happy out on the range or in his cabin sitting by the fire rolling his own smokes. He had a knowledge that comes only from experience, and just having him here gave us all comfort. It was like having your dad nearby when you were scared as a child. You knew that he would keep all the monsters at bay; it was that kind of feeling. He was born to be king when fate stepped in, changing everything. He had to leave his ancestral home in search of somewhere to fit in, a place to call home. He found that in the old west, and he wore it well.

Next to him stood Tanarr with his crooked smile and that spark in his eyes that were always hooded with green contacts. Those features along with his mischievous streak all came together to make him irresistible to almost every woman. His love for Ms. Lera had cost him. This love that she could never return, this love that he could never forget, taught him to love the game of love but never to give his heart to any other. His personality was larger than life; I thought he could talk the birds out of the trees. His lawyer lifestyle fit him perfectly; he always crossed every t and dotted all the i's, especially if that *i* happened to be a pretty girl. His look was all G.Q.; he could have been their cover guy. But unlike Zoul, the closest thing to a horse he was going to get nowadays was the horsepower under the hood of his sports car.

My heart skipped a beat as my eyes fell softly on Corbin. *My knight in shining armor, my Southern gentleman, my superhero; he's everything I thought I would never find.* Corbin specialized in antiques and commerce, which fit his personality. I was so glad he liked antiques as much as I did. We both loved things slow, easy, and old. With his handsome face, framed by that thick chestnut brown hair that had those great gold threads all through it, a perfect body and a kind heart…how could I keep from falling in love with this man? I couldn't wait for my momma to meet him; she was going to love him. I bit my lower lip; I hoped. What would she think if she were to find out his secret? *Stop it, Katelynn!* I gave myself a good mental shake. *Play only with the cards you're dealt; don't go courting trouble!*

I cleared my throat and my mind only to find all three of them giving me an odd look; I guess I had been staring at them. I gave them a sweet smile and went straight on with my conversation.

"You three are the very ones I have been sent to look for." They gave each other a knowing look. "Calldoon has asked to see all of you together." I said. They each nodded. This bond they shared was strong, making the four of them the closest thing to family that they had. I was sure that was why Calldoon had asked to see them together. His family, this band of good men, this odd brotherhood: they were all he had left to share his last hours with.

They slowly turned and filed into Calldoon's room. I could see the dread on Corbin's face. I could tell he was not looking forward to this final farewell. As each man passed over the threshold into Calldoon's room, he pasted on his best face for their friend. They weren't about to let him see any darkness on their faces. I knew that I would not be privileged to what would be said in their inner circle. What would be said in that room would stay with the four of them. The door closed behind the last one. The only thing I heard was the light-hearted humor of Tanarr.

"Okay, lad, this is no way to get a little extra action from the ladies," he said.

The laughter faded as the door closed.

I flopped down at the kitchen counter on the same stool that I had sat on earlier. I let out a long huff of air. Doulsie came up behind me, and lovingly she rubbed my back.

"Child, would one of yer big mugs of coffee be of comfort to ye?" she asked.

I huffed again.

"It wouldn't hurt," I said with a whine. "As long as you'll join me."

Doulsie looked around the kitchen.

"Methinks I could be persuaded to stop fer a wee bit."

She returned shortly with a mug of coffee in one hand for me and buttermilk in the other hand for her. She climbed onto the stool beside me

"How was the lad doin' when ye left him?" she asked.

I shrugged.

"As well as can be expected," I took my mug of coffee from in front of her. "Thank you," I said, taking a sip. "Only I don't know what to expect."

"Nor do I," Doulsie said with a shake of her head. "I never thought that anything could do harm to them." She smiled over the top of her buttermilk. "Ah, but he is a fine lookin' lad with his brown eyes."

"Yes, he is," I said with my hands wrapped around my mug. We both sat there in silence, lost in our own thoughts. I wasn't sure how much time had passed when we heard the door to Calldoon's room come open. I made a dash for the hallway with Doulsie fast on my heels.

The three men were standing there completely consumed in their conversation. Doulsie and I walked up to them. They had either grown so comfortable with us in this place or they were so worried about their friend that they didn't even notice us until I spoke.

"Everything all right?" I said, catching them off guard, so off guard that Tanarr just stood there, blinking, speechless. Zoul took a startled step back, and Corbin almost jumped.

"I'm so sorry, Katelynn; I didn't see you there," Corbin said.

"I know if it were under different circumstance, I would enjoy getting to sneak up on you guys," I said.

Corbin wrapped his arm around my shoulders as I slid my arm around his waist.

"How's he doing?" I asked.

Corbin only shook his head.

"What can we do to help?" Doulsie asked. She had just now stepped up to the circle.

"I don't know," Zoul said in his slow way. "Keep him comfortable. Sit with him. Let him talk. You two flutter over him; you know, that thing you women do so well."

"Wait! This sounds like you're not going to be here," I said.

"None of us will," Tanarr said.

I turned to look at Corbin.

"What is he talking about?" I asked.

"The three of us are going to Kee-Ka-Na. We are going to have a word with that High Priest. First, we are going see if he knows anything that will help Calldoon or if he can advise us in any way. We can't just stand around and do nothing. While we're there, we are going to see exactly what our options are with Blake. He has crossed the line for the last time," Corbin said.

"I'm going with you," I said.

Zoul looked at Tanarr, and Tanarr looked at Corbin. Their unspoken words were loud and clear.

"Not this time," Corbin said. I started to protest, but Corbin put his finger over my lips. "I know you could handle it, but we will be moving fast, and we need you three to be here for Calldoon. None of us know what will happen next. He should not have lasted this long, so please be here for him. We will be gone only as long as it takes, and not a moment longer. Our best hope is that the High Priest can help."

I nodded my understanding.

"But wait! What if Blake comes sniffing around while you're gone?" I asked.

"The castle will let you know if he does," Zoul said with a slow nod, his hands shoved in the pockets of his jeans.

"Then Deireadh will know how to handle him," Tanarr said with a wink. "She'll look out for you all; trust her."

"Do you think she's up to it?" I asked.

"Certainly," Tanarr said with his crooked smile beginning to spread over his face. "She assured me that she is just fine."

"Did she now?" I said, giving him a wink and a grin. "And is there anything else that she was assuring you of?"

"Kate...lynn!" Tanarr said, stretching my name out.

"When there be something that we need to be knowin', Deireadh will be tellin' us," Doulsie interjected with a giggle and a jab into my ribs with her elbows. I did a little giggling of my own.

"Okay, you two stop torturing Tanarr so we can get back to our problem at hand. We three are going to have a little talk with that priest if you three will take care of Calldoon," Corbin said.

"Ye have no need to fret about the lad, fer I be lookin' out fer him as if he were me very own babe. Think no more of it, and know we have it all under control," Doulsie said with a nod.

Corbin leaned over and gave me a quick kiss on the cheek then gave Doulsie a pinch on the cheek followed by a light pat.

"I can see that he will be in good hands," he said.

"When will you be leaving?" I asked.

"As soon as possible: we each have a few things to attend to, then we will be off." I opened my mouth to protest, but Corbin stopped my words before they could find their way to my lips. "I will find you before we leave."

My shoulders dropped in relief, I was not going to let him go without saying our goodbyes and getting a see-ya-when-you-get-back kiss; I learned that from Ms. Lera.

Our circle of concerned conversation broke up so the men could get on with what they needed to do. We were a strange lot of friends: no, not friends but family. We may not have known each other for long, but that made no difference; we were family. That unique difference in each of us, that sometimes scary but always safe feeling that we each brought to the mix, was the mortar that held us together. Much like this old castle: she was very much alive. If even one stone were missing, she would worry until she had recovered the missing piece. We were very much the same; we watched over and protected each other with the very fiber of what we were. If one were missing, we would worry about and look out for him or her until the missing family member was restored to us; that's what family does.

Each person walked off in a different direction to take care of his business. As they walked away, they took a small piece of my heart with them. I looked at the man who stood by my side; I loved him deeply. Now that there were only the two of us left in the hallway, this dark, heavy worry began to seep in as though it wanted to completely consume me.

Corbin must have felt my mood change. He gave me a soft squeeze.

"Katelynn, it's going to be all right; we will be back before you know we're gone."

"I doubt that," I said with a huff.

He arched his eyebrows and pulled back a little.

"You don't think we will be back?" he said.

"No, that's not it," I said.

"Then what?" he asked.

"It's, it's so much more. It's that I miss you already, and Tanarr has told me how dangerous that orchid and that place are for you all, and then there's Blake." I was talking so fast that I couldn't breathe, and my words were began to run together. All of a sudden, Corbin grabbed me by both of my shoulders and kissed me soundly.

"What was that about?" I stuttered.

He gave me a little wicked smile.

"It seemed to be the only way to make you stop talking; you were running out of breath."

"Oh, Corbin. I'm just so worried! There is way too much that can go wrong," I said.

"I know," he said, taking me into his arms. "But we simply can't just wait here if there is help to be had for Calldoon. As for Blake, he has gotten away with too much for too long. Look at all he has cost us: first Navar, then Lera, now Calldoon, and you know he keeps coming after you. That I'm not going to risk. And that doesn't even scratch the surface of all the people he has tortured over the centuries. He's evil to the core; the time has come to stop him."

I snuggled my face against his chest.

"I know in my head that you are right; however, in my heart I'm scared. I would like very much for you and me to take off and leave this all behind, just be you and me forever," I said.

"Ah, that's a lovely dream, my love," Corbin said, rubbing his face in my hair. "You know as well as I that Blake would destroy all those we love as well as constantly hounding us. Do you really want to live like that?"

"No. I know you're right, but I still would love for us to run away," I whispered.

He smiled and gave me a hug. There, within the circle of his arms, I felt so very safe.

"Someday we will. As for now, I must take care of what I must," he said, his voice dripping with regret. He tilted my chin up and gave me a kiss. "I will find you before we leave," he said as he released me, leaving me in the hall just outside Calldoon's room.

Standing there alone in the cold, stone hall, I began to feel as sorry for myself as I could. After all, here I was as far away from my beloved South as I could get. The man of my dreams was headed off to possible doom. I was to stay here with an old lady who may have been spunky but was still old enough to be my grandmother, and a fairy who was recovering from a near-fatal cut, and it was just a tiny cut at that. There was a dying vampire that we were supposed to take care of, and how, may I ask, just exactly how do you take care of what you don't understand? Then there was this vindictive, mean vampire who was out to get me for what I knew, except that he didn't realize that I knew diddly squat. Oh, and let's not forget the cherry on top of this crazy sundae; the one who as supposed to protect all of us from the bad guy was the fairy, and only yesterday she was half dead from a tiny cut. *Oh, yeah, I feel safe!* I thought. I let out a huff of exhausted air. *And let's not forget that we're all under the safeguard of a talking castle.* I guessed that would be the stem of the cherry on top of this crazy sundae!

Somewhere in the back of my mind, I heard a voice.

"It's all right, dear. We will be fine. I will watch over all my children. We will all be safe." It was the castle; she was trying to reassure me as best she could. In a way, it was working; the darkness that had invaded my heart was beginning to fade.

"You're right," I said, giving the stone walls a pat. "We will be fine; thank you."

"You're welcome, child; now take a deep breath, for Master Calldoon is in need of your assistance," the castle said.

I smiled and took a deep breath.

"Yes ma'am," I said as I turned to check in on Calldoon. I gave a soft tap on his door.

"Enter," came a week voice from the other side. I pushed open the door.

"Katelynn," Calldoon rasped with a motion for me to come closer. I hurried to his side, took his hand in mine, and knelt there. With my other hand I brushed his hair off his forehead.

"Is there something I can do for you, my friend?" I asked.

He closed his eyes and took a deep breath. His eyes came open slowly as he tried to focus on my face. Calldoon smiled.

"When ye first arrived, I must be tellin' ye I was a wee bit suspicious of ye."

"No!" I said with as much humor as I could muster.

"Yes, yes, I was. I be hoping that ye be willing to forgive me that transgression," he said.

I rubbed his forehead.

"There is nothing to forgive," I said. He smiled. "After all," I said with a little stutter, "I might have been a little suspicious of me, too. I mean, you had never seen me before, and here I am, claiming this beautiful old place for my own. Why, shucks! I might have called the police on me if I had been you."

He laughed; then a bout of coughing took his breath. It took him just a moment before he could talk again. I gave him all the time he needed.

"I would have had it not been for Sir Corbin. I knew him at once," he said with a smile.

"I hope you don't mind me being here?" I asked softly.

He raised his hand to cup my face.

"How could I ever mind an angel fluttering about?" he said.

I bent and gave him a kiss on the cheek.

"You may call me an angel, but from all I can see you are and have been the angel: a guardian angel for a very long time. I'm pretty sure that this place," I said with a wave of my hand, "would not be here if not for you. Everyone here depends on you. They adore you, and they need you. So you see, you have to get better."

He shook his head.

"No. I fear 'tis not to be; she will be for some other to care for now."

One small tear escaped my eye. Calldoon continued.

"No. No, there is no time for such as that. For now, I need to tell you where everything is, but first, may we go outside? It has been a long time since I've strolled in the sunlight without fear."

"Fear?" I said with a big question hanging in the air.

He started to sit.

"Yes, fear. You must know the pain that comes with the sun on our skin," he said.

"Oh! Oh, yes, I do know. Both Corbin and Ms. Lera explained the intense pain that you feel when exposed to the sun," I said. He smiled at the thought of Lera.

"I can still not believe that she would put herself through all that she did just to help the likes of us; none of us were worth that." He stopped. "No, there was one who was worth it." He paused again. "Lord Navar: he was worthy of all."

"You stop that!" I said, interrupting him. "She told me on more than one occasion that you all were a band of good men. I think she thought you were all worth a lot, so I'll hear no more of this," I said.

He put his hands up and chuckled.

"Yes, sweet Katelynn, ye may win," he said with a smile as he tried to stand but sank back to the bed. He looked up at me.

"Shall we give this one more try?" he asked.

"Do you think this is a good idea?" I asked. "I mean, it's just that you look so weak."

"I may be weak, but if it be me time to go, let me go in the sunlight. The Lord has given me one more chance, so I'll be takin' this chance. I may not have long, so let me enjoy life while I can. Why don't we have ourselves a picnic in the sun while we're at it?" He smiled a big smile. "That be something I thought that I would never get to do again, ever." He stopped and closed his eyes. "Ah, a picnic in the sunlight with a lovely lady! Please indulge me this one small request."

I could not believe my ears. It was such a small request for an ordinary man but a vampire…a vampire wanting to eat food in the sunlight? I didn't know if I should be scared or happy for Calldoon. Was this a good thing or a bad thing? I didn't know. But there was no way I was going to refuse what might possibly be his last request.

"Okay," I said. "Just tell me what to do and how to help."

He started to get up again. When I reached for his arm, he held up his hand.

"I can do this; only stay at my side," he winked. "Just in case."

"You got it," I replied.

He had on a pair of plaid flannel pajama pants and a soft long-sleeved T-shirt. He looked down at his feet and wiggled his toes.

"Ye may need to help me with me shoes," he said with a nod to his feet.

"Shoes," I said as I looked around, then I turned back the other way. "Where are they?"

He laughed.

"In the closet," he said, nodding toward the closet.

"Well duh! Where else would they be?" I retrieved the shoes. We got them on his feet and made our way into the kitchen. When Doulsie caught sight of us coming around the corner, she dropped the pot that was in her hand. It hit the floor with a clatter.

"Saints preserve! Child, what be ye doing?" she asked.

With his arm draped over my shoulders, Calldoon answered her.

"We, my fair lady, are going on a picnic. 'Tis a fine Scottish day, and I'll not be wasting it. If ye be in a mind to, ye are most welcome to join us," he said.

Doulsie clapped her chubby hands together.

"Oh, bless be! 'Tis a grand idea! The two of ye be makin yer way on out, and I'll be getting' the basket packed!"

"That's a fine idea, for it may take longer for us to get to our spot on the grass than for ye to fix the basket," Calldoon said as we slowly made our way to the door.

It was beautiful out in the bailey, the courtyard or just the plain old yard (whatever you wanted to call it). We chose a spot just between Deireadh's rose garden, the castle wall, and the kitchen door. I spread our blanket on the grass in the full sun. True to her word, Doulsie appeared with a basket in tow. She came over, sat down between us, and began pulling things out of the basket, spreading the blanket with more food than an army could eat.

Calldoon laughed.

"How many are ye expecting?" he asked.

"Oh, my," she laughed. "I could not help meself. This be the first time ye will ever be tastin' me cookin'. I only wanted ye to be havin' a good sample." Doulsie said as she reached over and took his hand in hers. "How be ye faring this day, son?"

He smiled.

"'Tis good." He closed his eyes and tilted his face up to meet the glow of the noonday sun. "Ah...," he said. "'Tis real good."

Doulsie grabbed a plate and filled it to overflowing.

"Well, then, just ye wait till ye wrap yerself around me very own cookin'," She held the plate up to him, her face beaming with pride. The fragrant aroma swirled around his nose, causing his eyes to pop open.

"I do believe me mouth is watering," he said with a little surprise. He reached over and took the plate in one hand and a fork in the other. With the first bite, a mix of surprise mingled with pure pleasure showed on his face. He savored each bite. I enjoyed watching Calldoon so much that I had completely forgotten to fix myself a plate. At last Calldoon took a break from his feast.

"Katelynn, are ye not going to eat? It's very good!" He took another bite. "And I do mean very good."

Doulsie sat there with a smile that went from ear to ear.

"Oh, my, where be me manners? Here we go!" she said, piling a plate full for me.

"Wow! Ms. Doulsie, I can't possibly eat that much!" I said in protest.

"'Tis so good I just might be eatin' what ye don't," Calldoon said in between large bites.

"You had better slow down there, pilgrim, or you're going to pop, and how will we ever explain that to the guys when they get back?" I said as he shoveled another forkful into his mouth.

"I should think that they all three would be quite envious of meself!"

I took his fork and plate. "Nevertheless, you, sir, are not popping on my watch!"

"Ah…," he said with a pout. "It's only that it has been so very long since I've eaten, and it tastes so good. Can I have just one bite?" he pleaded.

"No," I said with my eyebrows arched. "You will make yourself sick." I set the food on the other side of me. "Now, let's just enjoy sitting here in the sun. I think you might need to digest for a little while, anyway," I said with a giggle.

He leaned back on his elbows and stretched his legs out in front of him.

"Ah…'tis a fine day to be," he said.

"That it is," Doulsie and I both said. "That it is."

Doulsie and I exchanged curious, worried but optimistic looks. Could it be that this was the calm before the storm? Was he desperately living out his last wish? Or maybe, just maybe, he really was getting better. Only time would tell.

Chapter Forty-Two

The smell of new construction softly awakened me into the new day. It was nice to have my new bathroom complete enough to be workable. It was by no means finished, but I could at least take care of business without having to take a long hike.

With a stretch and a yawn, I began to come fully awake. There was a soft knock at my door. Surely Deireadh wasn't up to being my lady's maid yet? *If she thinks I'm going to let her do that, well, by gosh, she's got another think coming.* I was grumbling while I was fishing around on the floor for my fuzzy slippers. Ah ha! There was one of them under the chair. The other was hiding just under the nightstand. I snatched them both up and plopped my feet in, then wrapped my housecoat around me and cinched it in tight with the belt. I grabbed hold of the doorknob and gave it a hard pull. It came open quickly.

"Now Miss Missy, just what do you think you're doing?" I said in my best stern voice. "Oh!" I said as surprise flew all over me. That familiar soft baritone voice that I loved so much filled the air. Corbin laughed.

"I do believe that is the first time that anyone has ever call me a," he paused. "What was that? A Miss Missy?" he laughed.

I turned a little pink then a darker shade of red.

"Well, I...," I tried to tuck my wild hair back behind my ears and straighten my housecoat. "Well, I...," I began to stutter. "I wasn't expecting you." His eyebrows shot up. I whacked him with the belt of my housecoat. "Stop that! You know what I mean! I thought you were Deireadh, and besides, look at me! Wait, no; don't look at me!" I started to close the door, but he stopped it with his outstretched hand.

"What are you talking about?" he asked.

"Me. I'm a mess," I said, trying to hide behind the door. "I just got up, and my hair isn't even combed."

Corbin laughed.

"Like I haven't seen your hair tousled." He winked. "You know, I wouldn't mind being the one responsible for that look."

"Oh, you!" I said, springing from my hiding place. He laughed again.

"I knew that would get a rise out of you," he said.

"Arrr!" I growled and stomped my foot. "You knew I thought you were Deireadh."

"I assumed that. I don't think I have ever had anyone call me a Miss Missy. What is that, anyway?" he smiled.

"Arrr…have you come up here just to aggravate the dickens out of me, or is there another reason?" I said with a wink and a flip of my messy hair.

He smiled and started to reply then stopped and held up his hand.

"No, I'm not going to go there," he said as much to himself as to me. "There is a real reason that I'm standing in the doorway of the most beautiful woman I have ever met."

"You have my attention," I said with an eye flutter.

He threw his hands over his heart.

"If you keep fluttering those eyes like that, I just might forget what it was."

I rolled my eyes.

"Too corny?" he asked with a shake of his head.

"Just a bit," I replied with a nod.

"Okay, the real reason that I'm here is to say that we are ready to leave," he said.

My arms fell to the side.

"Already?" I whined.

Corbin nodded.

"We will return as quickly as possible, and when we do, we will hopefully have some help for Calldoon and some ideas on the best ways to handle Blake."

I threw my arms around his neck.

"I will miss you something awful," I said with my face buried in his neck.

"I know. I will miss you, too, but this has to be done. When we're rid of Blake, we can all go on with our lives. Now," he said, holding me at arm's length, "you stay within the walls of the castle, and know where Deireadh is, as much as anyone can know her. She and the castle will be your best protection. Blake will sense that we are all gone, and he might try something. The castle will confuse him somewhat, and Deireadh can completely confuse him, so whatever you do, stay close, okay?" he asked.

"I can do that," I answered back with a sharp salute, "but I have to tell you something. Doulsie, Calldoon, and I had a picnic outside in the sunlight. Calldoon had a really good time. He ate food and enjoyed the sunlight without pain. Is that a good sign?" I asked excitedly.

"I stopped by to see Calldoon and tell him where we were going and why. He told me what a good time he had on his picnic." Corbin paused and smiled.

"Thank you." He gave me a soft kiss on the cheek. "It does appear that he is getting stronger. I'm just not sure what this could mean. It's one more piece of the puzzle; I only hope the High Priest holds the rest of the pieces." He took a deep breath and didn't say a word; he just stood there looking at me.

"What?" I asked.

"Nothing...I just love looking at you, messy hair, crooked bathrobe, and all," he said with a smile that would melt any heart.

"Why, Sir," I said fanning myself with my hand, "I do believe I just might be blushin'!" *Eye flutter, eye flutter.*

He reached over and cupped my chin in his hand.

"We must be off," he said as he placed a soft kiss on my lips. My arms dropped to my sides in defeat.

"This minute? I thought we would have more time, at least two or three days," I said with a huff.

He cocked his head to the side and arched his eyebrows.

"We work a little faster than most," he said.

"I know, but still," I said with a stomp of my foot.

He slid his arms around my waist, pulling me close.

"Think of it this way," he whispered into my hair. "The sooner we leave, the sooner we will be back."

"I know," I said with a pout and a huff. "I'm so worried about you." I closed my eyes and leaned my forehead against his chest. "I know I've said it before, but there is way too much that can go wrong."

He tilted my chin up, and I opened my eyes.

"That is true, but so much could go right, and at the end we would be free of this evil: free to do as we please. So much wrong would finally be made right."

I wrapped myself as close to him as I could get, and a head nod was my only answer. Abruptly, he gave me a stiff pop on the backside and a big kiss.

"Now, we must be off." He stopped, took me by both shoulders, and looked me straight in the eye with more seriousness than I had heard from him in a while. "Remember...you must stay within the walls of the castle and always know where Deireadh is. Do not forget this!"

I put my fist on my hips gave him my best "duh" look.

"Well duh! I'm not daffy, as my Grandma used to say. I got it, okay? I got it. Don't go strayin' about." He just looked at me. I rolled my eyes "Arrr... good grief! You know, poking around where I shouldn't be?"

"You've got it," he said with a nod of understanding. "Stay here." With that said and one last kiss, he was gone. I was left standing there looking down a long, empty hall hoping and praying that they would be safe and back home soon.

"I love you, be safe!" I called after him. My words echoed off the walls of the now vacant hall.

I retreated into my room and riffled through my closet until I found my favorite old, worn out jeans; they fit me like an old friend, and I needed that feeling today. Next, I searched for my Crimson Tide sweatshirt. It wasn't flattering; it had some paint spots and a few spots that were holes. But that was okay; it was kind of how I felt.

I felt like I had a few holes in my heart and in my very being, but I come from good old Southern stock. I knew I would be fine, and so would Corbin. I just knew it. I turned around and around looking for my sneaks. Ah ha! There they were, peeking out from under my bed. I slipped them on and tied them snugly then ran a brush through my hair and pulled it back in a ponytail. I was trying my best to get cleared out before Mr. Roberts arrived to continue working on my bathroom.

I made up my bed and straightened everything up. I gave myself a good look in the mirror, pasted on a big, toothy grin, and pinched each cheek for color. "Okay, Katelynn; suck it up! Get on with things; he will be home before you know it."

I opened the door, took a deep breath, and headed out into the hallway, but not before I stopped and gave the door a good pat.

"Now, girl, you behave today; let Mr. Roberts do his work," I said in a whisper, just in case anyone was nearby listening.

I took off down the hall and bounded down the steps. I was about halfway down when I met Chuck Roberts coming up the steps.

"Good morning to ya, Katelynn," he said with a tip of his cap. "How's everything going today?"

"Fair to middling," I said as I got closer.

He stopped in front of me two steps down.

"What? You should be doin' great! Your new bathroom is almost done! It's a beautiful day! You own all this and more; it just don't get much better than that!"

I looked at him and smiled.

"You know what? You're right! I'm sorry; it's just that I have a lot on my mind."

He put his toolbox down.

"Is there anything I can help with? I got pretty darn good ears."

"Nah, but thanks anyway," I said. "I'm going to check on Calldoon, then I'm finding me some breakfast."

"Oh, yeah; I heard that Mr. Calldoon wasn't feeling so good," Chuck said.

I looked over the railing in the direction of Calldoon's room.

"He's not top limb, that's for sure," I said.

"Has he seen a doctor?" Chuck asked.

"No," I shook my head. "Doulsie is taking care of him," I said.

"Ah, she probably knows as much or more than most doctors. Let me know if I can help," Chuck said.

"I will; thank you. I'll tell him you were asking about him," I said. He nodded, picked up his toolbox, and headed on his way.

I rubbed my hand over my forehead then down over my chin. *Doctor*, I thought to myself. *A doctor! Yeah, that would be great. However, the only person who might have been able to help had been murdered by Blake in her room at Silver Cove.* I took a deep breath. "Oh, Ms. Lera, I miss you so much." I shook my head. "I sure could use your help right now." I let out a soft sigh.

"It will all be fine, child; we will all be fine."

"What?" I said, grabbing the railing and stopping in midstep. Then I heard it again. As realization sank in, I smiled at the soft whisper of the castle.

"Thank you. You know, it's going to take a while to get used to this kind of conversation," I whispered. She was trying her best to reassure me that she was on the job.

"Go to the kitchen," she whispered. "Those that ye seek are all there."

"Thank you again," I whispered with a smile.

In the kitchen, just as the castle had said, were Doulsie, Deireadh, and Calldoon all sitting around the kitchen table. Doulsie had her frosty glass of buttermilk and a golden chunk of sourdough bread spread thick with butter and jam. Deireadh was sipping on her tea. *It must be that mix that Doulsie keeps just for her: that mix of chamomile and fairy fern*, I thought with a shiver; it had been nasty stuff.

To my surprise, Calldoon was sitting with a large plate of eggs, potatoes, sausage, fresh tomatoes, toast, and a steaming mug of coffee in front of him. I slid into the chair beside him. As I sat there in silence, I noted that his color was much better today; as a matter of fact, it was almost normal, like human normal.

I watched with my mouth agape as Calldoon consumed the entire meal; not even a shred of potatoes was left. The three of them chattered while he ate.

Doulsie ate her last bite of bread and drained her buttermilk, and then she smiled over at me.

"Child, you be quieter than a church mouse," she said with a wink.

Never taking my eyes off Calldoon, my reply was almost a stutter.

"It's...it's just that he is eating again, and he's eating a lot!"

"I know," Doulsie said, slapping her little pudgy hands on the table. "I be knowin' the lad all me life; never have I ever known him to put even the smallest of morsels into his mouth." She shook her head. "Himself got up this morning; the fever was broken. He told me and Deireadh that he be starvin' and not just for his usual."

She swallowed hard, looked side to side then whispered behind her hand, "ye know, blood."

I nodded my understanding.

Calldoon cleared his throat.

"I be sittin' right here: me, myself, and I. I've not gone anywhere, nor have I gone deaf."

"I'm sorry! My Momma would tan my hide for doing this to you; it's just plain ol' rude," I said as I reached over and patted his hand, which was impatiently drumming on the table. "By the way, how are you feeling this morning?"

A smile spread across his whole face.

"I feel…," he stopped, still beaming from ear to ear.

"Go on," I said, rolling my hand. "You…feel?"

"That's it! I feel! I feel hunger, pain, thirst, discomfort; I feel everything!" He lowered his voice. "Most of all, I feel hope. I do believe with all my heart that I've been cured."

"Really?" I asked.

"Yes," he replied with a hope-filled voice. "I do believe it to be true. I know that only time will tell."

I bit my bottom lip as I thought.

"You know, it could be possible. If I remember my visits with Ms. Lera correctly, it was the amount, not how it was refined, that made the difference. If this woman brushed the tip of the ring on your shirt, it would have caused a portion of the nectar to spill. And the ring only contained the exact amount of the nectar to be lethal, then it would no longer have the strength to kill. Perhaps, just maybe, it left the perfect amount to cure!" I said.

"Do you think it could be so?" Doulsie asked, clapping both her hands to her cheeks.

"Yes, actually, I do," I said as the depth of what I had surmised came clear in my mind. I stood and began to pace, then my smile began to take over my face. "I think," I said with a little giggle, "that Blake may have accidently created the thing he feared the most. I think he may have come up with a shortcut to the cure." I walked around behind Calldoon and put my hands on his shoulders.

"I want you to take it really easy until the guys get back." I leaned down and gave him a kiss on the cheek. "They are going to be so surprised to see you like this." I looked at his handsome face. "You know what? Not only has your fever broken, but I think the aging process has stopped. You look great. This is so exciting!" I said as I slid into my chair. "By the way, is there any of that food left, or did you give it all to him?" I nodded to Calldoon.

Doulsie smiled.

"Nay, child there be plenty, iffin' ye have a mind to fix ye a mess, help yerself!"

"Well, I have a mind, and I don't mind helping myself," I said as I took a plate and began to load it up with a heap of deliciousness. The rest of breakfast was filled with light-hearted chatter, funny stories, and laughter.

When we were finishing up, I had to bring us all back to our real problem, as much as I hated to. I took my coffee mug in hand and drained the last drop. I still held my warm mug in my hand; it just felt good.

"Deireadh, if you don't mind, can you please let us know where you are at all times? Corbin said that we will be safe if we all stay close in. The castle will take care of us somewhat, and between you and her, we'd be fine."

Deireadh smiled her sweet little smile and nodded.

"Nice it be so…need to be…I'll be close as ye need…this ye may count," she said.

"Thank you," I said, taking her hand. "You know what I think? This place and all of us really need you a lot. I know one red-headed vampire who needs you even more."

She ducked her head.

"Think ye so…could he think of one such as I…in that manner of the heart?" she asked.

"Well, duh! He can barely talk when you're around, and when you're not around, all he wants to talk about is you. Yeah, I'm pretty sure on this one," I said.

She covered her mouth with her hand and giggled.

"Think I do," she crinkled her little nose, "a little flutter be he."

I looked at Calldoon, who was shoveling the last forkful of food into his mouth, and then I turned to Doulsie.

"Flutter?" I asked with a little head shake.

They both shrugged their shoulders.

"That's fairy for 'he rocks,'" Calldoon said, holding his fork up to make his point.

"Me thinks it means that he be the cat's pajamas," Doulsie said with a smile.

"Same thing," Calldoon said.

"Ah…she likes him," I said as we cleared our dishes. The easy chatter returned.

"I have an idea; how about if Calldoon has a little rest and we all meet in the garden for a little lizard time?" I asked.

Calldoon, Doulsie, and Deireadh each gave me an odd look and in unison said, "Lizard time?"

"Yeah, you know: lie around, soak up some sun like a lizard on a rock," I said.

Deireadh giggled.

"That's funny."

"Never in all me days have I heard talk like that," Doulsie said with a shake of her head.

"I can see it; I understand where ye are goin'," Calldoon said.

"Lizard time it is, then. I'll see y'all in about two hours," I said.

Everyone nodded their approval. As we each went off in our own direction, I felt Deireadh catch my arm.

"If need of me ye have, the garden be where ye may seek me," she said.

"Thank you," I said with a smile. "That really makes me feel better. Now I'm going to check on Mr. Roberts and see how my bathroom is going."

Chapter Forty-Three

I took the steps two at a time.

"Wow, what a difference a morning makes!" I said, my steps as light as my spirits. "I truly think that Calldoon will be fine. Deireadh is almost one hundred percent. She loves Tanarr and he loves her. Could this morning get any better?"

I entered my room to the sound of Chuck Roberts singing away. I recognized the song; it was an old church hymn. I began to sing with him; we even harmonized. I came in just as he was in mid song.

"*Amazing grace, how sweet the sound,*" I kicked it up a notch, "*that saved a wretch like me. I once was lost, but now I'm found, was blind but now I see.*"

When we finished the song, Chuck stopped and looked up at me.

"Well, I'll be a suck-egg mule! You're dang good, and ya know the whole song!" he said.

I put both hands on my hips.

"Well, yeah! You are looking at the girl who filled the third space on the first pew in the choir loft, singing for the First Baptist Church youth choir of Ela, Alabama, and yeah, we were good," I said raising my chin and fluttering my eyes.

"I'll just bet you all were. Anytime you would like to belt one out with me, just holler, 'cause that was a sack full of old home fun," Chuck said.

"Were you in a church choir?" I asked.

"Nah. I never stayed in one place long enough to get involved in such." He stopped and put his hand over his heart, "but my mama had the voice of an angel. I know that Heaven stood still and the Lord smiled when her voice reached his ears. She loved the old hymns; I think she knew them all." He smiled and blew a kiss toward the heavens.

"Is your mom still in Tennessee?" I asked.

"No," he shook his head. "Heaven," he said with a sad smile.

"Oh...I'm sorry," I said, regretting the intrusion.

"It's okay. She's with her Lord, and I know she gets to sing all the time now. That's why I like to sing while I work; it makes me feel close to her," he said.

"What happened to her, if you don't mind?" I asked.

He put his hammer down.

"We were coming back across the Smokeys from Tennessee back into North Carolina. We were almost to the top. There was this strip where the edge of the road was close to the edge of the cliff, and there were no guardrails. The next thing we knew, there was a car coming straight at us. I don't know if the driver missed the curve or if he were drunk or just plain ol' sky buggin'. Whichever it was, he was full on our side of the road. Dad swerved and the shoulder broke off. The next thing I knew, we were going over the edge. My brother and I were yanked out of the tumbling car by this man; the rest went over the edge. It was the oddest thing; I don't know how he did that. He didn't say a lot, but he stayed with us till help came. We heard the emergency workers coming up the mountain. As soon as we saw them, the man was gone. Mama didn't make it, and Dad just barely did. If it had not been for that stranger, I know my brother would have died. His side of the car was completely destroyed." He stopped. "There is something that's been chewing at my gut."

"What's that?" I asked.

"That man of yours?" he said.

"Yeah?" I said, half afraid of what he was going to say next.

"I know it's crazy, 'cause we're about the same age, but he looks exactly like the man who saved me and my brother. I know we were just tow-headed youngins when that happened, but the first time I saw him, I got the willies. He looks so much like that stranger. I tried not to stare, but it sure took me back. Still, in the back of my mind, I knew it couldn't have been your man," Chuck said.

I didn't know what to say so I went another way.

"Isn't that weird how that works? How some people can look so much like another? I know there was this one girl in my hometown who looked just like me; people were getting us mixed up all the time," I said.

"Yeah, that's funny," he said, picking up his hammer and going back to work. I closed my eyes and let out a slow breath.

Katelynn, you are such a liar, I thought. *You don't even know anyone like that.*

Trying to change the subject, I ran my hand over the door case.

"This looks great!" I said.

Chuck looked up from his crouched position where he was working on the baseboard, hammer still in hand.

"Thanks. I think it's turning out pretty good at last, after she finally decided that I was one of the good guys and let me work on her," he said.

That was an odd statement, I thought. I wondered if he had any idea what he was in the midst of? I squinted my eyes and gave my head a little shake.

"What?" I asked.

He shrugged his shoulders.

"Ah, you know. Sometimes these old places take on a life of their own." He patted the wall. "I know that she's not really a living, breathing entity, but it feels like she has a soul; a very old soul," he said.

I was hanging on his every word.

"Yeah, I know what you mean; she is quite a wonderful old castle," I said, looking around the room, "and you are doing a magnificent job with her."

"Thank you again," he said with a tip of his cap. "I don't mean to be rude, but I need to be getting back to work. I'm burning daylight."

I gave him a sharp salute and flipped my cap onto my head.

"You got it. I only came up here to get my cap. I know you're really busy, so I'll scoot. Calldoon, Deireadh, maybe Doulsie, and I are going to meet in the garden for some lizard time."

"Enjoy the sunshine; it's a nice day," he said as the hammering began.

I was the first one to arrive in the garden. I dragged a couple of chairs from the shade into the glorious sunlight. I fussed with them until they were positioned just right, and then I found two more chairs and hauled them over so Doulsie and I could have a seat, too, just in case she had the time to visit with us. I stood back with my hands on my hips. *Ah, perfect!* Everything looked just right for a day of lizarding. Out of the corner of my eye, I saw Calldoon and Deireadh coming around by the rose garden, and from the kitchen came Doulsie with what appeared to be a pitcher of lemonade and four glasses on a tray.

"Oh, let me help you with that!" I said, scrambling to her aid.

She smiled as I took the tray out of her hands.

"I be thinkin' that we might like a touch of ye homeland," she said.

"That's so sweet of you, Doulsie, 'cause I do love lemonade. My Grandma use to make it for me when I would stay with her in the summer; sometimes she would even make it in the winter. We would drink in my quilt castle that we would build over her dining room table." I smiled at the memory.

Doulsie looked up at me sideways with a twinkle in her eye.

"Child, did ye ever think that ye would be ownin' yer very own real castle now?" she said with a chuckle.

I gave a little laugh and shook my head.

"No. I must admit, I didn't see this coming at all. It truly is all about that glorious curve in the road."

I set the tray down on the little table that Deireadh had brought from the potting shed. We each took a seat with our lemonade in hand.

It was nice, but I liked my lemonade quite a bit sweeter. You might even say that this was a little tart. How was it that Grandma used to put it? Sour enough to make a pig squeal! I took another sip. *Yeah, that's it, make a pig squeal!* I thought. Trying hard not to let my lips pucker, I drank the whole glass and bragged on it to the last drop. It was just so sweet of her to make something for me with her only purpose being to make me feel more at home. *She melts my heart.*

We all sat there for a pretty good while basking in the plentiful sunlight, enjoying the company of what had become fast friends. Then, all of a sudden, I heard that voice in the back of my mind.

"Beware; evil is afoot."

The hair on the back of my neck began to prickle. Deireadh must have gotten the same message. We both began to nervously look around like two field mice when the hawk is flying. My spine went stiff like someone had run a steel rod down my back. I looked over at Deireadh.

"Did you hear that? Do you see anyone?" She gave me a quick nod followed by a head shake.

"What be the matter, child? What is it that the two of ye be speakin' of? For there be not a saintly soul about us," Doulsie said with her head back and her eyes closed.

"Yeah, but it's not that saintly soul that worries me. It's that one with a black soul that scares the dickens out of me," I said under my breath.

"What's that ye be sayin'?" Doulsie said, cupping her hand around her ear to help her hear a little better.

"Nothing," I said, not sure if I had heard anything at all or if perhaps it was just our active imaginations. I looked over at Deireadh, who still looked as uneasy as I felt. No, this was not our imagination. Brief though it may have been, Blake was here. The castle's warning was spot on; Deireadh and I both knew it.

Chapter Forty-Four

Janet made herself comfortable in the big, overstuffed chair. With her lipstick freshly applied to her perfect lips, she took a long drag off the joint she had just rolled. Blake always had the best weed, and my, my, how she did love a good smoke. He not only had the best weed, but he could give you anything else your carnal mind desired. Blake had small stuff like weed all the all way up to big stuff like people: people to do with as you pleased, and one of those people was Janet. *I'm not sure why he keeps me around*, she thought, rolling her joint between her thumb and forefinger as she contemplated her fate.

She kicked off her shoes and had a very one-sided conversation with herself.

"Janet, ol' girl, you've come a long way from that two-bit hooker barely scraping by, not knowing whether the next john would kill you or worse. The first time I saw Blake when he found me in the back room at that party, I thought my prince had arrived." She let out a huff. *Don't kid yourself, girl*, she thought. *He's no prince; he may be charming at times, but he's definitely not a prince charming. This dude is some kind of dangerous. I need to remember that. Someday, he's going to keep his promise and give me that bite; then no one or nothing will ever hurt me again. If they try, I'll just do what Blake does. I'll eat them*, she thought as she took another long, slow drag then exhaled slowly with a rather wicked grin.

Blake came storming through the back door. He slammed it so hard that everything in the house shook, including Janet. She jumped to her feet so fast that she dropped the joint. It rolled to the edge of the chair where she promptly crushed it out with her bare foot, flinching as it seared through her flesh.

"JAN-ET!" Blake roared, slamming things about as he crashed through the house. He came on her so furiously that her breath caught in her throat. He began to circle her, a move he had perfected and was quite notorious for. It made humans uncomfortable and nervous. He liked them like that, if one could say he liked them at all. They were week creatures that got on his last nerve. However, they were, unfortunately necessary, for they were his favorite snack.

"I thought you said you had completed your mission," Blake snarled.

Janet had a blank look on her face. She blinked, trying her best to collect her thoughts. She was not exactly sure what he was talking about.

"M-m-mission?" she stuttered as she began to shake all over. "What mission?"

He ended his circling, stopping in front of her. His face was ridged. His eyes were almost glowing that deep burgundy color. His hand shot out, grabbing her by the throat. Ever so slightly, he began to squeeze. As he did so, he lifted her off the floor. Slowly and methodically, he began to speak.

"Your mission: you know, the one where you were to execute one vampire, the stoic Mr. Calldoon. The mission that you said was so easy. What was it that you said, putty in your hands?"

She began to choke.

"Blake, stop! You're hurting me!" she sputtered.

"Yes, I am," he replied with a hint of humor. "This is mild to what I'm going to do to you if you don't start explaining."

Janet tried to stay calm and tried not to struggle. She didn't want to get him the least bit excited. She well knew what he was capable of.

"Blake, honey, please put me down, and we will see what is going on," she pleaded. Slowly her feet began to touch the floor as he lowered her. She rubbed her throat and cleared her voice while stalling for time. "Now," she said, clearing her throat once more. "Start at the beginning; tell me what has brought all this on."

Blake strolled over to the window with his hands behind his back. He looked out, not really seeing the view for the anger that boiled within. Without turning around, he began to speak.

"I thought I would swing by the castle and see how the girls were holding up after Calldoon's untimely death and to see if I could find out why the men had all left all at the same time. I assumed it was because they were so distressed at the passing of an old friend." Slowly he turned. "And what do you think I found there?"

Janet shook her head, remaining silent for fear that she would set him off again. Blake threw his head back and laughed a crazy kind of laugh: one that sent a chill down her spine.

"No, no, I don't guess you do," Blake said as he sat down on the couch beside her where she had melted as fear had gripped her soul. He slid his arm around her like a boa constrictor and began to squeeze. "I found none other than Mr. Calldoon sitting there in the sun, drinking lemonade with two, no, *three* happy ladies." He gave her a hard squeeze and an even harder shake. "Now, can you tell me what's wrong with this picture?"

Janet swallowed and started to answer, but Blake angrily began talking over her before she could respond.

"Let me tell you; the first thing we see is happy women. Next, they're all drinking lemonade; how many times will you find a vampire enjoying a tall glass of anything that's not covered in warm skin? Then he is sitting in the sun, smiling, eyes closed, face up, enjoying it. That never happens to any of us. Last but not least," he reached over to Janet's face and began squeezing until her perfect lips were shaped into a little oval. He could feel her teeth biting into her cheeks. He could smell the blood as it began to ooze into her mouth.

Ignoring the alluring aroma, he applied still more pressure until he heard one of her teeth pop, felt her flinch with pain, and saw the tears began to puddle in her eyes. He started to speak as she began to tremble.

"Here is the thing that troubles me the most; HE IS STILL ALIVE! You lied to me!" he yelled in her face. Then his voice lowered, his tone changed, and his eyes got a look that made Janet think that he was going crazy, scary crazy. He moved in so close that his lips were touching her ear. "They must die: all of them. I've already taken care of Navar and Lera," he laughed. "I will get them all. Who do they think they are to simply cast me out? Me? Me! That castle should be mine!"

"Lord Navar," he slurred the name in anger, and little pieces of spittle sprayed in Janet's hair and face, "thought he was so good, better than all the rest of us. Did he think that I could or would deny what I am, a powerful vampire? Ha! They will all feel my power!" He tightened his grip on Janet. "One more of them should be out of my way: the one who set me up, had it not been for your incompetence. I will get him, and next will be Katelynn; I must do it before she can do anything with that cure, if she has it. One by one, I'll get them all; I'll have my revenge. They will all see who is the better man." He threw his head back and laughed.

She shook her head as best as she could. He released her face. He was so caught up in his thoughts of revenge that he had forgotten that he was still applying pressure. He would now allow her to reply to his accusations.

"No, no, I didn't," she said, rubbing her face. She swallowed the blood that had pooled in her mouth; the fear that consumed her did not allow her to feel any of the pain from her now broken tooth. "I did exactly as you told me to." He arched an eyebrow at her.

"No, my pretty; if you had, he would be dead," Blake said in a condescending tone.

"I swear I did," she said in a weak voice, for fear had threatened to completely still it. "I did it to the letter, just like you said. I played the wounded bird and threw out a few compliments. When he picked me up and started to carry me down the road, I slid the cover on top of the ring over and jabbed it into the back of his neck. He dropped like a rock."

Blake rubbed his chin.

"Hmm…what went wrong? You didn't prick yourself or hit your jeans?" he asked.

"No, I didn't," Janet said with a white-faced shake of her head.

"What about his collar? Did you scratch it across the back of his collar, perhaps?" he asked.

She paused, trying her best to think.

"No, I don't think so; maybe." She threw her hands up in the air. "I don't know." she reached out and touched his cold arm. "I'm sorry. I didn't mean to disappoint you. I did my best."

"Your best?" he said, his voice dripping with sarcasm. "That would explain the failure," he hissed.

"Hey!" she fired back. "I don't see anyone else standing in line to do your dirty work!" Her fiery personality came roaring back. "Besides, I keep keeping my end of the bargain, and you never do."

He began to be amused at the fire he saw in her eyes. That fire was what drew him to her, the same fire that made him know that she was the one for him: no scruples, all fire. *Yeah*, he thought, *that's my girl.*

"It's okay," Blake said, rubbing his forefinger across her face. She slapped his hand away.

"It's okay? It's okay?" she yelled in his face. "It's nowhere close to okay. I jump through all your hoops, do whatever you ask, from being your arm candy at some fancy party to being willing to commit murder for you, all for you. All I've ever asked of you is to make me like you; give me that bite. That's all I ever wanted." Her fists were clenched at her sides. Her stance was strong, bold, and distinct. He reached out and dragged her into his arms, smiling and nuzzling her neck.

"That's my fiery wildcat; I knew you were still in there."

"Arrr…," she let out her breath and leaned against him. "You…," she said as she thumped his chest with her fist. "One of these days!"

"One of these days, what?" Blake said. "You're going to leave me? I don't think so. I have everything you want." He leaned in and whispered in her ear. "The whole house reeks of weed. As soon as we dispose of Calldoon, the rest is yours." He flashed his fangs at her.

"Really? Promise, this time for real?" she said, curling around him like a kitten after fresh catnip. He tilted her face up to meet his.

"First thing in the morning, go get that tooth fixed," he said, and then he lowered his head, giving her a long, slow kiss and savoring the remnants of blood in her mouth.

Chapter Forty-Five

By the time I was ready to turn in for the night, I was really tired. As soon as my head hit the pillow, the whole day came rolling back, from eating breakfast with Calldoon, seeing how well Deireadh was recovering, drinking lemonade while basking in the sun, experiencing the horrible feeling of knowing that Blake had invaded our circle followed by the comfort of the knowledge that the castle could watch over us, and finding out that Corbin had saved Chuck Roberts and his brother. *Wow*! It had been our first full day without the men, and we had survived.

As sleep overtook me, my last thoughts were, *Corbin, I miss you. I can't wait for you to get back. Be careful. I love you.* That last thought was slurred as sleep consumed me and dreams engulfed me. Some were warm and comforting, others were disturbing and hard. In and out all night long, I saw cold amber eyes in my face and smiling faces, and I felt warm arms holding me and keeping me safe.

A loud crash of thunder followed by a crack of blinding lightning brought me straight up in bed. All thoughts of sleep and dreams were abandoned; this was one bad mama storm. The power flickered. That put me to scrambling; I wasn't about to be caught by myself with no lights. *Yeah, yeah, it's daybreak, but I don't care, 'cause this is one bad storm*, I thought again.

After one more crash of thunder, my feet landed in my slippers and my housecoat went on all in the same movement. I really didn't like storms. I swung open my door and ran right into Deireadh. I screamed, and she screamed. I grabbed my housecoat, pulling it up around my face, and I saw her grab her face.

"Oh me goodness, wings and flutters! Scare ye I did not mean," she said.

"Scaring me doesn't even come close to how I feel," I grabbed the door case to steady myself. I took a deep breath and exhaled slowly. "It's all right; we're all right," I chanted. "It's only a storm, a perfectly natural occurrence caused by the convergence of two weather masses: hot and cold fronts or something like that, right? Right. It's only weather, and this is a good, strong castle," I babbled as I patted the door case.

"Katelynn, farest thou not well," she said, patting me on the back. "Truly a storm it be only: nothing more. Pass this it will do. Came I did only, telling ye the men, lighting the gas torches they are. For true it will be, no power will we have; the storm, she will see to that."

"No power?" I squeaked.

Deireadh looked about the room.

"All will be good, for it is now all but day," she said, looking toward the window.

I shook my head.

"Oh, no! It may be day out there," I shakily pointed at the window, "but in here, in those long halls with no windows, IT'S DARK! It's as dark as Paw-paw's root cellar, and I didn't like it down there without a light, either." I closed my eyes and took a deep breath. "It will be all right." I opened one eye. "You did say they were lighting all the torches, right?" I asked.

"Yes, say it I did," Deireadh said with a giggle. "Fine and safe ye be. Come now; our morning meal we will have as one."

"Okay, but you might as well know that I'll be sticking to you like glue," I said, linking my arm through hers.

She patted my arm that was draped over her forearm.

"Glue ye may be. Promise I do; safe ye will be. See this ye will."

In the dining hall we all had breakfast by candle light, Just as Deireadh has said, the power had gone out, and even though enough light could have come in through the large windows, the storm had made it dark and gray. Every time the lightning cracked, I jumped. Sitting there with my friends made it a little easer, but it was still a bad storm. I had a forkful of eggs that was on its way to my mouth as a large boom of thunder made me jump. My eggs tumble back down to my plate.

"Isn't it funny how I love a soft rain?" The lightning crashed, and I cringed, "but this kind of storm completely unnerves me"

"Hmm…," Calldoon said. "They are opposite sides of the same coin. Much like good and evil," he reached for his coffee cup. In the short time of his recovery, he had taken a true liking to a good, hot cup of coffee with a little cream and a little sugar. "Good stuff," he would say.

He set his cup down. "For although there could never be one without the other, the coin could not be without both sides. As long as the sides remain evenly strong, there is a good chance that all will turn out good, but if evil should ever gain the upper hand, the world would be in danger. For this reason, Corbin and the others must be successful." He shook his head. "Blake is gaining too much power, and this one who is working with him, this woman, this human. She is true evil: not a powerful evil but evil nonetheless. If Blake should ever choose to change her, or infect her, as you call it, it would be bad for all of us." He paused and looked me straight in the eye. "This could be bad for the world."

I pushed my plate back, no longer hungry.

"Do you think he will?" I asked.

Calldoon just looked off in the distance.

"At this moment, no: she is more useful to him in human form. We," he paused and let out an amused chuckle. "I guess now I should say 'they' can't feel her."

"But," I said, holding up my hand to make my point. "You have something on us all; you know what she looks like."

Ms. Doulsie began clearing the table.

"That be quite enough of all this gloomy talk. They all think that ye be dead and buried; they will not be lookin' for ye anymore. The storm is liftin', and so shall our spirits today; she will be a good day. Methinks that it will be a good day to be about cleaning out the closets and cupboards."

Calldoon, Deireadh, and I all made a face.

"Ah, really?" I said. "Cleaning closets?" I said with a whine.

"Yes, ma'am: closets," Doulsie said, dusting off her hands and giving us a sharp bob.

We pushed back from the table, looking like children who had been banished from the playground to do their much-dreaded homework.

"Come, come, children; we don't need to look like the whole bugged world has come crashin' down upon on us; 'tis only that the storm has made it no good fer bein' out and about this morning, and we need to be keepin' our wits about us." She tapped her head. "We need to be keepin' our minds busy. It'll help; ye'll see."

"Yes, ma'am," we all said in unison as we trudged along behind her.

"Here: if we're all going to the kitchen, then at least let me carry the dishes," Calldoon said, stepping in front of her to take her load.

"Then I be the one to wet and scrub them," Deireadh said.

"Well, then, if Doulsie cooked, Calldoon is carrying, and Deireadh is washing, then I will dry them and put them away," I said, bringing up the rear.

"See? I told ye we'd be havin' a good day," Doulsie said.

I began to whistle the song that the seven dwarves sang as Snow White saw them off to work.

"Catchy that what ye be whistling," Deireadh said, looking back at me.

"You don't know this tune?" I laughed. "I know I'm a bad whistler, but I thought everyone knew this. It's from *Snow White and the Seven Dwarves*; they sang it as they marched off to work. I'll add the words." I cleared my throat. "*Hi ho, hi ho, it's off to work we go. Hmm, hmm, hmm, Hi ho, hi ho.* Sorry, I can't remember all the words," I said, scrunching up my face.

"'Tis a funny little song. One day meet we may, the dwarf will teach us, the song of their work," Deireadh said with a big smile. "Like them we will!"

My smile faded as I realized she thought they were real. I stopped, and everyone else stopped with me.

"No, no, sweetie; they're not real. It's a cartoon. Walt Disney took an old fable and turned it into a cartoon," I said.

"Car…toon?" Deireadh asked, tilting her head to the side.

How do I explain a cartoon? I thought.

"Well, they take a picture of a drawing in all different positions, and when you run them all together really fast, they look like they are moving." I looked at the other two who had the same blank stare on their faces. "Do you mean to tell me that you have never seen a cartoon?"

"Yes, we have," Calldoon said, pointing between himself and Doulsie, "but Deireadh has not. She told us there was something wrong with keeping little people in a small box."

She crossed her arms over her chest.

"Tell me then, like it would ye, if keep ye we did in such a small box?"

Calldoon laughed.

"No matter how many times we try to tell her that they're not really living in there, she won't listen." He cupped his hand around the side of his mouth and leaned in. "I think it's a fairy thing."

"Hear that I did, for a fairy I may be, and me hearing 'tis far better than most. Know this; ye should by now, as long years we have shared." She giggled. "Ah, but remember you canna'. Don't mess with a fairy," she said with another giggle and a finger wag.

We all laughed at their banter.

"All right. That be enough messing about; we have work to do," Doulsie said, pushing us all own our way.

We obediently followed her into the kitchen and went straight to work. We made Calldoon sit and rest while we got the dishes done. Just when we were about to crack open the cabinets and get to cleaning, Rosey came running around the corner.

"Ms. Doulsie, Ms. Doulsie!" she yelled.

"Yes, child, I be here; ye do not have to scream the rafters down on us all."

"Sorry, ma'am; there be a pretty lady in the courtyard," Rosey stopped, still standing there and rocking back and forth on her heels.

"Well, child, do not just stand there in the midst of me kitchen. What is it that she has need of?" Doulsie said.

"Oh, sorry, ma'am; me thinks she be seekin' employment," Rosey said.

"We've no spot for her; shoo her away," Doulsie said.

"I tried, I did, but she'll not leave till she talks to ye. She truly wanted to talk with Master Calldoon, but I'd be tellin' her that the master is not feeling up to such," Rosey said with a wave in the direction of Calldoon. He smiled and nodded his appreciation at her efforts to look out for him.

"Bring her on in if that be what it takes so we can get on with our task at hand," Doulsie said with a huff of irritation.

Rosey left and immediately returned with the most beautiful creature I had ever seen in tow. The two of them stopped in front of Ms. Doulsie. Rosey gave a quick curtsey, and the enchantress stood there straightbacked and stoic like a regal princess. Rosey stepped to the side.

"This be Ms. Mary Margaret O'Tool."

She stood there with her hands clasped in front of her, giving each of us a sweet condescending smile and a brief nod. When she spoke, it was with an odd accent: not Scott, not English. It sounded almost forced, but it was an accent nonetheless. Sweetly and properly, she began.

"I be from the house of Douglass O'Tool. We have a long heritage of service to the highest heads of the courts. I come here seeking employment. I've been told by this child," Rosey made a face at her behind her back, and Doulsie gave Rosey a disappointing cut of her eyes. The rest of us tried to hide our amusement. Ms. O'Tool continued, never missing a beat, "that the master is not well. I do hope that he is doing better."

Calldoon cleared his throat and stepped forward.

"I may assure you that he is quite well as of now."

Ms. O'Tool fluttered her eyes at him.

"And you be?" she said.

"I am himself in person. I be Master Calldoon."

"Really?" she purred, stepping closer and placing her hand in the center of his chest. The moment she did so, it sent a shock of memory through his very being. He took in her sparkly green eyes, her curly red hair, and those rosy cheeks. He could find nothing familiar about her, so he pushed it to the back of his mind. Still, something kept chewing at the pit of his stomach; perhaps this was a normal mortal reaction to a beautiful woman.

He inhaled deeply. She smelled like a spring day when the soft breeze was sprinkled with the fragrance of the newly blooming flowers. *Goodness*, he thought to himself, *this is the first time in a long time, a very long time, that the smell of her perfume was more intriguing than the thought of her taste*. It felt good to have such thoughts. He smiled; *it's good to be human*.

She abruptly dropped her hand. With a flip of her curly hair, she turned and left.

"I've left all me paperwork with the child; it has all of me references and numbers; everything is there," she said, turning back to give Calldoon a smoldering look. "If only you have a want for me, that is," and she was gone.

We let out the collective breath that I think we had all been holding.

"All righty then, now, that was quite an introduction, wasn't it?" I asked. Doulsie turned back to her work.

"It be bloody too bad we've got no space fer her," she said.

"You know, I think that we can make a space for her," Calldoon said, rubbing his chin.

"No, no, no space," Doulsie said, rubbing her hands down the front of her newly donned apron.

Calldoon draped his arm on her shoulders.

"Doulsie, old girl, don't you need a lady's maid?"

"Oh no, no, no!" she chuckled. "'Tis quite a comical thought: me with a lady's maid. What be her task, laying out me old run-over shoes or fetchin' me a fresh apron? Oh, she could pluck the fat hen so I could roast it for yer dinner." She turned and pinched Calldoon's cheeks. "No, son, there'll be no fancy beauty waitin' on the likes of meself!"

"Ah, come now, Doulsie, it could work!" he pleaded.

Doulsie rolled her eyes, turned, and went back to work. Deireadh and I tried to hide our amusement that threatened to spill over into full-blown laughter. Calldoon threw his hands up in the air.

"Ye can't blame a guy for trying!" He stopped and turned all the way around. "May I ask you girls something?" We nodded. "Did she seem familiar to you?"

"No; I have never seen her before," I said, "I'm sure I would remember her."

"I remember her not; this one has never crossed me path," Deireadh said as we all went back to work.

Chapter Forty-Six

The small car left through the front gate, crossed over the arched bridge, and drove out through the countryside. When it was a good two or three miles away, definitely out of eyesight and earshot, the driver whipped the little car into a wide space on the side of the road and brought it to a screeching halt.

"These contacts have got to go!" she said out loud as she began fishing the green contacts out of her eyes to reveal her own hazel-colored ones. She rubbed her eyes and blinked a few times. "Ah, now that feels better!" Reaching up, she took a handful of curly red hair and gave it a jerk, tossing the curly mass to the floorboard and giving her head a good shake, which allowed her own bleached blond hair to bounce back into its perfect shape.

Looking into the rearview mirror, she took a makeup remover towel and began scrubbing at her face, removing not only the light freckles and rosy cheeks but also the pale skin tone that she had so very carefully applied to reveal her natural and healthy suntanned skin. She reached into her purse to retrieve her raving red lipstick; she didn't even need a mirror to apply it perfectly. She used the mirror simply because she liked looking at herself. "Janet, ol' girl, you should have been an actress!" She blotted her lips together and blew herself a kiss.

"You're good!" she said out loud. "I know Blake isn't going to be happy with me for coming to the castle, but I had to see for myself. Hmm. Not only is he not dead, but he's doing great! He looks better than he did before. Now he has color, and he's warm! If I didn't know better, I'd say he looked human." She engaged the clutch, threw the small car into first gear, and took off, sending gravel spraying off onto the grassy shoulder.

Janet opened the back door of the country house and threw her purse and keys on the table so quickly that the keys didn't stop; they slid over the table and right off onto the floor.

"BL-A-KE!" she yelled. "Where are you?" she asked even louder, running from one room to the next.

"I'm here," he said nonchalantly, stepping right in front of her. "You don't have to yell. I have excellent hearing."

Janet jumped and screamed.

"Jeez! I wish you wouldn't do that. One of these days you're going to scare the life out of me!"

Blake let a little cynical laugh escape his lips.

"I may drain the life from you, but never will I scare the life from you. You see, that would be a complete waste of human resources." He side stepped her, giving her backside a good hard swat as he started to walk away.

"Ouch!" she squealed then raised her chin. "Well, if you don't want to hear what I have found out…." She defiantly turned to walk the other way. Blake grabbed her arm and roughly turned her back to face him.

"Where have you been? What have you done?" he bellowed.

"Now you're interested in what I have to say, are ya?" Janet said, trying to be coy.

"Don't play with me!" he hissed.

"Fine, then," she said with a huff. "You're just no fun today." She was completely annoyed with him for not wanting to play her game. "If you're ready to listen, I'm ready to talk."

He gave her arm a hard shake.

"Well, get on with it!"

"Okay, okay!" she said, tucking a strand of bleached blond hair back in place that had been dislodged during the shake. "I thought—" Blake let out a snicker. "Hey!" Janet said with a frown and a stern finger wag. "Do you want to hear this or not? I do have other things I could be doing."

"No, please do go on. You have my full attention; I can't wait to hear what you thought," Blake said, his voice dripping with sarcasm.

"Okay, then. As I was saying, I thought I would go check it out for myself. I wanted to see what was going on. So I went to the castle." She said the last part quickly.

Blake's eyebrows shot up.

"You did what?" he roared as he began to pace.

"You heard me," Janet said with a hint of defiance edging her voice. "I didn't stutter." Blake began to growl as he paced. "Chill out, dude. I had a disguise, and a really good one at that."

"Really," Blake huffed.

"Yeah, really," Janet said, propping her clenched fists on her hips. "Green contacts, curly red wig, freckles, pasty white skin. You wouldn't have known me." She ran her index finger across his cheek.

He snatched her hand from his face.

"No one recognized you?"

She shook her head.

"No, no one," she paused, waiting for the praise that never came.

"Well, what are you waiting for? Go on!" Blake said impatiently.

Janet rolled her eyes, let out a sigh of disappointment, and continued.

"I drove right up to the castle, walked in, and told the little house girl that I needed to see the master of the house. First she said I couldn't see him, and that he was sick. I insisted she take me to see whoever was in charge. She took me to see this old fat woman. I think she was the head cook." She gave her shoulders a shrug. "I don't know what you call her. Anyway, just guess who was standing right there beside her? Mr. Calldoon. He introduced himself to me, even let me lay my hand on him."

Blake arched his eyebrow.

"Yeah, that's right." She walked up to Blake and placed her hand in the center of his chest. "Just like this. I walked up to him and put my hand on his shirt." She smiled up at Blake. "I did that so I could see if he was still cold: you know, like he was before." She paused, forcing him to ask her for more information.

"Well?" he said.

She fluttered her eyes.

"He was warm: very warm, warm as any man I've ever laid my hands on."

"Hmm…so it appears that he has not only survived but is now recovered." He turned back to her. "How did he look?"

Janet scrunched her face up as she thought about it.

"He looked a little older, maybe a little flushed." She smiled, "but I do have that effect on men." Blake glared at her. "Other than that, he looked great," she quickly added.

Blake began to pace, rubbing his chin.

"Let me think; he now looks older, and he is warm to the touch. To all appearances, he is human once more." He stopped and whirled to face her. "How can this be? By all rights, he should be dead. If I recall, from all that I overheard in small bits of conversation between Katelynn and others, it's the amount of nectar that makes the difference. You must have hit the tip of the ring on his shirt, releasing some of the nectar into his shirt, therefore leaving only enough to eliminate the part that makes him a vampire and leaves the human part. I must think on this. Leave me!" he said with a dismissing wave.

Chapter Forty-Seven

Sitting up in front of the fire in my room, I reflected on the day. Dinner was over, and everyone was tucked in and safe for the night. We had more fun cleaning out cabinets and closets and under counters than I had thought possible. We laughed at and with each other most of the day. It all started with the beautiful redhead and the effect she had on Calldoon. We picked at him, making all sorts of jokes at his expense. This went on for most of the day; it was good not to worry about anything or anyone for one whole day.

I curled my feet underneath, leaning my head back against the corner of Navar's splendid chair. I smiled into the fire.

"Maybe Corbin will be back tomorrow. I do hope he is safe," I whispered into the fire. The fire had begun to burn down. I yawned and stretched. "Might as well call it a night." I showered, brushed my teeth, and climbed into bed.

The next thing I knew it was morning. The soft sound of Deireadh's voice wafted through the door.

"Waitin' breakfast is, eat we will not till with ye be. Care for some food ye may?" she asked.

"Ooh, that sounds good!" I said, kicking the covers off my legs. "Come on in while I get dressed," I yelled as I threw my jeans and a denim shirt over my arm and headed to my almost-completed bathroom. "How's it going this morning?" I yelled through the bathroom door, filling the empty time while I got dressed.

"Well does it go," Deireadh said with a giggle. "Master Calldoon, in morning he be, telling he be, Ms. Doulsie, that need she does, the little redhead. Pretty she is, sparkly he thinks her to be."

I came out of the bathroom, still fighting my hair into a ponytail. Deireadh was staring out the window. She was so deep in thought that she didn't even look around as I walked by. I sat down in the chair to put my sneakers on.

"Whatcha thinking about, girl?" I asked.

Slowly she turned and walked over to my chair. She ran her hand across the top edge. "I need a word there be," she paused and snapped her fingers. "Ba-fubbled I be." As she went on, her voice got lower. "The redheaded girl, this of I speak, something there be. Of what I know not, but there be something."

I jammed my hands into my jeans pockets.

"You know, something did catch my eye. Did you see some blond hair around her ear? It was sticking out just a little around the edge of her left ear."

Deireadh clapped her hands together.

"Ah, yes, thought I did see that as well."

The more we talked, the more we each remembered.

"Was it me, or was she blinking a lot?" I asked.

Deireadh gave a sharp intake of breath.

"Ooh, think do we that she be wearing those things in her eyes like Tanarr wears when out among them? Think do we that she be one of them?"

I tapped my fingernail on my front tooth.

"No...if she was, the castle would have told us. If she was, we would have got that wiggy feeling."

She got an odd look on her face.

"Nay...lay hands on that red curly mop we did not."

"No, I didn't mean it like that, although it could have been a wig. What I meant was, you know, we get that," I paused, not knowing how to put what I wanted to say. "You know," I shivered, "That something-evil-is-here kind of feeling."

"Ah," she said with a nod of recognition. She stopped in midstep. "And was me eyes trickin' or deceivin', see it did ye, color on her neck and her face, the same it was not. Even in the light of the kitchen, which be not good, see it was not the same." She touched the corner of her eye. "Me thinks that me eyes was bein' true, now that we put all together in the same sight."

"Well, it looks like we have a true mystery on our hands, but first and more important to me, anyway, we have a starving girl on our hands, and her name is Katelynn Anthony. If I don't get some food in me soon," I threw the back of my hand to my forehead, put on my best Southern accent, and fluttered my eyelashes. "I surely I think I shall simply fade away." We both giggled.

"Know this I do, we'll not be havin' such." She got behind me, put both of her hands between my shoulders, and began to push. "Off with the two of us so no fadin' have we."

We all had breakfast; however, this morning we ate around the kitchen table because Ms. Doulsie said it made no sense to cart all the food into the grand hall and then have to cart it all back. We all agreed with her. It reminded me of being at my Grandma's house: the smell, the sound, and the love. I watched with great joy as Calldoon ate his food. It was amazing to see how quickly he had recovered.

As I sat there listing to the family-like conversation, my mind began to wander, thinking of my own family back home and dear sweet Ms. Lera. I wondered what she would think of Calldoon's recovery. After all, I remembered her telling me all about her bout with the orchid and how she and Navar had both gone into a coma. I wondered if the difference was as simple as not altering the nectar. Maybe the less tampering with it, the better; could they key be in the amount only? I was sitting there with my coffee cup halfway to my mouth when somewhere in the recesses of my mind, I heard my name being called. I realized it was Ms. Doulsie. I shook my head and blinked my eyes.

"Yes? I'm sorry; my mind drifted," I said.

"Are we that boring, child?" she said with her buttermilk in hand.

"No," I said with a smile. "It's just that I felt so much at home, it made me think of being at my Grandma's."

"Ah," they all said at once. I rolled my eyes at them, and they laughed. We finished our breakfast with all of us participating in the conversation.

When our meal was over and the dishes were cleared, Doulsie shooed Deireadh and me out into the garden with a list of herbs she needed for the evening meal. It felt good to be out in the warm sunshine after the previous day's storm. The air had a crisp feel as we stepped out the door; things smelled clean and freshly washed. I had to stop and smile. Now this was the way to start the day.

With snips in hand, we began going down our list: basil, chives, rosemary, and a few thing I didn't know how to pronounce. We soon found everything she needed; I set my basket down and placed my snips beside it.

"Deireadh, do you think Calldoon is doing as well as he looks?"

"Ah, that I do. For the first time since here I be, and knowin' himself. Just for ye knowin', a long, long time that be." She smiled. "Laughin' he be, real laughin'. Never before have I this side of himself seen." She stopped, set her basket down by mine, and stood up straight, shielding her purple eyes from the bright sunlight. "Or think, maybe hope it be more like, to be so. What think ye?" she asked.

"I think you're right; he is doing so well." I reached over and put my hand on her shoulder, giving it a little rub. "Hope has a power of its own, so we'll all keep right on hoping that he continues to get better."

The day went on uneventfully, thank goodness. It was almost a relief when dinner was over and we were each tucked in our rooms. It wasn't that I didn't enjoy everyone's company, but sometimes I needed the peace and quiet that only comes from being comfortable with yourself and having time to think. Grandma used to say, "You got to be comfortable with yourself before you can be comfortable with anyone else."

I enjoyed some time by the fire; I sat for a little while just thinking about everything, from the events of the day to worrying about the men and being happy for Calldoon. Then I read a little and prayed a lot. I said a prayer for all my old friends and family back home, one for my new ones here, and another for my love who was on a mission of his own.

"Please be careful," I whispered.

Chapter Forty-Eight

"Ow!" The pain that resonated from the crick in my neck woke me up. I was stiff and cold, and both my feet were asleep. I had fallen asleep in my chair. The fire had gone out, so the whole room was as cold as a tomb. Slowly I began to unfold myself and try to climb out of my chair. "Ow! Ow!" I said as I rubbed my neck and walked around, trying to stretch out my legs and get the circulation back into them. "Ow!" I hated it when I did something like this; it made everything hurt for a while.

I stumbled past the mirror, stopped, and looked back. "Oh man, I look bad!" I looked closer, "Really bad." I had gone to sleep without showering or brushing my teeth, and I still had all my clothes on. This was not a good start to a new day.

I heard a firm knock at the door.

"What?" I yelled at the door with more irritation in my voice than I meant.

"Chuck Roberts. Miss, I'm here to start work on the bathroom," he called back. I stumbled to the door and pulled it open. "Whoa, bad night!" Chuck said. "You look like my little brother after he'd been out all night with the good ol' boys."

"Nothing that fun," I said pushing my unbrushed hair back from my face. "I fell asleep in my chair." I pushed my chin to the left and then to the right, and my neck protested with a loud crack. Chuck winced.

"That didn't sound good," he said.

"No, but it felt good. I'll tell ya what, Chuck," I said, hanging onto the door. "If you'll head on back downstairs and have a cup of coffee with the gang, I'll get me a quick shower and see if I can't make myself more human. At the very least I'll look and smell better, but it may take a little while for me to feel better."

Chuck gave me a wink and dropped his toolbox at the door.

"No problem. Take your time. I haven't had my quota of coffee for this morning." He gave the bill of his cap a nod. "Besides that, if I play my cards right, I just might get to talk with that pretty little lady's maid of yours." He made his eyebrows jiggle up and down, turned on his heels, and left.

"Phh…," I let out a long huff of air causing my hair to flutter around my face, gathered up my stuff and headed off to the bathroom. "This is going to feel good, and I am not going to hurry."

The hot shower felt wonderful, and I didn't even care that the light fixtures weren't up or the baseboards down. All that mattered right now was hot water: lots of hot water.

Stepping out of the shower with my hair wrapped in a towel like a turban and a large bath towel wrapped around the rest of me, I began to brush my teeth. This was going to take a while because I never went to sleep without brushing my teeth. My mouth felt like my Grandpa's mule had died in it.

Freshly scrubbed, hair washed and curled, teeth brushed and flossed: I was starting to feel human again. As I stood in front of the closet, it occurred to me that today would be a good day for a nice walk. Reaching in, I grabbed a plain T-shirt, a long-sleeve flannel shirt, jeans, and my boots. I put my clothes on quickly and topped it all off with a cute little headband that let my freshly curled hair tumble down my back.

I took the steps two at a time, inspired by the delicious aroma wafting up to greet me. My spirits began to soar. You only get this kind of feeling from a fresh scrubbing and a hot breakfast that's waiting for you.

I rounded the corner into the dining room; sitting at the table were Calldoon and Chuck. There was no sign of Deireadh.

"Hey, is there any more of that coffee left?" I asked.

"Sure," Calldoon said as he stood to pull out my chair for me. "We have a whole pot awaitin' for ye!"

Chuck drained his cup and set it back on the table with a thud.

"Looks like my time is up. I best be getting to work!"

"You don't have to leave on my account. Sit; have another cup!" I said.

"Oh no, Miss, that's not it. Not at all, but if you want that bathroom finished, I'd best be getting started." Chuck stood, slapped his cap on his head, and gave the bill of it a quick nod. "Tell Ms. Deireadh I hope to be seeing her again."

"Deireadh had breakfast with you?" I asked.

"That she did," Chuck said with a wink and a nod.

"Where is she now?" I asked, looking around the room.

"To the kitchen went she, your breakfast for to fetch," Chuck said with a smile, looking toward the kitchen. "I swear, that girl has the oddest accent." He looked back at me. "It sounds like," he paused, and I could see him looking for some kind of comparison. "I know! If Yoda, you know, the little green guy from *Star Wars*, married a leprechaun, and they lived in the south and had children, she's what they'd sound like. But cross my heart and hope to die, when I'm sitting across from them purple eyes with the light bouncing off that sparkly red hair, she could be chewing me out in any language and I wouldn't care so long as I got to gaze upon that face."

He let out a deep sigh and tipped his cap. "Calldoon. Katelynn," he said, and then he turned and left the room.

I gave Calldoon a smile. He shrugged his shoulders and shook his head. "I know. It's the strangest thing ever did I see. She can turn a man into mush. I can see that now that I'm no longer a vampire. How odd it is, for it seems that I have-a-a-hmm…I don't know how to explain it. I have more everything!"

"I know. Ms. Lera explained it like this. She said that the orchid leaves you with a little bit of itself. You're like a super human but still a human nonetheless." I wagged my finger at him. "Don't forget that. She said that is what killed Navar; he forgot he was mortal."

Calldoon looked up at me, and his eyes were cold as steel.

"We both know what and who killed Lord Navar. When the others get back, we will take care of him."

The truth that he spoke sent us both into a dark spiral of silence. In that silence we sat, drinking our coffee and not saying a word, only thinking or perhaps plotting.

I jumped when my breakfast slid in front of me.

"Good morning," came the familiar voice from behind me.

"Good morning to you, too, Deireadh. This looks great and smells even better!" I said.

"Believe you may, it is what it is. Doulsie made it for ye. I only be carrying it, promise," Deireadh said.

I had to try hard not to laugh, as she was so serious. I patted the seat beside me.

"Have a seat while we finish our breakfast, and thank you both. I know I'm going to enjoy this."

"Welcome," Deireadh said as she took the seat offered her.

There before me was not only a feast for the palate but also a visual feast. My plate was adorned with beautiful flowers from the garden; the colors of the flowers complimented the color of the food. It was simply beautiful all the way around.

I took a big bite. *Who would have expected that the best quiche I have ever had would be here in this stately old castle?* I thought.

"Mmm, this is de-lici-ous!" I said to anyone who cared to listen. "So," I said with a fresh berry on its way to my mouth, "Ms. Deireadh, I think that one Mr. Roberts has a terrible crush on you."

She put her hand over her mouth and giggled.

"Help it I cannot. This be why I stay with the roses. For they care not for the looks of one's face, care they do only for sunshine and rain. They unfurl their beauty and release their fragrance. In return, lookin' for nothin' they are.

Care not what ye have they do. Ah, but the eyes of man, lookin' fer something they be, expecting somethin' they are."

"So, can I fix you up with him?" I asked with a hint of humor in my voice.

She stood up so fast that she almost flipped her chair over.

"Listening was ye not. I've no interest in a man of mortal. They canna' see past what they want. Prefer the likes I do of one like Sir Tanarr, aged he is. He sees, does he, beyond the pages of time. His face looks carved by a master, good, kind, strong, handsome."

She had such a star-struck look on her face that Calldoon and I had to laugh.

"I think that someone has a crush on Sir Tanarr," I said.

Deireadh slapped both her hands down on the table.

"Who? Tell me, if ye can," she said, squinting her eyes.

I leaned in close to her.

"You!" I said. "You're practically drooling!"

She giggled.

"So it be. Miss him I do. Canna' wait fer his return, 'tis me. Oh…," she said like a thought had just popped into her mind. "Should I be fer usin' me gift to be, from the head of Mr. Roberts, removing me?"

"No, no, no. I can talk to him. He's a real Southern gentleman; you know, a nice guy. If you tell him you're not interested, he'll leave you alone." I said. I knew she didn't need to expel that kind of energy. She didn't know how much she had left, so with that in mind I didn't want her to waste one speck of it if I could handle it myself.

The dishes were cleared away, and we enjoyed one last cup of coffee. Looking over the rim of my cup at Deireadh, I asked her, "Would you care to go on a walk with me after we finish our coffee?"

"I like to walk, too," Calldoon said, letting his cup land a little too hard on the table. We both gave him a look, and he knew what it meant. He threw his hands up. "Okay, fine! I'll stay in and rest, but tomorrow, I'm going on a walk." He stood and gave us a good finger wag with his eyebrows almost touching each other; he was not happy with us. "And neither of ye can stop me," he said with his eyes landing on Deireadh. "Not even ye, little fairy, for ye have no power over me anymore. At least, I don't think ye do." He looked over at me, and I gave my shoulders a shrug.

"I don't know. Ms. Lera never encountered a fairy, or if she did, she didn't think I would need to know about it, because she didn't think I would ever meet one. No, I'm all but sure if she had met one, she would have told me. I think, maybe? Unless Blake didn't give her the chance to tell me. Either way, I guess you're on your own with this one."

"Arrr…," he growled, and then he turned and left the room.

I turned back to Deireadh and leaned over the table.

"How about that walk?" I asked.

"A pretty day it be. A reason to not, I canna' think," she said.

"Great! Let's help Doulsie with the dishes, then we'll be on our way!" I said as we carried the remainder of the dishes into the kitchen. Ms. Doulsie tucked one of the dishcloths into her apron and waved her hands at us.

"Don't ye be bothering with me dishes; the day is young, and so be you. Ye need to be out and about. I got these ol' things. Shoo! The two of you, go! Be one with the day! Some fresh air will do ye good."

"What do you say, Deireadh? I'll grab my backpack, throw some snacks in, and meet you in the courtyard?" I asked.

"Sound it does like a fairy circle full of leprechauns, that much fun. Food this ye will not need, not for me, fer I will be munching on some fairy fern while out we be." She smiled. "What a giggle we will have."

I grabbed my backpack, stopped by the kitchen, and threw some snacks and a couple bottles of water in. *I can't wait to be outside in the fresh air. It feels like forever since I went on a walk.*

"You children take care out there; I'll be expectin' ye in fer dinner," Ms. Doulsie yelled across the kitchen.

"We'll be careful," I said, putting the last thing in my backpack. "I'm sure we will be back before dark. See ya later!"

In the courtyard, I found Deireadh sitting on one of the benches and swinging her legs while she waited for me. I stopped right in front of her.

"Ready to go?" I asked.

She stopped swinging her feet and looked up at me.

"Think I have, perhaps be this not a good thought. Thinkin' we could, just perhaps, run into things we should not."

"Ah, come on, Deireadh! It will be fun! We won't go far; we'll stay within our borders. I promise we won't step one foot off our land. We'll be fine; come on!" I pleaded.

"Well," she said with a tilt of her head. "If promise ye do, that before dark we be back," she paused, giving me a stern look. "We will the castle be back in before dark. I can see no harm."

"Woo hoo! Let's hit it!" I said, taking a large step toward the gate.

"Hit whom?" I heard Deireadh say from her perch. She had not left her spot on the bench. "I see no one to pummel."

I turned and grabbed her by the arm, dragging her from the bench.

"It's only an expression. It means we're going to get going. You know, our feet will be hitting the trail."

"Ah, see this I do. Me thinks it be time to hit it!" she said with big smile as off we went.

We walked and walked. It was marvelous. The air was crisp; the sky was blue except for one little puffy cloud that kept collecting friends. Deireadh shielded her eyes, looking up at the sky.

"The clouds, gray they be growin', dark. Think we might should be turnin' back."

"Nah, it's just one little puffy cloud. It will be fine; it's gonna float on by. Besides that, I'm not ready to go back yet. If it comes a little shower, we'll run for the trees. It will be okay; you'll see," I said, pulling my backpack up on my shoulders and heading toward the tree line.

"Yes, see we will," Deireadh said casually.

We were making good time, enjoying each other's company as well as the beautiful day even though ominous clouds kept following us. That pretty little fluffy cloud had now collected a lot of friends and was no longer so pretty. We had made it almost to the edge of the woods when, as Deireadh had predicted, it began to rain: a soft rain that threatened to get much stronger.

Just at the edge of the tree line I spotted a small shelter. I didn't know why it was there, as it seemed to be an odd place for one. All I knew was that I wanted to get out of the rain right then, and it was close.

We made it to the shelter without getting completely soaked. We tucked ourselves in and waited for the rain to pass. Finally the clouds began to break up, and the rain stopped.

"Look, look!" Deireadh said, pure pleasure beaming from her face. "Be there yonder a rainbow!"

I looked in the direction she was pointing. My breath caught.

"Oh, my! That's just about the prettiest thing I have ever seen!"

It was not just a rainbow; it was the biggest, brightest, prettiest rainbow ever. It was truly magnificent. It stretched the spans of the whole field, from tree line to tree line. We sat there watching it until at last it faded and vanished from sight. I sighed.

"That was the best show ever!"

I picked up my backpack and began rummaging through it.

"You know, I think I'm going to have a snack and some water before we go on." I dragged a bottle of water out and gave it a little shake. "Will you join me?" I asked.

"No, thank ye," she said with a shake of her head and a wink, "for yonder there be a fairy circle, sittin' just inside the woods it be, far not at all. See from here now. Food and water there be for the likes of me, awaitin' for the takin'."

"By the way, what do you eat?" I asked.

She smiled and twirled around, making her hair shimmer in the sun.

"Nuts, berries, and raindrops: true feast, if a fairy ye be!" With a wave and a smile, she was off.

As I sat there on the makeshift bench watching the sun come out, the fog started to get thick as the earth began to dry herself. What a beautiful place, so green and lush! My mind began to wander. I could see fairies and leprechauns frolicking on these fog-laced hillsides. I took another bite of my snack and a big gulp of water.

*Hmm, question…*I thought. *If I'm out here with a fairy, who by the way looks nothing like I thought a fairy would, well, maybe a little like one, only taller, a lot taller, and I now own my very own charmed castle, could there be leprechauns running around out in the forest? That's not too far of a stretch considering what I'm already in the midst of, now is it? Just think! How cool would that be, little pocket-sized green people, granting wishes and giving out pots of gold?*

A flash of something caught my eye in the deep of the fog. I stood up and squinted my eyes, trying to see through the thick and murky air.

"What was that?" I said out loud. "Deireadh?" I whispered into the mist, just in case it was not her. I didn't want to be too loud. "Deireadh?" This time I whispered her name even more softly. Now I was a little freaked, so I retreated to the far corner of the shelter.

Could it be a leprechaun? I thought. I let out a huff. "Yeah, right!" I said as I got a grip on my courage and my reality, deciding to step outside of the shelter. *It's probably only a rabbit or a deer*, I thought.

Panic gripped my heart as something brushed my shoulder. A chill ran down my spine.

"Corbin, if that's you, stop it! You're freaking me out!" I said out loud. Something brushed the back of my neck.

"Guess who?" came a sadistic voice with evil undertones. There could be no mistake; it was none other than Blake.

"What is it you want, Blake?" I hissed. "Ms. Lera along with all her secrets are gone," I lied.

"I well know that the defanged Lera is no longer among us. As for her secrets, ta, ta, ta," he said with a mocking finger wag. "I'm not so sure about all of her secrets." He now showed himself and began to circle me. "I think perhaps you may hold her secrets. Am I right?"

I lifted my chin.

"I have no earthly idea what you're talking about!" I said with as much disregard for him as I could muster.

"Well, if that is the case, then I have been wasting my time, and I don't like to do that. Just so this all is not a waste, let's me and you dance, hmm?" Blake said with an evil smile.

"I wouldn't dance with you if you were the last person on the planet, and besides, there is no music," I said, trying to dismiss him.

He leaned in close, still not touching me, but he was so close I could feel his breath on my ear as he whispered, "We don't need music for this dance."

I broke out in chill bumps. I heard a deep rumble of laughter.

"I see that I still have an effect on you," he hissed.

"Yeah, but not in the way you're thinking. There is a big difference between desire and disgust," I said, giving him a sideways glare.

"Yes, but which one is it?" he said, stopping in front of me. "You can't tell me that is disgust. I can hear your heart racing; your blood pressure is rising. I can smell it," he said, arching one eyebrow. "So you tell me. If it's not desire, then it must be fear!" He grabbed me by both shoulders and jerked me in close, so close that we were nose to nose. "Do you fear me, little girl?" he laughed. "You should!"

I took my hand, placed it in the center of his chest, and pushed, giving myself a little space. I tried to act coy: tough, showing no fear. I squared myself, hooded my eyes, and lowered my voice.

"All this fresh air must be mucking with your senses because it's neither of the two. If you think for one minute that I desire you, well, that turns my stomach!" I said with a snarl. "And if you have delusions that I'm afraid of you," I threw my head back and laughed out loud, "boy, then you couldn't be further from the truth!"

He began to circle me once more, stopping behind me.

"Me thinks the lady doth protest too much!" he whispered into my hair, "for I know that you are all alone. I could do with you as I please; there is no one to stop me!"

I spun on him, catching him off guard.

"Now that's where you're wrong!" I knew that Deireadh was somewhere close; at least, I hoped she was. With that in mind, I gathered as much bravado as I could paste on, hoping he couldn't see through me.

He circled me once more.

"What a brave little girl you are," he said at my back. "But I grow tired of this game. Tell me all that Navar's woman told you, and I'll leave you be." With lightning speed he pulled me hard against his chest, wrapping his arm around my shoulder until his hand rested just under my ear. He began to stroke the throbbing artery that threatened to explode with white hot fear.

Deireadh, where are you? I screamed in my head.

He spun me around to face him and grabbed my chin.

"Tell me!" he screamed in my face. "Or be prepared to endure the wrath of my anger!"

I tried to shake my head free, which only caused him to tighten his grip.

"I don't know what you're talking about!" I managed to say.

His eyes turned darker.

"In that case, if I can't have what I've come here for," he had an evil seductive smile on his face, "I'll settle for you."

My breath caught in my chest. I would not go quietly like a sheep to the slaughter. I was determined that he would have to work for this meal. I started to fight with everything in me, kicking, hitting, scratching, and screaming. He only laughed.

"Keep that up," he said as he tightened his grip. "I like it. I can play as long as you like," he chuckled. "Although we both know how this will end." Blake slowly lowered his head toward my neck. My heart was pounding in my ears, and my body went limp. My mind went into slow motion. *This cannot be happening. I'm going to end up with Corbin, and we are going to live happily ever after with our three kids and a dog named Spot.*

When Blake got close to my ear, I barely heard him say in an evil snarl, "So much for happily ever after!"

One tear formed in the corner of my eye.

"Farewell, my love," I whispered as I started to close my eyes for what would be the last time.

A flash and a sparkle caught my eye. Everything stopped. I could feel Blake's breath on my neck, but he wasn't moving. Ever so slowly, sparkly fingers curled over Blake's shoulder. His face was blank.

I heard Deireadh's bubbly voice.

"What be this in the palm of me hand? Can this not be as it appears? Bother are you this lady of human form? For the circle of the fairy she be a true friend, beg of her, her forgiveness."

Blake obediently responded, "Forgive me my trespass. What may I do to make all things right?"

Deireadh cocked her head to the side and placed her index finger on her chin. *She is having way too much fun with this*, I thought.

"Think I am, what needs to be, feel better, it will make us." She clapped her hands together just under her chin. "Decide have I, hand out yer fat wallet, to the fair lady ye must give, appease the spirits you may."

Without saying a word, Blake reached into his back pocket, pulled out his wallet, and handed it over to me.

"Does this appease m'lady?" Deireadh said with a mischievous grin. I bit my lower lip and rolled my eyes, trying my best not to laugh out loud. She reached out and took the wallet from his hand and placed it in mine. "This will do fine, believe it do, that it will." She turned back to me. "Require any more of this wingless creature do ye? If no be ye answer, take leave of us himself must."

"I'm good," I said with a mix of humor and relief.

She lifted her sparkly hands and waved him away.

"Then be gone ye may, but be gone with great haste. One more thing I have of thee," she leaned in and gave him a good finger wave right in his face.

"Bother us no more this day." With that said, she waved him away. He took off with amazing speed.

After Blake left I crumpled into a heap of nervous laughter.

"That blows my mind how you can do that!" I said, wiping tears off my face from laughing so hard. She smiled a big cocky smile.

"Great fun 'tis, seein' someone such as himself, so high and mighty thinks to be of himself. No one can best him, thinks he thinks." She reached over took my hand with the wallet in it, and with one swift movement she raised our hands to the sky. "Show him did we," she said with a giggle. "As fer me handiwork, last it will not. By the morrow, puff! Gone it will be. Back with us to herself we must be; her protection need we. Not knowin' he was here, the end of you it could have been. Barely heard ye I did; herself makes our knowin' stronger."

I gave Deireadh a sideways look.

"Are we talking about the castle?" I asked.

"No other would I be, for only herself can aid us like she, safe we be within her arms. So be off with us before the dark falls upon us when none is safe."

"You got it, girlfriend. I don't want to be out here with the creepy things. That would be either two or four or however many legs they have. When I'm no longer number one on the food chain, I want strong walls and even stronger locks around me, especially at night."

We made our way back to the castle as quickly as we could. Even then, it still took quite a while to get back; we had walked much further than I meant for us to.

"Ta-da!" I said as we crossed the arched bridge onto the castle grounds. The very first person we ran into was Ms. Doulsie; she looked at us over the tops of her little glasses.

"I'd be thinkin that the two of ye be into some mischief," she said.

"Us?" I said with an innocent eye flutter. Deireadh could no longer hold back her laughter. I had Blake's wallet in my hand; I gave it a couple of bounces in the air.

"What have you got there?" Doulsie inquired, still peering over the top of her glasses.

"Ah, to the victor goes the spoil," I said with a grin. Before the wallet landed in my hand for the third time, Calldoon caught it.

"If this is what I think it to be, there is going to be one very confused vampire wandering about." He brought the wallet to his nose and gave it a good sniff. "I do believe I smell fairy tomfoolery at hand."

I stepped close to Deireadh.

"Can he really smell what we've been doing?" I asked out of the corner of my mouth.

Calldoon stepped up behind us, draped his arms over our shoulders, and stuck his head between us.

"For starters, I may not be able to smell what ye two have been up to, but I do have perfect hearing, and it does not take a keen sense of either to know that if this fine fat wallet belongs to one Mr. Blake Klavell, then ye two dears have just thumped the hornet's nest."

Calldoon gave us both a good squeeze and a little shake then stepped past us to stand by Doulsie, who was slowly shaking her head.

"Girls, tell us that ye have not done this thing?" Doulsie stopped and leaned in toward Calldoon without taking her eyes off us. "Who be this Mr. Blake Klavell? Do we need to be fearin' him?"

"Only one of the most vile creatures, if not the most vile," Calldoon said, still standing straight and not moving.

"He be one…of…," Doulsie began, and Calldoon finished her statement.

"Yes, he is a vampire, but not like us. I mean, not like Lord Navar, his knights, and Zoul. This one, he is evil to the core. He is evil, and now this evil will be furious when he comes out of this fairy fog and discovers that he has been beguiled by a fairy."

"Oh, Calldoon," Deireadh said with a wave of her hand and a giggle. "Remember he will not."

Calldoon shook his head.

"He may not remember the whole encounter. However, he will know that he has no memory of where he has been or what he has done, and he also has no wallet. He is a smart man. It won't take long to add up all the facts." He nodded. "Then he will know, and he will come looking for ye."

Deireadh looked at him from under her sparkly lashes.

"Worry, worry too much ye do. Think him to remember, I do not. Good am I, at what I do," she giggled.

"That may be true, but ye two need to stay close in until everyone gets back so that the castle may help keep an eye on ye. I truly do not trust Mr. Klavell. I have seen the horror of his evil; it will haunt me until the end of me days." A deep sadness touched the corners of his eyes. "I canna' protect ye anymore. He is a smart man; it will not be long until he realizes that we have a fairy. Then he will figure out a way around it. Ye know that I'm right, so stay close: no discussion."

Neither of us challenged him further. We only dropped our heads with a quiet, "yes, sir."

Giving each of us a stern look, he issued a final warning. "Now, be off with ye two; it will soon be time for the evening meal. Stay within the protective circle of the castle, and do not antagonize Klavell further. As for his wallet, I have not decided what be the best to do with it."

After our dressing downs, Deireadh and I each returned to our rooms. I opened the door to my room and headed straight to Navar's big chair. There I flopped in front of the fireplace.

"Oh, man, I hope we didn't screw up, although it sure was fun making Blake jump through a hoop or two!" I had to laugh a little, but what if Calldoon was right and Blake would figure everything out? If he knew that we had a fairy on our side, it could be bad. Just how bad, I didn't know.

I shivered. I couldn't think about that, not when my guardian was so far away. I stood and walked over to the window. Looking out over the countryside, my mind began to wander. *Where are the men? Are they safe? Will the High Priest help them?*

At the sound of a knock at my door, I jumped like I had been shot. My heart was pounding.

"Y-y-yes?" my voice broke. "Who is it?" I said, clearing my throat and my thoughts.

"'Tis only but meself. Here I am. Sent to fetch ye I was. The food 'tis hot and awaitin'," Deireadh said through the door.

I opened the door, inviting her in.

"Scarin' ye was not in me plannin'," she whispered.

"You didn't scare me, but you sure did give me a start. I was lost in my thoughts," I said.

"Had yer mind gone to be with yer man?" she said with a faraway look in her purple eyes. "This feelin' I know. Feel it I do of sparks, stars, and dandelion tops, when of thoughts Tanarr in my heart comes."

"I hope they're all okay. I'm beginning to get worried about them," I said with a sigh. "Let's just put any and all bad thoughts out of our heads. There is no need to court trouble. They will be back as soon as they can, and they will be fine." I linked my arm through hers. "So instead of worrying about what we can do nothing about, let's go see what wonderful things Doulsie has prepared for us today."

At the table we all enjoyed a beautiful, tasty assortment of vegetables and breads along with a large, well-seasoned, perfectly cooked beef roast. After the meal was over, someone from the kitchen brought out a tray with a fruit tart browned to perfection and a large pot of coffee. We sat for the longest time, eating tart and sipping coffee. Conversation was light, with no thought of the day's events. Not one word was mentioned of Blake. As the evening went on, a very unladylike yawn caught me off guard.

"Oh, my! I must be a lot more tired than I thought. If you all will forgive me, I think I'm going to call it a night." I pushed back from the table as Calldoon got up to help me with my chair. "Thank you, and good night. I'll see you all tomorrow," I said as I left the dining hall.

I slowly climbed the stairs; my feet felt as if they were made of cement. I smiled as a vision of the commander at Silver Cove Retirement Center came to mind. He had once offered to have a pair of cement shows made for Blake if he got out of hand with me. I'd be happy to have the commander watching over us right now. I had to admit that I was worried.

Chapter Forty-Nine

I got ready for bed, turned back the covers, crawled in, and pulled the thick comforter up over my nose. I went straight off to sleep, but as we all know, there's sleep, and then there's sleep. I drifted off deep into dreamland, and not a happy dream at that but a scary, restless dreamland. The fog was as thick as it had been today after the rain.

Blake rose up out of the thick milky mist, only this time he had us trapped. We were completely unable to move. I couldn't even move my arms. Blake circled Deireadh, making horribly scary threats. She, too, was frozen with fear. She couldn't move; she just stood there blinking, for her fear of Blake had stolen her voice.

Blake circled her once more, this time stopping behind her. Taking hold of both her wings, he ripped them from her back and cast them to the ground. Shock spread across her face, and tears rolled down her cheeks. That was the last I saw of her before she crumpled to the ground. I couldn't no longer see her or even hear her; she was completely consumed by the fog.

Blake's full attention was now bearing down on me. Fear gripped my heart. I didn't know if he planned to simply kill me, cruelly toy with me like a cat with a mouse and then kill me, or worse, infect me, changing my life forever and leaving me a shell of living death. Whatever his plan was for me, I knew it would not be simple or painless.

The closer he got to me, the harder I fought, but I still could not move. I tried to scream, but just as with Deireadh, that same fear had stolen my voice. My screaming was deafening, except that I was the only one who could hear it. The closer he got, the harder I screamed. Still, not a sound came out of my mouth. I could hear his feet crunch in the grass, hear his evil laughter, and feel his breath on my skin. I tried to scream once more as fear gripped my very soul.

My door slammed into the wall; the explosion it caused when it made contact jolted me back to reality. My heart was racing. I couldn't think. *Why are all these people looking at me? What has happened?* Fear began racing through my veins as the blood drained from my head.

"What's going on? Why are there so many people in my room?" Their faces began to blur, and the room started to spin. "I think I'm going to pass out," I said, trying my best to catch a breath in between words.

"Not on me bloody watch," Doulsie said as she slapped a cold, sloppy wet cloth on my face. "Shhh, shhh," she cooed in my ear as she rocked me back and forth while lightly patting the moisture off my face. Coming fully awake, I began to push against her.

"Okay, okay! I'm fine."

"Are ye sure, child? Ye still be a wee bit pale," Doulsie said, reluctant to release me from her parental care.

"I'm sure," I said, looking around the room. "What, pray tell, is everyone doing in my bedroom?"

Calldoon clapped his hands, and everyone cleared out except for him, Deireadh, and Doulsie. Deireadh came around, taking a seat on the bed by Doulsie and me. With Doulsie on one side and Deireadh on the other, Deireadh reached over and patted my hand.

"Scream, scream ye did. Scared we were, so very, running from all places we did," Deireadh said with such a worried look on her face.

"Screaming?" I asked.

"Oh, child, ye sounded like a herd of banshees, woke the whole house. Everyone came running from every place," Doulsie said, waving her wet cloth around in the air.

"We knocked and knocked and yelled yer name, and when ye did not answer I had to kick the door in. That, for the record, is not such an easy task with meself no longer a vampire full of all kinds of strength and all. But when ye did not answer, I had no other choice." Calldoon walked around in front of me. "Are ye doing all right now?"

"I'm fine. It was just a bad dream," I said with a huff of relief.

"Bad dream?" Doulsie said, gathering me back into her arms. "There, there. Tell us all about it, for in the tellin' twill chase away all the badness."

"Nah, it was only a dream," I said with a shake of my head. "A really scary, really bad dream, but still only a dream."

"Come now, child, it was a bit more than just a dream. It was a dream that had ye wailin' till ye almost brought the roof down on herself. Tell us; let us help shoulder the fear, for when ye spread it out, it not so hard to carry, am I right?" Doulsie said with a warm smile.

"Okay," I said, sitting straight up in the middle of the bed. "There was fog…a lot of fog. Deireadh and I were trapped in the thick stuff. Then Blake appeared. The next thing I knew, my door was smashing into the wall and my room was filled with people." I sweetly smiled. "The end."

There was absolutely no way I was going to tell them that Blake had ripped the wings off Deireadh, leaving her crumpled in a pile of tears: no way. So I fudged a little and told a little white lie. Well, not even a white lie: it was more like I left out some of the details, gory details.

Calldoon made his way over to the door.

"If ye truly be fine, then I'll be turning in. Nowadays I need me rest; that has been the hardest thing to get used to," he smiled. "Aye, but I do love a good night's sleep." He came back over to me and took me by the chin. "As for you, missy, 'twas only a dream, so climb back into bed and go back to sleep. This time, only sweet dreams: no screaming. Ye almost frightened the life out of me, and I only just now got it back." He winked. "Good night, ladies."

Doulsie gave me one more hug.

"Are ye sure that ye have no more need of old Doulsie?"

I smiled and nodded.

"I'm sure. It was only a dream. I'm good."

She slid off the bed.

"Well, if ye be sure, methinks that I'll be takin' meself off to bed." She stopped at the door, turned back, and held up one hand. "But if ye have a need, just call." She smiled. "I know for sure that I'd be hearin' ye. We all be herein ye, fer ye have quite a set of lungs on ye, ye do." She blew me a kiss. "I'll be seein' ye in the morrow."

I smiled at Deireadh, the only one left in my room.

"I really am fine; you don't need to stay."

"Need I don't, stay I will be doin' if ye will but allow. Scared ye still be," she said.

"Okay, you're right. I am still a little shaken up. It's just that, my stupid dream was so real I could smell it. How weird is that? It's like I had smell-a-vision in my head."

Deireadh took the seat on the bed that Doulsie had vacated.

"Strong he be. In ye head he can get. Let him in do not. Stronger ye be; win ye can," she said. I could see the concern in her purple eyes, but her next statement caught me completely off guard. She was playing with a string on the bedspread. Her voice broke ever so slightly as she spoke.

"I be knowin' this all for invading me own sleep 'twas the same dream I am believin'. Wings are no more, ripped from me own back, cast to the side. Afraid I am, coming for ye he was. There on ye I saw." She put her hands over her ears. "Screaming, screaming 'tis what brought them all." She closed her eyes then slowly opened them, looking me straight in the eye. "Know I did before I woke; the dark one, he is coming for ye." She shivered. "Still feel ye fear, for it mingles with me own. Comes not the sleep, so if fine it be then stay I will. Feel better we both will."

I reached over and patted her hand.

"That's really not necessary. We're completely safe," I said.

Her eyes fluttered open, large and round. Her eyebrows arched up. The emotion on her face was sadness, or perhaps it was fear.

"No, no, here on the rug I be, quiet as a mouse. See ye will. Send me not away, not knowin' me to be here, ye will see." She kept talking faster and faster. *It's fear*, I thought. I reached over and touched her forearm.

"Shh," I whispered. "We're okay. He can't get to us here."

She began to calm herself.

"Think I do, thump the hornet's nest we did. Vexed him we did," Deireadh said so softly that I almost didn't catch what she said. I laughed and gave her a hug.

"Thumped it? Heck, yeah, we thumped it! And if he messes with us again, next time we'll squash not only the nest but we'll whip the dang hornets, too!" I said with more courage than I felt.

"Still, stay I may?" Deireadh said with a plea in her voice.

"Sure, you can stay, but you're not sleeping on the rug. You can sleep on this end of the bed, and I'll sleep on the other. This old bed is so big we'll hardly even be able to see each other," I said as I got off the bed and grabbed her a blanket from the top shelf of my new closet along with a fresh pillow. She curled up at the foot of the bed. I snuggled up at the other end under the covers, and the next thing we knew, we were both sound asleep.

Chapter Fifty

The fog that had been Blake's life for the last eighteen to twenty hours began to lift. As the sun rose, the fairy's spell lifted. He shook his head, trying hard to figure out where he was and what was going on. He made a motion to get up only to discover that Janet was wrapped around him like a strangler fig; any time she got the chance, she did this to him. *What is it they say? Keep your loved ones close and your enemies closer? I'm not sure which one of those groups I fall into. Either way, I don't care for clingers*, Blake thought. He pulled her from his chest; she protested slightly before she rolled over and curled around a pillow.

Blake walked over to the window. The sun had just begun to peek over the edge of the horizon. He ran his hand through his thick black hair. *What is wrong with me? If it were not for the fact that I have not consumed alcohol in several centuries, I would swear I had a hangover. To the best of my memory this is somewhat like how that felt. My mouth feels as if something vile has taken up residence in it. My memory for the past few hours is nonexistent. My brain is still a little fuzzy, as is my whole being.* He stood there for a while just trying to think.

Janet rolled over to reclaim her prize only to discover that he was nowhere to be found.

"Blake?" she whispered. "Blake?" this time a little louder.

"What?" his reply was flat and cold.

She flipped the sheets back and patted the space beside her.

"Bring your hunky self back over here. Your lovey dovey is lonely without her sweetie poo."

Blake looked over his shoulder with a snarl of disgust.

"What has gotten into you that makes you speak so ridiculously?"

She slipped out from under the sheets and crept over to Blake like a jungle cat, sleek and on the prowl. She slid her hands over his chest.

"Ooh," she purred. "Is my Blakie-wakie regretting what he said last night?"

In a flash he grabbed her wrist. His eyes darkened.

"What are you talking about?" he hissed in her face.

A quick tear came to the corner of her eye.

"You are!" Janet said with a quiver in her bottom lip.

"I am what?" he said with a vile tone as he gave her a hard shake.

"You're regretting what you said," she avoided his hard stare.

He let a huff of disgust escape his chest. He hated tears; they were a symbol of weakness, and he had no tolerance for weak humans. He grabbed her by the shoulders, pulling her off the floor. He brought her so close to him that she could feel his breath on her skin.

"One more time I'm going to ask you. What are you talking about?" Blake said each word hard and slow; his tone was dripping with venom.

"You, you were so different last night!" Janet stuttered. Confusion whirled on her face. "You were sweet and kind. You said that you cared so much about me that all you were and all you had was mine." She paused, looking into his eyes and searching for a hint of the man he had been the night before. When she could find no sign of that man, she sadly finished her story, for she knew it was only that: a story.

"You said you loved me," she said as her head dropped in defeat. "I should have known it was only one of your games. There is no such thing as a happy ending, not for people like me."

Blake tossed his head back as evil laughter rolled up from the pit of his very being.

"Love?" he laughed. "Love! What a sad, weak human emotion. I'll never saddle myself with such foolishness. It makes one weak; it makes you say and do things you know you should not, give away things you should keep. Be glad you have been spared of love. And know this; I have no need, want, or time for such. Now, leave me; I need to think." He pushed her hands from him, rejecting all that she had offered.

"Fine," she said through clenched teeth. "I don't need you, either." Her shoulders were squared as she started to walk off. Blake laughed and grabbed her, pulling her back hard against his chest. He leaned down and whispered into her ear.

"I didn't say I don't need you; I simply said I don't love you." He took her chin in his hand and kissed her slowly. While his lips were still on hers, he said, "Need you, that I do." He quickly released her. As she started to walk away, he smacked her hard on the backside. "Don't be so pouty, hmm? You don't love me, either; you only want me and all that it encompasses. So don't get all holier than thou on me. I know what you really want, and it has nothing to do with hearts and roses; it's all about gold and power. You know, you should thank me for saving you from the humiliation of love."

He pulled her back once more and tilted her face up to meet his. "Now, don't ask me to feel things I cannot or will not, and I won't ask you to feel things you'll only pretend. We'll go back to the way we have always been: totally and completely self-absorbed. After all, we like each other that way," he said with a snarl. "Love," he smiled, "will only bite you and make you wish you could die. However, if I decide to bite you, you will die: white ash dead. It would serve you well to remember that."

She gave him a sweet little smile that didn't quite reach her eyes.

"Of course, you're right. What was I thinking?" She turned once more to make her escape.

"Speaking of things you want, pitch me my wallet; I have something for you. I went by my holdings yesterday and collected from all of them." Holdings was a soft way of saying brothels, escort services, meth labs, marijuana farms, opium fields, and drug pushers. Blake jiggled his eyebrows.

"Business was good this month."

Janet went to the nightstand where he kept all his stuff. She moved his keys, some papers, and some odd change.

"It's not here," she said, still looking through the drawers.

"What do you mean, it's not there? Of course it's there; that's where I always put it," Blake said over his shoulder.

"That may be; however, it is not here," she yelled back at him.

Blake came over. He searched through all the things that Janet had just perused.

"See! I told ya," Janet said with her hands on her hips.

"Hmm. I must have left it in the car," he said.

She ran her hand up his arm.

"Ooh, what is it? What is it?" she impatiently asked. All thoughts of their past conversation were gone. She really, truly, deep down inside was only looking out for number one; no one else was.

"It's your allowance," Blake replied.

"How much?" she asked, trying hard not to drool or rub her hands together.

He stopped his search, all but positive he must have left his wallet in the car.

"Remember, I said it was a good month."

"Yes, yes!" Janet squealed.

"Your allowance this month is a cool mil," Blake said with a seductive purr. It wasn't even one percent of what he had collected. "Ah, it's good to be the king." He shrugged his shoulders. "King pin: it's all good." Blake grabbed Janet in a crushing hug. "How does it feel to be queen pin?"

Her only reply was a satisfied purr. It did feel good to be able to buy and sell your problems. *I guess he really is right*, she thought.

"I am king," he whispered in her ear just as he released her, causing her to fall back on the bed. "Now leave me!" he barked.

"Hey, but what about my money?" Janet asked with a pout.

"It's in my car." He stopped and gave her an unconcerned look. "I'm certainly not going out to the car at this moment. It will keep; now go!" He wouldn't have gone to get it now even if he had wanted to; it was the principal of the thing. She would not be telling him what to do.

With a huff of irritation, she left the room. Blake began to pace.

*What has happened to me? I must think. Let me see, I went by my holdings, grabbed a quick snack. Ah…*Blake thought with a smile of remembrance. *She was a sweet little thing*, he thought as he tossed his head back and laughed. He raked his hand through his hair and walked over to the window. *Then I found little Ms. Katelynn all by herself at the edge of the woods.* A chuckle rolled up out of his chest. *I do love messing with her! She never backs down regardless of how the cards are stacked against her. It's a shame that do-gooder Corbin got to her before I could work my magic on her. She would have made a good mate. She is one tough chick, or at the very least, she would have made a sweet addition to my best escort service.*

Let me think. I had her trapped, he smiled, slightly tilted his head up, and closed his eyes. *Hmm. I could smell her blood pressure rising. We did a little verbal sparring. I was moving in to rough her up a little: shake her up, see if I could rattle her cage.* He ran his hand over his face. *Then what?* He did some more pacing. *I have no memory; if I didn't know better, I'd swear that they had a fairy…could they?* He shook his head. *No. It's not possible, for the age of fairies has long passed.*

Giving up on finding any reasonable explanation, Blake pulled on a crisp, clean new shirt. He decided that searching for the known was less taxing than torturing himself with the unknown.

Outside, he went through every inch of his car from the glove box all the way to the trunk: nothing! "What did I do with that wallet?" He dropped down on the hood of the car and wracked his brain, trying to remember, but again, he came up with nothing. *What had happened in those hours after I first found Katelynn?* Blake sat there replaying the events of the previous day over and over.

He became so flustered, and that fairy thing kept coming back to his mind.

"Think, Blake! Think!" he said out loud as he smashed his fist into the hood of the car. "Okay, if you can't remember yesterday, let's go back a little further. What was that wizard's name who stayed at the castle? Hmm. He had a daughter, and if her mother was human, she would have been a fairy. *Think, man, think!* "Her name was Deireadh, I think."

He was still mulling all this over as he walked back in the house. "I can't recall the wizard's name, but I'm pretty sure the girl's name was Deireadh. I just don't know if this is of any importance." Blake hadn't noticed Janet standing there, drink in hand.

"What about the last one?" she asked.

"What are you rambling about?" Blake asked, only half paying attention to her or what she had said.

"Hmm, if you ask me, you're the one rambling," she said with a huff.

Blake's irritation level was already at the breaking point.

"You were saying something about the last one!" he all but yelled at her.

"Well, you were the one that was muttering Deireadh," Janet sassed back at him.

"So?" Blake said in a mocking tone.

"So, Deireadh means the last one!" Janet proudly announced with a cock of her head and a look that said *Ha! I know more than you do…this time, anyway.*

"How did you know that?" he asked.

"I read it in some book," she replied with a shrug. "It's Gaelic for last one, or that's what the book said, anyway."

"Ah…," Blake hissed just under his breath. "If I am right, then they do have a fairy. That has to be it! If my guess is right, her name gives her fate away in that there are no more; she is alone."

Janet set her drink on the counter.

"What on earth are you talking about?" she asked, now so confused that her head hurt.

"I'm talking about the one thing that can make a vampire do its bidding. The only thing that can completely control a vampire. The only thing that can render a vampire powerless." Blake stopped and propped his hip against the counter with his head in his hands.

Janet waited for him to finish what he was saying. She finally demanded an answer.

"I give up. What is it that is so all powerful?"

Blake slowly raised his head and lowered his gaze to meet hers. His next words made her jaw drop with surprise and disbelief. He squared his shoulders.

"FAIRY!"

Janet burst out laughing, twirling around the room and waving her hand like she was handling a wand. "You can't be serious? You're afraid of a wand-toting, wing-fluttering, itty-bitty fairy?" she said, flopping down in a chair and dissolving into laughter. The laughter stopped when she saw the fury on Blake's face that was followed by a low hiss of vile words. Janet didn't even understand the language, much less any of the words, but the depths of his anger frightened her.

"Oh no, you truly believe in fairies?"

Blake pounced on her, pinning her between the chair and the table.

"You foolish little girl! Are you so blind that you can only see what is right in front of you? Do you not understand that which you cannot see is more powerful? That we live among the unseen, among those that can blind at will. Only a short while back, would you have believed in vampires? If someone had told you that such lived in the human realm, would you have believed?"

She had stopped laughing and started listening.

"So you're telling me that there are fairies?" She measured about two inches between her thumb and forefinger.

Blake rolled his eyes and shook his head.

"This is not a fairy tale. Do you see me running around in a cape and sleeping in a coffin?"

"Well, no," Janet said. "That's Hollywood."

"Correct," Blake said as he began to pace. "If there is a fairy, she can make herself quite invisible to me, but if, as her name implies, she is alone, well…. One thing I learned a long time ago is a fairy by herself is vulnerable. She can be trapped." He looked away and smiled. "I had myself a good time with a fairy; a long time back, I caught myself one."

Janet knew in her heart that it could not have possibly gone well for the fairy. She didn't want to know but couldn't help it; she had to ask. It was like a bad car wreck that you just couldn't look away from.

"What happened to the fairy?" she asked, trying hard to swallow the lump of disgust that had formed in her throat.

Blake laughed his cynically vile laughter, the kind that made the hair on Janet's arms stand on end. He leaned down so very close to her face.

"Do you really want to know?"

Her only response was a pale-faced denial head shake; she had heard enough. Blake walked over to the window then back to a still pale Janet who was unable to move.
"I need you to make another trip to the castle. See who's there. Make close notes. Let no one touch you."

Janet tilted her head to the side.

"What do you mean, 'let no one touch me'?" she asked.

"Arrrgh!" Blake growled. "You stupid human!"

With that insult hurled, Janet had had enough. She jumped to her feet, causing her chair to go sailing. It hit the floor with a crash, cracking the back. With her fists on her hips and her voice pitch rising rapidly, she began her own rant.

"I may be just a human, but that's only because you keep going back on your end of every deal!" She pointed her finger at him. It shook a little with anger. "But I am not stupid. The last person who called me stupid, who underestimated me that much," she paused, dropped her hands, and raised her chin. "Well, they still haven't found that body."

She turned to retrieve her drink. With her back to him, she began to mutter and make faces into her wine glass.

Blake grabbed her arm and spun her around.

"What did you say?!" he demanded.

"I said," she said, raising her voice, "if you dig that hole deep enough, ain't nobody finding it. Twelve feet will do it every time!"

Her statement caught him off guard. He tilted his head to the side and just stood there for a while as all she said came full circle. He began to laugh.

"You are a true jewel with that quirky sense of humor. Ah, but it's that little evil side that I do so love; it assures me that you and I are perfect for each other. Someday, I will keep that promise: someday soon, but not today. As I was saying, I need you to go back to the castle. And before you ask me why, I'm going to tell you, so hold on to that temper. Yes, it must be you," he said, pulling her into his arms "for they won't be looking for a human. I couldn't get within the walls without that chatty castle telling."

Janet thought that was an odd statement, but she decided to let it slide.

"As for not letting anyone touch you, if a fairy lays hold of you, she can, if it is her gift, strip you of your memory. I think that may be what happened to me."

Janet held up her hand to stop him.

"Okay, okay. If there is a fairy, if she has this gift, and if she is in the castle, just how do you propose I get in?" she asked.

"How did you get in the last time?" he asked.

Janet thought for a while.

"The last time I put on a disguise and told them I was looking for a job. Not just any job but a lady's maid job."

"They bought it?" Blake asked, his voice edged with sarcasm.

Janet glared at him then punched him hard in the gut.

"Yeah, they bought it! I got all the way in and saw all of them! I swear, just when I think you're going to be nice, the real you comes out. I've had it, and I think I just might change my mind. I think I'll leave and forget all about this! Who needs it?"

He tightened his grip around her, pinning her arms to her side. She was trapped in more ways than one. He pulled her in hard.

"You won't," he mockingly hissed in her ear. "But you will go to the castle today or, I think, we will both go," he said with a hint of humor. "Let's see how much we can muddy the waters."

Chapter Fifty-One

Kaaaaate-lynn.

"What is that? It sounds like someone singing!" I heard myself say somewhere in the dreamy haze of my sleepy world. Someone was singing. Kaaaaatelynn. "Ah, what a lovely little tune, so soft and sweet!"

I lingered there, enjoying the peaceful state, feeling safe, soft, gentle, and calm. "I think I shall stay here forever, swinging on my flower-laced rope swing suspended from what I can only assume is a large tree." I didn't care what was holding me up as long as it didn't let go.

Like a needle scraping across a record, everything came to a screeching halt when someone or something touched my arm. My eyes flew open, and I began to scream. My heart was flying.

"Shh, shh," finally seeped into my brain as my eyes began to focus. I ran my trembling hand over my face and took a slow, deep breath.

"Oh, thank goodness and gophers, it's only you," I said as I let my breath out slowly.

Deireadh leaped onto the bed, retracting her feet; you couldn't even see a toe.

"Gopher, did ye say? Like them, thinks me not; get down!" She shook her head. "Not while there be a wild gopher roaming about!" she said as her eyes darted about the room.

"Deireadh, it's only an expression. There is nothing in the room, only you and me, okay?" I said, now fully awake.

She timidly touched one foot to the floor, still not sure that there were no wild gophers hiding under the bed.

"So sorry I be. Frighten ye not, this I did not mean. My intent it was not. 'Tis only that noonday is fast approaching. Doulsie did so tell me that need to rise ye do, starving ye will be," Deireadh said, still looking around for the gopher.

"Well, now that you mention it, I am a little peckish," I said as my stomach let out a loud growl.

Deireadh's eyebrows shot up.

"Peck-kish?" she repeated.

I kicked the covers back and slid out of bed.

"Yeah, I always thought it was an odd saying. My Grandma used it lots. It only means that I'm hungry, very hungry."

"Ah…," Deireadh said slowly as she mulled it over in her head.

I got dressed, and we quickly made our way down the stairs, guided by the interesting aromas that had wafted up to my room.

After I ate, it seemed that everyone had their day planned. Deireadh said that she needed to care for the roses; she had been neglecting them for too long. Calldoon had castle business that required his attention. As for Doulsie, there was always something in the kitchen that called for her skills; she never had time. That left me alone to entertain myself, so I decided to head back to my room.

Even before I got to the top of the stairs, I heard Chuck Roberts singing an old hymn followed by the sound of a hammer making contact with a piece of wood. Upon second thought, it sounded more like the distinct thud of a thumb. My suspicion was confirmed by the wailing that followed. I had to fight hard to suppress the giggle that flirted with the back of my throat.

When I got myself under control, I opened the door. There stood Chuck with a scowl on his face and the side of the offended thumb in his mouth. At this point all bets were off, and I burst out laughing.

"Hey! It ain't so dang funny! I dang near smashed her off," Chuck said.

"Oh, I'm sorry! Is there anything I can do to help?" I said, taking a step toward him and trying very hard not to start laughing again.

"No! I'm fine," he said, still nursing his thumb.

"Okay," I said, raising both hands in a gesture of surrender. "I was only trying to help, and now I think the best way to do that is to get out of your way."

"Hmm," was his only reply.

"So I'll just grab my baseball cap, my purse, and head back out my door." I flipped my cap on my head and my purse over my shoulder, and out the door I went without giving Chuck any more grief, leaving him with all the time he needed.

Let's see, what I shall do with myself today? I thought as I made my way back down the stairs. *It's such a beautiful day.* No sooner had that thought run through my mind than a truly yummy one replaced it. *Ooh! I have my purse. In it is my wallet, and inside that it is my driver's license. And down in the kitchen, hanging on a hook, are the keys to Tanarr's shiny red Ferrari. It must surely have a killer stereo in it. I know he wouldn't mind if I took it for the tiniest little spin around the block. Okay, so there are no blocks out here, but I'll just make a quick trip to town.*

Doulsie may need something from town, like milk or eggs. I could pick them up for her. Yeah, that's it! I'll make a store run for her.

I ran into the kitchen, grabbed the keys from the hook, and bounced the keys in my hand. "Doulsie, do ya need anything from town?" She peered at me over the top of her little glasses. "You know, like eggs or milk?" I asked as I gave the keys another bounce.

"Good heavens, no, child! We have chickens and cows here! We sell eggs and milk to town."

"Oh…," I said, my voice dragging with disappointment.

"But if ye be needin' to go for a ride in Tanarr's shiny little automobile, methinks that he would not mind, so go," she said with a wink and a wave. "Ye be a young lassie with a hankering to feel the wind in yer hair; go."

I clutched the keys in my hand and smiled, trying my best to be cool.

"You know, I think I will. It's a pretty sunny day. I won't be gone long. What could possibly go wrong? A flat tire? A speeding ticket at the worst?" I said with a shrug of my shoulders.

In the back of my mind lurked Blake, but I wouldn't go far. And besides, I refused to let my fear of Blake take over my life in any way. *I will do as I please!*

I slid under the steering wheel. It smelled of new leather and expensive men's cologne, or wealthy vampire; whichever, it smelled good. I slipped the key into the ignition and gave it a turn, and the engine roared to life.

Taking hold of the gear shifter, I engaged the clutch, pushed it into first gear, let off the clutch, gave it a little gas, and promptly killed it.

"Dang it!" *Okay, this is not like driving the farm tractor. Let's try this one more time.* I turned the key and engaged the clutch, and this time as I came off the clutch I added equal pressure to the gas pedal. Slick as a button, I was off. *Oh yeah, this is going to be fun!* I thought as I turned up the stereo.

Tanarr had the XFM on some classical station; Bach came blaring through the speakers. *No, no, no; we need some guitar-screaming, bass-thumping, head-banging rock and roll.* I found the perfect station after just a few turns.

With the windows down and the music pounding, I hit the gas, racing through the countryside. *I can drive however I please for a good while; for the next thirty miles at least I'm on estate lands. After that, I have to behave.*

"Wow! A girl could get used to this!" I said into the wind as I saw the castle disappear from sight in the rearview mirror. I knew that Corbin had told me not to step one foot outside of the castle, but technically my feet weren't stepping anywhere. I gave myself a wink in the mirror. *I don't see what could go wrong?*

Chapter Fifty-Two

Blake and Janet made their way toward the castle. Without warning, he made a sharp turn onto a narrow road. It was barely a road and was more like a trail instead.

"Where are you going?" Janet screeched while grabbing for the door handle along with anything else she could to right her balance.

"I want to show you something," Blake replied calmly as he maneuvered the car around rocks, limbs, and holes.

"What on earth can possibly be on this trail?" Janet asked.

Blake brought the car to a slow stop.

"What is this?" she asked, peering through the front windshield.

"They call it Rundaingne" Blake said as he opened his door and slid out, never taking his eyes off the structure. "The word means, strength of will."

Janet scrambled out close on his heels.

"Who are 'they,' and what exactly is this place?" she asked with wide-eyed fascination. Janet slowly ran her hand down the side of one of the large stones. It was cold, smooth, and powerful. She looked to each side to discover herself at the edge of a large circle composed of huge stones all standing on their ends, each a little different but all still very much the same. She stepped into the center of the circle. The air crackled with a frightening kind of energy.

It was a warm, humid wind that flirted with the edges of her bleached blond hair, even though the day was quite cool and airy outside the circle. *How odd*, she thought as she walked around within the bounds of the stones, slowly turning. She could not quite comprehend what this was. "What is this place?" she repeated.

"It is a monument," Blake said with steel composure as he absorbed the aura of the stone circle like a dry sponge dropped into the ocean.

"A monument?" she said as she stopped to give him a look of disbelief. "To what?" Taking one more turn, she looked all around the circle, trying to understand what she had gotten herself into.

"To death and power: the power of the one with the will to control it," Blake coldly replied.

"Really?" Janet said, turning slowly to give him a mocking look. Blake was so occupied by the circle that he did not even catch her jab, so she decided to push it even further. "Who built it? You?"

"No," he said, walking around the edge of each stone. "Some say the ancient Druids constructed it; others say it was placed here by aliens."

"ALIENS!" Janet laughed. "Little green men? That's a good one!"

"Yes, it is quite humorous, seeing as how I know for a fact that it was the first of the two," Blake said, still inspecting each stone.

There was no way that Janet was opening the can of worms that could be involved with that statement, so she remained silent.

"Ah, the Druids. They are masters within this circle," Blake said with a wave of his hand.

"Masters of what? Large rocks?" Janet asked, scoffing at the boldness of his statement.

Blake spun, quickly advancing on her as he spoke.

"Everything, anything, all things, past, present, future."

Janet instinctively took a step back.

"What do you mean, present?" she asked, swallowing hard at the lump that had formed in her throat. "Are you saying that there are still Druids, practicing Druids? Hmm. That would explain why it's so clean in here. It looks like it has just been swept and scrubbed."

Blake shook his head.

"If no one stepped a foot back into this circle ever again, it would remain spotless."

"How?" Janet asked, now getting completely caught up in his telling.

"It's the power," he said, clenching his fists and raising them to the stones. "Can't you feel it?"

"Feel what?" she innocently asked.

"Power, pure power; this place radiates it. It almost vibrates with power."

She walked around within the bounds of the circle, trying to visually ingest everything he was talking about.

"This power you're talking about: is it evil, or is it good?" she asked as she began to feel the power whirling around her. It was as if the more she believed, the more she could feel it. Her own will was beginning to work within the circle.

"Let's just say this is the only place on earth where a goody-two-shoes fairy has no power," Blake said as a crazy evil smile started at the corner of his mouth and quickly spread over his whole face.

"How do you know this?" Janet asked, trying to sort everything out in her head.

He rubbed his hands together.

"Well, well," he almost chuckled, "just where do you think I had myself a fairy at?"

"NO!" Janet said in a breathless hush.

"Oh, yes, right here, as a matter of fact. Right here on this very spot," he said, splaying his hands to encompass the place where he stood. "She put up quite a fight." He paused and narrowed his eyes. "And this is the same place where I'll take care of Katelynn's fairy."

Janet's hand flew to cover her mouth.

"You're not going to kill her, are you?"

Blake threw his head back and laughed.

"Blake, you're not, are you?" she pleaded.

"This is where you come in," he said, ignoring her plea. "I need you to lure the fairy here."

"No, I won't! I will not be part of this. I know I've helped you with some really bad stuff, but a fairy, and quite possibly the last one at that?" she shook her head. "No, no, no. I will not!"

"So what's the big deal?" Blake said with a shrug. "We've been just fine without dinosaurs, and I'm pretty sure we'll survive without a blasted fairy!"

"NO!" Janet said as she started to step out of the stone circle.

Blake grabbed her by the hair.

"No, did you say?" He wound her hair around his fist till he hit scalp, then he gave her a hard jerk back against his chest. He craned her head around, forcing her to look at him. "No? Do you think you have the right or the power to say no to me?"

Janet grabbed his fist with her hair tangled around it, trying to ease the pain he was causing her.

"Stop it, Blake! You're really hurting me!" she pleaded.

"Good!" he hissed. "Maybe this little pain will serve as a reminder to the real pain that I can inflict if I so choose!"

"Yes, yes, Blake, honey! Anything you say, I'll do it! Please let go!"

He released her hair with jerk, taking a good deal of her hair with him and causing her to fall.

She sat there on the ground refusing to cry, determined to do whatever he asked of her regardless of the cost. This journey had already cost her her grandmother, the only person who had ever loved her. Blake said he had killed her for her, but she knew that he had done it for his own vile reasons. The cost had also included her self-respect, not that she had much of that left, anyway. And now she would be responsible for the end of the fairies. What other price would she have to pay before she got her prize?

She took a deep breath, ready to do whatever she was told.

"Okay, what do you want me to do?" she said with a huff of defeat and a sweet little smile that only touched her lips.

He knelt beside her

"Ah, now, there's a good little girl!" he said as he ran his knuckles down the side of her face. "Here's what you're going to do—"

She stopped him in mid sentence.

"How will I know her? And why do you hate this fairy so much?"

Blake stopped and rubbed his chin.

"Let's just say that the fairy has charmed this vampire for the last time. No one fools me more than once, and this fairy has gotten me twice now." Blake stood and reached down, offering Janet his hand. When she took the offered gesture, he yanked her to her feet, bringing her hard against him and almost knocking the breath out of her.

Still gripping her wrist, he hissed into her face. "Only one other has done so. I don't take kindly to such. That's something you might want to archive in that small space you call a brain."

She chose to let that jab pass unchallenged.

"Was the first one to pull one on you also a fairy?" she asked.

"Yes," his reply was flat and cold.

"What happened to her?" Janet asked.

Blake threw his head back and laughed.

"She was delicious; perhaps a little sweet for my tastes, but I enjoyed every drop!" He laughed again, this time a little more crazily than before.

Janet was cold as a stone as Blake unfurled his plan. She tried hard to catch all the details, but other thoughts kept running through her head. *This dude is getting crazier by the day. I think he is headed over the edge. I only hope he doesn't take me with him.*

"Got it?" Blake barked at her.

There was no reply from Janet; she was still lost in her own thoughts.

"GOT IT?" he said again, this time with a force that jolted Janet back out of the recesses of her fear-riddled mind.

"Got it," she replied. *I hope*, she thought.

"Now, get in the car; we have a fairy to tend to."

Chapter Fifty-Three

Rosey came running into the kitchen at top speed, so fast that she didn't even bother to close the door. Instead, she let it smash into the wall.

"Ms. Doulsie! Ms. Doulsie!" Rosey said in between pants.

Doulsie dropped her dishcloth and made a dash for the frantic girl.

"Child, what's the matter with you?" Doulsie asked, taking the young woman in her arms.

Rosey began shaking her head and pushing out of the hug.

"'Tis not meself. 'Tis Ms. Katelynn, the Lord of our castle!"

Now she had Doulsie's full attention. She took Rosey by the shoulders and looked her squarely in the eyes.

"Ms. Katelynn, you say? What kind of blarney is it that ye be rattlin' off?"

"No, Ms. Doulsie, there be a lady yonder in the courtyard. Told me she did to come get Ms. Deireadh, that Ms. Katelynn was in sure danger and needed her help, her help only," Rosey stated the facts as she knew them.

Doulsie began stripping off her kitchen apron.

"Take me to this lady."

Rosey shook her head.

"No, Ms. Doulsie, she said she was in need of Ms. Deireadh, that she be the only one that could help."

Doulsie, knowing of Deireadh's special talents, questioned Rosey no further.

"Then fetch her we will," Doulsie said. Taking Rosey by the hand, they went out the back door that led into the rose garden. They found Deireadh taking care of the beautiful roses. Doulsie and Rosey both made a dash for her as soon as they spotted her. Rosey was the first to arrive, but Doulsie spoke up first.

"Deireadh," Doulsie said, trying to keep the fear out of her voice.

Deireadh looked up from her task.

"Problem, there is. Help I can, ye have only but to tell," she said with a smile.

Doulsie took both of Deireadh's hands in her own.

"Listen to me, child; it be Katelynn. She has a need of ye special talents. There be a lady in the courtyard. She will take ye to her," Doulsie gave Deireadh's hands a motherly squeeze. "Godspeed, child, and if ye be in need of help, send word. Calldoon and meself will come runnin'."

Deireadh smiled.

"Know this I do." She gave Doulsie a peck on the cheek. "Fine be we," she whispered, then she turned to Rosey. "Take me to this woman. See we will, what be the problem."

Janet was pacing in the courtyard, hoping that she wouldn't screw this up. *Blake will be so mad at me that he might forget that he needs me*, she thought. As soon as she spotted Rosey coming with a sparkly redhead in tow, she knew this must be the fairy. She was in complete awe of the magnificent creature. *She must have been here somewhere the last time I was here*, she thought. *Why didn't I see her? What a shame! She is truly, amazingly beautiful.*

Rosey and Deireadh stopped right in front of Janet. Before either had the chance to speak, Janet grabbed Deireadh by the hand.

"Come on, come on! Katelynn needs you! She's in big trouble!"

"Trouble of what nature be she in?" Deireadh asked.

"No time to explain!" Janet said with a wave of her hands. "We're wasting time! We can talk in the car," Janet said while she hurried around to get them both in the car.

"Sure, sure," Deireadh said, getting caught up in Janet's facade of concern. It wasn't completely fake concern; she was concerned all right, but only for herself and no one else.

Deireadh slid into the front seat of Janet's car. She had been so worried about Katelynn and so rushed by Janet that she couldn't hear the castle trying to warn her about the mischief that was afoot.

The castle tried to alert Calldoon, too, but all she could warn him of was that there was a stranger about and that she felt that this stranger was up to no good. Calldoon dismissed the thought; after all, there was always someone new about. *People come and go around here all the time*, he thought.

In the car, Deireadh began to question Janet.

"Katelynn, where be she?" she asked.

"It's not far, just down the road a little," Janet replied with a flip of her hand.

"Find her, how did ye?" Deireadh flatly asked.

Janet nervously glanced over at her. She was now glaring at her, with no emotion whatsoever on her perfect face. Janet could see suspicion in her glorious purple eyes.

"Oh, you know!" Janet said with a shrug of her shoulders.

"No," Deireadh said in a matter-of-fact way. "Knowin' this, impossible 'twould be. Tired I grow of this game play ye. True of be, what seek ye of meself?"

"It's here, it's here!" Janet said, quickly changing the subject as she whipped the car onto the little dirt road. "She appeared to be hurt, so I told her that I would get you. I promised I'd hurry. It's just ahead, where I left her, that is. You'll see; she's right there!" Janet said as she brought the car to a slow stop at the edge of the stone circle.

"See her, I do not," Deireadh said, carefully looking through the front windshield.

Janet opened her door and slid out.

"She's over here, see? Come on!"

In the throes of her concern for Katelynn, Deireadh had not noticed where she was or how much danger she could be in. She squinted her eyes.

"See her this I do not."

"Come on," Janet urged. "She is right over here."

Deireadh stepped out of the car and around the large stone. There to the far side of the stone circle was a figure crumpled on the ground, not moving.

"I put a blanket over her to keep her warm," Janet said when Deireadh paused. "We better check on her!"

Deireadh moved closer. She reached out to touch the unmoving body under the blanket. Just before she made contact with the lifeless figure lying before her, the form she assumed that was Katelynn, a strong male hand shot out from under the blanket, trapping Deireadh in a vice-like grip.

Blake's trap had sprung. Shock and horror emanated over Deireadh's whole being as she realized that the dream she and Katelynn had shared may come true, for she was powerless within the boundaries of the circle of stones. No one knew where she was; no one would come for her.

Blake laughed his wicked laugh, the one that Janet was haunted by. He loved to see fear in the eyes of his victims, and it gave him special pleasure to see fear in the beautiful purple eyes of this fairy who had tricked him not once but twice.

He bounced to his feet effortlessly, never breaking the painful grip he had on Deireadh's wrist. He began to drag her around within the circle of stones; his evil games had begun.

Janet could no longer stomach watching the horror that was unfolding before her, and Blake was so caught up in his cruelty that he didn't even see Janet slip away.

Chapter Fifty-Four

Wow! I thought, *Now this is one sweet ride. And I thought Judd's homemade go-cart was fun*. Momma hated us being on that thing. She used to say, "You young-guns are gonna get your necks broke on that dang thing!"

I had to smile at the memory of the fateful day I put the go-cart right under Grandma's car. We had spent days helping Judd build the thing, then we selected the perfect hill to launch it from. We all pushed and pulled and pushed till we finally got it to the right spot. I won the game of rock, paper, scissors: the game that determined who got to ride first. I climbed in and pulled Papaw's goggles over my eyes; after all, we didn't know if the go-cart would take flight. I took a firm grip on the steering wheel that we had found at the dump, where we had gotten most of the parts.

"Ready?" Judd yelled from behind.

"Ready!" I yelled back as I adjusted my grip on the steering wheel.

Judd gave a yank on the cord, and the lawn mower engine that we had reclaimed came to life.

"Let go!" I yelled over the noise of the engine as I stomped on the gas. I took off like a slow bullet and sounded a bit like a mason jar full of mad bumblebees. And that's how I wound up under Grandma's car. After they pried me and the go-cart out, I hopped over to Momma, who was working in her flower garden.

"Momma, I think I might want to go see Doc. Taylor."

Momma didn't even look up from her work.

"Well, then, you might want to go see your father, 'cause I told you to stay off that blasted thing. A week's worth of burring is all it's worth," she grumbled, digging even harder in the dirt.

Momma never called Daddy "Father" unless she was really mad.

I decided I was fine, and the go-cart was fine, but I did learn two things that day. One, if you're going to ride a homemade go-cart, don't be the first one, and two, if you are the first one, make sure that the brakes work.

I laughed and shook my head. What fun we had! It was amazing that any of us made it to adulthood. I slowed the Ferrari as I got closer to the castle; after all, no one needed to know how I liked to drive. When I got to the arched bridge that went over the creek at the edge of the castle, I shifted down into first, slowly crawling over the bridge and into the courtyard.

I turned off the engine and slid out from under the wheel. As I walked around the front of the car, I placed a kiss on the tip of my finger then put the kiss on the top edge of the fender.

"Thanks for the ride! What a ride it was!"

Even before I got to the door, Rosey came running to me, grabbing me around the waist.

"Oh, Ms. Katelynn, we all be so glad that Ms. Deireadh found ye before 'twas too late!"

Confusion whirled around me.

"Deireadh? What?" I asked.

Rosey pushed back.

"Ye've not seen her?" she asked.

I shook my head; her eyes darted from side to side.

"Oh," she whispered and hurried off before I could ask any more questions.

I pushed the door closed behind me. There it was: that soft voice whispering in my head. *There's tomfoolery about.* I think that's what she said; I didn't catch it all.

"Tom…who?" I whispered. "Did you say Tom Foolery's foot?" The castle was trying to tell me something. "Who the heck is Tom Foolery?"

About the time I got it, one of the house boys walked by.

"Tomfoolery 'tis but messin' about," the young man said as he continued on his way.

"Thank you," I said.

Again one of the staff passed. "Glad to see ye home safe and sound, m'lady," she said with a bob and a nod.

Have I stepped into the Twilight Zone or something? I thought. *It's always a little odd in here, but what is everyone talking about?*

I rounded the corner and ran smack dab into Doulsie. She looked like a chicken that had had its feathers rubbed the wrong way.

"Oh, saints preserve us!" she said, grabbing me in a big bear hug. "Fiercely worried about ye I was!" She looked around. "Where…where be Deireadh?"

I shook my head.

"I don't know. People keep talking about her coming after me or something like that. I was out for a drive, and you know she never leaves the castle. I'm completely confused. What on earth is going on?"

Doulsie stepped back, adjusted her little glasses, and folded her hands over her apron.

"This woman come barrelin' into the courtyard, flutterin' about, sayin' somethin' about how ye be in a cartload of trouble: the kind of trouble that only Deireadh could help with. She said that ye yerself had asked her to fetch Deireadh, and only Deireadh, so fetch her we did."

"She, who?" I asked.

"The woman who came to fetch Deireadh," Doulsie said in a matter-of-fact way.

"Doulsie, what was her name?"

Doulsie had a blank look on her face.

"I do not know," she said with a shake of her head. "I did not ask. No one did; we all be too scared fer ye."

"Where did they go?" was my next question.

Doulsie only shook her head.

"Wait, Rosey!" she said.

"What about Rosey?" I asked.

"Rosey talked with the woman. Might be that she would be knowin' something. ROSEY!" Doulsie yelled at the top of her lungs. A very reserved Rosey stepped into sight when she heard Doulsie's call. With her head bowed, the usually perky girl was now very somber.

"Ma'am," she said with a bob.

Doulsie walked over to the young woman and lovingly took her by the chin, gently raising her face so they could look each other in the eye.

"Child, fret not, but think hard. Did the woman tell ye her name or where she was a takin' Deireadh?"

A tear rolled down Rosey's face.

"No, ma'am, I did not ask, and she did not say. She only told me to hurry, that m'lady was in danger."

Doulsie wrapped Rosey in a bear hug.

"'Tis all right, child, for none of us knew."

"Well, this is not good," I said as I began to pace back and forth. "Hold it. I'll be right back." I got just outside the door then stepped back and poked my head back in. "On second thought, go get Calldoon and meet me in the dining room in about fifteen minutes."

I made a mad dash to the library. As soon as I got there, I dragged a chair over to the bookcase and climbed to the top corner shelf. I had my hand on the book whose spine read *The Truths of Those That Be*. I just knew that if I could get to the secret room, the castle could help us find Deireadh.

I retrieved the big blank book and climbed back down. I placed the book on the desk. Next I pulled Navar's ring out; I always kept it on a chain around my neck. I held the ring up to the light. "Okay, Go-Brath, we need your help, I know that there needs to be the three of us, but you only have me. I hope that I'm enough," I whispered.

I was about to climb back up on the chair to engage the lock to the secret passage when I heard that soft voice in my head.

"*Shhh. Calm yourself, for it makes no difference if there be three or one not this time, for I cannot help you. The fairy is no longer within my walls. I can only tell you that she left through the front gate. The woman who whisked her away was not true, but she was scared, very scared. She had been here once before, only she was disguised. I have one more warning; not only is the fairy in danger, but you, too, are in danger. The same evil that pursues the fairy will also come for you.*"

The voice in my head went silent.

"Thank you," I whispered.

I made my way back to the dining room, all the while trying my best to come up with a plan. By the time I got there, I still had nothing. As soon as I walked in the room, all eyes were on me.

"Okay, the plan is—I don't have a plan. I thought I did, but I don't," I said, pulling out a chair and flopping down. "Anyone got an idea?"

Doulsie, Calldoon, a couple of house staff members, and I all sat around the table trying to come up with a place to start looking for Deireadh. Rosey came sliding around the corner.

"Ms. Katelynn, Ms. Doulsie, Master Calldoon! Come quick, come quick!" She took a deep breath. "'Tis the woman, the one that came to fetch Ms. Deireadh. She is back, back in the castle!" She shook her head and rolled her eyes. "I meant, she be in the courtyard. Come, come quickly, for she looks like she may take flight. She looks feared for her soul!"

We all sprang to our feet so fast that some of the chairs fell back, clattering on the stone floor. We must have looked like an advancing army as we all piled into the courtyard. I could see fear on the face of the woman. I stopped because she had begun to retreat to her car; I knew if we lost her, we wouldn't have a snowball's chance of finding Deireadh. When I stopped, everyone else did as well.

"Hi, my name is Katelynn," I said with my hand extended even before I got close enough to shake hands.

The woman squinted her eyes.

"I know," she said.

"Can you help us find our Deireadh?" I asked as calmly as I could.

She started to answer when Calldoon charged forward.

"Tell us!" he yelled at the woman, which only made her retreat further into her car.

"I shouldn't have come. Blake is going to kill me, and you will never believe me, anyway," she said more to herself than to any one of us.

Calldoon stopped when he got a good look at her.

"It be ye!" he whispered.

She cocked her head to the side, giving him a good look but one that did not indicate recognition.

Calldoon repeated his statement.

"It be ye! Ye're the one who saved me!"

"Look, dude, I don't know who you are or what you're talking about, 'cause I ain't never saved nobody except this fairy chick, and that ain't turning out so good. I'm just gonna be on my way. Good luck to you all, see ya!" She ducked into her car.

"No, wait! Please" I almost yelled, effectively stopping her with my plea. She pulled herself back out of her car and looked at me with the saddest eyes I had ever seen. I held my hand out to her.

"Please help us find our friend; she is very special to us all."

The woman took a step toward me.

"She's the last one, isn't she?" she softly asked. I nodded, and she came closer. "She's trapped in the old stone circle."

I heard both Calldoon and Doulsie's sharp intake of breath. My head turned in their direction. Doulsie had gone two shades of pale.

"Rundaingne." I heard Calldoon mutter so softly that I could barely hear him. I couldn't tell if it was fear or awe. I turned back to the woman in front of me. I extended both of my hands.

"Help us."

She reached for my hands. As soon as I had both her hands in mine, I knew we would find Deireadh. I only hoped that we wouldn't be too late.

"Come on, let's sort this all out," I said.

She shook her head.

"No, there is not enough time for tea and sweet talk. If we don't hurry, we'll be too late!" A tear came to her eye. "I didn't mean to hurt her. I'm sorry!"

"It's okay," I said, trying not to panic. "Is it all right if we follow you in my car?" I asked.

"Yeah, that's great. That way Blake won't know I brought you. I'll stop just short of the circle, and you guys can drive straight on. If we work this right, I might come out of this alive, but if we don't get a move on it, that fairy won't," Janet said, sliding into her car.

The three of us piled into my small car, and we were off. I stayed close on her bumper; there was no way I was going to lose her.

"Okay, I saw Doulsie turn two shades of pale, and I heard you say Rundaingne," I said to Calldoon as our eyes met in my rear view mirror. When I said "Rundaingne," his eyes darted from side to side, resting on the scenery that was flying by. I thought for a while that he was not going to answer me. I heard him take a deep breath then exhale slowly.

"Have ye any knowledge of the stone circle?" he asked at last.

"Only what I saw on the National Geographic channel. Let me see if I have this right. They are large stones that are set in a circle. No one knows who did it because the stones are so large, and they don't know what their purpose was, either. Some experts say they are some kind of calendar, others say they are clocks, and still others say they are some sort of worship structure," I said, still staying on the bumper of Janet's car.

"Very good," Calldoon said with a nod.

"Well, when you don't have a life other than work, you watch a lot of TV, or at least I didn't used to have much of a life. Now I seem to have way too much life." I gave my head a little shake. "Man, it's either feast or famine!"

Calldoon and Doulsie both chuckled.

"Well, ye definitely be feastin' now!" Doulsie with a giggle in her voice.

"So…," I said, waiting for one of them to tell me what was going on. Neither said a word. "Okay, someone tell me what we are walking or driving into?"

Doulsie remained quiet, only turning paler as she stared straight ahead. Calldoon finally softly began.

"Rundaingne is one of the stone circles. However, it has more power than most."

"Power?" I interrupted.

"Yes, power. Do you know what Rundaingne means?" Calldoon asked.

I shook my head.

"It means power of will. The one with the stronger will and power will gain even more power over his foe, whoever or whatever that foe may be."

Hope began to spring up in my heart.

"Let me think," I said, putting my hand to my temple. "If Deireadh can hold strong, she could win over Blake, right?"

Calldoon nodded.

"Yes, if she knew about the power of Rundaingne."

"What do you mean, if she knew?" I asked as my newfound hope began to dwindle.

"You must remember she is but a fairy, and the last one of her kind at that," Calldoon said.

"What do you mean, she's only a fairy?" I asked, giving him a hard look in the rearview mirror.

Calldoon looked out the side window, staring at nothing in particular as far as I could tell.

"Being the last of her kind, there be none to tell her about it. And even if there were, fairies never took much care about things that the rest of the world would think important. That's how Blake tricked the other fairy into the circle."

"What happened to her?" I asked.

Calldoon shook his head.

"It didn't go well; to be quite frank about it, she did not survive. Deireadh's father and I found her lying there within the circle, or what was left of her. I've tried me hardest to purge meself of the memory of the carnage," he stopped and closed his eyes, leaning his head back. "'Twas like nothing I had ever seen before. He had to have been fiercely angry with her, or perhaps he is just evil to the core. I had seen his handiwork before, as I have told ye, but this? This was far worse."

"Oh…," I whispered.

Chapter Fifty-Five

We drove in silence until we turned onto the dirt road. As we had planned with the woman in the car in front of us, she pulled to the side of the road. I saw her get out of her car, so I stopped and rolled down my window.

"It's just ahead; you'll drive right up to it. As far as I know, it's all that is out here," Janet said, looking off down the road.

"Thank you," I said with a wave and a smile. The three of us drove on. In no time there before us it stood. The hair on the back of my neck began to prickle, and fear gripped my heart.

"What's the plan, guys?" I asked, staring at the structure looming before us. As the last word passed my lips, we heard a bloodcurdling sound. "What was that?"

Doulsie turned to face me, and in whispered tones she replied, "Me thinks…it be…Deireadh." She swallowed hard.

I heard Calldoon scrambling to exit the car.

"I don't know what be the plan, but I do know that Sir Tanarr will have our heads if anything should happen to Deireadh, for ye know he has fallen in love with a fairy," Doulsie said.

I turned in my seat and put my hand on Calldoon's arm to stop him.

"Wait, Calldoon; we have to have a plan. You're no longer a vampire, remember?"

"Ah, this is true, but I also know the secret of the stone circle. And my will is as strong as his, if not stronger. We," he said, giving us a nod, "will distract him. When I give ye a sign, at that point, ye grab Deireadh and take her to the nearest fairy circle."

"Fairy circle?" I said.

"Follow Doulsie," he said.

Doulsie nodded, and we slid out of the car as quickly as possible. The cool air swirled around us. It smelled of damp leaves, babbling creeks, and moss:

that wonderful deep wood smell. On another day, I might have thought this to be a beautiful place. It reminded me of a fairy tale, but this was all too real.

My breath caught; there it was again: that sound. It brought us all to a halt. It was followed by a sound that I would never forget: the deep, thoracic laughter of Blake.

From that point on, we did not speak to each other. Calldoon waved his hands, instructing us to go around the back of the stones. One of us went to the left, and the other went to the right. Calldoon stayed in the center. Blake was still so engrossed in his torture that he had no idea we were there.

On Calldoon's signal, Doulsie stepped from behind the stone she was hiding behind. With her hands folded in front of her, she rocked back and forth on her heels.

"Whatcha doin'?" she calmly asked, much like a small child who had come upon a group of children playing marbles.

Blake was caught so off guard that for a while all he could do was stand there and stare at her. To his disbelief, there standing before him was this sweet little old lady. He was on her in a flash with his hand around her neck.

"Who are you?" he growled.

Doulsie smacked the top of his hand, again catching him off guard.

"If ye'd be letting me go, I might be of a mind to tell ye."

Blake growled and tightened his grip. Next Calldoon gave me a sign. I peeked out from behind my stone.

"Yoohoo!" I called from across the circle then popped back behind the stone. Blake whipped his head around, releasing Doulsie. As soon as he did so, she slipped behind another stone. I popped out on the other side.

"Yooho—!" before I could get my whole yoohoo out, he had me around the neck. Blake pulled me close to him; we were nose to nose.

"It's you!" he hissed. He was so angry now that he was almost shaking.

"Hey!" Calldoon yelled as he ran across the circle and ducked behind the other side.

Blake whirled in the direction of Calldoon's voice. No sooner had he gotten to that side than Doulsie stepped out. She had moved all the way across. Blake had made a dash for her. It was working; we had him completely confused.

I stepped out next, and this time I was a little closer than I had intended to be. He grabbed me around the waist, pulling me hard against his chest. With my back to him, Blake took my hair, yanking my head back so hard I couldn't breathe. He jerked my head to the side so his lips were against my ear. I could feel his cold breath on my skin.

"I should have killed you when I had the chance!"

I could barely speak; he had my head at such an angle.

"You're too afraid of Corbin to do anything to me. You know he would never let you get away with hurting me," I rasped.

Blake laughed and spun me within the circle of his arms.

"Oh, really? If your Corbin cares so much for you, then where is he?" He grabbed my chin. "Methinks that Sir Corbin has grown tired of his sweet little Southern flower," he laughed again. "I think it may be my turn with a Southern belle," he stopped and cocked his head to the side. "I don't think I've ever had myself one of those: not for a while, anyway!" he laughed, giving my chin a hard shake.

He released my face and grabbed my wrist, dragging me to the center of the circle. I almost tripped over Deireadh. I could tell that she was still breathing, but just barely. As he dragged me around, he began to chant.

"Ollie, Ollie ox and free! Come out, come out, wherever you are, unless you want to see something bad happen to your precious Katelynn!"

Doulsie stepped out from behind her stone with her lips pursed and her hands folded over her belly.

"Oh, what a brave lad ye are, bullyin' around little girls. Like to see them cry, do ye? Ta, ta, ta!" She made a little clicking sound as she shook her head.

Blake growled, making a lunge for her. Since he still had a grip on my wrist, I slowed him down. Doulsie slipped back behind her rock. From the other side of the circle, Calldoon stepped in front of one of the large stones.

"Blake!" he yelled. "Do ye remember me?" Blake spun around, still holding firm to my wrist. He tilted his head to the side and gave Calldoon a good look. "Yeah, that's right; 'tis me, the young armor bearer: the one who got ye banished from Go-Brath all those many centuries ago. Ye thought yer assassin had done me in, but not so; she saved me instead."

"So you're nothing more than a mortal again?" Blake said as he advanced on Calldoon. "This time you'll be no challenge at all!"

"There are some things ye might like to be aware of," Calldoon said, dodging Blake's advance quite effortlessly.

"Oh, really? And what would they be?" Blake snarled, never releasing his grip on my wrist. "A human has nothing to barter with. The vampire holds all the cards, so you lose!"

"Ah, one would think that be true. However, although yer assassin did hit her target, she missed her mark. As ye can see, I be alive and well!" Calldoon bragged. I could tell by his mannerisms and tone of voice that he was making fun of Blake, and so could Blake. This only served to make him even angrier; it also put him a little off center.

"Yes, you are alive and well, but now you are only human and no threat to the likes of me!" Blake snarled.

"That is true; I be human. Now listen closely; this is where it gets interesting. I am human but not quite, fer the gift that the orchid left me is superhuman strength, speed, and so on. Plus I can taste again," Calldoon made his eyebrows jiggle up and down. "And there is one last thing. I know the secret of the stone circle. My will could be stronger than yours. Ye see, I'm like ye, only better!"

By now Blake was beside himself. I knew his pride would be wounded. It was more than he could take to think that this man, this human, had gotten the best of him. He dragged me to the center of the stone circle. I had to do a little side step to keep from stepping on Deireadh. He slammed me on the ground so close to her that we almost banged heads. Calldoon kept up his banter with Blake, giving me the chance to check on Deireadh.

I brushed my hand across her face. I could feel her pulse in her neck. This movement caught Blake's attention.

"Just what do you think you're doing?" he said, turning on us.

"I, I, I," was all I could get out.

Calldoon quickly got between us.

"Tell me; had ye rather be frightening little girls? Is this what ye have come to? Are ye too afraid to play with the big boys? Ye know, there was a time when I feared you," Calldoon said, poking Blake in the chest with his index finger. "That time has passed!"

"Deal with me now!" Blake yelled, charging Calldoon with the fierceness of a lion.

Calldoon took a few steps back, clearing the way for us to escape.

I bent close to Deireadh's face.

"Can you move?" I whispered as I gave the two warriors a sideways glance. They were so locked in battle that I think I could have brought a full ambulance right into the center of the circle and they would not have noticed. "Deireadh, can you move?" I repeated my question.

"By meself this I canna' do. Escape while ye may. Feared I am, the end. Go, go now," Deireadh said. She took a shallow breath and closed her eyes. "Go," she softly whispered.

I looked up at Calldoon with pleading eyes. He was effectively avoiding Blake's blows.

"Ye two need to leave now! Go to the fairy circle!" Calldoon yelled.

I shook my head.

"She can't move," I said.

"Then we'll be movin' her!" Doulsie's voice came from just over my shoulder, causing me to jump. I grabbed my chest.

"Oh, Doulsie, you scared the beejeebus out of me!" I said.

"That's all good and dandy, child, whatever a beejeebus be. Fer now, we need to get Deireadh to the fairy circle. Ye take her under one arm, and I'll take the other. Together, we can get her to safety." Doulsie got in place and gave me a quick wink.

"Now!" she said.

To my surprise, she was light as a feather; I could have carried her all by myself. As a matter of fact, I had carried grocery bags that weighed more than she did.

We carried her to just outside of the stone circle. I stopped.

"We need to be gettin' her on to the fairy circle!" Doulsie said, her voice cracked with fear, for I knew that all she loved was in danger. I looked back at the battle that raged only a few steps behind us.

"But what about Calldoon? Blake will kill him!"

"That he canna' do," Doulsie said as she brushed the glittery red hair from around Deireadh's face.

"But he can! Don't forget Calldoon is not a vampire anymore; he's just a man!" I said with frantic wild-eyed gestures toward the two men who were fighting in the heart of the stone monument. "We all have to remember that!" I almost yelled.

"Shh! Calm yourself, child. Calldoon will be fine. There is something he has told no soul save meself. The orchid granted himself a gift; its gift has made him…stronger. The best I can say of himself is now he is an immortal," Doulsie said, cradling Deireadh like a child.

Frustration had converged with confusion to give me a pounding headache.

"Okay, I give up. What are you talking about? And what is an immortal?" I asked.

"It is a creature of legend and folklore. Methinks they could not exist." She brushed the side of Deireadh's face. "There be many things in this land that should not be."

"I don't understand," I said, kneeling by the two of them.

Doulsie looked up at me.

"If ye take all the bad things away, keep all the good stuff, and roll them all into one person, that person would be the state where the master resides now."

I looked back at the stone circle, and sure enough, Calldoon was holding his own.

"Wow!" was all that would come out of my mouth. I heard Doulsie's sharp intake of breath, which pulled my attention back to her and away from the battle that raged at our backs.

"Doulsie, what is it?" I asked.

"We need to be getting her to the fairy circle as quickly as we can," she said.

I reached over and picked her up.

"Let me carry her; she doesn't weigh as much as my purse." I straightened up with the sparkly fairy in my arms. I started to take a step forward.

"Wait, Doulsie. I got a couple of questions. One: where are we going? Two: how far is it?"

Doulsie thought for only a breath before answering.

"There be a fairy circle in the dark forest just beyond the castle herself."

"Here's the deal; I'm in pretty good shape, but not that good. I could never make it that far carrying myself, much less anything else." I gave my head a nod toward the car. "Let's drive really, really fast."

"Good idea, child!" she said with a nod.

With great difficulty, Doulsie climbed into the back seat of my little rented car. After she was in, I very carefully placed Deireadh in the front seat and buckled her in for fear she would slip out of the seat. Doulsie reached between the seats, holding onto her shoulder to help steady her.

"Which way, Doulsie, which way?!" I yelled.

"Back toward the castle herself!" she yelled back.

I threw the car in reverse, whipped it around, then shifted into drive. I hit the gas so hard that the tires spun trying to grab some traction; this sent a spray of small rocks, sticks, and dirt flying into the air.

Chapter Fifty-Six

Back on the main road, I glanced back over my shoulder.

"It's getting dark. Can you find this fairy thing in the dark?"

Doulsie waved her pudgy little hand toward the road.

"Ye best be watchin' the road, for ye will be needin' to turn on the head-lamps."

"Oh yeah," I said, reaching to flip on the headlights.

"I could find the fairy circle in the dark with me eyes covered," I could hear the smile in her voice.

I gave a sigh of relief as we crossed over into Go-Brath's lands. It felt good to be back on home territory. Safety seemed to wrap itself around us, even though we still had a lot to contend with. I glanced over at Deireadh.

"She ain't looking so good, Doulsie," I said.

Doulsie reached between us and patted her arm.

"Hold on, child. We'll soon be to safety," she cooed. "See the road to the left?" she said, pointing so hard and fast that she ran her little finger into the window. "Ouch!" she yelped as she grabbed her finger.

I leaned forward, looking as hard as I could into the dark.

"I don't see a road," I yelled, rolling down my window with the hope that I could see better if I stuck my head out the window. The cool night air whipped across my face; the fragrance of this land I had grown to love brought hope back to my heart. Then…great! The fog began to roll in.

"Doulsie, I can barely see the road in front of me with the headlights! How am I going to find a side road in all of this stuff?"

She took a deep breath,

"Calm yer heart. Listen to me; turn when I say so," Doulsie said.

I nodded.

"There it be. Slow the auto; turn now," she said.

"What!?" I squeaked.

"Turn now, right now!" she said with firm assurance.

"Okay…," I said, giving the steering wheel a blind yank to the left. We hit what I could only assume was the side road. We hit it with a bounce and a bump, then we kind of leveled off as my headlights landed full on what was more of a path than a road. I soon began to realize that we were on the same trail that Deireadh and I had walked the day before when we had our encounter with Blake. Deireadh had told him to give us his wallet, and he did. The warning that Calldoon had given us came back to mind. "Thumped the hornets' nest," he had said, and what a hornet it had turned out to be!

"Stop now! Ye can drive no further!" Doulsie said.

I brought the car to a full stop, jumped out, and ran around the front of the car. The headlights caused a ghostly flicker against the trees. I jerked open Deireadh's door. She looked lifeless. I picked her up, and she let out a moan in protest.

A sigh of relief escaped my lips.

"At least she's still alive!" I said as I got her firmly settled in my arms. "Where are we going?" I turned to get my bearings before we headed off into the forest. "I sure hope they can help her there!"

Doulsie scrambled out of the backseat much faster than she had gotten in.

"Come, come, quickly, quickly!" She moved faster than I had ever seen her move before.

It only took a few steps inside the dark forest before we lost all traces of the lights from the car.

"Wow, Doulsie, can you see?" I asked. I could only barely see her, and she was right in front of me.

"Don't need to; 'tis just ahead," she said.

"Really? Ahead of what?" I asked, hoping that I wouldn't step in a hole and break both my neck and Deireadh's.

"There it is! See? I told ye I could find it with me eyes closed!" She stepped to the side as if she were introducing me to royalty. "Here she be."

My mouth gaped. There before me was magic, for lack of a better word. This magic made a circle out of dark green grass and little mushrooms. The grass was not regular field grass; it was dark green and rich but not too tall. The mushrooms were little white sparkly morsels. It was beautiful. It made no sense that I could see any of it in the pitch black dark, but I could. The air in the circle was lit by sparkles that shimmered in the air; it sparkled much like Deireadh's hair. *This is crazy amazing!* I thought.

"Now what?" I whispered.

"Follow me," Doulsie said as she stepped into the circle.

Inside the circle the air was fresh and cool, and the fog was nowhere to be seen. There was a feeling about it, an energy, an emotion. As my heart began to soar, I knew that emotion was hope. Nothing else but hope could feel like that. This feeling cared for and caressed us as we walked across the soft grass; we were safe. We were home.

"Wow! I've never felt like this anywhere before," I whispered as I gazed around within the heart of the circle.

Doulsie sat on her knees and patted the grass in front of her.

"Place her here, but take ye great care."

Slowly I placed her exactly where Doulsie had instructed. With Deireadh's head resting in Doulsie lap, we sat there. After a while, I took a deep breath and let it out slowly.

"What are we waiting for?" I asked as I watched the sparkles float to the floor of the circle. Doulsie didn't answer. I could see the concern on her face.

I looked down at Deireadh. My hand flew to my mouth, and a tear threatened to spill over my lashes "Oh, no! Doulsie, she's not breathing!" There was still no reply. "Doulsie, she's not breathing. Did you hear me?" She began to coo a song. It must have been in her native tongue, but I didn't know what language it was. I didn't understand one word of it.

She sat there singing her peaceful little song, and all the while she was lovingly caressing the side of Deireadh's face.

I reached over and took Doulsie's other hand. I gave it a little squeeze just to let her know I was there for her, whatever happened. She didn't even look up at me.

"We need to be patient and give the circle time for its magic to soak in," Doulsie softly said.

Deireadh took a deep breath, and her eyes came open. I didn't move as hope came roaring back. She held that breath just before she collapsed back onto Doulsie's lap.

"D-O-U-L-S-I-E!"

She reached over and patted my leg.

"Calm, child, calm. 'Tis working," she said.

I turned my head to look at Doulsie, who still had not taken her eyes off Deireadh. I gave my head a little shake.

"Doulsie, in my world when a person's eyes roll back in their head like that and they stop breathing, that person is dead."

Doulsie smiled her sweet little smile.

"Ah, but you see, fairies don't live in the mortal realm. The rules that apply to the both of us do not apply to them. You will see. Wait fer the circle to do her job; she knows what a fairy needs."

We sat in silence for a while as the air shimmered around us until my curiosity got the best of me.

"Doulsie, can you tell me how you know all of this?" I asked.

She smiled, and a small tear ran down her little cheek.

"I know what I know because she is my child."

My mouth gaped, and my eyes widened.

"Say what?" I said when at last I found my voice.

Slowly she turned her eyes from Deireadh to me.

"I be her mother," she whispered, wiping at the tears that kept sliding off her lashes.

This was such an unexpected turn of events that I didn't even know what to say. I just babbled.

"What? How?"

Doulsie smiled.

"I will tell ye, but ye must never tell another soul." I nodded my oath. "Ye canna' tell by the looks of meself now, but I used to be quite fair of face with flowing red hair and a waist so small that a lad's hands could go around it with ease and did," she said with a wink. "When Lord Navar had just finished his beloved Go-Brath, a wizard was passing by. In his fashion, Lord Navar invited the wizard to the grand ball, given to celebrate her completion; this would be the same wizard that charmed her. Ah, what a handsome man he be: not too tall, not short but well put together, much like Tanarr."

"He had gray eyes; never had meself laid eyes on such, and dark brown hair with red shades in it when the sun shone upon him." She reached down and twirled one strand of Deireadh's sparkly hair around her finger. "It sparkled much like hers does. I fell deeply in love with this wizard, and he with me." She looked back at Deireadh, bent, and placed a kiss on her forehead. "This sweet child is what our love made."

"But I thought that she was hundreds of hundreds of years old? How can you be her mother?" I asked trying my best to keep all the players straight in my head.

"That she is," Doulsie said with a smile, giving Deireadh's face a gentle, loving pat. "And so am I." I'm sure she could see the questions in my eyes because she didn't even pause; she just went on with her story. "Ye see, when she was born we knew that she would be a fairy, for between a wizard and a mortal it will always be so. For this reason, we could tell no one of our beautiful child. We knew, too, that her father should be the one to help her grow; the time of fairies was to be no more, as was the time of wizards."

"Our world was a changing, and he knew how to care for her. As she grew, me heart was so filled with fear and sadness that she would be left all alone in this big world." She shook her head. "I could not stand the thought. One day in me grief I begged her father to charm meself so our child would not be alone. He granted me this wish, but with a twist. Meself could be there for her to care and watch over her. The twist to me charm? I must never let her know that I be who I be."

"Why, Doulsie? I would want to know if you were my mother! You're the best, sweetest mom ever!" I said, sliding my arm across her shoulders and giving her a little hug.

"Ah, that be kind of ye to say, but if a fairy knew, she would be tellin' all, for a fairy canna' keep a secret. 'Tis their nature; they canna' help it."

"Would that be a bad thing?" I asked.

"Oh yes! 'Twould be very bad, fer humans are no good with such; they would surely have us banished," she said with an edge of sadness in her voice.

"Hey! Not in my castle!" I said with pride.

Doulsie shook her head.

"'Tis sweet but 'twould last for only a season, and the season would pass; we could live longer than you and even your children."

"Oh! I didn't think about that," I said.

"You see, we had to protect her for all time," Doulsie said.

"Can I ask you something?" I asked, not knowing whether to go on or just to let it go.

Doulsie nodded.

"Why is it that you appear to be so old, and Deireadh is so young?" I asked.

"I was old when I asked fer the charm," she looked at me over the top of her glasses. "If I had had me wits about me, I'd been askin' for the charm a wee bit sooner!" she laughed. "Himself taught me all 'twould need to know of how to care for her. As long as she is, so be I. I love her so much," she added with a smile.

"Wow, that's, just, wow!" was all that I seemed to be able to get to come out of my mouth.

"Ye be the only person I've ever told me story to," Doulsie said.

"You mean that Calldoon doesn't know?" I asked.

"Until of late he be not knowin' I was even about. Who has a care of the help? After all, I be but a lowly cook." Her voice was soaked in defeat.

"Doul-sie! I swear! I can't believe you said that. You are so much more than just a cook. You do everything. Your cooking, I might add, is some of the best food I've ever had. You make sure all the staff members are in place and doing what they should be. Why, that place couldn't run without you! We are all quite blessed to have you with us!" I said.

"Thank ye, Ms. Katelynn. I am what I am. I'm quite happy to be so, but the best of all is I know that I be her mother and she is my daughter. In the knowin' of that, there is enough," she said.

A peaceful silence settled over as we waited…for what, I didn't know. It looked to me like all hope was lost. There had been no change in Deireadh since she had taken that last deep breath. But here we sat, and here we would stay until Doulsie decided otherwise.

Chapter Fifty-Seven

A brutal slam smashed Calldoon's back against the largest stone, almost knocking the breath out of him. Blake was channeling all of his anger toward Calldoon.

Calldoon pushed himself off the stone and tauntingly proclaimed, "Is that the best ye can do? Why, I've had little girls push me harder than that! Is that all ye got? If I promise to buy ye a new dolly, do ye think ye can play better?" Calldoon said all of this as if he were talking to a small child, and one that was not too bright at that.

He got the reaction he was looking for; the statement was like throwing gas on a fire. Blake exploded, losing all thought of control and therefore forfeiting the power of the stone circle as well. Blake charged him like a raging bull. Calldoon easily sidestepped his charge. Calldoon's power was growing; the circle was working for him.

With his right fist, he caught Blake in the stomach, doubling him over like a wet washcloth over a clothesline. All of the air went out of him in one great whoosh. Blake crumpled to the ground. Calldoon stood over him. Was the battle won? Was it over? Could he now claim the full power of the stone circle and the victory?

He turned to walk away, but before his foot could step out of the stone circle, an iron hand clamped down on his shoulder. It felt as though it might rip the flesh from the bone and forced Calldoon to his knees. The voice that hissed in his ear was Blake's.

"I have always been stronger than you, and I always will be, lest you forget, stable boy! Navar's boot shiner!" Calldoon was on his knees. "That's right! Bow before me, pup." Blake was so angry that saliva had collected in the corners of his mouth. "We'll see who has the upper hand now!"

"Hey! What's going on over there?" came a voice they both recognized. Calldoon smiled as Blake spun on his heels.

"So you have returned!" Blake hissed. Little pieces of saliva were flung in all directions like a mad dog snapping at the wind.

Corbin strolled to the center of the stone circle, daring Blake to meet him there. Blake could never resist a challenge. This left Calldoon unattended, giving Zoul the chance to help him to his feet and out of harm's way.

"I have returned, indeed, and…," Corbin said dramatically and as animated as an actor on the stage, "I have something for you: a gift, as it were. A gift from the High Priest of the kee-nan-twa."

If it were possible for Blake to turn pale with his spray tan intact, he did.

"What is this?" Blake roared, as if he didn't know and fear what Corbin held in his hand.

"Well, let me see," Corbin said, holding a full hypodermic needle out so Blake could easily see it. "Some might call it revenge for all the evil you have inflicted over the years. Others will call it vindication for their loved ones who did not deserve what you did to them." Corbin hooded his eyes. "I call it justice, sweet justice at last for my best friend, a good man who only sought to help those who could not help themselves. And let's not forget Lera. She would have given all that she was to help us, and you destroyed her for your own selfish reasons. Hate and evil controls you, and now I'm done with you." Corbin made a quick lunge forward, thrusting the needle like a well-balanced fencing sword.

Blake jumped to the side, his temper cooled by a cold splash of reality; his very mortality was in the balance. His reflexes along with his willingness to compromise had returned.

"Let's talk about this!" Blake pleaded. His tone had changed; he knew he was outnumbered and outplayed.

"The time for talk has passed," Corbin said as he circled Blake looking for just the right spot to inflict the most damage with the least effort.

Blake decided it would be in his best interest to escape the circle. The stone circle that had been the source of his power earlier had now become his prison; each time he tried to escape, Zoul or Calldoon would only shove him back into the center.

Calldoon spoke up. "This is for all the small villages ye terrorized!" He crossed his arms over his chest, firmly taking his stand.

"For killing all of our hopes when you murdered Lera: she was our hope," Zoul said, mimicking Calldoon's stance on the other side of the circle. They stood there like the ancient stone guardians of the past, present, and future. It seemed that evil was outnumbered and had to answer for all the wrongs it had imparted.

"It is now time to pay for all you have done," Corbin said as he made one last stab with the needle. This time he hit his mark. The shock that spread across Blake's face was unmistakable. He clutched at the needle that was protruding from his chest. He didn't say a word as he crumpled to the ground. The three men stood over his lifeless body.

"Well, that's that. We've done what had to be done." Corbin said as he extended his hand toward the other men. The three men exchanged a firm handshake over the lifeless body of their centuries-old enemy. He had won a lot of battles, but they had won the war.

"We will need to see if the women made it to the fairy circle with Deireadh. She was in poor condition; Blake had almost done her in," Calldoon said, not being able to hold back a swift kick to the side of the thing that had caused so much pain and loss.

The men were so enthralled in their conversation and concern for the women that they didn't even notice the grimace that flashed across the monster's face.

Calldoon, Zoul, and Corbin left the stone circle to find the women. They knew that Tanarr was already there; however, their work here was done…or was it?

Chapter Fifty-Eight

Janet emerged from her hiding place where she has witnessed the entire battle. Now as she stood over Blake's lifeless body, to her surprise she was truly sad. She knelt at his side. Lovingly she stroked his forehead. He had been a force to reckon with: handsome, forceful, strong, and oh so rich. All of this was edged with an evil cruelness that she wouldn't miss.

A tear escaped the rim of her lashes and ran down her cheek, landing on his face.

"Oh, Blake! Now what am I to do? I never meant for this to happen. I just didn't want the fairy killed. Looks like I messed up all the way around, and you? You never kept your promise. If you had, I'd be strong and safe!" She pounded her fists on his chest.

To her horror, his iron grip clamped around her wrist. Her breath caught in her chest, and fear ripped through her very being.

"Blake? Blake! You're alive! I, I thought you, you were gone!" Janet stuttered.

"You did this to me!" Blake rasped.

Janet said nothing, as fear had completely stolen her voice.

"Now, come close. Collect your promise before it is too late." Blake, now weakened by the power of the orchid's nectar, had little time left and even less power. "Come closer," he whispered.

Janet leaned down, so near that her ear was almost touching his lips. With his last ounce of power, he reached up and took hold of her head with both hands. Holding it still and close, he sank his fangs into the soft white skin at the base of her ear. Pain and joy all washed over her, for now she would have an ultimate power over all.

"You will need help," Blake said. She could barely hear him; she was too focused on bracing herself for the pain to hit its full strength. She was waiting for that bone rattling, can't-breathe pain followed by the need for blood.

"Janet, listen to me," he raised his voice as much as he could. "You will need help. Seek out Savar."

"Who is he, and where do I find him?" she asked, still only half paying attention.

"It's not a he but a she—" was the last thing he said before his eyes rolled back in his head and closed for the last time.

Janet sat there within the arms of the stone circle holding the lifeless form of Blake. The air within the circle had changed. It was now cold and heavy, as if the stones themselves were mourning his death.

Janet cocked her head to the side.

"This ain't so bad," she said out loud as she rubbed her hand over the bite wound. It stung a little. "I thought this was some big pain deal." She gave her shoulders a shrug and smiled down at Blake. "You know what? You don't look so scary now! And how exactly and where exactly am I supposed to find this Sa . . .var?" she said as she continued her conversation with the stones and the body of Blake.

"Hey, didn't I hear stories about how you had this crazy craving for blood? I'm not feeling it. Are you sure you bit me right?" She rubbed his hair back. "Would someone please tell me what to do with you now? I can't just leave you here like this." She paused and put her hand to her face.

"Oh, wait! I think I have a blanket in the car." She gently lowered his head to the ground. "I'll be right back; don't move. What am I saying? Like you're going anywhere." As she started to leave the circle, she looked back over her shoulder. "It just seems wrong not to cover you," she said, making her way to the car.

"Where is it?" Janet said, throwing things around in the backseat of the car. "Ah ha! Here it is." She wadded it up under her arm, gave the door a slam, and headed back to the circle. Once back within the parameter of the giant stones, she noticed that the attitude of the stones had changed again. She couldn't quite put her finger on it, but something was different. She chose her steps with care; something was not right. She was almost to the other side of the circle.

"Hey, what the?" She turned around and around; the blanket dropped along with her jaw. "Where did he go?" Janet said, spinning around one more time. Blake had vanished. "Okay, this is just weird. Maybe I'm asleep." She picked up the edge of her blanket. "Yep, that's it. I'm asleep." She dragged herself along with her blanket back to the car.

In the car she, threw the blanket into the backseat, put the key in the starter, and fired up the engine. She tilted the rearview mirror down so she could see her neck. "I don't see the big deal; I really think I'm asleep. It will be my luck he'll have the locks changed and all of my stuff out on the porch. He's just messing with me!"

Chapter Fifty-Nine

Still quietly sitting within the heart of the fairy circle, I was the first to break the silence.

"Is she going to be all right?" I asked as I reached over to take Deireadh's hand.

Doulsie smiled.

"That she is."

"Oh, but Doulsie, how do you know that?" I asked, trying to keep the worry out of my voice.

"I know what I know, and if it be our time to be no more, so be it," she sadly said.

"Doulsie!" I said with a squeak. "Please don't talk like that!"

Doulsie looked down at her daughter; Deireadh's head was still resting in her lap.

"It will be what it will be," she said with a sigh.

I started to say more, but my words were silenced by the sound of a twig snapping. I whipped my head around and squinted my eyes, trying my best to see into the darkness.

"What is it?" Doulsie nervously asked.

"I don't know," I said, slowly coming to my feet. I turned around; all I could see were the small shimmers within the fairy circle.

"Katelynn, child, can you see anything?"

"No, Doulsie, nothing: nothing at all," I answered her worried question. Then, I heard it again: another snap, this time on the other side. "All right, that's it! I have had just about enough of this!" I yelled into the dark as I protectively stepped in front of Doulsie and Deireadh.

That's funny, I thought. *Like I could protect them or even myself from the stuff that lurks in this part of the woods.* I felt like Little Red Riding Hood trying to protect the little pigs from the Big Bad Wolf. He was probably going to eat all three of us. *Oh well, if that's the case, I won't go down without a fight.* "I hope you choke on me!" I yelled into the dark.

Doulsie turned her head to the side.

"Katelynn, child, did ye say ye be choking?"

"No, but if whatever is out there thinks it's going to enjoy snacking on me," I turned my back to the dark, "I promise it I'll kick and scream till it chokes." I turned back around. "So bring it, or are ya just a big chicken?" I yelled, stepping close to the edge of the dark green grass that formed the circle.

Feeling much braver and a little cocky, I turned my back on the dark and gave Doulsie a wink. Before my wink was done, a male hand went around my waist and the other clamped over my mouth, pulling me to the edge of the circle. I could see panic on Doulsie's face.

I began to kick and flail my arms as hard as I could. I made hard contact with who or whatever had a hold on me. That knowledge brought pure fear to my heart; it had to be Blake. No one else could take a blow to the shin and other places and not flinch.

He dragged me closer to the forest. Just before we stepped out of the circle, I heard a familiar voice over the pounding of my heart. As realization sunk in, I stomped his foot and chomped my teeth into his hand. This caught him enough so off guard that he released his grip just enough to allow me to spin in his arms. I shook my finger in his face and gave him a good finger wag.

"What in the Sam Hill do you think you're doing? You almost scared the living daylights out of me! Arrrrrrgh!" I said with a growl and a foot stomp. "Tanarr, I could just...Tanarr! Tanarr!" I gave him a big hug then looked around. "Where's Corbin?"

There it was: that crooked smile that could get him almost anything he wanted.

"Nice to see you, too, m'lady. Spiderman isn't with me. He's...shall we say, taking care of some old business," he said with a smile. "Now, what's going on over here?" he said, picking me up by the shoulders and setting me to the side. He stopped still in his tracks as his eyes fell on Deireadh's still form lying there in the center of the fairy circle.

"She's been like this for a while," I said, looking over at the beautiful but wounded fairy. "I don't know what to do. Doulsie keeps telling me that she is going to be fine, but I don't know." I shook my head.

Tanarr slowly walked over and knelt at her side. He started to reach for her but stopped and looked to Doulsie for approval or permission. She granted his silent request with a nod. He slowly, gently picked her up. His breath caught, and a grimace crossed his face as Deireadh's head slipped forward and landed roughly against his chest.

"What are you going to do with her?" I asked.

Tanarr shook his head.

"I don't know," he said, looking down at her. "What happened to her?"

"Blake." As I said his name, I saw the muscle in Tanarr's jaw tighten. His eyes darkened as he slowly turned them toward me. I now had his full attention. "We played a harmless trick on him." I looked down. "He didn't think it was so funny. I kind of borrowed your car, and while I was gone, Blake and this woman tricked her into thinking I needed her. Fortunately the woman couldn't stand to see a fairy killed, so she came to get us."

I paused, looking down at Deireadh. "This is how we found her, there with Blake. He had done this. We left Calldoon doing battle with him. Calldoon told us to take Deireadh and leave. He said to take her to the fairy circle...I hope he's okay," I said, looking off into the dark.

I turned back to Deireadh, who was draped in Tanarr's arms. "The woman saved her life. I know beyond a shadow of a doubt that Blake would have killed her. He almost did anyway."

Doulsie interrupted us by clearing her throat. She then patted the ground at her side.

"Ye may hold her if it pleases ye, but sit we will till the magic of the fairy dust does her work."

I sat on one side of Doulsie, and Tanarr settled on the other with Deireadh cradled in his arms. We formed a small triangle. Tanarr leaned down and lightly placed a kiss on Deireadh's lips. As he did so, she moved ever so slightly in response to his kiss. I put my hand over my mouth.

"Did you see that?" I whispered.

"Yes, child, I did," Doulsie said with a smile.

"I think it was the kiss," I said, more to myself than to anyone else.

"Don't go be givin' Sir Tanarr so much. 'Tis but the power of the fairy dust and the circle herself. I told ye it would take care of her; it always has," she said with a nod.

Tanarr looked up and flashed us one of those crooked smiles.

"Nah, it was the kiss," he chuckled.

Deireadh's eyes fluttered; we all held our collective breath. She looked to me first, then next at Doulsie. Then she turned her beautiful face up to Tanarr. She smiled and snuggled against his chest. I put my arm around Doulsie's shoulders and gave her a squeeze.

"She is going to be all right," I said, looking down at Doulsie. A tear ran down her face.

"Fine, that she is. Now, let's be goin' home," Doulsie said as she struggled to get to her feet. I stopped and helped her get up.

Before we had made it to the edge of the fairy circle, Corbin and Zoul arrived.

"Corbin!" I squealed and hurled myself at him, landing my target perfectly. For what was a short eternity, we held each other, not wanting to let go and not daring to move. I felt safe for the first time that I could remember.

Tanarr interrupted us.

"Did you take out the trash?"

"We did," Corbin replied. He flicked the end of my nose with his finger. "We'll continue this later," he said against my lips, ending our reunion with a soft peck on the lips. With his arm protectively draped around my shoulders, Corbin turned his attention toward the others. "If it had not been for Zoul and Calldoon, I couldn't have done it. Wait," Corbin looked around. "Where is Calldoon? We all left Rundaingne at the same time."

Zoul's strong hand came down hard on Corbin's shoulder.

"Well, son, I think we forgot that he is no longer one of us," he said in that slow, easy way of his.

"Should we go back and find him?" Corbin asked.

"There'll be no need fer that," we heard the breathless voice of Calldoon coming from out of the dark woods. Calldoon joined us at the edge of the fairy circle. He stood there panting with his hands on his knees like an out-of-shape runner. He raised his head and scrunched up his face. "Me thinks me lungs may burst within me chest!" He cocked his head to the side and smiled. "'Tis a good feeling!"

Corbin smiled a sad smile back at him and patted him on the shoulder.

"I can't wait until we can run out of breath together."

Doulsie dusted off the back of her dress.

"All right, now, boys, this little talk can be done back at the castle herself. Fer now, this child be needin' to be tucked into bed so meself can care fer her properly," Doulsie said in a take-charge, motherly kind of way.

"Come on. I'll help you get Deireadh in the car," I said, motioning for Tanarr to follow me.

Tanarr pulled Deireadh in close to his chest and leaned his head on top of hers. "If it's all right with everyone, I think I'll carry her home."

We all smiled at him as he left the edge of the circle heading toward home.

"Ah," I said, clutching at my heart. "Our little boy is in love!" I couldn't resist glancing over at Doulsie. She was smiling that parent smile; a smile that said, "You're doing good, and I'm proud of you." I reached over and slid my arm across her shoulder; she patted my hand. "Let's go home," I said.

Calldoon stood up straight.

"Sir Tanarr may want to walk home with his lady love in his arms, but as fer meself, I'll be taking the car."

I looked up at him, shook my head, and patted the side of his face.

"I think you're getting soft on us; that was only two or three miles. We're going to have to put you in training," I smiled. "We can take the car, but you have to sit in the front seat," I rubbed my hands together. "I get that little back seat," I turned around and wrapped myself around Corbin, "with my hunky, sweetie of a Spiderman."

Corbin jiggled his eyebrows.

"You'll get no complaints from this Spiderman."

Calldoon rolled his eyes.

"Saints preserve us from lovebirds," he hooded his eyes and lowered his voice, "or be it lustbirds."

"Now, now! That be just about enough of that kind of talk!" Doulsie gave him a good finger wag. "Not only are ye in the front seat but ye be driven that auto."

"Me!" Calldoon said.

"Yes, you, fer ye know I canna' control such a thing," Doulsie said with her hands on her hips.

"Yes, ma'am," Calldoon said with a salute. "Yer humble chauffeur, at yer service." He gave her a deep bow.

"Oh, pish posh! There be not a humble bone in yer body! Now, be on with ye! We'll be back to herself and safe before ye know it," Doulsie said with a nod.

When we got close to the small car, Zoul stopped and rubbed his chin.

"Folks, I think I had just as soon walk rather than crawl into that thing. If it's all the same to you, I'll see you back at home." He gave us a cordial nod and took off.

The rest of us climbed into the little rental car. It felt good to be back in Corbin's arms. I snuggled against him. We tried to steal a kiss or two, but every time we tried Calldoon would hit a pothole or run off the edge of the road. I gave him a hard look in the rearview mirror. He just smiled, and I could see the humor dancing in his eyes.

"If ye be hittin' one more of them potholes in the road, I'll be followin' Zoul and walkin' the rest of the way home," Doulsie said, clutching at the dashboard.

"Okay, okay. I'll behave! I was but messing with our two lovebirds," Calldoon said with a laugh, pointing over his shoulder.

Corbin gave me a hug and a wink.

"I don't mind getting bumped around and rubbed together; I don't mind at all. Keep it up; I kind of like it," Corbin said with a big goofy grin.

"Hmm, that takes all the fun out of messing with ye if ye like it," Calldoon said. We all laughed, and Calldoon avoided all the rest of the potholes.

Chapter Sixty

Calldoon brought the little car to a slow stop in the courtyard of the castle. We all pried ourselves out of the little subcompact car. I understood the full meaning of that now. Even if you were packed in there with someone you loved, it was still really compact. I had just gotten straightened up when we heard Zoul.

"I thought I had been abandoned," he said with a lazy smile.

"What do you mean, abandoned? Aren't Tanarr and Deireadh here?" I said, straightening out myself and my clothing all at the same time.

"Nope. It's only me and the castle people," Zoul said, sliding his hands into the back pockets of his jeans.

"They should have been here way before us," I said, turning to Corbin. "Oh, no! You don't think that something could have happened to them, do you?"

"I don't know," Corbin said as we all turned to look back in the direction we had just come from. I looked over at Doulsie, and she was smiling.

"They be fine," was all she said.

There we stood staring into the darkness and waiting. But waiting for what? I hoped we were waiting to see Tanarr come walking through that gate with Deireadh in his arms and both safe and well. We stood there for what seemed like forever, but then finally we saw them at the far end of the bridge. Arm in arm, they walked over the bridge.

My breath caught in my throat, followed by a soft sigh. It was like watching the ending of a sweet fairy tale. You know, a good one where Prince Charming rides off with Snow White, or Cinderella gets to dance as long as she wants with the man of her dreams?

I could tell Deireadh was still in pain, but the smile she gave Tanarr was so sweet. I reached over and took Doulsie's hand.

"She really is going to be fine," I whispered.

Doulsie smiled and nodded.

"She be more than fine, for she be in love." She took the back side of her hand and brushed a tear away before anyone could see it. But I saw it, and I understood. Deireadh stumbled, and we all rushed toward her. Tanarr scooped her up before anyone of us could even get close. He cradled her close in his arms and placed a kiss on her cheek, holding her snug. Zoul was the first one to their sides.

"Son, why on earth did you make her walk? I thought you had better sense than that!"

Tanarr gave him a look that said, "Are you serious?"

"Yeah, I got tired of carrying her, so I made her walk" Tanarr said, giving his head a shake.

Zoul gave him a look right back. "Really!"

"No, she asked to walk over the bridge. She said she wanted to show her new friends that she was not hurt. She said that she loved having friends; this was new to her. What was it she called it? Befeiberly?" He shrugged his shoulders and shook his head. "Whatever befeiberly is."

Deireadh had slipped back into an unconscious state. Doulsie stepped forward and took Tanarr by the upper arm.

"Bring her this way; we'll be puttin' her in me room."

Tanarr looked a little suspicious.

"I can take her to her own room, or even one here in the castle; there are plenty of vacant rooms."

"No, no, no; ye will not be takin' her to that drafty ol' pottin' shed or even a room far down the hall. You'll be takin' her to me own room, do ye understand me words? Fer she will be needin' around-the-clock lookin' after," Doulsie said, daring anyone to dispute her concern.

"Yes, ma'am," Tanarr replied as he obediently followed her through the door and down the hall.

This left Calldoon, Zoul, Corbin, and me standing out in the courtyard. Calldoon let out a loud yawn followed by a big stretch.

"I think I'll be callin' it a night after I grab meself a big, thick sandwich and a cold pint, that is. Then I'll be tuckin' meself in."

"Good grief, man! It's not even ten thirty yet; what's gotten into you?" Corbin said, giving Calldoon a whack on the back.

"First you can't run for any space at all without getting winded, and now you're turning in with the chickens," Zoul teased.

Calldoon stretched and gave us all a big smile.

"Life, boys. It's called life. It's truly exhausting being human." He turned and headed toward the kitchen. "I hope you both get to try it again," he said back over his shoulder.

Zoul dropped his head and kicked the toe of his shoe in the dirt.

"Me too, my friend, me too," he said, more to himself than us. He slowly raised his head; a sad look had touched his eyes. "I need to go hunt. Since I met the brilliant Lera and the beautiful Katy," he reached over and took my hand, placing a light kiss on the top of my knuckles, "and alas, my beloved Kassandra, I will not take human blood. But nevertheless, I need to feed because for now, I'm still the same. I do hope that's going to change, right Katy?" he pleaded with a nod.

"I'm going to give it my best shot, or let me say, *we* will give it our best shot," I said, flashing him a smile. In return, he gave us a quick nod, and he was off into the lonely darkness, which, as he had told me before, was nothing more than a metaphor for his existence.

Corbin had his arm draped around my shoulder. He gave me a squeeze.

"I'll bet that you wouldn't mind a big sandwich and a hot cup of coffee?" I smiled up at him.

"You know me so well," I said as we walked into the castle.

"Oh, pardon me, m'lady, Sir Corbin," Rosey said as she almost plowed into us in her hurry to the kitchen.

"Hey Rosey?" Corbin yelled after her, effectively halting her flight. She turned and slowly came back to us.

"Yes, Sir Corbin? Something fer ye?" Rosey asked with her head bowed.

"If it's not too much trouble, could you please bring Katelynn a sandwich, a pot of hot coffee, and some fruit up to her room?" Corbin asked with a smile.

I bent down and whispered in her ear.

"If there is any of that chocolate cake left, I would love a chunk of it."

She smiled up at me as I stood.

"Yes, m'lady." She motioned for me to come close. I granted her that request. She cupped her hand over my ear as she whispered back.

"I'll be fetching ye a very big chunk," she said with a smile. I gave her a wink, and she turned and hurried off.

Corbin and I walked up the three flights of stairs to my room. When we got to the top, I let out a puff of air.

"Either I'm more tired than I thought, or someone has added a few more stairs to this last flight. Either way, I'm beat!"

Corbin pushed open my door and scooped me up. This time I didn't protest; I was just too tired. He carried me over and gently placed me in Navar's big, comfy chair. He looked down at me.

"Would you like a fire?" he asked.

"That would be wonderful," I said with an eye flutter.

"One fire, coming up," he said, rubbing his hands together.

By the time we had the fire going, we heard a knock at the door.

"Yer food, m'lady," Rosey called from the other side of the door.

I opened the door. There stood Rosey, her eyes cast down. I took my finger and placed it under her chin, raising her face to meet mine.

"Thank you, Rosey," I said.

"Ye be very welcome, m'lady. I be so sorry fer all the trouble I caused. I did not mean to bring harm to Ms. Deireadh. 'Twas all me fault!" Rosey's words came tumbling out all at once along with a few tears. I took the tray out of her hands and set it on the floor beside us.

Rosey's hands covered her face as she began to sob.

"Oh, please forgive me!" she said.

I gathered the young woman into my arms.

"Shh, shh," I whispered into her hair as she continued to sob on my shoulder. "Rosey, listen to me. It was all my fault. Had I stayed here where I should have been, none of this would have happened." I held Rosey at arm's length. "So dry those eyes, and know this was not your fault, okay?"

She sniffed a couple more times.

"Thank ye," she said as she started to leave. Then, quick as a wink, she whirled back, giving me a hug. After that, she was gone. I turned back to Corbin, who was still smiling at me.

"What?" I said.

"You're so good with everyone here. Navar would be so proud to know that the person Lera chose to continue their work and care for all they loved is so loved by the very thing she cares for. And they do love you, from the youngest child right on up to Go-Brath herself."

"Ah…," I waved my hand, "they're easy to love," I said, picking up my tray and giving the door a kick closed with my heel.

"If someone like Blake had gotten control of all this, it would not be the same happy, peaceful little slice of heaven. Instead, it would be a torturous hell. Even if it had fallen into the hands of a corrupt human, it would have been bad." Corbin shook his head. "That's why Calldoon is so protective of this magical place."

I set my tray down on the table and took a big bite of my sandwich followed by a large gulp of my really good coffee.

"It's easy loving all of this; how could I not?" I said.

"That's why Lera chose you; it's in your blood," Corbin said.

"It may be more in my blood than you know," I said through another bite of my sandwich.

"What?" Corbin asked.

"It's something Deireadh said about wizard blood running deep in my past." I took the last bite of my sandwich and dusted off my hands. I got up and slid into Corbin's lap. With my backside seated in his lap and my feet dangling over the arm of the chair, I put my arm around his neck and rested my head on his shoulder. "I don't want to talk about that right now. I want to hear about your adventure. I'll bet it was more exciting than a jar full of fireflies on a dark summer night!" I said, snuggling against his neck.

Corbin wrapped his arms around me.

"I don't know if I can remember anything when you're this close and feeling this good, not about the Amazon, anyway." He leaned in and gave me a soft, slow kiss.

I pulled back.

"Now, don't go distracting me! I want to hear what happened. Was the High Priest of the orchid willing to help?" I pushed back just far enough to see his face. "He wasn't the same guy, was he?" I asked.

Corbin smiled and nodded.

"Indeed, he was the same; he was gracious but suspicious. Immediately he knew Zoul as the lost prince of Kee-Ka-Na and Tanarr from his time in the village with Lera. As for me, that took a little convincing. After we explained why we were there, the High Priest began to pace with his hands behind his back. After a while he stopped and looked to the top of the trees. He said that he had heard of all the evil that this dark one had brought on both human and vampire. He was surprised that he had not had this request sooner."

"He said that he had been saddened when Lera had told him of Navar's death, and he wanted to know if her work was going well. We told him that Blake had killed Lera and been responsible for Navar's death, and that he had almost killed Calldoon with the nectar of the orchid that was in a ring, but that he had survived. When we told him that, he got an odd look on his face. He asked us one more time if Calldoon had survived. He remembered the day the King, Zoul's father, had asked for the ring to be constructed. It was with great sadness that he made his request, for he knew in his heart that his beloved son could never return."

"He also knew that if he did, there would have to be a way to stop him as quickly as possible for the good of all. So the ring was forged out of the purest of gold, sadness, and the power of the Great One. It was meant to keep a lethal portion of the nectar fresh and pure for all time, or as long as it is was needed. The priest told the whole story of the ring, never taking his eyes off of Zoul. It's like the priest wanted Zoul to know how his father loved him and just how much this decision had hurt him."

"Zoul confirmed that his father had told him that on the day he returned, the King would be the one to administer the blow with the ring. Zoul knew how much his father loved him, and he knew how much it cost him to protect the village."

"The Priest said that he had wondered what had become of the ring. He knew that it had been stolen and hoped that it had been lost. He again asked whether Calldoon had survived the encounter with the ring."

"When we said yes, he made one more trip across the floor and back. He went to a shelf and got a scroll, which he brought back to the table. He invited us over as he unfurled the scroll on the table. It was in a strange script, one I had never seen before. He began to translate for Tanarr and me as Zoul read along with him. It was, after all, Zoul's native language." Corbin paused for a while, looking into the fire. It looked to me like he was lost in the memory of where he had been, or maybe he was trying to figure out how to explain what the Priest had read off that scroll.

"Okay, Corbin, I give. What did the scroll say?" I said, wiggling a little in his lap just to remind him that he was still sitting here in the castle with me and I wanted to hear the rest of the story. It was my way of reminding him that he was back home.

"He said that it read, 'He who survives the orchid is blessed by the flower, for now and evermore, he will be immortal. Not predestined to good or evil, the receiver of the gift will decide what his truth will be.' "

"Do you believe him?" I asked.

"I guess so, maybe. Maybe not. It could be only tribal folklore; you know, a fairy tale," he said.

"And we all know how true a fairy tale can be, now, don't we?" I said with a tilt of my head. "You do believe him, don't you?"

"I guess, maybe. I don't know. But I am sure that time will tell," Corbin said in a somber tone.

I yawned and snuggled up around his neck.

"I'm sorry, but I'm full and warm, and I feel safer than I have in a while. Now I think I'm getting sleepy."

"I'll leave then," Corbin started to move.

"No, please, just hold me. Tell me more about what happened," I said with a sleepy plea.

"Okay," he said, cradling me close. I relaxed and let his soft baritone voice lull me off to sleep.

Chapter Sixty-One

In that dreamy state of half awake and half asleep, I snuggled against Corbin's white linen shirt only to discover that the white linen shirt was just my pillow and not Corbin. My disappointment brought me fully awake. I rolled over to find a beautiful white magnolia on the pillow beside me with a note tucked in the heart of the flower. I pulled out the note and unrolled it.

My Dearest Katelynn,

This magnificent flower that lies at your side pales in comparison to you. Corny, I know, don't laugh. I thought I'd try my hand at romantic poetry. Epic fail, but I know how you love big white flowers, so I couldn't resist. I need to hunt; sorry I couldn't be here when your eyes opened to greet the first rays of the new day. I will be back as soon as possible. I have instructed the staff to have a pot of hot coffee set outside your door. By the time you're ready to come downstairs, I hope to be there.

Love, Corbin

I kicked the covers off and ran to the door. Just as Corbin had written, there was my pot of coffee. I grabbed the tray, brought it in, poured myself a large, steaming cup, and took it with me into my freshly finished bathroom. Ah, yes! Hot coffee in my new bathroom; now this was sweet!

I grabbed my jeans, a denim shirt, and all of my shower stuff: gel, shampoo, a shower pouf, and a big fluffy towel to finish it all off. It was going to be nice not to have to carry my stuff all over the castle just to get a shower. I stepped into the shower, and everything had a place, from my towel all the way to my little pouf. I sighed with contentment.

I was out of the shower and dressed with my hair clean, dried, and hanging freely down my back. I refilled my coffee cup and headed down for breakfast. My heart was particularly light this morning. After all, the bad guy was dead. Deireadh was mending. Calldoon was doing fantastic.

I wondered about that immortal thing. *What does that really mean?* I was going to have to do some research. But how does one do research on something that no one knows about or thinks could be possible? It was one more item to add to my list of things to look into.

Best of all, the men were all back home and safe. Home, I thought. Doulsie is home. Deireadh is home. Calldoon is home. I stopped with my hand on the beautiful hand-carved railing, smoothed by time; there was no telling how many hands had slid over it in the exact same way.

I looked down this grand stairway that flowed into the sprawling entrance hall. The doorway was flanked by two suits of armor that were polished to perfection. Navar's coat of arms was displayed with pride above them, and the gray marble floor peaked out from under a hand-woven rug. Everything in this place amazed me, from the paintings by the old masters, sculptures sculpted with love, and talent by the unknown artists. The craftsmen that built this place were fantastic; the only thing that I could say was, Wow!

Both inside and out, Go-Brath always took my breath away. It was amazing. I still couldn't believe that it was mine, but even though all of this belonged to me, it wasn't home. Home is and will always be Ela, Alabama, and I felt home calling me back. I needed to see Momma and Daddy. I needed a hug. I wanted to sit on the front porch, sip some sweet tea, wave to the neighbors, wait for the sunset, and listen to the night bugs. I needed to go home.

I made my way to the dining hall. Just as his note had said, Corbin was sitting at the table waiting for me. He smiled when he saw me, and my heart skipped a beat. He stood and pulled out my chair. I took the seat he offered. As he pushed my chair in, he leaned down, kissing me on the neck and causing little prickly bumps to run up and down my arms.

"Good morning, my love," he whispered in my ear. "Are you ready for your breakfast?"

"You know me. I can always eat, but first I want to ask you something," I said. Corbin took his seat.

"What's put so much worry on that beautiful face that I love?"

"Well, it's not worry; it's more like homesickness," I said, running my finger around the rim of my cup. "What would you say if I said I want to go home?"

Corbin leaned back in his chair.

"I'd say you are home. This is yours; it's all yours," he said softly.

"I know that, kind of. Well, it still hasn't sunk in, even though I know on paper that it's mine. But in my heart, home is where Momma is. Home is in Alabama," I said.

Corbin gave me a sweet understanding smile.

"Stop that," I said, giving him a good finger wag.

"Stop what?" he said with an innocent smile.

"Stop smiling at me like that, or I will forget what I was going to say," I said as I reached for my coffee cup.

"I'm not trying to sidetrack you. I understand. I always wanted to go home, too," he said with sad undertones in his voice.

"Thank you for understanding. I do love this place, and I will come back, but I need to go home," I said.

"Then home we shall go. We will get a few things in order here. You have good people to leave in charge; I don't see a problem," he said.

"Good morning." We both turned to see Tanarr and Zoul coming to the table.

"May we join you?" Tanarr asked.

"Sure," I said.

"Take a chair," Corbin said to the two men.

"Thanks," Zoul said with a nod as he and Tanarr both sat down across from Corbin and me. No sooner had they gotten settled than my food arrived. Eggs, bacon, toast, and juice. I already had my coffee; it only needed a refill.

"How is Deireadh doing this morning?" Corbin asked.

"Very well, thank you for asking. She said she would be in to join us," Tanarr said.

I closed my eyes and let out a little breath of relief.

"That's so good to hear! I have been worried about her. If we had been any later, it would have…," I couldn't finish that statement; the implications were just too scary. "I know if it had not been for that woman, she saved Deireadh's life. I know she did. I will be forever grateful to her."

"Did you know her?" Tanarr asked.

I shook my head.

"She looked familiar, but I don't remember meeting her before. Calldoon seemed to know her; he was saying something to her. I couldn't quite get all they were saying. There was so much going on in the courtyard when she returned," I said, sipping at my newly filled cup of coffee.

The next one to join us at the table was Calldoon.

"Top of the morning to ye all," he said with a nod. "May I?" he asked permission as he pulled out the chair beside me.

"Oh, yes, please," I said.

As soon as Calldoon had gotten settled in his seat, the train of food began, starting with some fruit and sweet rolls then eggs, bacon, sausage, potatoes, bread, butter, and jam. I don't think there was anything left in the kitchen when he was done. He washed it all down with a quart of milk.

"Stars and bars, son! If you eat like this all the time, that would explain why you couldn't keep up with us!" Zoul said.

Calldoon smiled and wiped his mouth.

"'Tis a glorious thing to have me taste back. One would think that I'd be getting a pot around me middle," Calldoon said, heaping his fork with a mix of ham, eggs, and potatoes.

Corbin glanced over at Zoul then leaned in so he could see Calldoon's face around me.

"Let me ask you something."

"Sure," Calldoon said with another forkful of food on its way to his mouth.

"Other than this unbelievable appetite, have you noticed anything else out of the ordinary?" Corbin asked.

"Not really," Calldoon said with a shrug of his shoulders. "Well, maybe. I seem to be a little faster and perhaps a wee bit stronger than the average. I'm thinking that it is just maybe a little leftover from what I was."

"Not likely, but I do have another theory. Have you ever heard of an immortal?" Corbin asked.

"I have, but I don't think that such could be. It's not likely that one could just go on as he is, unchanged by time or anything, Doulsie and meself had a conversation about this very thing just the other day. She is convinced that that is what I be." He shook his head. "Not likely." Calldoon didn't even look up from his food. He was not the least bit interested in the line of conversation.

"Calldoon, look at me," Corbin said, trying his best to get Calldoon to focus on what he was about to say.

Calldoon put his fork down and straightened his shoulders.

"Ye have me full attention, for if I must be honest, I do believe that this immortal is what I have become, whether I want to believe it or not."

"While we were talking with the High Priest of the kee-nan-twa, we told him that you had survived the attack," Corbin said.

"But Lord Navar also survived," Calldoon interrupted.

"There is a difference. Navar was injected with a manipulated version of the nectar. You received pure nectar; it should have killed you. The Priest retrieved an old scroll. It was written in the ancient language of the Kee-Ka-Na. In this scroll there is a line that reads, 'he who survives an attack of the orchid is thereafter blessed by the flower itself and shall live from thereafter forever and ever unchanged. In other words, he shall be an immortal'," Corbin said.

"What is to become of me if this be the truth?" Calldoon said as he looked around the table seeking an answer.

Corbin ran his hands across his face.

"I don't know, my friend. I don't know, but we will do some research on it. For now, you're fine. You are no longer a vampire, nor are you completely human. Until we figure this out, enjoy your new life. Have fun. Eat cake. Run in the sunlight. Find a pretty girl and fall in love. Do all those things you couldn't do before," Corbin said with a wink.

"It's going to be all right," I said, giving his back a good rub.

Calldoon pushed back his plate.

"I think I'll be takin' a walk. I need to think." He had gotten almost to the door when he turned and came back to the table. Calldoon took one thick slice of bread, filled it with what was left on his plate then topped it off with another thick slice of bread. "No use wastin' good food just I because I want to think."

We all laughed at the sight of Calldoon trying to keep the eggs and potatoes from falling out of the bread. Tanarr leaned forward.

"Lucky son of a gun has the best of both worlds." Tanarr's head came up at the sound of a soft giggle at the door. His face lit up like a Christmas tree. He jumped to his feet and made his way to escort Deireadh to the table. As they approached, Tanarr pulled her chair out for her. He then helped her secure her seat.

Bending down, he gave her a soft kiss on the cheek. His "Good morning" was whispered with the kiss. Their exchange was so soft we could barely hear it, but we did. It took everything in me not to sigh and swoon; it was so sweet to watch the two of them.

Tanarr took his seat just as Rosey was bringing Deireadh her modest breakfast of toast and tea. I took one look at that steaming cup of tea. I would have bet my Aunt Martha's hat box that it was the same stuff I had gotten a hold of. *Yuck!* I involuntarily shivered.

"How are you feeling today?" I asked.

"Better," she nodded. "A good nurse have I," she smiled up at Tanarr. Then she turned her purple eyes on Corbin and me. She was so breathtakingly beautiful; the only flaw was a gash about four inches long just below her eye. The evening before, she had had cuts and bruises all over, and her wings had been ripped. The fairy circle had completed its magic; her wings were totally repaired, and most of the bruises were gone. The worst that was left was this cut and whatever battles she fought on the inside.

Her cup of tea was on its way to her mouth when her hand began to shake, sloshing a small amount of tea onto the table. "Blake-monster," she said.

Tanarr slid his arm around her.

"It's all right, sweetheart. He will never harm you again. He has been taken care of," he said, giving her a soft squeeze.

Deireadh set her cup down on the table.

"Good, good. Breathe I can," she said, lifting her cup again. Just before it got to her perfect lips, she looked over the rim of her cup, shrugged her shoulders, and giggled just a little. "Methinks, keep we might, the fat wallet."

We all laughed.

All heads turned at the sound of feet shuffling at the entrance of the dining hall.

"Sorry to interrupt, ma'ams, sirs," Chuck Roberts said. He was standing in the archway with his tools in hand. I couldn't tell if he was coming or going.

"Come on in! Have a cup of coffee with us," I said.

"I'd love to, ma'am, but I've got to start another job. I just wanted to stop by and see how you were likin' your new facilities," Chuck said with a little pride in his voice. He adjusted his cap. "If I could be so bold before I go, I'd take great joy in giving you a tour of your new bathroom." He bobbed his head. "If that would be all right with you."

I put both hands flat on the table and looked around at everyone.

"Guys, that's a tour I'm not going to miss! I'll be back shortly," I said, pushing up from the table. All the men stood. I gave my eyes a roll and decided not to protest the long-trained gentlemanly gesture, but then on second thought, I couldn't pass on giving them some grief. I turned back, gave them a sweet little smile, and said, "Ya'll do know I'm coming right back!"

I chuckled as I slipped my arm through the crook of Chuck's arm. I gave Chuck a nod.

"Let's go see what you have created up there," I said with a smile, and with that, we were off.

When we arrived at my room, Chuck stopped at the door, allowing me to enter first. I gave him a quick bob, mimicking Rosey.

"Thank you, kind sir," I said before crossing the threshold.

After we stepped into my room, I waited for Chuck to take the lead. He quickly did so, walking around the fireplace, through my bedchamber, and straight to my finished bathroom. He stopped at the door, gave the door case a good pat, and then extended his arm for me to give it a good once over.

"I tried to give the opening a good arch like the rest of the doors, making it look old but well-cared for in compliance with the rest of the room."

I nodded my approval as he talked on.

"Don't you just hate it when a new addition to an old room winds up looking like a fresh cut then becomes an ugly scar?" he asked as we walked into the dressing room. "In here, I tricked it up a little."

He picked up a remote and aimed it at the wall with the mirror. When Chuck pushed the first button, half the mirror slid into the other, exposing a walk-in closet where my clothes would hang. I almost laughed out loud. It was a little bit overkill for my holey sweatshirts and jeans, as well as my T-shirts.

Next he aimed the remote to the left and pressed another button. A different wall slid into itself to expose a room full of little cubbies and shelves.

"What are these for?" I asked as I walked around the small room.

"Chuck had a blank look on his face.

"Shoes?" he said with a shake of his head.

I hit my forehead with the heel of my hand.

"Well, duh! I knew that!" I said quickly, but I really didn't. I just didn't want to look so small town. If I were to be honest with myself, I had never seen anything like this.

Chuck hit a third button, and little trays slid off the wall. I was a step ahead on this feature but only because we had talked about it during the construction. Calldoon and I had laughed about it as we watched the trays slide in and out.

"Trays for my sparkles, right?" I asked.

"Very good!" Chuck said with a smile.

Each tray was lined with dark burgundy velvet, and the shoe cubbies contained the same fabric to keep the shoes from getting scratched by the wood, according to Chuck.

We proceeded from the closet into the bathroom. Chuck beamed with pride.

"I think this is some of my best work!" he said with his chest puffed out and his hands on his hips. Everything was perfect. To the left, there was a double sink in black marble, as we had discussed. The front of the cabinets were as dark as the marble bowls, and they were trimmed with a hand-carved wooden rope. All of the fixtures and hardware were brushed nickel.

There, nestled between the beautifully crafted cabinet doors, was Navar's crest. It was magnificent; not one detail had been left out. It looked just like the one that hung over the doorway in the grand dining hall. *Why have I not seen this before now?* I ran my finger over it.

"Wow! Where did you get this?" I asked, not even trying to keep the awe and admiration out of my voice.

Chuck squatted down beside me, balancing on his toes.

"I was at home the other night thinking about these sinks when it just came to me. So the next day when I came in, I took a quick picture of that big shield in the dining hall with my cell phone. When I got home, I downloaded it to my computer and used it as a pattern to follow. Then I found a good chunk of soft wood," he smiled, "just right for carving. After I created the design with craft paint, I finished with two or three good coats of clear polish."

"Why did I not see this last night?" I asked, still inspecting the crest.

"That's 'cause I only just now put it on there," he said as he stood up.

"Well, it's beautiful! It looks just like the big one downstairs. I'm very impressed. You are a true artist in every sense of the word!" I said as I stood up.

"I sure am glad that you like it, miss. I must admit that I was a little worried that I was overstepping my place, seeing as how I didn't ask or anything."

"I sure am glad you did! What a nice surprise!" I assured him.

We continued with our tour. To the right was a large, black-marble tub complete with a whole array of jets. The elegant hardware looked like a nickel-plated swan. Above the tub was a spacious skylight that flooded the room with light. I pictured myself up to my nose in bubbles, soaking my worries away.

Back to the left sat a black, porcelain toilet. It was new, but it looked very old. The tank was hanging high on the wall with a chain that you pulled to flush. It looked right at home in this old castle.

At the back of the room was a very large, very beautiful multi-head shower well-hidden behind a breathtaking stone wall. The wall was ten to twelve feet long, and a small waterfall trickled and tumbled down over the rocks into a small catch pool that had plants and rocks all around, bringing some of the outside in.

"I love it!"

Behind the rock wall was a shower I could live in; it could be just a regular shower head or a full-on rainforest. *Oh my goodness!*

Last but not least was the floor. It was made of white marble held together with black grout. From the floor to the skylight, the entire room looked light and spacious.

I turned around and gave Chuck a big hug, catching him completely off guard. He took a step back.

"Whoa, there, little missy! What's that for? You know you got a feller down there in the dining hall, and I sure don't plan on getting on the wrong side of his donkey!" Chuck said with a little embarrassment in his voice.

I reached up and gave his cheek a pinch.

"Oh, you," I said as I turned back around. "Chuck, this is amazing! I mean, I knew that you would do a good job, but this is a great job!"

I'm glad you're happy with her, but now I best be getting back to my real job," he chuckled. "I got a bridge to build. Let's head on back downstairs to the dining hall so I can say my goodbyes."

When we got to the entrance of the dining hall, Chuck stepped in and tipped his worn cap.

"Folks, it's been a hoot working here and a true pleasure to get to know ya'll, but I reckon it's time for me to be pushing on," he said as he turned to leave.

I walked him out.

Chuck stopped to pick up his toolbox and then turned back to me.

"I'd still like to take that pretty little redhead to dinner," Chuck said quietly.

I looked over my shoulder, smiled at every one of them, and then looked back at Chuck.

"That girl comes with a whole sack of stuff! Besides, I think she is off the market," I said with a shake of my head.

Chuck looked back at the table of friends. Tanarr and Deireadh were sitting with their heads almost touching.

"Yeah, I reckon that slick lawyer won his case this time," he shrugged his shoulders. "A good-looking lawyer one-ups a rough carpenter every time: my loss."

I gave him a sisterly pat on the arm. *Good grief, it's like patting a tree trunk!*

"That's okay. When I get back home, come see me, and I'll introduce you to my cousin, Meg. You two are perfect for each other; she's a sweet girl."

He rolled his eyes.

"Great! Just what every man wants: a sweet girl."

I put my hands on my hips.

"Well, I never! Not only is she the sweetest girl in the whole town, she just happened to win Miss Alabama her junior year in college, so there!"

"Oh, my bad," Chuck said. "But wait! Isn't this your home now?" he asked.

"No. It does belong to me, but home is Ela, Alabama, in the good old U.S.A.," I said with a hint of pride in my voice. "She's nestled in the heart of Dixie, and I miss her. I miss homecoming at church, the Fourth of July picnic followed by the fireworks, harvest festival and, of course, the Christmas play," I said with a smile of memory.

"Wow! You ain't been here that long, now have ya?" Chuck asked.

"I know. That's my point; I don't want to be here that long," I said.

"So it sounds to me like you'll be heading back soon," Chuck said.

"Yeah. I haven't told anyone but Corbin. I plan on leaving in the next day or two," I said with a wink.

Chuck gave me a wink back.

"I won't say a word, but it'll cost ya. When ya get back home, I would like to meet that sweet, pretty cousin of yours. You can be betting I'll be looking you up."

I gave his upper arm a friendly rub.

"You just give me a holler, and I'll leave the porch light on for ya," I said with a smile.

Chuck looked over at the others sitting around the table.

"It was a pleasure meeting you folks. It's time for me to be moving on. Everything is all done, so I'll say my goodbyes." He tipped his hat, and he was gone. *I really do hope that he will come to see me when I get home.*

"So it seems that you have gotten everything fixed the way you like it and all settled for the stay in the master suite," Zoul said.

"Well…," I said with a squeak. "I have something to tell you all. I've told Corbin." I reached over and took his for hand for support; he gave me a comforting smile. No one said a word as they waited to hear what I had to say. I took a deep breath and trudged on. "I have decided to go home," I said quickly.

"You're leaving?" I heard Calldoon say from the doorway. He had returned from his walk.

"Come on in, Calldoon," I said, patting the seat beside me. "You see, I miss home. This is your home, and you all have everything under control. You do the best job ever at caring for all of this, and you don't need me to interfere. Doulsie is wonderful at tending the kitchen. She doesn't need me. Tanarr takes care of all the legal things; he doesn't need me. Deireadh has all the gardens under control; she doesn't need me. There are those at home that do need me, and I need that, too," I said with a smile.

Deireadh looked so sad that I got up and went to her side.

"Don't look like you have lost your best friend!" I said.

She looked at me with her big purple eyes with one tear trailing from the corner. It rolled down her cheek.

"But losin' my only friend I am. Never a best friend have I. Lose you I do not wish," she said.

"You do know I'm coming back, right? I'll be back and forth. I can't stay away from my new family, not for long," I said, giving her back a soft pat.

"Family?" Deireadh whispered.

"Yes," I said with a smile. "Family."

Suddenly Rosey came sliding around the corner. All heads turned in her direction to see what was going on.

"Ms. Katelynn, Master Calldoon! Everyone come quickly! She's back! She's back!" Rosey breathlessly yelled.

"Good grief! What on earth has gotten your britches in a wad, girl?" I said.

She came running over to me and leaned in to make her point.

"'Tis her! 'Tis the woman who took Ms. Deireadh away!" Rosey said with wide-eyed panic.

"Really?" I asked.

"Yes! She be in the courtyard. She's askin' fer ye to come talk with her," Rosey said.

"Me?"

Rosey said nothing; she only nodded her head with her eyes as big as saucers. She was still breathing a little hard from her panic and her run all the way from the courtyard.

"She be askin' to speak with ye all."

We all looked at each other.

"Well, guys, what do we say? Do we send her away, or do we hear her out?" I asked.

Tanarr was the first to speak.

"I say we bloody send her away before I have her for dinner," he said with ice in his voice.

"Tanarr!" I scolded.

"Well," he said, "she almost killed Deireadh." He slid his arm protectively around her shoulders.

"In reality, she saved her, too. Blake was the one who was trying to kill her," Calldoon said, looking down at the cup that he had been playing with. "She also saved me."

Tanarr rolled his eyes.

"No, she didn't. She was trying to kill you. Your body just had a different idea, and you need to keep that in mind when speaking with her or about her. I don't trust her with anything."

"Okay, but we need to know what to tell her," I said.

"I think we should hear her out, see what the little lady has to say. It might be an interesting little tale," Zoul said.

"I'm with Zoul," Corbin said. "I would like to hear her side."

Deireadh sat there not looking up from her plate with her hands folded in her lap.

"Deireadh, what do you want to do?" I asked.

She looked a little surprised.

"Me? Speakin' to me be ye? Me thoughts no one wants to know," she said, looking up at me sideways.

"I think yours are the most important. You are the one she took away; you're the one she put in danger," I said.

"True that is. Came after she did. Left me she could not. Here I be only by her grace. Her courage overcame her fear. See her we shall if it be up to meself," she said with a smile.

"Fine, then," Tanarr said, pushing away from the table. "Let's go see this woman."

Chapter Sixty-Two

Out in the courtyard stood a very nervous looking young woman. I was the first to approach her flanked by the other five, well, six if you counted Rosey. When we got close, we all stopped. I turned to Rosey.

"Go get Doulsie, please," I said.

"Yes, m'lady," Rosey said, taking off like a shot.

I stepped closer to the young woman.

"My name is Katelynn, and yours is?" I asked.

"My name is Janet Jenkins," she said.

I blinked my eyes a couple of times.

"Where have I heard that name before?" I asked

"You were my grandmother's nurse," she answered my question.

"Mrs. Jenkins from Silver Cove? You're her granddaughter, the one that made that beautiful shawl? She was so proud of that shawl. I'll never forget the look of love in her eyes when she spoke of you. You're that Janet Jenkins?" I asked as disbelief filled my heart. "It really is a small world."

"Yeah, that's me," she said, shoving her hands into the pockets of her tight jeans.

"What happened to you? How did you wind up with Blake?" I asked, still trying to wrap my mind around all of the turns that had brought us to this point.

"That's a long story, and it's not why I'm here." She looked around like she didn't know whether to run or stay.

"Then would you tell us why you are here?" I asked.

"Yes, by all means; tell us now or stop wasting our time," Tanarr said though clenched teeth.

"Look, I know you have no reason to trust me," she stopped, looking off at nothing in particular. I didn't know if she was waiting to be thrown out or if she was collecting her thoughts. She took a deep breath, crossed her arms over her chest, and began again.

"It's just that I didn't know where else to go after Blake bit me."

"What?" Calldoon said, stepping forward.

"Yeah," she said. Janet tilted her head to the side, exposing what was left of an obvious bite. "He did this right before he died."

I had stepped forward to inspect her neck.

"Hmm. That's odd; he doesn't usually leave a mark," I said, probing at the mark on her neck.

"He didn't take much time or care," Janet said, giving her shoulders a shrug. "I have watched him drain a person and never leave very much of a mark, but this time he was dying. I guess that was the difference."

"So Blake is dead?" Tanarr asked.

Janet nodded.

"The last thing he told me was that I would need to be guided. He told me to find Savar." Out the corner of my eye I caught the men all glancing around at each other. I didn't know what had made them so nervous, but something had spooked them. Janet shook her head. "First, I don't know where to find her, and besides, I don't think it's working."

"What do you mean, you don't think it's working?" Calldoon asked.

"Blake had been promising to bite me for a long time. You know, so I would have all that power. I really wanted it bad, so I knew what would happen. I had done my homework. I knew about the fierce pain that would signal the start of my power, how the sun would affect me, and last but not least, I knew about the thirst for blood." She shrugged. "Nothing, not a thing. I even feel better than I did before. He had ripped my neck pretty badly," she stretched her neck out and pulled at her shirt collar. "You can see for yourself that it is mostly healed. What's happening to me? Can anyone tell me, please?"

Calldoon reached for her hand. At first she flinched and pulled away.

"It be okay; I won't hurt ye," he whispered.

Janet held out a trembling hand. Calldoon reached for her hand and wrapped it in both of his.

"I think I know what has happened to ye," he said.

"You do?" Janet asked with hope in her voice.

"Yes, 'tis almost the same as what happened to me. I do think that the end will be the same," he said, looking at only at Janet.

By now Calldoon had all of our attention, and Janet was hanging on his every word.

"Let me explain. I do believe that just as I won the battle with the orchid, now, in a strange way, so have ye. When you injected me with the nectar of the flower, somehow I must not have gotten the full dose of the orchid nectar. The tip of the needle must have caught on the back of my shirt, releasing some of the nectar and giving me a smaller portion. It allowed the nectar to kill off the virus that caused me to be a vampire, but it left me with this…," he paused and smiled, "stronger, healthier body, much better than before. They tell me that I now be an immortal. I think that ye got the same small dose from the dying Blake. When Blake bit ye, he had so much nectar running in him, it was like ye got both the vampire virus, as Katelynn calls it, and the nectar all at the same time. Yer body, like mine, didn't let go of everything; it kept some of both," Calldoon explained. "Is it clear what I'm saying?"

Calldoon turned to me. "Do ye think it makes sense? Would it not be the same?"

"The same what?" Janet asked.

I could see confusion clouding her eyes. Calldoon gathered both of her hands in his own.

"We be immortals," he said.

"What the heck? I got shorted again!" Janet said with a huff and a stomp of her foot.

"No. We have the best of both worlds. We will not die, but we don't need blood to sustain us. We can eat what we want and walk in the sun without fear," Calldoon said.

"But I wanted the power, the wealth! I wanted all that Blake had!" Janet said.

"I canna' know what being an immortal is all about, but we will find it out together," Calldoon said as he stopped and looked around at all of us. His eyes were begging for permission.

Deireadh was the first to speak.

"Yes, need they do each other." She smiled at Janet and stepped forward to give her a sisterly hug. "Welcome," Deireadh whispered.

Janet pulled back.

"I almost got you killed," she said.

"Ah, but ye did not…'tis that a fear of something. Takes over us it will… do things we would not do. It makes us what we are not of our own. A good heart it is that beats within your chest." Deireadh looked around at all of us, inviting us to welcome Janet.

One by one, all the way to the reluctant Tanarr, we all agreed that she was welcome to stay. By now Doulsie had arrived. It was important to me to find out what Doulsie thought of allowing this woman to stay among them. After all that had happened, I wanted the mother's opinion. It was important.

I slipped my arm through Doulsie's arm.

"What do you think?" I whispered.

"If Deireadh can forgive her, so then will meself," Doulsie said, turning her little face to me. She peered over her little glasses. "I may forgive her, but ye can be sure that meself be a watchin' her!" She looked back at the woman standing before us.

"I think that's a good idea," I said with a nod.

After we had all agreed to let Janet stay, Deireadh turned her to face the entrance of the castle.

"Welcome to castle Go-Brath! Well ye will do here, for each have lived a little out of time and place. For each of us are lost in years and have borrowed seasons that we should not, so come be a part of us."

We all went to the dining hall so we could sit and discuss what we could do to help with this situation. We each took a seat; it reminded me of a world summit. Worry crossed some of the faces, others smiled at the thought of guiding a new broken soul. And as for me, I was lost, totally and completely.

"Okay, guys, I want to know something," I said, and with that statement I had the full attention of every person in the room. I went on with my question. "When Janet said the name 'Savar,' why did each of you flinch a little?"

There was silence. No one said a word.

"Fine, but we aren't leaving here until I get an answer."

Corbin cleared his throat.

"Savar is the very epitome of evil; she is beautiful to behold in every sense of the word, but beneath all that loveliness lies the blackest and darkest an evil that mankind could never imagine. She is a vampire whose very presence will ensure mayhem and destruction. She doesn't ever get her hands dirty with any of the messy stuff; she is the instigator, the one who puts it all together. The one who pulls the strings. When she starts to insert her will, it's like a snake charming a bird; they can't escape. It was rumored that she warmed the bed of Genghis Kahn; she's the one that planned his ruthless attacks. If any of his men got out of hand, she, shall we say, took care of them. She became priceless to him; he would do whatever she said."

"I heard that she was Adolf Hitler's secret lover for a time," Tanarr said.

"I saw her with the King of Kenrcha," Zoul said.

"King of what?" I asked Zoul.

"Kenrcha. It was a small island nation, long vanquished. History will not record it. It was gone before written history appeared. This king was so cruel. He and Savar reveled in the many torturous things they could inflict on his people. They dined regally on his subjects."

"Was the king a vampire?" I asked.

"No. He was just so charmed by Savar, so under her spell that he cultivated a taste for human flesh so he could be a part of her world in some way," Zoul answered, folding his hands on the table.

"Why didn't she just bite him and make him like her?" I asked.

Tanarr protectively slid his arm around Deireadh as he started to speak. "Ah, you see, that would take all of the fun out of it for her. She likes being the cat in her little game of cat and mouse. She never wanted anyone to have more power than she has. She's a dangerous snake in the grass," Tanarr said as his fist landed hard on the table, causing me to jump. "Blake would have loved to have turned her loose on us."

"What ever happened to that little island?" I asked.

"Between the famine and the wars that were instigated by Savar, they soon destroyed themselves, all except for Savar and the king. When there were none left to snack on, like the black widow spider, she ate her mate. When she had finished off the king, she moved on to her next victims," Zoul explained with a look of disgust.

"Eee…," I shivered. "You're telling me that she's still around?" I asked in hushed tones, remembering what my Grandma had said about not speaking of evil.

"Around and doing very well," Zoul said with a nod.

"Why did Blake tell me to find her?" Janet asked with a puzzled look and a little squeak of concern in her voice.

"Because evil will always seek out evil. In a lot of ways, he saw you as his child. So naturally, he would want you to have a mentor to guide you in his ways. He knew no better person to send you to than Savar. She is, after all, the best of the best at what she does. They were a pair for a while; they almost burned each other out." Corbin raised his chin, closed his eyes, and took a deep breath. "Blake had no way of knowing that you wouldn't want to be just like him, that you wouldn't buy into his plan."

Janet covered her face with her hands. She began to cry.

"What am I going to do? I have no money and no place to live. I am lost!"

Deireadh left the room and soon returned. In her hand she had Blake's fat wallet. She placed the wallet on the table in front of Janet.

"Help ye, this may, to Blake it belonged." She fluttered her purple eyes. "Took it we did, tricked him, a good idea it not be." Deireadh rubbed her hands together. "Ah, what great fun it be. He be not so strong when jumping to our commands. Take it. Use it."

With trembling hands, Janet reached for the wallet. She slowed opened it. Her jaw dropped, and her eyes popped.

"There must be hundreds of thousands of dollars in here!" Janet stuttered as she put the wallet back on the table. "I can't take this!"

"Why not?" I asked.

"It's not mine!" she replied.

"It probably wasn't Blake's, either. Besides, he isn't going to need any money where he is, and you do. That solves your money problem for now," I said with a smile.

"You may stay here; that would solve your housing problem, and the rest we will figure out as we go," Calldoon said with a reassuring nod.

Janet sat there looking at the wallet lying on the table.

"Thank you all so much. I don't know what to say. I promise I will do my very best to make up for all I've done. I won't let any of you down." She turned to Deireadh. "Dear sweet little fairy, I do hope that you know I never meant for you to be hurt. Blake threatened me. I didn't know what else to do, so all I could do was what he demanded. I am so sorry."

Next she turned to Calldoon. "You are noble, strong, and good: everything that Blake was not. I am sorry I let Blake use me to the point that I almost killed you. Thank goodness your body had better sense than I did. I will spend the rest of my life making up for that," Janet said, smiling up at him.

"Ye released me from a horrible existence. I know it be not yer intent, but the results were the same. I thank ye," Calldoon said, taking her hand and kissing the top of her knuckles.

"Right," Tanarr said with a roll of his eyes and an irritated huff. "That's enough of the love fest. I'm still not sure I trust you." He paused. "I will be keeping my eye on you."

"Fair enough. I will prove that you can trust me; you'll see," Janet said. She extended her hand for a handshake. Tanarr met her halfway with an outstretched hand of his own. "I promise," Janet said.

"I will be holding you to it," Tanarr said with a firm handshake. There was still no sign of trust in his eyes.

Doulsie got up, walked over, and took Janet by the arm.

"Come, child. We'll be getting' ye a room of yer own, and till we can get to town, I think I can be findin' ye some suitable coverings. They will not be the height of fashion, mind ye, but they well make do till we can get better."

"Thank you…," Janet paused.

"Doulsie. Me name be Doulsie. Ye may call on me anytime," Doulsie said with a smile as they made their way to the doorway.

"Thank you, Doulsie," Janet said as she obediently followed Doulsie down the hall.

I took the last gulp of my almost-cold coffee.

"Wow, what a morning!" I said, putting my cup back on the table.

"I still don't think we should trust her," Tanarr said with deep furrows creasing his brow and an icy tone in his voice.

Zoul whacked him on the back.

"Don't be such a worry wart; we'll keep an eye on her. Besides, we have all made our share of mistakes; she did apologize." Zoul narrowed his eyes. "I think she meant it."

"That remains to be seen," Tanarr replied.

I pushed back from the table.

"Guys, I'm going to start my packing," I said.

"Are you still leaving us?" Calldoon said as disbelief spread over his face.

"Well, yeah. I can't help you if I stay here. I need to go back home; that's where all of Ms. Lera's papers are. There may be something in them about all of this. I'm coming back, you know. I have this super new bathroom that's spider free, so I will definitely be back," I said, pushing my chair back under the table.

"If ye must go, then we will help ye, for the sooner ye, leave the sooner ye will be back," Calldoon said.

As I started to leave, all the men stood.

"You don't have to do that, guys; sit!" I said with a roll of my eyes.

"Help ye I will," Deireadh said.

"Thank you. Let's get it done," I said, dropping my arm over her shoulder.

The rest of the day was spent packing, telling stories, and enjoying the laughter of true friendship. Later that evening, there was a soft knock at my door.

"Who is it?" I called, not forgetting the lesson I had learned when I first got here.

"It's just Janet, Janet Jenkins," she answered.

Deireadh and I looked at each other and shrugged our shoulders. I pointed at the door and mouthed, "Is it okay?" She smiled and nodded. I opened the door.

"Come in, Janet. We're packing some of my things."

"Oh, then I won't bother you," she said as she started to leave. I reached out and took her by the arm.

"You're not bothering us," I said with a nod. "Come on in. We're laughing as much as packing."

Janet came in and took a seat on the edge of the bed.

"Can I ask you something?" she said.

"Absolutely," I replied as I took the neatly folded sweatshirt that said "I ♥ Scotland" from Deireadh. I tucked it into the corner of my case on top of the other shirts, giving it a loving pat before turning back to Janet, who was fiddling with the corner of the bedspread.

"Are you leaving because I'm here?" Janet asked without looking up.

"What? No, I made this decision before you came," I said.

"But you have so much here! Why on earth would you want to leave this place?" Janet asked.

I stopped packing and looked around at all the beautiful things that surrounded us. From Navar's grand sword to my newly finished bathroom, it was all quite impressive.

"Yeah, this is all nice," I said.

"Nice? This is way more than nice. This is over the moon. This is the nicest I have ever been in, and it blows my mind."

I took a seat by Janet on the edge of the bed.

"Do you know what this doesn't have?" I asked Janet. She only shook her head. "This doesn't have Momma and Daddy, my little brother, or my crazy cousins. I need a hug from Momma, that family type hug that says, 'We love you more than any other thing in the world': that hug that lets you know that you are needed, you're important."

Janet had began to tear up. I had forgotten about Blake killing her grandmother until then.

To lighten the mood, I added, "You know what else I miss?" Janet shook her head. "I miss the eccentric little old lady that lived next door." I laughed. "She always wore three dresses, with the longest one on the bottom. She had long conversations with her old tabby cat on her front porch swing, and she made the best cookies you have ever tasted. She made them fresh every day, and she shared them with me on that same swing. I told Ms. Sara everything on that old porch swing." I smiled at the memory. "I can almost hear the creak it made as it went back and forth. The birds would be singing, and sometimes Rowbee would come by." I laughed. "Rowbee was this blackfaced bumblebee. He would stop right at my nose, and he would just hang there buzzing, like he came to tell me something. Ms. Sara would say, 'he has good news for you.' He would hang there for a little while, then he would take off."

"Other neighbors would stop by to visit while we were out there. I think that porch meant almost as much to me as my Grandma's did. It had this wonderful old jasmine vine that wound and wove around the corner post all the way into the gingerbread trim that hung at the top of each post. There was a bed of black-eyed susans at both ends of the porch. In between and all around the steps were so many types of flowers. Ms. Sara used to say that every house should have jasmine and black-eyed susans. I don't know who loved the flowers more: me or the hummingbirds."

"Across the porch from the swing were two big wicker chairs with big puffy pillows in them. A glass-topped table sprawled in front of the chairs. In the center of the table was a big glass pitcher of lemonade or iced tea. The outside of the pitcher would always fog up because the lemonade or tea was cold and the air was so hot. Sometimes we would leave a message on the pitcher. Ah, but the best part of all was sitting on that swing. When you heard the screen door creak, you knew that warm cookies were on their way. It was the best."

"You see, I'm just homesick; I had been in upstate New York for a while and now here, so it's time to go home. But," I said with wide eyes, "I will be back. Like I told Calldoon this morning, I'm going to do some research on this immortal thing," I said.

"Speaking of Calldoon, is he really as nice as he seems?" Janet asked. Deireadh nodded.

"Yes, kind he be. Bring ye harm he would never." Deireadh smiled. "Like ye he does."

"Do you think so?" Janet asked.

"Oh yeah! He is the one that stood up for you when some of the others wanted to send you packing," I said.

"How could he possibly care anything about me, after what I did?" Janet said.

"Sees something in ye he does. Trust him this I do," Deireadh said.

"Really?" Janet asked.

"Really," Deireadh and I both said at the same time.

"Take your time; get to know him. I think you will find that you have more in common than just the immortal thing, which by the way is a big thing." I reached over and patted her hand. "He's a good man. Give him a chance. And now I have to get back to packing," I said as I got off the bed and retrieved my last bag out from under it.

That night at dinner we all sat around the table. I had insisted that Doulsie join us, although she put up one more battle.

"I be no fine lady, not good at curtsyin' and such. I don't like the boys to be kissin' me hand. I be best fer the kitchen, only fit to be stirrin' yer pots," she said as she fussed around the kitchen.

I plopped my hands on my hips and cocked my head to the side.

"Doulsie, if I hear you talk like that again, I swear I'll pin your ears back. Do you hear me? You and I both know that you are way more important than that." I softened my voice. "Thank you for trusting me with your heart, and know that I will never betray that trust. Putting all of that aside, you are the heart of this crew. We love you, and we need you. I would really like to have the whole family together tonight." I reached for her hand. "Come join us, please?"

She smiled and reached for my hand. We walked into the dining hall together.

At dinner the air was filled with laughter and light-hearted conversation. It was wonderful. As the evening began to wind down, my curiosity got the best of me.

"Janet, may I ask you something personal?" I asked.

"After all you have done for me, you may ask anything," she replied.

"Okay. If it's not too personal, can you tell us how you found yourself with Blake?" I asked, leaning forward just a little because I really wanted to know what could have brought her to this point.

You could have heard a pin drop. No one said a word; they hardly even breathed. *Yipes!* I thought, *Maybe I have stepped over the line.* But I didn't just want to know; I needed to know. Before I left my friends with her, I had to know. "I know that you had a great family, a great family with lots of money. Your grandmother bragged about you; she loved you so much."

Sadness washed over her face.

"You're right. I had it all. In high school I got mixed up with the wrong kids. I started to drink, and next came drugs. I got mad at Mom one night because she wouldn't let me go to a party." Janet shook her head. "She knew that some bad stuff was going on. She tried to stop me, but it was too late. So that night, at the ripe old age of seventeen, I ran away from home. I had no money and nowhere to sleep, and that's when I met Jackson." She took a deep breath.

"He was a pimp; he promised me the world. He got me deeper into drugs. The next thing I knew, I was turning tricks for a roof over my head and all the drugs I wanted, and I wanted a lot. I was an escort at this big Hollywood party; that's where Blake found me. He didn't promise me the moon; he promised me the world, the moon, and the stars all wrapped up with a pretty bow on top, and I believed him." Her head bowed and her hands dropped to her lap. "I've done some really disgusting things with him and for him. If you want me to leave, I'll understand," Janet softly said.

Tanarr rolled his eyes in disgust that was edged in hope: hope that just maybe this young woman had some redeeming qualities. "Enough; there will be no more talk of leaving. After all, someone will have to look after you two oddballs."

"If that not be the pot callin' the kettle black," Doulsie said with a huff.

"And what does that mean?" Tanarr asked.

Doulsie shuffled in her chair.

"'Tis only with ye being yerself and yerself bein' in love with who ye be in love with. Methinks I never seen an odder pair than ye two."

"Whatever are you talking about?" Tanarr said with his crooked smile trained full on Doulsie.

She looked all around. I was convinced she was making sure that there was no one lurking about, and then she leaned in toward Tanarr.

"Phhh! A vampire and a fairy? Never have I ever!" she said with a chuckle and a wink.

"What makes you think that there is anything going on," he stopped and smiled at Deireadh, who only giggled and covered her face, "between the two of us?" Tanarr asked, still smiling.

"Even the very blind could see that the two of ye are quite taken with each other. Sometimes methinks a good whack to the head, and ye might just give her a kiss," Doulsie said with a nod.

Deireadh covered her mouth and giggled some more.

"Well, now, you're getting a little sassy for a mortal," Tanarr said, giving her cheek a little pinch.

Doulsie and I exchanged knowing looks. I gave her a wink to reassure her that I would never divulge her secret.

Corbin laughed.

"Just because they're mortal doesn't mean that they are docile. You got to be on your toes around here," Corbin said. We all laughed. Out of the corner of my eye, I saw Calldoon reach for Janet's hand and give it a soft squeeze.

Ah, I thought, *Calldoon has fallen for Janet. I hope she doesn't hurt him.*

"But that is the risk you take for love," came that soft voice in the back of my mind. The castle had joined us for dinner.

Chapter Sixty-Three

The next morning I was up early, showered, and dressed for travel. I was heading home; the thought brought a smile to my face. There was a knock at my door.

"Who is it?" I asked.

"It's me, your friendly neighborhood Spiderman."

I swung open the door.

"Get in here, you," I said, reaching up to give him a kiss. In his hands was a tray with a pot of coffee and a big fat pastry.

"Doulsie said you would need this," Corbin said, holding the tray up.

I took the tray out of his hands and set it down on the table.

"She is right about that, but I need this, too," I reached up, slid my hands around his neck, and gave him a long slow kiss. It was a kiss that said thank you for all you do for me, thank you for coming here with me, and thank you for going back home with me. I knew I couldn't have done anything without him.

"Wow! What would I get if I brought two pastries?" he said with his forehead touching mine. We both laughed, and I gave him one more peck on the lips.

"She is right," I said as I poured myself a cup of coffee then took a seat in Navar's grand chair so I could enjoy my pastry. Corbin sat in the other chair.

"You know, I'm going to miss this place," I said.

"You don't have to go," Corbin said.

"Yeah, I do, because as much as I will miss this place, I miss home more," I said.

Corbin got up and picked up three of my bags.

"Wait," I said. He stopped with the three bags in his hands. I reached up, put both of my hands on each side of his face and gave him a sweet kiss. Just before my lips left his, I whispered, "This is my tip for my very capable bell boy." Three bags hit the floor as his arms slid around my waist. He pulled me in close.

"I've got a tip for you," he whispered back.

"What's that?" I replied, snuggling up closer.

"If you keep this up, I may never let you leave this room, much less the castle," he said, giving me a smile that could melt the coldest iceberg, not to mention my heart.

I fluttered my eyes and put on my best Southern accent.

"But sir!" I put my hand to my heart. "If I don't get my little old self back home, I'll never get to work on all the things that need our attention!" Eye flutter, eye flutter.

"I know, I know!" he said with a huff as he picked the bags back up. "In that case, I'd better get started."

"Thank you. I love you," I said as I stuffed the last bite in my mouth. I dusted off my hands only to discover I had sticky stuff all over them. I went into my new bathroom, washed my hands, and gave the room one more good once over. I made sure there was nothing left that I would need. I brought my last bag out and placed it on the bed.

There was a soft knock on my door. I didn't even have to ask who it was. I knew that knock.

"Come in, Deireadh."

She opened the door and giggled.

"'Twas me, how did ye know?" she asked.

I smiled at her. "No one else in the whole castle knocks like you."

She smiled a sad smile.

"Have something for ye I do."

I stopped, took a seat on the edge of the bed, and patted the space beside me.

"Come and sit with me," I said.

She smiled, taking the space offered her. She took my hand in hers and slid her beautiful ring onto my finger. My breath caught.

"I can't take this!" I said in disbelief that she would consider giving something like this up.

"Take…I hope ye will…. Remind ye it will of things that will never be again, of a time long lost. Need it I do not, for there be no more fairies to need a queen. A remembrance 'tis all it be, so remember." She closed her sparkly hand over the ring on my finger. "A true friend never have I had before. Nice it is. Remember." She leaned over and gave me a kiss on the forehead. "Return soon to us." With that said, she was gone.

I carried my remaining bag down the long flights of stairs for the last time. Rosey met me halfway, where she presented me with a single rose.

"Ye will not be forgettin' me now," she said with a curtsy.

I patted her soft face.

"Rosey, I could never forget you, and I'll be back before you know it." She smiled and hurried off in typical Rosey style.

The next person to meet me was Charles, the stable master's young son whom I had ordered chocolate cake for. I well knew how he had wrapped everyone in the castle around his precious little finger. He stopped right in front of me and held up a beautiful wooden box. Navar's crest was hand carved on the top of the box; each detail was perfect. I set my bag down and took the box from his hands.

"Oh, my goodness, Charles! This is beautiful!" I said, running my finger over the top of the box.

"I made it meself," he said with pride.

"You did an amazing job!" I said. I started to hand the box back to him.

He put his hands up to stop me.

"'Tis for ye."

"Oh, wow! Thank you. I'll keep it forever," I said, hugging the box to my chest.

Charles blushed and ran off toward the kitchen. He stopped halfway there and came running back. He wrapped his little arms around me and almost squeezed me in half. "I love ye," he whispered just before he ran off again.

At the front door I stopped to take one last look at this grand place before I said my goodbyes.

"Take care out there, child," came that soft whisper in my head. The castle was saying her farewell.

"I will," I said softly.

"Come back to us soon," she whispered, "for the days of man are numbered and fleeting. Before you know, they are all used up. We are left with only memories of those we love. Don't forget us."

"I won't. I will be back." I rubbed the door case; it was my farewell hug to herself.

I put my last bag in the car.

"Ready?" Corbin asked.

I nodded.

"But first, let me give out some hugs." I turned around and began my embraces. I started with Calldoon and Janet. Next were Tanarr and Deireadh, followed by Doulsie and all the way down to the smallest children of the staff. I took a step back to give them all one big smile.

They all looked so sad; a tear had escaped and rolled down Doulsie's pudgy little cheek.

"Hey, what is this all about? I'm not dying," I tilted my head to the side and put my hands on my hips. "Does someone know something I don't?"

They all looked shocked and shook their heads. I held up my hands.

"I'm kidding, only kidding. I will see y'all soon; really I will." Corbin held the door open for me; I blew them all a kiss as I slid into the front seat. I waved like crazy as the car started and pulled out of the gate.

As we drove down the road, I looked over my shoulder out the back window. The flags of Go-Brath were fluttering in the wind; it looked like the castle herself was waving goodbye. Pride welled in my chest.

"What a beautiful, magical home she is. What was it that Deireadh told Janet? They had all lived in stolen years, they had borrowed seasons they should not have been allowed?" I said with a sigh.

Corbin squeezed my hand.

"Are you all right?" he asked.

I smiled and nodded.

"Yeah, I'm fine. I just wanted one more look. She truly is a grand old place." I turned back around in my seat, trying to absorb everything we passed: every rolling hill, every tree, every cloud. I didn't want to forget even one stone in all of the stone walls. All of a sudden I caught a flash of something out of the corner of my eye.

"What was that?" I asked.

"What was what?" Corbin said.

"I don't know. I caught something black out of the corner of my eye. Phhh...," I said, mimicking Doulsie. "I'll bet it was just a big ol' crow after a bug."

Corbin reached over and brushed a strand of stray hair back out of my face.

"You're probably right," he said with a wink.

Chapter Sixty-Four

One of the border guards for castle Go-Brath caught sight of something off in the distance. On approach he discovered it to be one of the most beautiful creatures he had ever encountered. This creature was definitely female, with long black hair so black that it was almost blue. Her skin was as white as snow. The guard had to laugh at his comparison, for he could tell this was no sweet little village girl. The closer he got, the more sure he was on that point; this was a woman of the world.

He stopped his Jeep just a few feet from where she stood with her back to him. Slowly, methodically, she turned to face him.

Her eyes, what an odd color! the guard thought. *Not black, not amber.* They were almost burgundy and defiantly hypnotic, and he was trapped in her spell.

She was wearing a long black dress. It fit her like a tight racing glove. The dress was slit up her right leg all the way to her waist where it met leather lacing that didn't quite pull the fabric together, as white skin peaked out along the whole length of her body. It sheared off to the left, exposing her entire right shoulder and arm. The neck and left arm were covered all the way to her fingertips; it was one continuous piece of fabric. On her upper arm a silver snake with ruby eyes wound its way around the shapely limb that was shrouded in black.

The guard couldn't take his eyes off her; the trap was set. Unfortunately for him, he thought that he was in control. Foolish man! When mortal will battles with evil of her level, man is powerless; she could do with him as she pleased.

"What is your name, and what business have you on Castle Go-Brath lands?" the guard said, his voice cracking as he tried his best to get his mind focused back on the job he was set to do.

She lowered her gaze on him. Taking a step forward, she leaned against the open Jeep. She reached in with her covered arm and ran her hand down the man's thigh.

"I am in need," she hooded her eyes. "Are you capable?" she asked in a soft, seductive voice.

"I most definitely am," the strong guard eagerly said, throwing his legs over the edge of the Jeep and jumping to the ground in one swift move.

He swaggered over to the beauty before him like a jungle cat stalking his prey. Little did he know that he was the prey. He had her trapped between an outcropping of rock and himself.

"How can we assist each other?" he said with a wicked smile.

She returned his smile as she flipped the side of her skirt back to reveal the entire length of her. The man's mouth went dry, and the trap slammed shut.

Quick as a flash of lightning, she seized the guard by the throat and lifted him off the ground. He kicked and gurgled. She had intended to strangle him just for the fun of it.

"Ah, I have no time for this!" she said in disgust. "It always takes too long for peasants to die, and they always reek of garlic." She sniffed at the kicking, dying man. "Or whatever vile thing they have ingested last." With that said, she gave her arm a short, hard jerk, snapping the man's neck.

She dropped him like a rag doll. "I need no assistance from a mortal man." She turned to walk away then paused to look back over her shoulder at the crumpled man's body lying on the ground. "To answer your question, you may call me Savar!"

She threw back her head and laughed. The vile sound sounded off the rocks and echoed through the valley.